Three
Things
About
Me

Aliya Whiteley

Three Things About Me

MACMILLAN NEW WRITING

First published 2006 by Macmillan New Writing,
an imprint of Macmillan Publishers Ltd
Brunel Road, Basingstoke RG21 6XS
Associated companies throughout the world
www.macmillannewwriting.com

ISBN-13: 978–0230–00136–7 hardback
ISBN-10: 0230–00136–X hardback
ISBN-13: 978–0230–00744–4 paperback
ISBN-10: 0230 00744–9 paperback

9 8 7 6 5 4 3 2 1

A CIP catalogue record for this book is available from
the British Library.

Typeset by Heronwood Press
Printed and bound in China

For Liz and Justin

Prologue

Amie had not been raised to consider the idea of ever braving the world that existed outside. She had never even tried the handle of the small door behind the wall of runner bean canes, at the far end of the garden. But now she had no choice; her father had been deposed, and they were being kicked out of The Nation. No-one would tell her why. She only heard from them, in whispers, to try and redeem her father's soul, be careful with money, and look out for a good job.

◆

Charlotte had an escape plan in place. She knew this was the last time she would have to bear her manager's hand on her backside, and she smiled as she was swung round in the Viennese Waltz for the fifty-second time that evening.

◆

So much for abseiling, Hilary thought, as she observed the crumpled bodies of her instructor and her best friends on the floor of the natural valley below.

◆

'But I love you,' Gary said, his suitcase in one hand and his notice of expulsion from the university in the other. His ex-girlfriend took a step back, into the safety of her doorway. 'That's as maybe, Gary, but you're still crap. Crap in life and crap in bed. To be honest, I'd get more emotional support out of an automated penis.' She closed the door. Conversation over. Time to buy a train ticket home.

◆

Her son had written a best-selling, sensationalist account of his abusive mother. She had lost the house and car in a un-successful legal battle against its publication. In court her husband had revealed his long-running affair with her agent. She could not find anybody else to represent her since her last film had gone straight to video in Korea and Sweden only. There was only one thing left for Alma to do. Move to the middle of nowhere and find a pub.

◆

Sam Spurling looked down over the cliff edge at the barbed wire the kidnappers had erected around their hide-out. Then he took off his helmet and turned resolutely in the direction of his home town. He had just admitted to himself that he was getting far too old for the vigilante game.

◆

Fresh out of school with four GCSEs, Rose felt she had the world at her feet. She had seen her friends sign up for Allcombe college, but she had decided to start her career. By the time they got their next load of qualifications she would be earning a fortune, and perhaps even managing her own staff. All she had to do was pick a prospect from the local paper at the end of the summer season and send along her curriculum vitae. She had her pink interview suit ready in the closet. How could they fail to be impressed? 'Just Be Yourself!' it said in the information pack on employment she had been given. And that was what she intended to do.

Looking for a New You?

Great opportunities to break out, learn new skills and make new friends.

Realise your potential and join a winning team of customer service representatives working in brand new premises.

No experience necessary – just enthusiasm and commitment.

Relocation costs to Devon will be partially reimbursed for the right applicants.

Send a handwritten letter of application and your curriculum vitae to ...

◆

To: Rob Church, Customer Service Trainer
From: Rolf Chester, Head of Customer Services

Rob,

Sorry to say level of applicants was extremely poor. We've scraped together a first training team for you to start with – smaller than I would have liked. Names listed below:

Hilary Black
Samuel Spurling
Charlotte Jackson
Gareth Lester
Amie Doe
Alma Chippendale
Rosemary French

Any ideas about what you'd like to do?

Part One

Rob

'Okay, people, let's break the ice! Hopefully you all got your information packs last week through the post and have all had a think about your facts, so let's play Three Things About Me!'

Rob makes his initial evaluations of them, taking into account their appearance and speech as well as the two facts and one lie about themselves that they were asked to prepare. These first impressions are an important moment in the trainer/trainee relationship, and Rob tries hard to make insightful and valid observations, jotting them down on his pad. For the first trainee he writes:

Balding. And overweight too, Rob notes, in the way that middle-aged men are, with an extra layer over the top of the trousers. The remains of his blond hair, combed into strands across his forehead, are glued there by tiny beads of moisture. *A bit short. Awful tie. Bad teeth*.

'Hello. I'm Sam Spurling. I've got three facts for you all. I hope I haven't made it too easy for you. The first one is, I'm a computer expert. The second one is, I used to do, um, charity work before starting work here. The third one is, my father left me quite a lot of money and I don't need to work at all. Is that too much detail? Sorry.'

The voting reveals a majority for fact three as the lie.

'Actually, it's – er – fact number one that's the great big lie because I've never used a computer before. Never even switched one on! Hope people will help me out.'

Rob notes that Sam does not mention the history behind the two true facts, even though the third statement has attracted interest from other members of the group, particularly the girl sitting next to him.

Very pretty, Rob notes. She's very young, though. All people that young are pretty. She's very girly, wearing a pink suit with a short skirt. Its hem is above the rectangular table when she gets up, drawing attention to the elastic, bare skin of her legs. Her hair is blonde and it looks dyed. Is anybody naturally blonde any more? Suppose she could be. But her eyelashes are brown and her eyes are non-descript brown. *High voice. Strong local accent.*

'I'm Rosemary French. Yeah, is it that my favourite group is Westlife, or is it that I've got a grade A GCSE in Theatre Studies, or is it that my cousin is a DJ in Ibiza?'

The voting reveals a tie between facts one and three as the lie.

'Yeah, like anyone who'd known me for more than five seconds would know that fact one is totally wrong, 'cos the Sugababes have so much more talent, I mean, Westlife, they just do covers. And they're really old.'

Rob turns to the next trainee and beckons for her to begin.

Unusually tall. At least, for a woman, and she doesn't stoop to cover it. She's a serious brunette, with rimless octagonal glasses that Rob usually sees on nazi doctors in old movies. They don't suit her, and she doesn't wear a scrap of make-up. She has large shoulders. Her grey trousers have two perfect creases running directly down the front of each leg. *Well muscled. Strong features.*

'Hello everyone. My name is Hilary Black. My three facts are as follows: number one, I attend the gym every day without fail; number two, I'm the eldest of four sisters; number three, I'm a mayonnaise addict.'

The voting reveals a majority for fact one as the lie.

'Well, I am indeed the eldest of four sisters, and I do eat mayonnaise with everything, even roast beef. I don't attend the gym every day. Every other day. It's dangerous to overdo physical activity without letting your body take a break.'

Rob looks expectantly at the next person.

What a mess. A rumpled cardigan with a strange stain running parallel to the buttons, and a huge skirt in royal purple velvet. Looks like a T-Shirt under the cardigan; the tops of the letters of the slogan it carries can just be seen when she takes deep breaths, which is all she seems to do. She's wearing too much badly applied eyeliner, and her halo of grey hair sticks out like straw from her blended face and neck. Rob wonders how she slipped through the application process. *Overweight. Wrinkled.*

'Alma Chippendale. Okay. Fact number one is that I can eat three packets of Oreos in twenty minutes. Fact number two is that Alma Chippendale is my real name. Fact number three is that my husband left me for a younger woman. Go knock yourselves out.'

The voting reveals a landslide for fact two as the lie.

'So, you wouldn't doubt that I could eat a truckload of cookies or get dumped for a younger model, huh? Thanks very much. But you're right – I have changed my name. You wanna know why? Like I'd tell you bunch of losers.'

Rob gives a fake chuckle in an attempt to smooth over Alma's comment. Then he gestures to the next employee.

Shifty. He has black eyes and streaky ginger hair that reaches his shoulders. He's very thin and quite tall. His new suit does not really fit him; he looks like he's playing at being a grown-up with those gigantic shoulder pads. The comedy tie does not help matters. His long, thin fingers are always on the move and his fingernails are immaculately kept, quite long on one hand. *Very nervous. Can't stand still.*

'Hi … I'm Gary. Oh, Gareth … um … Lester. Um … Number one, I love cooking. Number two, I'm a guitarist in a band. Number three, I once met Eric Clapton.'

The voting reveals a majority for fact one as the lie.

'I do love to cook. I make a really good aubergine hotpot. I do a lot of the cooking at home. And I do play guitar in a band, I mean, it's my band. We're called Power Cord, as in, chords you play on the guitar and cords to plug in electrical objects, yeah? We're still working on the name. We're having a gig in the pub this Thursday, if anyone wants to come along … And I have seen Clapton live, but never met him. The gig was great, though.'

The next candidate leaps to her feet before there's time for Rob form an opinion.

'Hi, I'm Charlotte Jackson, I used to be in PR but it didn't meet my expectations so I'm giving this a go. My first fact is … I have a degree in Physics. My second fact is … I was born in Allcombe. My third fact is … I am fluent in German. The choice is yours!'

The voting reveals a majority for fact three as the lie.

'I was born in Allcombe, believe it or not, and I lived here until I left for university. I'm living with my parents right now. And I am fluent in German … I've just come back from two years working abroad. Everyone should try it … great experiences. Actually, the lie is the degree in Physics … I got mine in Business Management. I've just never been able to get my head round science.'

Rob lets his smile linger on her for a moment longer before turning to encourage the last person.

Extremely clean. She has light brown hair that falls to the middle of her back, and she wears it tied back with a navy blue ribbon. Her conservative suit is the same shade. She's wearing thick tights – it could never be stockings – and heavy shoes that squeak as she shifts her weight. She is reminiscent of the girl Rob teased once at school and felt sorry for ever after. *Great skin. No waist.*

'My name is Amie Doe. It's good to meet you all. I'm afraid the most boring one gets to go last! I hope I have the rules – I don't want to get it wrong. The first thing is – I am an only child. The second thing is – I have never been to school. The third thing is – my father was an actor in movies? American movies?'

The voting reveals a whitewash for fact three as the lie.

'You're right. My father never acted in movies. He wanted to, but other things came first. Now he's working as a builder. I am an only child and I had a private tutor, so I never went to school, not a real school. I would have liked to.'

Finally, Rob gets his turn to recite his stock facts. He has practised this speech so often that he doesn't even have to think before beginning.

'Right! Brilliant! I'd like to play too, so that we can all understand each other a little better, and to show that I'd never ask you to do something that I wouldn't be more than happy to do myself. My three facts are as follows. Fact number one: I've been working in Human Resources for five years. Fact number two: I really enjoy my job. Fact number three: I'm not going to do my very best to help you all pass this course.

'Before you start to raise your hands, we're not going to vote on this one. I'm going to tell you the answer, if you hadn't already guessed. The incorrect fact is fact number three. I want you to be sure that I am one hundred and ten per cent dedicated to getting you through this course and totally prepared for your new career as a customer services representative. It's not an easy job. It's a front line job. It's the most important job in this organisation. So anything that you need to get you through the next month, anything at all … just let me know.'

Rob flashes his dimples and makes sure that he meets the

eyes of each member of the group, working clockwise along the tables. He doesn't want them to think of him as a real person.

Initiation

Timetable of Events

9.00   Introduction
9.30   Health & safety

10.30 *Coffee and biscuits*

11.00 Background on banks – a fun quiz

12.00 *Lunch*

2.00   Tour of the Building
3.00   Personal welcome from Rolf Chester – video

3.30   *Coffee and cake*

4.00   General knowledge quiz with PRIZES
4.45   Summing up

Hilary

Monday, 30th October, 10.30 am

Her best friends in the world were dead.

The three friends she had thought would see her through the worst times. They had been the inseparable group at university – the girls that were the Lads – Hilary, Jackie, Jenny, and Dot; always there for a good night out, and why shouldn't they go travelling together when the finals were over, before real life began? And if she wasn't that good a friend with Dot, and Jenny had her annoying moments with that really whiny voice, and Jackie hadn't understood when she'd picked up a boyfriend out in New Zealand, it was all less than important now. Now they were only a memory.

The first coffee break of the day had taken an age to arrive.

Drinks were to be served in the restaurant, which was situated in the basement. Rob, the Course Leader, who had the most beguiling dimples when he smiled, but no personality whatsoever, summoned a lift outside the training area on the fourth floor, and squeezed them all inside it when it arrived. Hilary pictured the cable from which it was suspended as it began its slow descent and thought about how quickly this could all change into a nightmare scenario. There would be no goodbyes – just a sudden twang and a plummet.

The lift doors opened.

They marched through a long corridor made of what appeared to be strong cardboard fences, Hilary at the back of the group, until they reached the restaurant. This was a mass of tubular steel and polished glass, reflecting the industrial strip lights that were suspended from thin wires above. In the far corner there was a collection of bright green nylon sofas around a wicker coffee table, upon which were two trays of white plastic beakers and a large coffee pot with a screw-top lid. Rob encouraged them towards it.

'Let's all gather round here, shall we? Help yourself, everybody. I'll go and find the biscuits.'

The women squashed themselves together on the sofas while the the old man and the boy tried to look comfortable standing up. The boy was leaning at an awkward angle, as if he wanted to rearrange his crotch and was making a mental effort not to.

She was sandwiched between the instantly annoying Charlotte and the older woman, Alma, who took up far too much room with her folds of fat. With the Course Leader absent, a lack of anything to say had blanketed the group.

The argument last night had affected her equilibrium. He had called her an ostrich, telling her she was unwilling to face the truth. Steve, her New Zealand boyfriend and the one man who she wanted to understand her, had revealed in one hackneyed phrase just how little he cared about what really went on inside her head. She had slammed the phone down on him.

Everything she thought about life had changed. She knew now that one mistake could end it all. A slip with a knife, or a mis-step on a pavement that the County Council had, in typical fashion, neglected to level. An old harness. A fraying rope. Too many people in a lift. All were possible and she watched for them.

The Charlotte girl was leaning forward to pour the coffee, then handing the beakers round with calm efficiency. She smiled a lot and addressed each person by name – a management trick if ever there was one. She didn't fit with the rest of the group; she was already commanding them, although Hilary was sure they weren't aware of it. Charlotte was obviously no entry-level clerical worker. It was a mystery why she was in such a basic group.

'Hilary?'

Charlotte held a beaker out to her. Hilary grasped the rim and drew the coffee back. She felt her elbow collide with a soft part of Alma and, while attempting to counterbalance, her legs tangled with Charlotte's ankles. In a moment the beaker was out of her grasp and the coffee was up in the air.

The majority of it landed on the thick material of her trousers, from her left thigh up to the waistband, and for a second there was only the awareness of moisture. Then the coffee soaked through to form a slick on her skin and the heat penetrated in a sudden rush. There was no way to argue with it and no time to think. Hilary fought off Charlotte's hands and levered herself upright, grabbing the material with fingertips to keep it from burning through her flesh.

Charlotte was making noises. ' … so sorry, it just slipped, sorry, oh, sorry …'. Hilary didn't waste time listening – she started off towards the toilet in a crab-like sidle. The youngest girl of the group appeared by her side, making a kind of cooing sound that Hilary assumed she must have learned from her mother.

The toilets outside the restaurant were decorated in the standard magnolia, with three small cubicles and a pair of dryers. A row of rectangular mirrors above the sinks reflected Hilary's unusually flushed face back at her.

She slid into the middle cubicle before the blonde girl could follow her. The door lock was stiffer than she had expected; everything was sparkling in its newness. She banged the bar home just as the main door opened and squeaked shut again.

'It's Rose. Are you okay? Do you want me to come in?' The toilet door rattled.

'No, I'm fine.' Hilary unzipped her trousers and eased them down the puffy skin of her thigh. 'Could you hold these under the dryer?' She bent her knees and offered the trousers through the gap under the cubicle door. She got a flash of long nails painted in yellow glitter before the trousers were taken away. The dryer started with a wheeze.

Her stomach and thigh were candy-floss pink and swollen; it was impossible to touch the skin without wincing. The heat from the burn was intense and shocking. Hilary sat on the toilet seat and took deep breaths.

'Its not drying very quickly,' Rose shouted over the noise of hot air. Hilary didn't reply. She knew the correct course of action – she should splash ice-cold water over the affected area until numbness set in, but there was no way she was going to let Rose see her in her sensible cotton white knickers.

She heard the main door open and close again. A soft, hesitant voice said something indistinct.

'What?' Rose shouted, rather aggressively, Hilary thought.

'It's Amie. Charlotte told Rob what had happened. He sent me to ask how she is.'

'She's locked herself in the loo and she won't come out,' Rose said.

'Oh no,' Amie said in a small voice. Her shyness had led her to stick in Hilary's memory and she could be pictured easily. An image of an ugly girl with a slight moustache and no waist came to mind.

'I'm fine,' Hilary shouted, just as the hand dryer shut off.

'Its not going to get any better than that,' Rose said, her impractical high heels coming into view under the cubicle door. 'Not quickly, anyway. Is that okay?'

'Yes, thanks.' The glittery nails reappeared with the trousers and Hilary pulled them to her. The zip was hot but the material was still damp and sticky. The smell of cheap coffee floated up to her nose as she climbed into them. They clung lovingly to her burn and made her wince.

'They are all waiting for us,' Amie offered.

'Mmm,' Rose replied. Hilary zipped up and reached for the lock. It resisted her. She swore under her breath.

'What?' Rose asked her.

'Nothing. The lock is a bit stiff.'

'Are you trapped?' A gleeful edge appeared in Rose's voice.

'Hang on.' Hilary applied controlled force which did no good at all. A wash of fear powered her muscles and the bolt finally gave, leaving her with two ripped fingernails. She smoothed her jacket and opened the cubicle door.

Rose was fishing in her clutch bag. As Hilary started to run cold water into the wash basin, Rose produced a cigarette and a lighter decorated with cartoon drawings of elephants. She lit up casually, with a flourish that made Hilary suspect smoking was not something she did out of habit so much as the desire to impress.

Rose tilted her head back and exhaled, keeping her eyes fixed on Hilary. 'That's better. I needed that.'

Amie shifted on her sensible patent leather shoes, one hand still on the door handle. Hilary rinsed her hands and picked off the two broken nails. She wafted her hands in slow motion, fingers spread apart; she had heard that hand-driers encouraged the growth of bacteria, but there were no paper towels.

'Isn't this a no smoking area?' she asked her reflection.

Rose caught her eye in the mirror and nodded, one over-plucked eyebrow raised. She looked pleased that Hilary had noticed.

'The whole building is,' Amie said in her soft voice.

'I don't care,' Rose said. 'Do you care?'

Amie coloured and looked down. After another exhalation Hilary spoke up, more loudly than she had intended. 'If you want to smoke, that's up to you.'

Rose smiled, leaned into the nearest cubicle and flushed away the remaining half of the cigarette. Her clutch bag was reopened and a roll of mints produced, which she unravelled in order to place one between her teeth. She crunched it loudly. A spray of heavy perfume and cheap deodorant completed the job.

'We should go,' Hilary said.

Amie opened the door a fraction and waited. Rose came forward first and Amie stood aside for her, not meeting her eyes, rather like a house-cleaner giving way to a superstar. Hilary followed, giving Amie a weary and disapproving look from which the plump girl shrank away. Such soft behaviour left Hilary feeling annoyed, but she knew she was incapable of acting like Mother Teresa. She was not about to take Amie under her wing as a pet project, even to provoke someone so arrogantly stupid as Rose.

The lift took a long silence to arrive, and a longer silence to reach the top floor and the training room. Hilary spent the journey deliberately tuning out her two companions and trying to ignore the mental image of the cable that supported them all. She had a hatred of people who always took the lift, putting unnecessary strain on the mechanisms when the use of the stairs would do them good.

She would have taken the stairs herself but the trainer, Rob, had neglected to mention where they were. Although he was young and slim, he had obviously fallen into unhealthy ways, just like the rest of Hilary's generation. She would find the stairs tomorrow.

Sam

Monday, 30th October, 11.01 am

He hadn't expected the rest of the course members to be so young, or so clean. He had given up on personal cleanliness a long time ago, and it had been an effort to locate his flannel early that morning. He had seen crease lines of age in the mirror as he had shaved around them; he had ironed his shirt badly and discovered all his ties were crumpled.

When he had been a vigilante, an early start had never fazed him. He had believed in the goodness of what he was doing, and in his own ability to do it. His super gadgets had been created in the garden shed, and his costume made by his father, who was a whizz with the ancient sewing machine. It may not have been everyone's idea of self-employment but it had made him happy. Now his father was dead and he had accepted that the vigilante business was no domain for the ageing and alone.

Customer Services could be just as fulfilling. Who knows? He could picture himself aiding some confused old lady with money worries, advising her to remortgage or claim her government benefits. He could be an efficient administrator and feel he had earned his daily wage. He didn't want a job or a career. He wanted a new vocation, except this time round he wanted it on a nine-to-five basis, with free refreshments. He wanted to have spare time, and with it to discover a personal life for himself. Normality. As normal as he could get.

After the upset with the coffee and the disappearance of the two girls – women, he corrected himself – Rob had returned with the biscuits and they had all helped themselves. An uncomfortable silence had then been easily broken by the most professional of the girls – women – who was called Charlotte. She had questioned Rob in great detail about what teaching techniques and management practices would be used on the course. It was all in a new language to Sam, and he had felt out of his depth. Was this what they taught in schools now?

He had caught the eye of the older, plump lady and shrugged, turning his palms up to the ceiling. Humour had always been his way of coping. She smiled in return, but it was not a real smile. It was more of a lonely grimace. Still, at least she had responded. Perhaps the cruelty of age could be a bond between them.

It reminded Sam of the last woman who had given him a real smile; a beam of gratitude and reciprocation of feelings. He had stormed a bank under siege, crashing through a plate glass window and tackling one of the miscreants to the ground. The rest of the robbers had fled, leaving him with one temporarily stunned criminal and a very appreciative bank clerk. He could picture her as if it had happened yesterday. A redhead, long legs, in a dapper staff jacket and tight skirt, wearing quite the brightest shade of lipstick he had ever seen. Her tender kiss had left a mark on his cheek that his father had berated him about upon his return home. As Sam had told the old man then, thinking him old-fashioned beyond belief, he didn't work for reward but if it came he would surely be a fool to turn it down.

His father had revenged himself by putting the girl's telephone number through the washing machine. Still, Sam had never intended to see her again anyway. He couldn't have got involved back then. Duty came first.

All the trainees were now back in the training room, and yet Sam couldn't remember the ride in the lift or the return of the girls – women – after the spillage incident. Memory had overtaken him once more, as it often did in less demanding moments. He would have to concentrate hard during the quiz about banks. The subject-matter did not strike him as likely to be enthralling.

The other trainees were looking at him. The class was silent. Sam guessed that Rob had asked him a question while he had been lost in memory.

'Sorry. I don't know that one,' he replied heartily with a false scratch of his thinning, once-blond hair. Rob turned to the opposite desks.

Rob was speaking in the kind of voice Sam usually heard only when he passed mothers reasoning with small children in the street.

'Remember, you don't have to know the answers. Just have a guess and then I'll let you know what the correct answer is. This is just to get you thinking, not to find out how much you know about banking. And cheer up everybody! This is supposed to be fun!'

The people sitting across the room from Sam smiled faintly. Sam had never been in such a situation before. Rob may have been stressing the pleasurable nature of the experience but it was certainly far from that. Being asked a direct question had always brought out the worst in him.

The closest atmosphere he had encountered to this was when he had been captured and interrogated by a gang of pirates off the coast of Turkey. While on a daring raid at their hide-out above a popular Irish pub he had been knocked out and tied up aboard one of their leaking vessels. He had awakened with a monstrous headache and a closed eye, his mask ripped away and hanging loosely about his chin. He had never felt so exposed and vulnerable in all his years as a vigilante.

One pirate, an elderly Turk with a grizzled beard and blackened teeth, had been watching over him in the semi-darkness of the ship's hold, bilge water lapping around his ankles. He had soon been joined by more. The interrogation had been in broken English, hard to understand, and exhausting.

And then they had argued in their own language, making their guttural clicks and rolls. Sam had assumed this was over whether to throw him overboard immediately or continue their questioning with the use of more persuasive methods. Torture frightened him, but he knew he could withstand it. He had practised at home with pliers and the electrical cord off the iron.

Thank goodness they had not been able to reach a decision that day, or indeed the next day. Soon the lone guard had become complacent. One attack from Sam's secret weapon had effectively silenced him, and a small amount of spit dribbled over Sam's shoulder and down to his wrists had loosened his bonds enough to free his arms from captivity.

The swim to shore had taken six hours. Sam could remember clearly the sheer exhaustion and the elation he felt upon reaching the beach; he recalled he had refused to even towel-dry himself until the police had been informed of the pirates' whereabouts.

Ah, the good old days.

Rob was looking at him again. In fact, the rest of the group were looking at him with varied expressions of amusement, curiosity and annoyance. He twisted his mouth and looked back at Rob's chin.

'Sorry, Rob, don't know that one either.'

'Well, I'll tell you that one. It's actually seventeen. Can you believe that?'

Sam smiled back at him.

Charlotte

Monday, 30th October, 11.51am

He's so dreamy, she thought. So totally hunk from a magazine, little boy lost, superhero material, better than Brad Pitt, dreamy. And intelligent. The most important quality, intelligence.

Charlotte watched him under her clear mascara. He had perfected the social interactive skills necessary to make a worthy learning experience available to the pack of no-hopers that surrounded her.

She knew very little about him. Rob. Rob what? Robert? Robin? Perhaps one day she would call him Bobby. No, not Bobby. There was something cheap and British about a Bobby, and something Italian and expensive about a Rob. Roberto.

He was scanning the room with his blue eyes, checking he had everyone's attention with the kind of professionalism that reassured Charlotte she had indeed met a kindred spirit. He would not abuse the managerial role with inappropriate feelings and conversations. He would not make a sex object out of her when she was obviously mentally above everyone else in the room. He would not be like her last boss.

Charlotte reviewed what she had learned of her class mates. She had made a mental list and memorised the appropriate information. Such behaviour was the hallmark of a good manager. Just because she had been forced to drop to the bottom of the pig-sty once more did not mean she had to wallow in it.

Sam – ageing, unmotivated, does not pay attention
Rose – immature, unused to work environment
Hilary – accident-prone, not a team player, a loner
Alma – ageing, unmotivated, lazy
Amie – shy, unattractive, may be a slow learner
Gary – unappealing in every way. Why can't some men try
*   to make the best of themselves? Honestly*

Looking around the room at them all, Charlotte felt a pang of loneliness. When the previous job had become unbearable she knew she had run out of choices, but leaving Salzburg had meant leaving everything that she loved behind. She had been forced to abandon the friends she had come to rely on, and the career to which she had been dedicated. Public relations had been her life, her future, and Austria had been her home. So much for the night classes in German and the textbooks on social skills; some things could not be taught. Like how to fend off idiot managers who thought that PR stood for Pinching Rumps.

Charlotte knew that it was all still out there – the opportunity, the glamour, the light green domes of the churches and the jewel-encrusted rooms of the castle, dark and hidden within the belly of its thick black walls. But for her the location and the career had been intrinsically linked and both were now ruined. At least, until her complaint case was resolved.

So, to start again in Allcombe may be infinitely less glamorous but at least it was a new beginning.

The information was hard to take in. Charlotte had begun by taking notes but could not fight against the apathy of the group for long. Now she simply played the end of her purple fountain pen over the slick of her salmon-pink lipstick, watching how Rob would turn toward her and then away, his eyelashes flickering over her like a moth brushing over a naked bulb.

She was sure he liked her too. He was trying to remain professional – as was she, as was she! – but sometimes things are bigger than people. Charlotte needed something new in her life and she had hoped that the new thing might be love. And as long as things went according to her plan, love is what she would have.

The plan, perfected recently on a napkin that came with the packaged meal on the flight back from Salzburg, ran as such:

1. *I'll know the man on sight, and he will know me (a sign of recognition must pass!)*
2. *We'll get to know each other gradually, in a civilised manner (he will not get drunk and leap on me!)*
3. *He won't be afraid of the fact I want a career (he must be supportive even though he earns more than me!)*
4. *Under no circumstances will he show inappropriate behaviour in the workplace (he'll know how much attention to give me, and when!)*
5. *He'll be at least five feet nine inches and he won't ever mention my feet.*

Her old boss had continually pointed out that Charlotte had large feet. At five foot five and a little under nine stone, she was considered to be a petite lady. Many of her friends had commented on it; the term 'China Doll' had been used more than once, and she supposed she could see that. The upturned nose, the light blonde hair with a natural curl she worked hard to maintain with hot oil treatments, the blue eyes, the straight white teeth. She was careful with her appearance but every career girl knew that looks could get you things hard work could not. She could only play the system, not change it.

Her feet didn't fit with the image at all. A size nine was difficult to hide in any style of shoe, particularly the flat slip-ons she yearned to wear. So she wore high heels, and suffered looking like an average woman who only worked to find a man, so that her big feet would not look like plates. That was what her ex-boss, Mike Miller, had called them on numerous unsuitable occasions and with no prior warning – dinner plates. You could serve a suckling pig up on those. You could carry an eight-course banquet and still have your hands free.

The Bank Quiz had ended. Rob had done almost all of the talking and his voice contained a slight crack on long words, but he did not pause for breath and he did not let his smile slip, although the silence of the group could not have been a helpful indication for his training plan. He would have to be weighing up just how difficult the next three months were going to be. Charlotte felt a rush of anger at them all, sitting there, waiting to have knowledge pushed into their brains by Rob's hands. Didn't they understand they would have to do some work too?

'Right, we're coming up to twelve o'clock now and as it's your first day, and there's been a lot to take in, we're giving you a two-hour lunch break. We'll meet back here at two o'clock. Please try to be a few minutes early so that we can get started again at two o'clock sharp. Any questions?'

There was a general shuffling of chairs and the youngest member of the group, Rose, stood up. Rob turned in Charlotte's direction and raised his eyebrows, as if to say, 'What can you expect?', and Charlotte felt it was directed solely for her attention. It was a sign worthy of stage one of her plan. He obviously felt he was developing a bond with her.

A helping hand wouldn't do any harm at this stage. She cleared her throat over the noise of people organising their pencils and wrestling with their heavy winter coats. 'Is anybody else going to lunch in the restaurant here?' she asked the room in general, and then locked eyes with Rob. 'We could eat together?'

Rob smiled, revealing his first flaw – slightly yellowing

teeth. But that dimple was exceptionally cheeky, and nobody was perfect. He adjusted his shirt collar. 'That's a really good idea, Charlotte. The food's not bad at all, and they have themed meals on Mondays and Wednesdays. Who's in?'

Sam looked up suddenly from his desk, startled, and then gave a wide smile and a nod. The disquietingly slim, red-haired man called Gareth also smiled at her with a self-acknowledged shyness, rather like a water vole poking his head out of the river bank. The foreign girl followed suit. Basically, the misfits and loners grabbing on to an opportunity for someone else to organise them, Charlotte thought, and then mentally berated herself for being so unkind. They were her work mates and it was important to try to get along with them. She would have to make herself search for ways to build bridges.

Rob walked to the door and picked up his tan leather jacket and cream scarf from the coat rail. 'Great! Good thinking, Charlotte! I hope you lot have a great lunch together. I have to run. Meeting to attend. See you all at two.'

Luckily he was gone before he could have registered the open dismay Charlotte felt crossing her face. It was too much to ask that the other group members would not have seen it. She rearranged her features to show managerial calm and faced them. Sam was shuffling his feet, and Gary was biting his lip and wiping his hands on his trousers. The foreign girl was pretending to rearrange her unfashionable clothing. Charlotte couldn't tell if they had registered her feelings.

'I think I'll tag along.' Rose came up next to her, smirking, and disproving Charlotte's theory that young people, particularly women, were never aware of the social dynamic within the group environment. And now another person was joining the lunch break, which was shaping up to be an hour of silent people trying to swallow quietly. It was hardly going to be a tremendous networking opportunity unless she found an inexhaustible stream of wit and charm in the next five minutes. Still, sometimes that was what was required by the gifted in the work place.

Charlotte turned on a smile and tried to make it stick. 'Great! I'll meet you all in the restaurant? I just have to make a personal call, yeah?'

It was Gary who led the way out of the training room, and the others followed meekly. Rose brought up the rear, still wearing the smirk along with the unsuitable pink suit. Charlotte waited for her to pass and the rest of the room to empty.

Alone, she finally had the chance to examine the training room without the clutter of her colleagues. It was pretty much a perfect square in shape, she would guess, with a series of perfectly square tables for one arranged into a horseshoe that took up three quarters of the room. In front of them was the three-legged easel with white pages attached to it that was Rob's main teaching aid. Next to that, a television and a video recorder on a metallic black trolley. Behind it was a white board, screwed to the wall, with colouring pens lined up in its jutting lip.

From her position next to the door Charlotte could see the ageing buildings of Allcombe through the wall of unopenable windows opposite her. Beyond the grey-tiled roofs lay the small harbour, and beyond that lay the Bristol Channel. It was a clear, cold October day and Charlotte calculated that the glimpse of pale green she could see, floating beyond the sea, almost out of vision, was the coastline of Wales.

She closed the door and walked to the windows, retrieving her mobile phone from her soft, grey leather handbag. She always kept the phone on silent so as to not be interrupted during business hours, but the display told her that nobody had rung anyway. She searched the phone's directory for the appropriate number and pressed the 'dial' button. By the time she had placed the tiny phone to her ear it had already been answered.

'... Palmer Forth can I help you?'

'Yes, could you put me through to Mr Forth please? It's Charlotte Jackson.'

'Is he expecting your call?' the receptionist asked her.

'No, I was hoping he might be free to talk about my case for five minutes only. Is that possible?'

'Would you mind holding?' There was a click and the phone went dead. After a worrying pause, a string quartet leapt into life halfway through a lively and well-known tune, clearly chosen not to offend the listener. She was no good at identifying composers but it sounded like something Mozart might have written; instantly she was transported back to the candle-lit concerts she had organised in The Residence in Salzburg. There was a moment of happy memory. Then the rage and embarrassment she had felt over Mike Miller's treatment of her during one such concert leapt back up and stole her profession-alism away from her. She wet her lips and swallowed, pushing away the vision of his hand straying casually to her bottom.

'Ms Jackson?'

'Mr Forth. Hello.' Charlotte was reassured by his tone – polite yet focused. She was paying him by the hour and he would not waste his words. It allowed her to regain her con-centration. 'I wanted to ask you if there was any progress forthcoming?'

There was a dry cough. She had met Mr Forth twice, and she could picture him now, a 1970s man in a twenty-first century office. It was his age that had appealed to her. 'These things do take time, Ms Jackson.'

'The initial letter was sent?'

A slight pause as a file was examined and perhaps fingers counted. 'Nineteen days ago. Past experience tells me that we should wait until a full month has passed before attempting to chase up a response. I will reiterate to you – these things take time.'

'I'm aware of that, Mr Forth, but I'm sure you're aware that each day that passes is a day in which I am unable to work within the public relations industry.'

'There is no reason why this should affect your career. In fact, as we discussed previously, no reason why you should have terminated your position in Austria.'

'And as I told you then, Mr Forth, I could not continue to work under those conditions, and I cannot continue to work now. Public relations is all about effective networking and until this issue is resolved I cannot communicate in a professional manner with people who may well have heard about my ... case. I could not expect to be taken seriously.'

'Yes, well.' He coughed again, and there was surprise in his voice, as if he had not been expecting such vehemence. Or perhaps he had not been expecting any disagreement from her; he, after all, was the authority on the law. Charlotte felt foolish. She had made her youth and inexperience in this field obvious.

'All that aside,' she said placatingly into her mobile phone, 'I am more than willing to follow any advice you have to offer in this matter. After all, I am paying you for your years of experience and your high level of legal ability.'

'Indeed.' A note of warmth crept back into the cracked voice. 'Then allow me to recommend that we bide our time. In cases of sexual harassment it does no harm at all to allow the accused to draw his lines of defence. Let him approach us with an offer.'

'The money is not as important as re-establishing my credibility within the work place.'

'If he admits culpability then he will probably be sacked, Ms Jackson. I'm sure an examination of his behaviour is already underway by the human resources department of the company. They may well contact you directly in time.'

'I doubt they will, Mr Forth,' Charlotte told him. 'They were particularly reticent when I first informed them of the situation. That is one of the reasons I left Salzburg – in order to be taken seriously.'

'And so you will be, so you will be.' But his voice was un-interested, his mind, no doubt, on a different case. 'Now, time presses. I'll contact you in, two weeks, say? If not before.'

'Thank you very much.'

The phone went silent in that abrupt way mobile phones did when a call was ended. Charlotte folded it away into her bag. She was certain she was in the best of hands, but it did annoy her to not have her views taken seriously. However, Mr Forth was an old man, probably on the point of retire-ment, and constantly struggling with his own growing infirm-ities. She needed to give him respect and trust, unless he did something that would lead her to believe he was becoming mentally incapacitated.

'Oh, hello.'

She turned round on one heel and looked into Rob's handsome face, ruddy from the cold breeze outside, his jacket thrown over one arm.

'My meeting was cancelled so I thought I'd work on my training notes up here.' He took a step toward her as she remained silent, her knuckles white around the grey suede of her handbag. 'Is everything okay?'

It was definitely the sign of recognition Charlotte had been hoping for. He had come back for her. Now it was up to her to explore the potential of the situation. She put a sob into her voice. 'Oh, Rob. I wasn't expecting … to see anyone. You see, I just got off the phone with my … solicitor.'

'Now, now,' he said soothingly, and pulled out a chair for her, as any proper gentleman would. 'Is there anything I could help you with?'

'Could I tell you about my personal circumstances, Rob? I really need a sympathetic ear.'

'Of course you can. Come on, now.'

He patted the back of the chair, waited for her to sit, and then wheeled his own chair next to hers. His eyes were as sympathetic as she could have hoped.

'You see, it all began in Salzburg …'

Gary

Monday, 30th October, 3.54 pm

Coffee and cake had been cut short.

Actually, cake was an overstatement: a fondant fancie that had been sitting in a hot place for a day or so would be closer to the truth. Gary appreciated fine food and there had been precious little of that today. He had opted for a pork stir-fry special from the restaurant for lunch and he did not intend to make that mistake again. He decided he would prepare sandwiches every morning, but then he calculated that he would have to set his alarm clock ten minutes earlier and sleep won out over his stomach. He would rather have time in bed than a slightly more appetising lunch; sandwiches had never really been what he called a treat anyway.

Every minute or so a fresh wave of embarrassment and disbelief swept over Gary, whenever he remembered to remember it. He had told them all about his band, and about the gig. A group of total strangers, and he had told them something so personal about himself – something that represented all he wanted for his future and all he had hoped for throughout his past. His dream of being the best guitarist in the world, spread-eagled and pinned down for everyone to stand over and point at. He might as well have thrown his failed relationship with his ex-girlfriend Millicent into that ridiculous little group-hugging session. Then everyone could have had a really good laugh at his expense.

He dreaded the idea that somebody could now turn up at the gig to listen to him. Power Cord was a work in progress; he had hand-picked the vocalist, Donna, from a karaoke event in the local area. The drummer, the bass guitarist and the keyboard player were old school friends who he had looked up upon his return from university. They were only adequate, but he hoped that time and practice would improve them. The best way to make them gel as a band was to play some live gigs, but he had never really imagined anyone but a blank-faced audience, empty of anything but applause, watching them. They simply weren't good enough. So why had he said it?

Gary knew he was stupid. He knew he was full of pride that led him to demand attention and then, afraid of the truth, push people away. He knew he was a talentless man, and that he was ugly. Millicent had gone to great lengths to assure him that he was crap in bed, and Millicent had never lied to him. She had told him the absolute truth from day one. That was why he had fallen for her. It was the way she had looked at him over the pool cue in the student bar and told him that he was lucky to have been accepted on the mathematics course at Durham University, and he would probably fail the first year.

She had looked into his soul that night, and told him the absolute truth. She had always been right about him, and that meant she had been right to leave him.

Hilary shifted next to him and nudged his arm accidentally as she moved her fountain pen down and across the quiz sheet. He moved away from her, hoping she wouldn't notice. She smelled wonderful, like a field of wild flowers in a playful spring breeze, designed for his nostrils alone. It was surprisingly feminine and sweet, a secret side to her he had never imagined from the rigid back and wire-rimmed glasses from behind which she surveyed the room.

They had been put together to answer fifty general knowledge questions. Rob had informed the teams that there would be prizes for the top three scores. As there were only three teams Gary felt he had a good chance of a decent reward for his effort. However, Hilary had resolutely commandeered the question sheet upon its arrival and started filling in the answers at an amazing speed. She had made it crystal clear that no input from him was required. Still, his confidence slowly draining, he suspected he wouldn't have known the answers anyway.

The other teams were looking more co-operative, or at least they were all getting the chance to peruse the quiz sheet. Alma and Sam looked equally lost with the current affairs questions and Charlotte was making sure that every answer was conferred upon by a slightly less willing Rose and Amie. Rob looked over the progress with long scans of his ever-smiling eyes, occasionally brushing them over Gary's forehead.

Hilary was muttering under her breath. 'Sailors, fighting on the dance floor … Oh, man, look at those cavemen go …'

Gary was suddenly one hundred per cent focused on her words, to a point beyond embarrassment or forethought. He had to speak. 'David Bowie.'

'What?' Hilary asked him with a note of irritation.

'David Bowie. *Life on Mars*. "Take a look at the lawman, beating up the wrong guy, oh man, wonder if he'll ever know, he's in the best selling show, is there life on Mars?"'

'How does the tune go?' she asked him suspiciously.

Gary dared not look around the room to see if he was attracting anyone else's attention. He repeated the lines in a small, sing-song voice, hoping he could carry the tune recognisably. Hilary listened without looking at him, her head turned to one side to make a straight line from her ear to his mouth. Gary could see a faint fuzz of white hair extending from the tip of her lobe and across the straight line of her jaw, softening her face. He hadn't noticed how full and pink her lips were, or perhaps she had forgotten at that moment to keep them clenched.

She interrupted him half-way through the first chorus. 'Of course! I love that song! I just couldn't place it.'

'It's a great song. From the *Hunky Dory* album.'

'I love that song. I like David Bowie, but I haven't really heard a lot of it.'

'I could lend it to you,' Gary offered, and then immediately wondered why he was such an idiot that he continually put himself out there, asking for rejection, begging to give people a chance to despise and belittle him.

'That would be great. Are you sure you don't mind?'

He couldn't be sure he had heard Hilary correctly. 'Okay. No problem. I'll bring it in tomorrow.'

'Thanks. Do you know any of these others?'

She was actually pushing the paper towards him, asking for his opinion. She still hadn't looked him in the face, but this talking thing was good. Talking with a woman, a woman who wasn't finding him repulsive. He scanned the paper, found the lyrics section and noted that she had already correctly answered a lot of the music questions. She knew her stuff, particularly modern, 1980s and 1990s. A couple of the older tracks had eluded her.

'This one …' He tapped the page with his finger. '"I bet you're wondering how I knew about your plans to make me blue." That's Marvin Gaye. *I Heard It Through the Grapevine*. Good song.'

'You fill it in.' Hilary gave him the pen and twisted her body around to the back of her chair so that she was facing the window. Gary assumed they had reached the end of their conversation, but as he concentrated on trying to make his writing as neat as possible, she spoke again, in a voice pitched for his ears alone.

'Are you a sixties fan?'

'Yeah. I like a lot of stuff.' Was that too vain?

'I like Hendrix,' she said, even more quietly, as if divulging top secret information. Her eyes were staring through her steel-rimmed glasses, through the window panes and to the sky. She looked like she was miles away. Funny how she had become much more feminine to his eyes in the last five minutes. He realised that fact and instantly decided not to think about it ever again. Hilary was a work colleague, and he was not ready to be examining anybody's femininity yet. He wanted to be neutral for a while.

'I love Hendrix! What's your favourite track?'

'*Little Wing*,' she answered, and locked eyes with him. Gary felt a jolt of camaraderie.

'I've covered that. My band covers it. We've got it pretty good now.'

'Are you going to play it on Thursday?'

'Yeah.'

'I'll look forward to that, then.'

Oh God. She was going to attend his gig. He looked ahead and pretended not to understand while his mind raced through a million possibilities. What if the gig was crap? What if the gig was great and she loved it? What if the gig was cancelled? What if she didn't turn up on the night? The worst thing was, he wasn't sure which of his imaginings he would actually prefer to come true.

'This one is The Stones,' he covered hastily. '"I went down to the Chelsea drugstore, to get my prescription filled."'

'Of course! I should have got that one. It's … the one with the choir. *You Can't Always Get What You Want*.'

Gary wrote in the answer. He glanced at the rest. 'You've got all the others right.'

Hilary pointed to the top of the page. 'Do you want to check the current affairs questions?'

'I wouldn't know whether they were right or wrong. I don't keep up with that stuff.'

She smiled from the corner of her mouth, her attention still fixed out of the window. It was getting darker. It would be night by the time they left this room. 'I do. So we should have done pretty well overall.'

'Yeah.'

Gary froze as she leaned conspiratorially toward him. Even sitting down her eyes were level with his forehead. She must be a good two inches taller than him, and there wasn't a spare ounce of flesh on her. He found most women intimidating, but she had a power and control that made him want to run away and hide.

'Not that there's really any competition. Nobody else looks too sharp.'

'No,' he said, although secretly he was thinking that Charlotte came across as pretty scarily intelligent, and she was certainly leading the way with her team. Hilary replied as if he had spoken the thought aloud. He supposed he wasn't that difficult to read.

'That Charlotte girl gives a good impression, but it's all bullshit to impress the boss. That kind of skill has no practical application in the real world. You wouldn't catch me believing all that business speak. It's designed to make the worker a slave, to pull the wool over Mr Average's eyes, and it's certainly worked for her, wouldn't you say?'

'Yeah,' Gary chuckled dutifully, hoping that her quiet speech had been some sort of joke. Hilary paid no attention to him, so he guessed that he'd done the wrong thing. He cleared his throat and gave himself a serious expression.

'Right! Everyone! Time is up!' Rob tapped his watch as he spoke over the murmurings of the group. 'Pass your paper to the left, please, and we'll mark each other's. I'll read out the answers. One mark for each question answered correctly. And shout out if there's a problem, okay?'

Hilary received the paper from Charlotte's group and plucked the pen back out of Gary's fingers before he had a chance to react. She had a lot of Millicent's features. They had the same belief in themselves.

Confidence was something Gary knew very little about, apart from the fact that he found people who possessed it extremely attractive.

Millicent and Hilary also had intelligence in common; a sharpness that enabled them to make pithy and insightful comments about other people without ever being over-heard. And pride – they both believed what they said and trusted in their own instincts. They really were so sure of everything they were sure about. But in the looks department they were totally different. Millicent was short and blonde, with a pointed chin and a bigger chest than Gary had been expecting from her initial appearance, but behind both sets of eyes there was the same look: the glint of conviction.

As Rob made his way down the list of answers, Gary found himself considering the last conversation he had exchanged with Millicent, only a week ago. They had broken up in the summer and she was back at university now, but they still kept in touch, having decided to maintain a friendship on the basis of the character traits they admired in each other. So they had telephone conversations in which Millicent made it clear that criticism of those exact character traits was the duty of a friend, even though it was exactly the same criticisms she had made when they were a couple. Gary always listened attentively.

So the new job started in a week, she had stated. Had he made all the necessary preparations?

What preparations? he had replied.

She sighed. That was why he had failed at university. That was why he would never succeed at anything. He doesn't put in the necessary work. Background on the company, she informed him. An action plan. What did he want to achieve?

He needed the money, he had replied, unable to keep surprise from his voice. Apart from that, he had the band. Music was his career.

A little bit of realism, Gary, she had said in a dry tone. Try to think of the future. Try to understand that a woman wants more than empty promises and some second-rate rock ballads penned in her name. Why was he persisting in this fantasy?

That was when he had begun to feel angry with her. What right did she have to advise him on his behaviour any more, anyway? He only had fantasy left to hold on to. She knew his reality had been shot to shit. No career, no degree, no girlfriend, no money.

A softening of the voice, back to the little girl she used to become under his single duvet, and he had been persuaded once more that she only meant to help him. Only he had finally come to understand that it wasn't helping him.

Did that mean he was over her? In that case he had better consider taking the picture of her down from his bedroom wall, and maybe even making an extravagant gesture such as burning those light blue envelopes with the neatly signed letters inside that he re-read most nights. He would hate to be the kind of person who never got over stuff, but he suspected that, deep down, he was exactly that kind of person. Rob's voice intruded on his thoughts.

'So – hand the paper back to the original team and let's shout out our marks, okay? Sam, you go first.'

The marks revealed:

17 out of a possible 50 for Sam and Alma

41 out if a possible 50 for Charlotte, Rose and Amie
42 out of a possible 50 for Hilary and Gary

Gary saw how Hilary smiled widely at the losers, and how Charlotte took that as a personal insult, stiffening in her chair and freezing her face to a polite mask. It was the beginning of something that he didn't want to get involved in, but he felt that the last hour had tied him irrevocably to it, and to Hilary. Maybe he could stop this feud before it got started; maybe he could smooth things over and gain some respect.

He felt his heart grow warm for Hilary.

'I did say everybody gets a prize, didn't I? So don't worry, it really doesn't matter how you do,' Rob concluded cheerfully. 'You all get a wonderful prize. Here's yours, Sam, and yours, Amie. Everybody gets one. It's your name badges. As from tomorrow I'd like to see all of you wearing these so that we can all feel really committed to the team. Okay? Let's call it a day then! Let's get ready for tomorrow morning, right here, bright and early, for the real start of the training process!'

People collected their name badges and left, ten minutes ahead of schedule.

Amie

Wednesday, 1st November, 5.18 pm

She could never fit in with this scenery; this little town with drunks lying in the street next to the dog muck, the net curtains on the closed houses and the grimaces on the faces of the grey people.

Amie smiled as she opened the front door of the holiday cottage her father was renting. It wasn't a real smile, but she was determined not to burden him with her feelings.

Nothing could be done, anyway, so what was the point of moaning about it? He had left their home in Wales, the communal base of The One True Separatist Nation, and taken her with him for reasons she could not begin to understand, and he was not going to explain why.

The hall was little more than a small, damp closet in which to hang a coat, so Amie did that. She placed her raincoat on the peg next to her father's working jacket, banging her elbow on the staircase as she did so. In a clip frame hung next to the door of the room that served as a lounge, kitchen and bedroom her father had put a picture of the Wye Valley, cut from a magazine that came free with the newspaper on Saturdays. She always tried not to look at it and failed yet again as she passed it by.

The furniture in the main room had been rented along with the property. There was a sofa bed and an armchair in an orange tartan pattern. The curtains over the one window that managed to let in no light whatsoever clashed with the furniture: they bore a faded floral pattern in pink and green, with a layer of dirty lace to stop strangers looking in at them from the street.

The sofa began in the living room and ended up in the kitchen. There was a fridge and a cooker, both of which worked, and a washing machine, which didn't. The landlord's empty promises resulted in no action on that issue. The ripped lino blended into the turquoise carpet with a couple of inches of bare concrete between them.

Her father was exactly where she had expected him to be: on the sofa, which pointed directly at the television, his working boots still on and dangling over the arm toward the door. He was engrossed in one of the soaps that was usually on at that time. She could never remember which one. Over the last months he had lost weight on his face and gained it on his stomach and arms, and she had to admit it suited him. He had lost that pampered look that life as the Leader had given him; if only they hadn't lost everything else along with it.

He didn't look up as she entered the room, but at least he spoke to her. That meant it was one of his better days.

'How was your first day of work?' he said slowly.

'Fine, Papa,' she replied, not really wanting to go into the details. 'How was your day?'

'Not so good.'

'Why, Papa?' she asked him in her little girl voice. How she wished she could break out of the rôle of child and speak to him as an equal. After all, he had made her find work to provide half the income.

She knew they needed to have just one conversation as adults so that she could understand the situation fully, but she was afraid that, if she knew their real predicament, she would become paralysed and useless in the face of the information. Talking honestly with her father would be like asking her to tackle the Antarctic single-handed. He had never made any sign of wanting to deviate from his silence: not once. Even in the uproar and the dislocation, the rejection and the poverty, he was still, by his choice, her Daddy. She didn't want to respect that any more but she didn't know how not to.

'I'm fine, my darling. There's nothing to worry about.' As he turned his head on the armrest of the sofa to look at her, Amie saw how he held his left arm against his chest and tried not to move his shoulder. 'I stretched a little too much today.'

She wanted to examine his shoulder but knew he wouldn't let her. He never had before, and this pain in his arm had become a recurring problem recently. Amie settled for sitting in the battered armchair and leaning toward him. 'Perhaps you should go to the doctor,' she said tentatively.

He gave her a reprimanding squint. 'But you know what

they will say, don't you? They will tell me to stop working on the building site, and then what will we do? Do you want to live on the street, my darling?'

This was an old argument, but today Amie could offer a variation. 'I'm working now. I thought I could support us, Papa, and you could get some rest.'

He sighed. 'And you think the amount you earn will keep us in the luxury to which we have become accustomed?' he asked her wearily, gesturing around the room and wincing at the movement. He eased himself into an upright position, hunching over his knees, bearing his growing bald spot on the crown of his head to her, and she knew he had ended the conversation already in his head. She dared herself to push him further.

'How much money is this house? To rent?'

'More than you think!' he told her emphatically. Amie was swamped with the urge to demand a straight answer from him, to rip it out of him if she must. She was angry as never before; she was a burning hot needle that must prick the balloon. Her fists clenched and her square nails dug into her palms. Her chest was swollen with furious questions and her throat was choking with the fear that she might admit it.

Her father got up slowly, favouring his left side, and walked out of the room. Amie sat still in the armchair and willed herself to relax. Finally she had enough control of her voice to call out to him. 'Are you in pain, Papa? Shall I run a bath for you?'

There was a long silence before he replied. His baritone voice floating down the stairs from the one bedroom upstairs. 'No. I shall rest before dinner, thank you.'

Did she hear an edge of disappointment with her in his voice? Was she making his burdens worse? She was engulfed in a wave of shame, and vowed to do better, try harder, for him. She was the only person he had to rely upon.

Amie got up, straightened her skirt that scratched her legs as she walked, and took the four steps to the kitchen. She would make her father a special meal, she decided, then realised that was impossible as she opened the refrigerator. Sausages it was. Still. She could dress it up with a little interesting potato side-dish, maybe. Cooking had been one of her tasks in The Nation, and the only good thing she had found about life in the heathen world so far was Delia Smith on the television on Wednesday evenings. It was the only programme that interested her, unlike her father, who seemed to be living a different life through the screen. She wished the actors didn't look so false to her, so that she could join him there.

The potatoes had grown white, spidery roots but they could be cut off. Amie set to work. As she manipulated the peeler around the bumpy growths she let her mind stray, and was unsurprised to find it settling on her first day as a working woman. She couldn't remember a time when she had been so frightened, not even on the night when they had walked out of The Nation's communal house. Mingling with strangers, trying to fit in; it terrified her. She hoped she had not come across as peculiar to them.

The incident in the ladies' bathroom had stuck in her memory particularly. It was not Hilary, the tall, dark haired woman, that had interested her, but the young woman in the pink suit, Rose. Amie could picture her clearly, standing against the sinks nonchalantly, lighting her cigarette as a challenge to the rest of the world, eyeing her with contempt. Rose had a way of looking right through people, telling them that she already knew exactly what they were and had no interest in finding out more. She was everything Amie had imagined youth in democracy to be from the little information she had gleaned – insolent, sneering, permanently bored, daring, angry.

She was magnificent. Amie longed to be her.

It occurred to her that, if she phrased the request correctly and suggested it would be a chaperoned occasion, her
father might let her go to the musical rendition by Gary's
band on that Thursday. Maybe she could start to live a little
through her new job. She wanted badly to fit in, to be popular. This was a changed life and her father must surely see
that she had no choice but to change with it.

But then she remembered how she and her father had
never managed to once talk openly since the death of her
mother ten years ago, and Amie saw her chance to change
as a step away from him; a step she was terrifyingly willing
to take.

Alma

Wednesday, 1st November, 5.32 pm

Allcombe had once, for a period of about fifty years, been the
height of fashion, and the decaying evidence of that time
surrounded Alma as she shuffled homewards.

Victorians had loved this place. The local library was full
of books about it, and nothing else. It had been the seaside
town with all modern amenities, making it perfect for taking
the air and braving your pantalooned legs in the never less
than chill Bristol Channel. Minor royalty had even visited
for one summer, and a parade had been held on a Sunday in
July. Alma could imagine the parasols swaying and tall black
hats bobbing as wealthy couples had greeted each other on
that fine day, perhaps with children in tow; a little blond-
haired boy in a freshly-pressed sailor suit that he was careful
not to run in and his little sister, her face peeping through a
nest of curls under an itchy straw bonnet.

Now, as Alma dragged herself along that very same promenade in the direction of the seven flights of stairs between her and her draughty flat, she could not help but see the remnants of that time around her. The long, straight sea-front path ran parallel to the row of large and dilapidated hotels; they were dinosaurs with boarded windows and broken signs. The Imperial stood next to The Mirage, which stood next to The Grand, followed by The Grange, and then the The Claremont. Some remained as cheap family hotels, on the knife edge of bankruptcy, and others had long been closed and taken by squatters.

Alma could imagine waking up in a threadbare sleeping bag on a carpet that had once been royal blue, but now was thick with falling plaster and the strange stains of neglect. She could picture the once glittering chandelier overhead, faded to rust grey, swinging in the wind from the broken windows, and the empty bottles collected on the chipped sideboard that had once been used to place breakfast – kedgeree in a silver, shining dish as big as her hands put together. She didn't know why she could see herself there more truthfully than in her own past, even though there had been expensive fixtures and fittings to that life. Possibly, she admitted to herself, she had never really believed in the glamour of her past anyway.

At least the abandoned terraced giants proved that a golden age had once existed, as did the rotting bandstand with chains fastened around it and the grassed-over railway tracks from the trains that had stopped calling fifty years ago.

She had proof that Allcombe had been beautiful once; not so when she looked at herself. All she saw in the mirror over the sink she couldn't be bothered to clean was the head and shoulders, not of a has-been but of a never-was. The scattered photographs of her youth around the walls belonged to another person in another life.

The sun had almost touched the sea now and the long, grey shadows were blending into one. The bottle of whisky

Alma had picked up from the small supermarket just one hundred yards from her new workplace was an added weight under her long, thick coat, the pressure of it against her stomach reminding her of its promised comfort every time she moved. No, that was a lie. She would be thinking about it even if she was not carrying it right now. She was imagining it as she thought some women must imagine male movie stars, alone together in soft lighting. She had known too many movie stars to hold that dream any longer, but whisky and cigarettes still had a glamour.

Not all of the hotels were empty, Alma knew. Some had been taken over by unscrupulous businessmen and turned into private homes for the less fortunate at a minimum of expense. It was easy to see from the transparent material of the curtains and the occasional glimpse of ancient armchairs in front of peeling wallpaper that these institutions were hardly luxurious.

The largest of these, and apparently also the most shambolic, was The Paradise. It was the last hotel on the row, and had once been an exercise in grandeur. The gateposts were crowned with large cement pineapples in a flaking, yet still luminous, pea green. Past the gates, mock palm trees stood on either side of the main entrance in the same vibrant colour. The large sign on the front of the unloved building was in a typescript that had probably not been used since the 1920s – a florid series of curves obscured each letter to make the words practically illegible, and it had faded as an accompaniment to the declining fortunes of the hotel. It was now a nursing home for the elderly, and it suited its rôle well. It radiated age and neglect.

Alma had often looked through the windows as she passed by, usually as she had been walking home after closing time. The place was unreadable in darkness at that late hour, but occasionally she had glanced in during a midday walk to relieve her customary hangover and seen the residents collecting together for lunch in the ballroom, or a hunched body bending over the keys of a piano in a sitting room. The hotel must have been at least eight storeys tall, but the upper windows had always gazed out over the decaying sea front without giving any of their secrets away, however often she had craned her neck to examine them. Alma didn't really know why she looked, except perhaps out of habit now, and she knew she was the kind of person who found habits hard to break.

A light shone out from the first floor. That was unexpected enough to cause her to stop in her set path.

A woman stood in the window. Alma could tell that, in order to be standing so completely in view of the promenade below her, she had to be standing on the window sill itself; an impressive feat for someone who was obviously no longer capable of athleticism. With the light behind the woman, it was difficult to make out anything of her but an impression; a scrawny body and wispy hair remained after the rest of her had been hijacked by age.

Alma's first thought was of suicide but, even as her chin trembled at the thought of what was about to happen, she realised she couldn't be right. The window was closed, and anyway, the old woman looked more purposeful than desperate. She was standing so still and so patiently, as if her action was an end in itself. After a frozen second, Alma saw the piece of paper she was pressing up against the window pane and the bold black lettering that had been unevenly and insistently printed on it.

It read, 'HELP'.

She considered pretending she hadn't seen it, but her legs had already begun a slow walk up to the open gate. Alma passed the large pineapples and then the towering palm trees. The double doors were ajar and did not make a sound as she pushed them wider.

The empty reception room was the epitome of faded grandeur. The wallpaper had diminished to yellow streaked with grey, and it bore a row of rectangles in the shade of its original gold where the paintings that had once adorned it had been taken away. There was a large oval desk on the left in a dark wood with a layer of dust over the pens in their holders, the blotter and the brass bell. The balustrade of the staircase was made of the same wood, and curled around to the left, along with the track marks of the stair-lift that seemed to be the only recent addition to the room. Alma could see the frayed edges of the once plush carpet, red with golden leaf swirls, hanging over the edge of the stairs like cobwebs.

There were doorways on either side of her. Through them Alma could see rooms she had only glimpsed previously through the windows. The dining room had a stainless steel counter that did not look particularly clean even to her eyes, and a selection of mismatched folding tables and chairs scattered around, some with dirty plates showing some sort of congealed gravy and white patches of gristle still upon them. The sitting room opposite did indeed have a piano, an old upright, and a scattering of threadbare armchairs, each one with a carefully aligned antimacassar smoothed into place upon it.

The smell of overcooked meat mingled with the undertone of urine, but the strong, salty breeze blowing through the hall did much to keep both aromas at bay. Alma began to feel uneasy, as a trespasser in a horror movie. There was an extreme silence to the place that only occurred on the screen a moment before the killer appeared.

She reminded herself that she was far too old to feel threatened in any situation. One step followed another, and she was walking up the staircase and stopping at the first floor before she could give her imagination the chance to start in on her.

This was in no better state than the first floor. The wall-paper was the same, pale around the right angles that marked where it had been stripped of its pictures. The carpet had worn through in long, straight lines, making Alma think of the shuffle of slippers that must have caused those patterns. One brass tulip lamp attached to the wall further along gave out a dim glow that did little to lift the atmosphere.

The rows of doors were placed in the kind of symmetry that gave the corridor the appearance of a Stanley Kubrick movie scene, and they were all shut. Alma didn't know quite what she had been expecting – an open invitation, a pointing sign? She could guess at the right door but the last thing she wanted was to stumble into a dark room and knock over some geriatric's false teeth on a nightstand. How many lie-downs did the over-sixties need in one day, anyway? Surely they should all have been playing charades together or having a sing-along in the drawing room. She wanted to picture retirement as a holiday with good friends and an occasional back pain; at forty-eight she found herself already struggling to get out of low chairs and she didn't want to find out how much worse it could get.

There was no way to find out any more without a little trial and error. She guessed at the right room and tiptoed up to it. Alma considered knocking, but decided she couldn't bring herself to make the noise. The door, like all the others on the floor, was painted badly in standard white and had a cheap metal handle that was barely attached to it. She placed one hand upon it and turned it.

It was loose but silent. The door opened when she applied some force to it, sticking on the carpet beneath and making a swishing sound. She had guessed correctly. The electric light was on within, and it was much brighter than the corridor. Alma shielded her eyes.

'Come in, come in,' a desiccated voice said to her, and

then she felt a light touch on her arm, insistent, plucking the sleeve of her patchwork coat. She stepped forward as she adjusted to the glare, and heard the door being closed softly behind her.

There was no light-shade to cover the naked bulb that hung from the high, artexed ceiling. A single bed with a bed rail had been pushed into the corner behind the door, and next to it stood a small chest of drawers in a plain style with an oval mirror fixed above, a fine layer of dust sprinkled evenly over it. Cheap perfume and face lotion in dated bottles sat upon it, along with a plastic navy blue brush that was caked with grey hairs in a thick, tangled pelt. A brown armchair with a worn-through seat was pushed up against the window and a crumpled ball of white paper lay on the floor next to it.

The only colour in the room was supplied by a crocheted blanket that lay over the lower half of the single bed. It was huge and ugly, made of a thousand different colours from blood red to privet hedge green, whatever wool the maker could get their hands on she presumed, and it must have taken years to complete.

'I saw your sign,' Alma said, just to have something to say. 'Are you okay?'

She turned back to the door and looked at the old woman who was listening at it. She was tiny, with a slight hump and long blue fingernails that looked greasy, along with her squashed-up skin. Her grey straw hair was cut short and was thinning on the crown.

'They're killing us,' the old woman said. 'Take me out of here.' The paper-whiteness of her skin was a contrast to the sharp, steel-grey of her eyes, trapped behind pink-framed bifocals. She was wearing a bright mauve tracksuit with sky-blue fluffy slippers. She looked terrified.

Alma forgot the bottle of whisky she was holding to her

stomach under her coat. It fell to the floor and landed on the carpet, rolling to touch the toes of her shoes. She bent to retrieve it automatically.

'Would you like a glass for that?' the old lady asked her. Alma shook her head and held on to the bottle, unsure what to do next.

'They took Gladys away in a bin liner yesterday. I saw three of them carrying her down the stairs. They told us at breakfast she had left with her nephew but he wouldn't have taken her in. I said to myself, Dora, I said, that little shit hasn't taken her out of this shithole, something's just not right here, and I watched out of the door after lunch and that's when I saw them take her away. Help me move this chair back.'

Dora brushed past her and started tugging ineffectually at the armchair. It must have taken her hours to move it to the window; she had no strength in her muscles at all. Alma picked it up and let the old woman point out where it needed to go, a foot or so away, still facing out to sea. Then she watched as it took Dora thirty seconds to bend down to retrieve the sign she had made, lying in a ball on the floor. 'Help me eat this.'

She tore off a corner with shaking fingers and held it out. Alma took it and stood in disbelief as Dora tore off another strip and placed it firmly in her own mouth, mashing up and down with dedication. She ate the paper like a victim of famine, chewing as if she was afraid it would be taken away from her, and gestured for Alma to do the same.

'Let's just … hold on for a moment. Give me the paper, okay?'

Dora shook her head in token resistance but she didn't object when Alma took the ball of paper from her hands, even if she did continue to munch and then swallow defiantly. Alma didn't know where to begin to get to the truth, but the weight of responsibility was pressing on her for the first time in a long time. She couldn't tell if she felt caring or simply curious, but something was making it impossible to walk out of the room.

'Perhaps Gladys died in the night and they didn't want to tell you, to upset you?' she reasoned.

Dora's face slumped. 'So why was she carried out in a bin liner?' she asked.

'Maybe that wasn't her. Maybe they were clearing out her room.'

'Don't you think her son would have wanted to do that? He was always after her valuables. The relatives usually do clean out the room, after ...' In a moment the sharp and argumentative old lady had been replaced with a scared and frail pensioner once more. 'You're not going to help, are you? Why not? Why not?'

For one terrible moment Alma thought the woman was going to collapse. 'Of course I'm going to help you! Of course! But I can't just take you away with me!'

Dora had become a stuck record on the wrong speed. 'Why not? Why not?' Now she was crying, but it was not a disintegration; more of an outpouring of anger that she seemed unable to express in any other way. Alma thought that Dora would have grabbed her and shaken her if she had had the strength. Her desperation was catching.

'It's against the law, Dora. I haven't got anywhere you could stay. You hardly know me. You might need special medication. Anything could go wrong.' Alma reeled off all the reasons not to get involved that she muster.

'What's your name?' Dora asked her suddenly, in a complete change of attitude. She had stopped crying in an instant.

'Alma.'

'No it isn't.'

'What?' Alma was shocked into confusion.

'I know who you are … you're … you're…' Dora was staring at her, at the lines on her face, her double chin, her voluminous coat and her ankle-length skirt as if she could see through all those layers to the real person who lay within that disguise. There was a moment of fear that didn't seem quite real to Alma. She felt as if Dora was about to discover her, crouching in a small, dark cupboard, during a game of hide and seek. She was a small child again with a huge imagination that could easily turn a little old lady into a monster.

Dora turned her face to the window and the feeling passed. The promenade lights had been turned on and an orange haze was obscuring the emerging stars.

'Is there anyone I could call for you?' Alma offered. Dora did not look at her. She had slumped over, her hands on the window sill, exaggerating her age. Her fighting spirit had deserted her. 'A relative?'

'My daughter,' she replied weakly. A wild energy infused her. 'But she won't care! She doesn't care! She's in on it! She wants me dead!' Dora grabbed Alma's coat; she could feel the sharp knuckles just underneath her breasts. With one hand still holding the whiskey bottle and the other grasping the partially-eaten paper she couldn't react. If she could she didn't know if she would have comforted Dora or pushed her brittle body away.

The noise of the door being pushed across the carpet came from behind them.

Dora's grip tightened and then she scuttled backwards, behind her dressing table, trying to squeeze herself behind the oval mirror. Alma took a breath and then faced the man who stood in the doorway. She tried her hardest to emanate serenity, and the belief that she had every right to be there.

'What's going on here?' the man asked her in a loud voice that was cursed with the local, rolling accent. He was tall and thin, dressed in a white shirt and trousers with loud orange trainers that made his feet look very large. He had peroxide blond hair, large, straight lips and a weak chin, but the short sleeves of his shirt revealed an impressive set of muscles and he filled the doorway, eying her suspiciously. For the first time Alma wondered if Dora could possibly be telling the truth; this young man was belligerent, stupid and physically fit – a bad combination.

She thought fast. 'I just looked in to visit Dora here.'

'Visiting hours are over.'

'Really?' she said innocently. Years in the acting business had left her with a little rôle-playing ability, but she had to resist the urge to flirt. That tactic may have worked years ago, but this man didn't look desperate enough to go for an obese, ageing American.

'How did you get in?'

She shrugged. 'Door was open.' Two could play at question and answer sessions. 'Why was it left open if nobody was meant to come in?'

That met with a short silence. Dora cracked first. She must have bumped the dressing table; behind her Alma heard the squeak of old, protesting wood and then the clatter of falling glass. The smell of artificial roses flooded the room, overpowering.

'Sorry, sorry,' Dora gabbled.

Alma never took her eyes off the man as she spoke to her calmly. 'That's okay, Dora, mistakes happen.' With another person in the room it was easier to consign Dora to the role of Old Biddy, and Dora was reducing herself to that willingly.

'You're not a relative,' the man said. His voice was getting louder, carrying further.

'That's right.'

'Are you a friend?' he asked doubtfully, as if nobody ever came here under that title.

'Can I ask you a question?' Alma pressed ahead while her nerve held. 'Where's Gladys?'

Dora had no poker face. Alma could feel waves of terror radiating from her. If the window had been open she was certain Dora would have thrown herself out of it to escape the answer to that question. The man, she noted, wore a shocked expression, but why? He managed to cover his chagrin and stared at her with deceitful and guilty eyes.

'Gladys Clement? She's left to live with her son. He picked her up this morning.'

Dora gasped behind her, and knocked something else over on the dressing table. This time a waft of synthetic violets hit Alma's nostrils.

'Dora told me she'd died,' Alma said in a voice of mock concern, letting a slight accusation seep through. 'That wasn't right?'

He ignored the question and drummed his fingernails against the door handle, drawing attention to his muscular arms. Dora made a small squeak in her throat; the noise a mouse makes in its cage when the gigantic hand of its owner descends upon it.

'Perhaps I should get going,' Alma continued brightly.

He didn't move. She took a step forward. He still didn't move.

'I'm not sure about this,' he told them both. He looked extremely immoveable for someone who was meant to be feeling ambiguous about her presence.

Alma's mind flashed up an image from nowhere. She saw Tippi Hedren tiptoeing up the stairs to a white door, turning the handle and revealing a menace in the dark at the end of a Hitchcock movie. Alma could remember clearly the first time she had seen that movie, and how disgusted she had been that Tippi had let the door shut behind her, trapping herself in that room with the crazed birds, black-bright eyes and razor feathers and beaks darting into her. She had thought it a total fantasy that someone could be in a life-threatening situation and not react to save themselves. But perhaps real life was not so far away from the movies after all.

'Maybe you should check with someone?' she suggested. Her voice filled the small, white room with a confidence at which she was amazed. It was her last bluff. If he bullied her now, Alma knew she would do just about anything to escape the room, including leaving the old woman to her fate.

He weighed her words. 'Wait here.'

He left. In complete surprise, Alma froze. It was Dora who broke the spell. With an athleticism Alma would have applauded in a teenager she leapt across the room from her hiding place behind the dressing table and slammed the door so hard the floor trembled.

'No, no, no,' Alma heard herself saying. 'We have to go. Do you have a coat?'

Dora, one hand attached firmly to the door handle and the other clawing the wood of the door as if it had closed against her will and she was pleading to be let out, didn't reply. Alma dropped what she was holding on the bed and grabbed the crocheted blanket that lay there. She approached Dora slowly with it, as if to trap a panicking, injured animal, and placed it over her shoulders as she reached around her to remove her hands from the door.

There was nothing to her, physically, but Alma felt her stiffen up as she touched the tiny shoulders. The clawed hands fluttered back and a violent shrug tried to push her away. Alma grasped the door handle, greasy from Dora's sweaty palms, and opened the door even as she stepped back from Dora's hostility.

So she couldn't touch Dora, but she found out quickly she didn't need to. As soon as the door was opened Dora scented freedom. She took off, her hunched back swaying as she fled along the semi-lit corridor and began to tackle the stairs. Alma had to hurry to catch up with her.

They reached the soft turn in the stairs and looked down into the lobby. It was empty. Alma inched down the stairs until she could see clearly into both the dining room and the lounge. They were deserted. She couldn't stop herself from expecting that thriller moment, dreading the unknown things that sneak up and grip the back of the neck with icy fingers. It was ridiculous, but impossible to dispel.

She stepped forward. And stepped forward again. Nobody shouted, or appeared from nowhere to confront her. The only noise was the shuffle of Dora's slippers against the worn carpet as she followed, two steps behind her.

Alma looked to the main double doors; they were still open. Night had closed in quickly upon the promenade, but Alma could make out the curves of the mock palm trees and, dimly, the huge pineapples that adorned the main gates. She concentrated on the spikes of the left pineapple. It was no more than thirty yards away and every step was bringing it closer. She had to resist the strong urge to run, but she was already breathing hard and so was Dora. The noise they made between them was incredible, ringing in her ears, and she could not slow her breathing down. Her only option was to pick up speed and get out into the dark.

The night air was chill. As she hit it Alma wrapped her coat around her. The pineapple came into view clearly, and then they were past it, and the last rail of the promenade before the corner became the new goal. She was as close to running as she had been since her last gym session with her personal trainer a decade ago, and it was not coming back to her easily. Her stomach and the top of her legs wobbled un-controllably and her lungs gave out sharp groans of pain as she pushed herself forward. Dora was making similar noises but she didn't show any signs of slowing down.

Alma reached the corner first and grabbed on to the comfort of the freezing metal rail, burning her palms against it. She couldn't make herself go any further. If she had been fitter she wouldn't have dreamed of stopping until she was safely within her own flat, one of the new estate buildings that the local council had tried to hide behind the next hill. Dora came to a halt beside her. The woman appeared older in the darkness, and much frailer as she stood against the chill October wind in her multi-coloured blanket, bent nearly double and panting with effort.

Alma turned and looked back at The Paradise. There were no alarm bells ringing, no police cars drawing up outside with blue lights flashing. Apart from the main lights on the ground floor, the windows remained inscrutably black. It was impossible to think straight about what would happen next, except that some sort was judgement was unavoidable. Judgement always was.

Dora was trying to form words through her bad teeth and gasping breaths. 'You're … you're … Morrow. Jacqueline. You're Jacqueline Morrow.'

Hearing somebody else say her old name, her screen name, was enough for Alma. It released an explosion of memory into her head, an exultation of movie moments that she had never thought could have been so well-preserved by her pickled juices that she could relive each and every emotion, not as a faded watercolour, but as thick as the first time they had been smeared upon her.

She heard the introduction and applause from her appearance on *The Tonight Show*. She saw the crowd open up before her as she stepped out of her white stretch limo on Oscar night. She wore the tiny bikini that had made front page news around the world. She cashed her million-dollar pay-cheque, the first time that a female actor had been paid such a salary. She felt the kisses of her fantastically hand-some co-stars, both on and off screen.

She saw it all, wanted it all again, and then saw it fade away to leave her on Allcombe sea front once more, clutch-ing her bulk, dying for a cigarette and desperate for a drink. She realised she had left the bottle of whisky on Dora's bed.

'We've got quite a walk to my flat,' Alma told her gently. 'Let's get going.'

She pushed the hanging judgement of her own ridiculous-ness away until tomorrow and concentrated on how some-times, very occasionally, life could be just like the movies.

Hilary

Thursday, 2nd November, 8.28 pm

The answer may not be at the bottom of a glass, but it didn't hurt to look there. It was Hilary's third red wine and it ex-ceeded her limit for the week. It was only Thursday.

The Bosworth Slaughter was a well-kept pub that had a steady queue for the bar and the ladies toilets. It was situated on the corner of the road that became the pier if one turned to the left and the promenade if one turned to the right when emerging from its low oak door. For Hilary, it was only fifty yards from her own front door. She had bought the fish-erman's cottage on the end of the row that edged on to the pier when she decided to take the job in Allcombe. She con-sidered renting to be dead money.

So that made The Slaughter her local, but this was the first time she'd set foot inside it. Hilary didn't drink. She didn't like the slow disintegration it brought on; a creeping forget-fulness of who she was and why she didn't like the things she didn't like. The third glass was having just that effect, and she was losing the usual clench of her stomach muscles along with the rigid lines inside her head.

Hilary lifted her chin from her contemplation of the wood grain of the bench, distorted through the bottom of her wine glass, and looked around the pub.

It was one large room, a rectangle in shape with the bar set along one of the long edges, opposite the three stone steps that led back up to the main door and the street beyond. The small passageway that led to the toilets was on the left side of the bar, and three girls who looked underage to Hilary were lolling inside it in a disorderly queue, baring white legs in tiny denim skirts and shivering in tank tops as multicoloured bra straps escaped over their goose flesh. The barman, moving in a leisurely pace to pull pints and exchange notes for coins, looked over at them appreciatively now and again, stroking his patchy grey beard.

The bar was made of a dark, panelled wood with a brass rail running atop it, and also one attached to the floor in front of it as a resting place for the feet of the regulars who were making it clear they did not intend to give up their positions, no matter how pushy the young people became in their effort to get served. Yellow fairy lights were hanging in short loops over the bottles behind the barman, giving the spirits within a viscose orange glow that attracted Hilary's eye. It was the brightest spot in the room; a darkness settled over the thick, crude wooden benches that were lined up precisely before the parquet floored dancing area that was doubling as a stage for the night. Sleek black boxes of musical equipment and a metallic monster of a drum kit lay sleeping upon it.

Amie was sharing Hilary's bench in preoccupied silence. Her attention was across the room with Charlotte, Rob and Rose, who were playing an electronic quiz machine. Rob's blond hair and blue eyes were illuminated by the screen as he pressed the appropriate buttons with vigour. He was sandwiched between Rose and Charlotte, who were holding a giggling competition.

Hilary rolled her eyes and took another mouthful of wine, letting it pass over her tongue and lie in her mouth for a moment before swallowing. It had a sour aftertaste and she was fairly sure it was dyeing her teeth purple. She closed her mouth firmly and decided not to worry about it. She supposed she could see the attraction of Rob – he had looks, and a little bit of power. He had a smile that could charm a person that was interested in smiles. Hilary wasn't. Rob was only eye candy to her, in his faded denim jeans and beige leather jacket, emphasising his muscular legs and shoulders. She realised she was staring at him. She was as bad as Amie, Rose and Charlotte, who all appeared to be besotted.

Hilary turned back to the fairy lights behind the bar. She was letting the wine take hold of her, and she knew why. Steve. Her supposed boyfriend, Steve, sitting halfway across the world and using the wonders of modern communication to preach to her from his lofty position. The telephone had been ringing when she had walked through the door after work, and there had been no doubt from the start that the conversation was not going to go well. After four days of trust-building exercises and computer training for co-ordinationally challenged ape creatures, she had hardly been in the most receptive of moods for one of his sermons.

He wanted her to return to New Zealand. He wanted her to live with him, and he wanted her to get counselling for her apparent 'problem'. He just couldn't understand that experiences were meant to stay with a person, to mould a person, not just be brushed aside by a few tears on a therapist's couch. Perhaps the wine was making her more honest than usual, as for the first time she admitted to herself that she liked her problem and she wasn't ready to give it up just yet.

Somebody pressed against her arm and she moved away

as an instant reaction. Rose squeezed in next to her. Charlotte and Rob were arranging themselves next to Amie, who was blushing. She really did have a crush.

'The band should be on in a minute,' Charlotte told them all enthusiastically. 'I'll get another round in.' She pushed her way into the crowd around the bar before Hilary could tell her not to buy her another. Hilary watched her touch elbows and insinuate around thighs, blonde hair flouncing and black trousers and waistcoat emphasising her tiny waist. A flash of jealousy was instantly replaced by a cool dislike that Hilary felt could easily be nudged forward into hatred if nothing happened to change her mind.

Charlotte was now standing at the front of the bar, chatting with Alma, who must have been there for hours in order to get such a prime position. An old lady, entirely incongruous in a cream cardigan and mauve tracksuit bottoms, was sitting awkwardly on a bar stool next to Alma, leaning in to her as if she could find shelter in the lee of her bulk. Hilary wondered briefly if the old lady was Alma's mother; they were definitely together.

A spotlight was switched on, and the band emerged onto the dance floor from the whirlpool-effect glass-paned door which opened onto the beer garden. The band members had obviously been waiting outside for some time; their shaking limbs and sucked-in cheeks spoke of a cold night, but Hilary supposed it could also be due to nerves. They took up their positions, and the annoying and tuneless pop song that had been playing on the juke box screeched as it was silenced.

A short woman, thin as a paper-clip, with two nose piercings and long, black hair that was parted severely in the centre of her forehead, stepped into the direct beam of the spotlight with a large, old fashioned microphone held upright in one hand, her fingers clenching and loosening around it. The strong light made her skin appear the colour of milk, and her faded black T-shirt and drainpipe jeans had the appearance of a suit of armour for which she had been inaccurately measured up.

Around the edges of the spotlight the small preparatory movements of the band could just be discerned: a large drummer twiddling his sticks, a tall bass player leaning over his amplifier, a thin keyboard player moving his head from left to right repetitively, and a lead guitarist. Hilary knew that Gary was the guitarist, standing very still on the right of the lead singer, but all she could see clearly of him was his arm, bared to the weak bicep above which the folds of his black T-shirt fell. He was holding a silver plectrum between his thumb and forefinger, poised for action like an artist meditating over a blank canvas.

'We're Power Cord,' the singer said, with what she obviously hoped was nonchalance. Her long hair fell over her face as she bowed her head, putting the microphone behind the screen it gave her. Hilary was reminded of Yoko Ono in those terrible concerts with John Lennon, and she assumed that was the effect the singer was striving for. She half-expected the woman to fetch a blanket and ululate underneath it.

Therefore it came as no real surprise when Gary began the first riff with a fast, practised abandon, the amplifier cranked up high; it was instantly recognisable as *Day Tripper*, but at double the original tempo and played with plenty of attitude. Gary had skill, and Hilary was curious to discover that she had never really doubted it. The rest of the band followed competently and the woman sang with a wispy, ethereal voice that didn't suit the hard edge of the music but had a charm of its own, even though she missed as many notes as she hit.

Charlotte arrived back at the bench with a tray of drinks. Another glass of red wine was placed in front of Hilary, and another half-pint of cider in front of Rob. Rose and Amie were given identical bottles with a lurid orange liquid inside. Charlotte hadn't bought a drink for herself.

Hilary decided she wasn't going to drink the wine. She allowed her fingers to play with the stem of the glass as an accessory, tapping her unvarnished fingernails on it in time with the music.

There was a pause as the last note of *Day Tripper* faded away. The audience decided not to applaud, and Gary pushed on to the next track. The only part of him that was clearly visible now was his elbow. Like a naked mole rat, the pink, wrinkled skin would appear in the spotlight and then dive away again in time to the music. The tempo was slower, more suited to Hilary's mood. She thought she recognised the song within a few bars, but couldn't be sure until the singer had delivered the first line.

'Well she's walking, through the clouds ...'

Little Wing. Hilary had listened to it constantly after the accident in New Zealand: the deaths. The images had been vivid and warm in her mind at a time when other images had needed to be erased. For a split-second Hilary once more saw the snapping rope, heard the shout of the instructor that was cut off by the thuds on the valley floor.

She took a mouthful of wine in the hope of dampening the unpleasant warmth that was uncurling in her stomach, and closed her eyes, willing herself away from those memories with the music. Soon she was floating, imagining Gary's fingers picking out the tune with deft accuracy. She was on a weightless waterbed of wine and soft strings that she didn't want to get off; didn't want to remember that tomorrow was a working day, that people could die and had died on her, that Allcombe was not New Zealand and administration was not adventure training. That she was alone with only the ghosts of dead friends for company.

The song ended and this time there was a faint smattering

of applause, which Hilary thought was well deserved. She didn't recognise the next song, and she allowed it to wash over her without paying too much attention as she watched the other people surrounding her with the detachment of a scientist watching the Brownian motion of particles under glass.

Opposite her, Rob was tapping his fingers on the rim of his half-pint glass and smiling from left to right, listening to both Rose and Charlotte talk simultaneously. He would go far in the social politics of management. Amie was a statue, with an imperious upturned face, her attention focused on the spotlight above. She appeared to Hilary as an eminently boring person who did not merit much interest.

It looked like a winner was being declared in the fight for Rob's attention; Rose was sliding out from the bench and putting on her bleached denim jacket with deliberate lethargy, announcing her intention to leave. Charlotte raised an eyebrow and cocked her head, triumph written through her pert little movements. Hilary decided that she did hate her after all. It was exacerbated by alcohol, but it didn't make her feel any less venomous.

Rose said something that Hilary didn't catch and then turned and walked away from the group in a manly stride, her purple sequined clutch bag held under her arm. Hilary watched her go with a wobbly disinterest, noticing how she gestured to others standing around the room as she went. Rose was obviously popular with the local crowd, mostly girls and lads of her own age, dressed cheaply in lycra and lifting slender-necked bottles filled with multicoloured liquids to their greasy complexions.

As Rose stomped up the three steps to the main door in her platform trainers and disappeared from view, the song finished and another began – a slow number with a loose, climbing melody defined by Gary's sliding hands. Hilary's wine glass was empty again but she couldn't remember drinking its contents, however rubbery her teeth now felt. She recognised the tune, belatedly, as one of those heartfelt numbers by some old soul legend who had come to a nasty end. *These Arms of Mine*, her brain reminded her. 'These arms of mine, they are lonely, lonely, and feeling blue,' the paper-clip woman sang.

Hilary thought Charlotte and Rob made a cute couple, all dimples and glances under eyelashes, pretending to have a serious conversation with plenty of nodding but probably both wondering what the other looked like in underwear. The pub had filled up with couples of all descriptions. Everyone she could see was touching someone else, talking to each other about the light and happy memories that bound them together. Hilary could see Alma with her mother, Charlotte and Rob, others nearly touching, swaying in rhythm. The only thing she was swaying towards was the wood grain of the bench.

The house would be so dark when she returned to it. She was always such a stickler for turning out lights, saving electricity, but now she wished she could have forgotten just this once. She wanted to have a spot of brightness to aim for; a glow to welcome her in.

Hilary's empty glass was plucked from her fingers and Rob was telling her he would get her a fresh one. She didn't reply. The band had started a new song and Gary had moved further into the spotlight. She could see his shoulder, and occasionally his ear and cheekbone as he concentrated intently on his playing. He had a talent, and she could bear his company for that reason alone. He wasn't waiting for love, or romance, or a promotion that amounted to a worthless pat on the back. He had a different goal, and he was relying on himself to fulfil it.

She hoped he would seek her out when the band had finished the set. Hilary wanted to talk, really talk about herself before her cold house became her inevitable last stop that evening. Rob was placing another glass in front of her, and she took in another mouthful.

Sam

Thursday, 2nd November, 10.41 pm

Sam was on first name terms with Allcombe. He was a true local.

He had lived his entire life in the town, had never seriously considered leaving it even though he had travelled all over the world. To him it was The Ally, as it was to all the lifers. Even though it was impossible to be born there as there was no hospital, and they could not be buried there because the nearest cemetery was ten miles away in the next town, there was a core of perhaps twenty people, or four families, to whom the town belonged whether the other inhabitants knew it or not. To them, and to Sam, other places may be more exciting, offer more diversions or have a more illustrious history, but only The Ally sufficed.

His father's house – his house – was a four-floor, thin, stretched building on one of the 1930s hilltop estates on the way out of town. It had a good view of the natural cove from which the remaining fishing boats came and went on the tide, laden with tourists in the summer and empty lobster pots in winter.

Sam had a twenty minute walk to undertake in order to get to work every day. This enforced exercise was instrumental in reminding him just how unfit he had become. The walk tired him, and the work exhausted him; he would never have believed that the nine to five world could be so draining. After four days he was ready to collapse. A weariness that he had never experienced in the superhero business oozed through him. Even when he had kept watch for thirty hours without a break in a dingy alleyway across the street from the suspected hideout of the master criminal, The Whirler, he had been infused with adrenalin that had enabled him to function. In this job he could barely stay awake to two o'clock in the afternoon.

He was getting old.

He was getting old, and he was still so in love with youth. His eyes followed schoolchildren in the street and he aah-ed at babies in pushchairs, even though he could hear his dead father tutting at his feminine behaviour. He had always gone to the park on Sunday afternoons, sitting on the cold iron benches to catch a glimpse of a toddler stretching out anxiously towards the assembling ducks to throw bread to them, releasing the white sticky lumps with a jerky overhead throw and the tiny fingers splayed wide, the wellingtons set far apart to keep balance. He could not see enough of those red wellingtons.

It was a combination of exhaustion and obsession that made Sam miss the gig in the Slaughter. He had fallen asleep on the couch after the walk home from work and had not woken up until late in the evening, coming back to reality with a thick head, crumpled shirt and hunger pangs. A quick change and a cheese sandwich later, he had set out on the long walk back into town, but as The Slaughter and the lights on the pier had finally come into view, he saw something that made him stop and shrink back behind a public waste bin, pressing himself up against the brick wall, away from the electric glow of the neon sign of the fish and chip shop.

She was standing on the pavement in front of the pub, pulling a mobile phone from her bag and beginning an accomplished rap upon its inscrutable buttons, engrossed in the message she was sending. Sam indulged the opportunity to watch the innocent face, sweet as the down of a duckling, empty of a past. His father would have been disgusted with him.

She replaced her phone and began to saunter towards him, in the direction of the promenade. He realised that he knew her. Rose wasn't a girl he had really looked at before that moment; her attitude had put him off, he supposed, now he thought of it. Sam's eyes were drawn to purity, and he knew that he was highly unlikely to find such purity in the soul of an Allcombe teenager. He was certain they had all accumulated much more sexual experience than he had.

In that unguarded moment outside The Slaughter, Rose had been different. When she thought nobody was watching her, she was appealing in the way that the tiny pink tongue of a leopard was appealing.

The waste bin wasn't much cover and he was too dumb-struck to think quickly. Rose had seen him, and her easy steps became a strut, her head thrown back, a cigarette mystically appearing between her lips. She produced a lighter from her bag and was blowing a stream of smoke away as she came to a halt only a yard away from him.

'What are you looking at?' she asked him, amused. The tone of her voice suggested that she already knew the answer to the question.

'Nothing! Nothing.' There was a stiff wind ripping in from the sea and Sam had to speak louder than he liked. He knew already that she thought him useless and ineffectual. It used to be his disguise – his alter ego. Mild-mannered, tongue-tied Sam, destined never to amount to anything. Now that outfit enclosed him, appearing at the worst moments to straitjacket him into enfeeblement.

'You getting chips?' she asked next, with a more genuine interest.

'No,' he said stupidly.

'So what're you doing?' There was a sneer evident in her voice. He wanted to say to her, 'I saw you. I saw the lost look, the hair falling over your tiny face, and I know that was the truth', but he didn't dare. In this mood she could eat him alive, and suddenly that was interesting to him too.

'I was going to see Gary's gig. At The Slaughter.'

Rose shrugged and took another long drag of the cigarette, her fingers spread elegantly apart to draw attention to her over-long fingernails and glittering nail polish. 'Don't bother. It's crap.'

'Is it? Oh dear!' Sam said in bright concern, and she gave him a scornful look, raising her eyebrows before she turned her head away to gaze back in the direction of the pier. He sensed she was no longer interested in the conversation, if she ever had been. Perhaps she was wondering what to do next, or considering 'hanging out' down at the pier. He didn't doubt for a moment that she had many friends of her own age. She was that kind of girl: confident, popular, rude to people whom she considered to be in authority.

He found himself wondering if she took drugs. That was the cool thing now, wasn't it? He had once blown up a drug overlord's Columbian palace in the seventies so he knew that insignificant habits could quickly snowball into real crime, real degradation. That Overlord had begun by cultivating a cannabis pot plant in his flat in Slough, and look where he had ended up.

In Sam's imagination he saw the contours of her face age under the electric light from the chip shop sign, the eyes holding a drawn and empty hopelessness, the skin wrinkling and sagging, her fashion clothes becoming the skin-tight rags of a lady of the night. He felt a wave of conviction that Rose was heading for such an ugly fate and he wanted to tell her all he had seen and done. He wanted to make her understand what people did when they reached the bottom of their souls.

Sam knew she wouldn't have listened.

'What are you going to do now?' he asked her.

'Dunno.' She sniffed, and then dropped her cigarette stub on the ground, not bothering to tread on it. It glowed there until the wind caught the ash and extinguished it with an icy breath. It was far too cold to be standing around. 'Going home, I s'pose.'

'Walking home?'

'No, flying,' Rose snapped out, but Sam thought she was pleased with herself for thinking of the reply rather than genuinely annoyed at him for asking the question.

'It's not safe on your own,' Sam said weakly. She snorted through her nose. 'Perhaps I should walk you home,' he offered, reminding himself that he was older and wiser than her, although he really didn't feel either at that moment. He felt like the greasy chip wrapper that was curving itself around her slim bare ankles and falling underneath her day-glo trainers. He was fooling himself into believing he would still be able to protect her from the awfulness of life; she was going to laugh in his face, deservedly so.

'If you want,' Rose said, without any pause. She didn't even look at him before turning away and taking large strides up the steep curves of the hill that led back to the High Street and past their mutual work place. Sam caught her up, leaving the aroma of frying oil behind.

Rose was setting a frightening pace, but good manners dictated that Sam held a conversation while fighting his increasingly wheezy lungs. 'Where do you live?'

'Up the hill. I don't need you to do this.'

'No no. It's fine. I jus ... wanted to make sure ... you're safe.'

'Yeah, you said.' Unbelievably, she was lighting a cigarette without breaking her pace, the flare of the tip cutting through the darkness of the thick, hulking Victorian buildings that pressed in on them. The road was beginning to level out, but Sam knew the layout of The Ally intimately. A short walk along the High Street would be followed by another uphill sprint that he was dreading; that was where most of the residential estates had been built. If he had been alone he would have succumbed to a taxi by now.

'Are you ... enjoying your ... new job?'

'Are you?' she threw back with blunt disgust, and didn't wait for his answer. 'Might get better once the training's over, I suppose. Training's crap, though.'

'You ... think?'

'Best thing about it is Rob's arse.'

Sam jerked up his head and fought his breath. He knew girls – sorry, women – nowadays were independent and strident, but this was the first time he had heard one be so lascivious in tone. He had never, ever dared to air lustful thoughts himself, knowing too well what his father would have said to such language.

He was shocked to discover he had a half-hearted erection happening in his downstairs department. He hadn't had one of those since the hostage crisis of the Munich Olympics. He had been captured and tortured by Feather-Tickler Woman, who had stroked his inner thigh and demanded to know what government agency he worked for. Not that the incident had anything to do with the hostage crisis – it had happened to be on the television in her living room, and for some reason had stuck in his mind.

Now they were walking past the office, incongruous in its shiny new-ness, Sam a few polite steps behind Rose, trying not to stare at the smooth, bare thighs swaying against the sheen of her tiny pink skirt. The High Street was noisier than Sam had expected; he hadn't ventured out into Allcombe night life since his twenties, when he had learned quickly that club culture had not suited him. Disco had been all the rage then and he didn't remember the fashions being that different from what he was witnessing now.

Two hundred yards from the office, on the opposite side of the road, was a group of about twenty girls and boys – sorry, men and women – of the same age as Rose, Sam guessed. They were lolling in the street and against the crumbling building they had adopted, making careless noises that frightened him. There was something lawless about them, like a band of Technicolor gunmen in a fifties western, waiting with a sneer and a purpose. His legs had already turned to lead with the uphill sprint. Now they disintegrated into water.

Rose didn't slow. She crossed the road and Sam realised she was intending to confront them. He wanted to run but his body refused to turn away and his mind was telling him he could still be a crime-fighter if he thought positively, so he straightened up and kept pace with an expression he hoped was deadpan.

They were in groups of three or four, girls together with skin immune to the cold and hair immune to the wind, and lads in leather and denim with more stubble on one of them than Sam managed to scrape off the side of the basin in a week. Nobody looked at him with any interest.

Rose picked the tallest lad and stood, as Sam suspected was her habit, directly in front of him, invading his space. 'You could have fucking called me,' she spat, her bag clutched in one fist. Sam wouldn't have been surprised if she had swung a punch. The tall man squared up to her, but there was amusement in the line of his traditionally handsome jaw.

'See you've brought your dad along.' His voice was strong and steady, with the drawl on the vowels that all Allcombe inhabitants shared, but in him it was a carelessness that made the girls around him perk up in his direction. Sam was watching a power struggle.

Rose changed her approach. 'So are we going in or not?'

Sam realised belatedly that this was not a gaggle of youths but a disorganised queue leading in to the gloom of the building in front of which they stood. He could glimpse a long corridor leading to a door painted black, flanked by two large men in black suits with the stripes of white shirts visible around their necks and down over their chests and stomachs. The corridor was empty and unadorned, with a peeling dampness about it that didn't welcome a person in.

'Is this a disco?' he muttered to Rose, who was standing in front of him, excluding him from the group. He could see the heads of the taller ones, blowing clouds of smoke over the shorter ones, and the impractical shoes of the shorter ones as they spat chewing gum on the pavement.

Rose turned and fixed him with a cold eye. She looked unpleasantly surprised to find he was still there. 'It's a club.'

'Oh.'

'How old are you?' She pitched her voice to carry deliberately, Sam thought. A titter ran through her female friends.

The tall lad moved forward. Sam refused to meet his eyes. He had seen enough wildlife programs to know that direct eye contact could be deemed as antagonistic. 'Fuck off,' the lad ordered.

Rose sighed and rolled her eyes, like a mother pretending to upbraid a child doing something naughty yet adorable. 'I'm going in,' she said. She obviously had some leadership skills; people began to file in through the entrance at her command. Sam looked at his feet. They weren't moving, either into the club or away from the crowd, and he was certain they should be doing one or the other. When he looked up again Rose and the tall lad were giving him stares that he knew contained a message.

'Right then,' he offered lamely. 'I'll go on home, shall I?'

''Bye,' Rose muttered, and then she was walking through the entrance and down the long corridor, the last of her group tagging along behind her. Sam tried not to watch her go and failed.

The girls and boys receded without a backward glance. They weren't concerned about him, or about age or youth or respect or morality. Their lives were exciting and terrifying. Sam knew the hard work of keeping such a lack of concern in place was beyond him now; it had always been beyond him. He had been a superhero, and he couldn't defeat his will to care about other people, people who didn't need him any more.

He set off along the High Street in the direction of the taxi rank.

Charlotte

Thursday November 2nd, 11.38 pm

'*Gehen sie gerade aus,*' she said.

The computer screen showed a triangular sign with a red border. A black silhouette of a duck on a white background was inside it.

Charlotte opted for 'B' – Beware of Wild Fowl. She shoved the mouse into position and clicked the left button with characteristic efficiency while taking a mouthful of low calorie hot chocolate. She was tired and her head was buzzing due to the unpleasant pub atmosphere, but she was not going to sleep until she had successfully completed her daily mental list:

1. *Work Day. Nine to Five. Give my best!*
2. *Gary's musical evening. Remain sober and connect with team mates.*

3. *Arrange for Rob to walk me home. Swing conversation around to sex.*
4. *Revise for driving theory test. 45 mins.*
5. *Practise German. 15 mins.*

Another day nearly over with. She would sleep well knowing that everything was progressing according to plan. *'Ich möchte ein banane, bitte,'* she said.

The computer screen showed a circular sign with a red background. A large cross in blue had been painted upon it.

Charlotte opted for 'D' – No Stopping. She drained the last of the hot chocolate and tilted her wrist to examine the face of her slim gold watch. Eleven forty. She had left the pub, with Rob, at nine forty-five, after the culmination of Gary's musical set. Home by ten, then coffee until Rob had departed at ten thirty. She had turned the computer on immediately afterwards; that meant she had completed her tasks. She could go to bed.

It gave her great comfort to know she could divide any day into a series of tasks which kept the minutes passing easily and her sleep deep and refreshing. Life after Salzburg had become a line of these inner goals and not much else, but lately she had begun to think outside her self-drawn box once more. Although Rob was one of her objectives, he was also fast becoming more than that. He was becoming a real consideration without limits.

It did seem, if she had any critical comment to make after initial proceedings, that a certain chemistry was lacking between them. There weren't immediate sparks; it was more a gentle glow. However, Charlotte felt strongly that she had made her decision and she would stick to it. Chemistry, like love, was a commodity with which one must speculate in order to accumulate.

There was a light tap on her bedroom door, which then immediately opened. Charlotte found this just one of the truly irritating effects of moving back in with her parents. They were more than happy to revert to behaviour patterns that had last been aired before she had left for university. A lack of privacy was considered a regular feature of life in her parents' world.

Her mother's head appeared at a tilt around the door, a smile painted on it carelessly in a shade of frosted-coral pink. The rest of her face had already been scrubbed clean to reveal dull, grey skin with the texture of old lace that had not been looked after, but even so her mother was never seen without her lipstick. Age was something that had happened to her while Charlotte had been overseas. Now she was a stereotype of a woman in her late fifties, with more grey hair than blonde, more lines than smoothness, more sags than curves, more good wishes than actions.

'Are you busy?' she asked in a sing-song voice.

Charlotte shook her head, manoeuvring the mouse to hit the 'Shut Down' menu on the screen. Her work desk was positioned in the far corner of the room, and her single bed was between it and the door. Three small cuddly bears in graded shades of blue were lined up on her cream Egyptian cotton pillowcase, contrasting nicely with the sky blue curtains and the bookcase painted in the same shade. Behind the door was her solid oak wardrobe and dressing table, fixtures of her room since her birth, and upon the dressing table was her palmtop pilot, nestling between her expensive perfume and no-nonsense brand of deodorant.

'Your father and me are turning in now.'

Your father and I, Charlotte corrected mentally, feeling an instantaneous surge of annoyance. She nodded, hoping that was the end of the conversation.

'Rob seems like a nice young man,' her mother offered in a coaxing tone, edging her way into the room and closing the door. She perched on the edge of the single bed. Charlotte switched off the computer screen and arched her back, one hand fixed to the pressure point on the nape of her neck. 'Your father was glad you brought him in to meet us.'

'God, mother!' Charlotte countered. 'He's my boss! I've only known him for four days! We're hardly engaged!'

'Four days? Are you sure it's a good idea for him to be walking you home?' Her mother crossed her legs and pulled the lapels of her dressing gown together. It was a faded primrose yellow and it clashed horribly with Charlotte's room. Her mouth had assumed the long-familiar pout of distaste that Charlotte had begun to see recently in her own features whilst passing the tacky shop windows on Allcombe High Street. She was working hard to correct it with a few simple facial exercises first thing every morning.

'Do you think he's a serial killer? Does he look like a serial killer?' Charlotte asked her. 'I can take care of myself, you know. I've been living alone, in a foreign country, with no problems at all.' She slid her chair back from the plywood desk and stared at the folds in the curtain material. She hated this kind of conversation.

Her mother shifted on her thigh and cleared her throat. 'Me and your father were worried about that too.' She leaned forward, an earnest look in her grey eyes that made Charlotte squirm. 'Why did you come back so quick, Lottie? Did something happen out there?'

'Nothing happened!' Charlotte defended, aghast at the use of her ancient family nickname. If she hadn't been saving her money for the sexual harassment case bills she would have packed her bags and left for a hotel room that night. 'I'm fine. You're giving me a problem I just don't have!'

'What about those letters you get? The official looking ones? And the ones from Germany?'

Austria, Charlotte correctly mentally. 'Have you been reading my letters?' she demanded, trying to change to the role of interrogator. She already knew that her mother would do no such thing, even though she would be itching to; the woman had an irreproachable and unswerving internal morality.

'Well, I would never do that,' her mother replied, perplexed. 'I only wanted to be sure there's nothing wrong. I worry about you.'

'There's absolutely no need to.' Charlotte had control of the situation now. She faked an expansive yawn. 'I really need my sleep. Tomorrow is a working day.'

Her mother rose, adjusted the belt of her robe and shuffled towards her. Charlotte steeled herself for the grating, perfunctory kiss on the forehead that inevitably followed. There was a brief, light touch above her eyebrows that she closed her eyes against, and when she reopened them her mother was quietly shutting the bedroom door behind her.

Charlotte relaxed a little. Yet the house was small and full of uncomfortable memories of her childhood, most of which had been spent in self-imposed loneliness within this very room, with her books of foreign places and her jigsaws of grand landmarks to occupy her. She had thought she had left that life behind her; that university had changed her utterly. Any time spent in this place robbed her of the confidence which had been so difficult to acquire. A fluent speaker of the German language, a budding manager, an independent woman who can take care of herself? She was none of those in Allcombe.

She waited until she heard the creaking of her parents' bed and the click of their bedside lamp before she undressed, wrapped a towel around herself and slipped down the staircase and into the white-tiled bathroom. The shower cubicle, austere in the extreme cleanliness her mother imposed on it, promised to wash out the smoke and the sweat of the day. Charlotte dropped the towel on the cold linoleum floor and stepped over the spider plants arranged in pots around the lip of the cubicle, closing the plastic door behind her and turning the octagonal dial to allow the jets of freezing water to hit her.

She gasped, and felt her skin contract until the water began to warm. The hum of the shower and the pumping of her blood intensified the ringing in her ears from the loud music she had sat through earlier, running as an accompaniment to her thoughts. Charlotte rescued the shampoo bottle from the lip of the shower unit and began to massage her scalp as she began a blow-by-blow remembrance of the walk home with Rob. Just thinking about it was an antidote to the teenage worries her mother resurrected within her.

The band had finished playing and Gareth had arrived at their bench, flushed and nervous, pleased with himself and desperate for a good opinion from them. She had heaped praise upon him until he had relaxed and turned his attention to Hilary, allowing her to return her's solely to Rob. Amie had already left and the pub began to empty rapidly. Rob had told her the clientele were departing in order to reach Lusty's, the only local night club, before the entrance fee increased to £2.00.

Five minutes later, in the surprising peace of the deserted pub, with empty glasses between their fingers, it had only taken a whispered suggestion and a touch on the arm to persuade Rob to walk her home. On a cold night, an artful shiver resulted in the donation of Rob's leather jacket, still warm from his body. A stumble had resulted with his hand on the centre of her back, and those acts had given her the confidence to steer the conversation towards her intended destination.

'I'm still waiting for a response,' she said, after he had finished telling her that she should look for a pair of shoes that offered more lateral support for her weak ankles.

'From the solicitor?'

'That's right. I can't wait to get this issue resolved.'

'I'm sure.' Rob gave her a sympathetic smile as they walked in tandem along the promenade. 'It shocked me to learn that such terrible management exists. You're very brave to follow this up, to make sure that this man gets what he deserves.'

The softness in his voice was comforting and made her next statement easier to make. 'Thanks, Rob. But, you know, this has affected me more deeply that I ever thought it would. I find it so difficult to trust anyone. Particularly ... particularly men. I just can't get close to anyone.' She was surprised to hear her voice crack at the end of her speech. It was unlike her to lose control at such a crucial moment in her plan.

'I'm sorry,' Rob said, after a pause, and as his hand moved to squeeze her shoulder, sliding across the leather of his own coat that she had draped about her, 'all I can suggest is that you give it time. I mean, Charlotte, how long is it since you returned from Salzburg? And the issue is still unresolved. The court case has to be finalised. I'm sure you'll find it a great relief when it's over.'

'It's not just that. It was before, too. I mean, a year of sexual harassment. You don't just get over it.' Confusion and embarrassment overtook her. Her composure was far from what it ought to be. He had to be made to want to protect her, not pity her.

'Sssh. I'm sure the right man will come along and everything will fall into place, you know? You just need to find someone you feel comfortable with, yeah?' He squeezed her shoulder again and she allowed her head to drop against his chest for a moment.

'The right man ...' Charlotte stopped walking and turned, facing Rob as he halted behind her, standing close. 'But what if he doesn't know he's the right man? Or if he's too scared to tell me how he feels? What then, Rob?'

He gave her a melting gaze of reassurance, his eyebrows raised over his beautiful blue eyes. 'Don't you worry. How could he fail to want to tell you you're perfect for him? Men dream about true love too, you know.'

'Do they? Do they really?' she asked him earnestly. The eye contact was knee-trembling in its intensity. She parted her lips gently in hope, but he was too much of a gentleman to take advantage of a lady in distress. He moved backwards a fraction, uncomfortably, and Charlotte broke the moment to save him from any embarrassment. 'This is my parents' house. Would you like to come in for coffee?'

'Okay,' he said smoothly, without hesitation, and they had walked into the house with a new and precious intimacy established between them.

Of course, twenty minutes of sitting on the sofa making small talk with her mother while her father screamed at *Question Time* on the ageing television had banished all the warm and fuzzy feelings. A quick peck on the cheek had been the only goodbye mustered after Rob had drained his coffee at record speed, probably scalding his mouth in the process. She would have to see if he had any trouble forming his consonants tomorrow.

Charlotte applied her deep cleansing camomile conditioner to her hair and mentally compiled her list for Friday:

1 Work Day. Nine to Five. Give my best!
2. Find out what Rob thinks of me. (Ask him for reassurance.)
3. Phone solicitor for update.

She shook her head and erased point three. She had promised herself she would wait a full week before speaking to Mr Forth again. That meant she had to leave the Salzburg issue until Monday. Saturday and Sunday threatened to be long and boring days.

3. Find alternative weekend activity.

Perhaps she could make friends with a course mate who

could drive so they could get out of Allcombe for a few hours. She had no idea which of her associates had a car, or even where they might go. She just knew she couldn't spend forty-eight hours hiding in her bedroom from her parents' constant attempts to suggest family outings. These invariably involved buying a Mr Whippy from the none-too-sanitary ice cream van on the promenade or being given two bingo cards to watch in a room full of people who no longer possessed their own teeth, rudimentary bowel control, or any shred of self-respect.

4. Revise for driving theory test. 45 mins.
5. Practise speaking German. 15 mins.

As Charlotte rinsed out her hair she speculated on which of her colleagues were appropriate for a friendly relationship. Hilary and Rose irritated her the most; they could be easily dismissed from the running. The problem was, she really didn't know enough about those people who shared her days, and she couldn't remember the information they had given in the Induction as she had been practising her own speech instead of listening properly. A black mark against her, she mentally admonished. Although they obviously hadn't said anything interesting or she would have remembered it.

She turned off the shower and stepped out, retrieving her towel.

6. Find out who is actually interesting in my training group.
7. Correlate info with who owns/drives a car, and befriend.

She wrapped the towel around herself, brushed and flossed her teeth, and turned off the bathroom light behind her.

Gary

Friday, 3rd November, 9.03 am

To: Alma Chippendale, Amie Doe, Hilary Black, Gareth Lester,
    Rose French, Sam Spurling, Charlotte Jackson
From: Rob Church
Re: E-Mail

Hi All,

Welcome to the E-Mail system and to your new computers
and desks. I've arranged an hour of free practice, nine o'clock
until ten o'clock, when no monitoring of your mails will take
place. Use this time to acquaint yourselves with e-mail, and
please ask if you encounter any queries or problems.

At ten o'clock monitoring of E-Mails, as per company policy,
will be activated. E-Mail is a privilege which can easily be
revoked if it is abused – it is intended for use on WORK
ISSUES ONLY. Not for gossip or chat. Please bear that in mind.

There will be a training session at 10.15am which will
concentrate on cascading information re the in-house
computer system, the Client Interface and Data-Capture
system (or CID). This session will last until midday.

Rob

————

To: Gareth Lester
From: Rob Church
Cc: Alma Chippendale, Amie Doe, Hilary Black, Rose French,
    Sam Spurling, Charlotte Jackson
Re: Last Night

Gary,

Just a quick mail to let you know how impressed we all were
by Power Cord's gig last night! Kicking! It's great to know we
have our very own Eric Clapton right here in the training group!

NB. The company's christmas dinner is now only seven
weeks away and a talent contest is being held this year –

how would you feel about putting together an act to
represent our group? Maybe you could find out if anyone
can sing, dance or play an instrument? I'm really interested
to see what you can come up with – I'm certain it will knock
the socks off the opposition!

Congrats again on the gig.

Gary sat up straight in his brand new swivel chair and risked
a glance over the top of his computer screen towards Rob's
desk. Rob was looking straight at him, wearing a scarily en-
thusiastic expression with his thumbs raised, his hands ruddy
against the shiny pink material of his immaculate shirt.

He ducked behind his screen.

He decided to ignore the previous e-mail. Perhaps if he
didn't mention it, nobody else would either. The phrase 'talent
contest' brought to mind memories of Butlins holidays and fat
girls in sequinned leotards attempting the splits to Irene Cara
tracks: this was not something he wanted to get involved in.

Gary leaned over and fiddled with the chair control in
order to lower it further. He liked the cover his new seating
position gave him, although he was anxious about the
people who had been assigned to share his table. They would
not have been his first choice, but he supposed that was the
point. Last night Hilary had dryly stated that she thought
Rob was enough of a slave to management tactics to think
he'd be improving the group dynamic by seating together
the people who experienced a natural and healthy antipathy
towards each other.

Their new training environment was situated in the basement, along a corridor that was still in the process of being
built and was currently demarcated only by hessian-covered
screens with paintings by the Allcombe Juniors tacked upon
them. The restaurant was at the other end of the makeshift
corridor and the main boiler had to be next to them; most

people had already shed at least one layer of clothing as it became obvious this was to be the hot-spot of the building, at least during the winter months.

It was a large, open-plan area with nondescript brown floor tiles and overhead lighting in strips that ran along the length of the ceiling. Gary suspected the planners had realised this windowless underground room would impart a sense of dislocation from the real world to those working within it, for a large digital clock, the numbers broadcast in a steady red, kept count of the hours and days for them. As the only object of interest on the walls, it commanded far too much attention. So far he had seen everyone, including Rob, glance at its black outline at least twice. Right now it was reading 9.07 am, 3/11.

The team had been split on to three separate tables arranged at right angles to each other, and Rob's desk made up the fourth corner of the square. Gary was in the opposite corner from Rob, tidied away against the back wall, with Rose sitting opposite him and Amie seated on his left. Luckily, with his chair now lowered, he was not risking accidental eye contact with either of his table mates.

Rose and Amie scared him, although for different reasons. He had been aware of Rose for a few years now, her robust presence coming to his attention as he was finishing his A Levels and she was starting her GCSEs. She had been known throughout the school as the bully of her year, inspiring terror in other girls her age. Mental cruelty had been her speciality, by all accounts, making both her peers and the teachers powerless to confront her over something which left no physical evidence. More than one girl had been turned into a quivering wreck when beholding Rose striding through the corridors towards them; Gary had seen her effect upon them for himself.

He was hoping that she had grown out of it, but the first signs did not look good. It was ridiculous, but he was frightened of her in the same way that he was frightened of wasps and horror films. Just sitting opposite her heightened his apprehension and tightened his stomach, as if she would sting him or bite his neck if he did not keep his wits about him.

Amie was a type of woman he had absolutely no experience with, and he could not think of a single thing to say to her. He had heard that Wales was not much different from the West Country but Amie displayed none of the behaviour of local girls: no street-wise back-chat, no tiny outfits complemented by handbags just large enough to hold a multi-coloured condom, and no obligatory mobile phone. She couldn't even meet his eyes without blushing.

Currently Amie was looking at the computer as if she had no idea what it was or why it was flashing at her. He caught her casting glances to either side of her, watching what the others did and copying them tentatively, laying one white hand upon the mouse and moving it experimentally with widening eyes. What could he find to say to a woman who didn't know what a mouse was? She was horrifyingly removed from the modern world.

To: Gareth Lester
From: Hilary Black
Re: Talent show!

I'm sure you're overwhelmed at being given the opportunity to organise our effort for the talent show! How grateful you must be to Rob for coming up with such a splendid idea! I personally would like to volunteer my services as a sarcastic heckler from the audience. PS Have you got a hangover today?

Gary did, in fact, have a light stomach and a creeping headache from the excesses of the night before, but that was negligible compared with the relief he was experiencing over the jocular tone Hilary was using with him. Fast drinking before closing time had established a rapport between them and he had thought about it all night, hoping that she would not choose to resurrect her barriers in the light of day. She had unveiled such a wicked sense of humour to him. It made him feel that she saw through the people around them and deemed them unworthy of a serious response; such an attitude made the working world easier to deal with.

He looked over at her. She had been allocated to the table in front of his own, along with Charlotte, giving evidence to her theory that the people who had initially disliked each other were now the victims of enforced socialising. As he watched, she swivelled in her chair to say something to Rob at his desk behind her, and then turned back to her computer. Her attention was anywhere but on Gary.

He typed a reply to her message with his forefingers.

To: Hilary Black
From: Gareth Lester
Re: Talent show!

Hilary
A ha ha ha ha ha! Shall I tell Rob that you want to do a solo turn on the talent night as a comedian? But then, you would have to be funny for that, so maybe not.

Hangover isn't too bad. My parents were pissed off at me because I tripped over the umbrella stand when I got in last night and couldn't get up again. My mum had to help me to bed. How do you feel today?

He clicked on 'Send' and immediately began to regret it. Was it too familiar in tone? Did it make him look ridiculous? Would she laugh? And it wasn't exactly the whole truth; there was another event from last night that he desperately wanted to share with her but was ashamed to do so. He had called Millicent's hall of residence from a pay phone on the stagger home. He had let it ring for minutes, but with no answer. He didn't know this morning what he had intended to say last night, and he was relieved beyond measure that he hadn't got a chance to say it. He had enough to regret already; the umbrella stand incident would take a lot of apologising before he was forgiven.

To: Alma Chippendale, Amie Doe, Gareth Lester, Hilary Black, Rose French, Sam Spurling
From: Charlotte Jackson
Cc: Rob Church
Re: Getting To Know You

Hi everyone,
As we get the remains of this hour to utilize the e-mail system in order to become familiar with it, why doesn't everyone let the group know (via e-mail, of course!) the answers to a couple of simple questions:

1. What are you doing this weekend?
2. What is your ideal car? (and tell us what your current car is for comparison!)

I'll go first:

I don't have any firm plans this weekend so I'm open to suggestions if anyone would like to get together for some laughs and fun.

I don't drive!!! Really!!!!!! I'm learning at the moment, but I would like a new Mini when I pass, or maybe a Smart Car.

Looking forward to your replies!
Charlotte

The group had been together for a week and he already had a clear idea that this was typical Charlotte behaviour. He could guess Hilary would be rolling her eyes. Gary glanced over at the desk to the left of him. Sam and Alma were both bending over their computers with painful concentration, muttering to each other as they crawled towards typing their e-mail responses. It was lovely to see two older people bonding.

Gary was halfway through typing his own answers to Charlotte's questions when he received a new mail. Quickly he finished his reply, checked it briefly for spelling mistakes, and sent it to the group.

To: Alma Chippendale, Amie Doe, Charlotte Jackson, Hilary
    Black, Sam Spurling, Rose French
From: Gareth Lester
Cc: Rob Church
Re: Getting To Know You

Hello

I have a practice session with my band this Saturday so that should keep me busy. Probably I'll stay in bed on Sunday to recover from this week!

My ideal car is the E Type Jaguar. I can drive but I can't afford a car yet due to my (expensive) year at university. I have a loan to pay off before I can think about buying anything new!

Thanks

Satisfied, Gary clicked on the new mail.

To: Gareth Lester
From: Hilary Black
Re: Aaaaaargh!

Did you know that Charlotte Jackson is the evil love child of Florence Nightingale and Napoleon? She wants to conquer the world and heal us all at the same time! Thanks but no thanks. I have an idea – don't reply to her e-mail for a while!!! Let her sweat. It'll take the rest of the group an hour to type a sentence anyway. Have you seen Sam and Alma? Perhaps they're more used to an abacus.

Sorry about the trouble with your parents. Do they drive you up the wall? I bet you can't get much music practise done there?

He made sure Amie couldn't see his screen from her sitting position and typed a quick reply.

To: Hilary Black
From: Gareth Lester
Re: Aaaaaargh!

Doh! I already replied to Charlotte – sorry! But if you think Sam and Alma are confused, take a look at Amie. Even if she does figure out how to read her mail I bet she won't know what a car is.

Yeah, my parents do wind me up sometimes, and no, you're right, I can't practise a lot as they go mad at the noise. Still, I can't afford to move out yet so there's no point in complaining. And they're pretty cool, really. They didn't moan too much when I got kicked out of uni and had to move back in with them.

Do you think Sam's ideal car will be a Model T Ford?

Gary was quickly finding out that there was something ex-hilarating about chatting via computer. It had a confessional quality to it. He was aware that he was beginning to worry less about what was expected of him, and saying what he wanted to say instead.

To: Amie Doe, Charlotte Jackson, Hilary Black, Rose French,
    Gareth Lester, Sam Spurling
From: Alma Chippendale
Cc: Rob Church
Re: Getting To Know You

I thought computers were meant to make life easier.
I'm looking after an elderly relative (yes, older than me) who is visiting me, so that's the weekend tied up. I drive but I haven't got a car over here because I can't get used to stick shifts and where would I go anyway? Is there anything in an hour's drive of this place that's worth seeing?

To: Alma Chippendale, Amie Doe, Charlotte Jackson, Hilary
     Black, Gareth Lester, Sam Spurling
From: Rose French
Cc: Rob Church
Re: Getting To Know You

I don't want to learn to drive. Buses are cheap and there are
loads of cars already. I don't want a car. Friday and Saturday
nights I'm going down the pub with my mates, then
probably on to a club.

Gary sneaked a look at Rose. She was slumped back in her
chair, looking at her nail polish and displaying no interest in
her new computer or surroundings. She spoke to him suddenly, without raising her eyes from her cuticles.

'Do you want to go outside for a fag?'

Alma was the only other smoker in the group; Gary
couldn't find any satisfaction in being thought of as better
company than the abrupt American. At twenty minutes past
nine it was far too early to feel justified in taking a ciggy break,
but he was too much of a coward to suggest that to Rose.

'Not just yet, thanks.'

'Suit yourself,' she told him with spiky sibilance, and
grabbed her handbag from under her desk before sauntering
brazenly out of the room. Both Rob and Charlotte watched
her go and then exchanged a look which told Gary volumes
about how they viewed themselves compared with the rest
of the group. They were working on making themselves a
separate unit.

'Uh, Rob,' Sam said softly from the next table. He cleared
his throat and called again, this time at a volume Rob might
reasonably be expected to hear. The good-looking trainer got
up from his desk in top gear and crossed the carpet tiles to
Sam's side in record time. 'I can't seem to get this to send.'

Alma, her chins dropping and her arms crossed over her
impressive chest, muttered something in a derogatory tone

that Gary didn't hear, but it was obvious that Sam did. The older man recoiled backwards from her venom.

'Now, Alma, not everyone picks things up straight away,' Rob admonished. He began to lecture Sam in a patient, play-school voice. 'You need to put in your addresses, Sam. See?'

Perhaps Sam and Alma weren't going to become a sweet old couple after all.

To: Hilary Black, Charlotte Jackson, Gareth Lester, Rose
    French, Amie Doe, Alma Chippendale
From: Sam Spurling
Cc: Rob Church
Re: Getting To Know You

Hello everyone.
This is all a bit new to me. I hope I'm doing it right.

I don't have any plans for the weekend. I might go out for a drive, now you mention it! I have a Volvo. That's my favourite car, too. My Dad always used to say, flashy is no substitute for steady and safe!

Thank you

Sam

Gary looked around the room and then, against his will, looked at the digital clock. 9.32. Knowing Rose was propping up the wall outside and smoking a ciggie enhanced his own craving to bursting point, but he had set himself a deadline of ten o'clock. He tapped his fingers against the desk. He adjusted the contrast setting on his screen. He wrote his name on the underside of his mouse mat.

The flashing Inbox eventually provided a ready distraction. Gratefully he clicked upon it.

To: Gareth Lester
From: Hilary Black
Re: Why Don't You-?

Hi
You can call this a crazy idea if you like, but I've been thinking
that really I need some company in my house, and you hate
living at home. What do you think about becoming my house
mate? The second bedroom is fairly large and I can cover
expenses for the first month. When we get paid we can start
going halves on bills, food, etc. It should work out fairly cheap.

And the best bit is … there's a basement so you and your
band can practise down there whenever you like!! Let me
know if you're interested. No pressure, okay?

PS. What's a Model T Ford? Never heard of it.

Gary read it, and then read it again. It wasn't an offer he
needed to consider; he just wanted to check he hadn't misunderstood it. When he was sure Hilary really was asking
him to move in with her he dared to feel eternally grateful
to God for this magnificent opportunity. She must really like
him. He could put the past behind him and concentrate on
really liking her.

He made himself wait for a full minute before starting to
type his reply. He wanted her to think he had needed time
to weigh up his options before agreeing to her proposal.

To: Hilary Black
From: Gareth Lester
Re: Why Don't You-?

Wow! That just might work!
Seriously, though, are you sure you don't mind? Of course I'll
go halves on bills, food, etc. and I promise not to leave my
socks in the sink or anything, but you should really think about
this carefully. I mean, you hardly know me really although we
seem to get along really well … (I think so, anyway!)

So, that's great with me if it's great with you. Is it great with
you?

PS. A Model T Ford is a really old car. But you'd probably
worked that out anyway.

Was he giving her too much opportunity to back out? He was so ridiculously stupid; of course she was going to back out. He risked a look at her over the top of his computer screen. She was typing in an awkward style, not dissimilar from his own efforts, her attention melded to the keyboard. In her octagonal glasses Gary occasionally caught a flash of the electronic glow emanating from her screen. There was a severity in Hilary's appearance that suited her personality. Gary saw a strict morality in her. Yet again she reminded him of Millicent.

Gary resolutely pushed that thought aside and waited for Hilary's reply with increasing anxiety coupled with the pressing desire for a ciggie. The clock on the wall was now showing 9.47 in an ever brighter shade of red.

His Inbox flashed. He clicked it open and started to read.

To: Alma Chippendale, Amie Doe, Gareth Lester, Sam
    Spurling, Charlotte Jackson, Rose French
From: Hilary Black
Cc: Rob Church
Re: Getting To Know You

Hello
I was going to swot up on some reading re codes of conduct
in the banking industry this weekend, just to keep myself
ahead of the game.

I learned to drive when I was seventeen, got my HGV licence
at nineteen. I don't have a car at the moment but I'm looking
at buying a Subaru Impreza WRC next year.

It had taken Gary a line or so of confusion before he had looked back at the header and realised it was not a reply to his own mail. Still, he read it with interest. Was Hilary being truthful or pulling Charlotte's chain? He was fairly certain she had no interest in reading about banks, but then he couldn't picture her driving a truck either. Why would she take her HGV licence? Her mail raised more questions than it answered.

To: Gareth Lester
From: Hilary Black
Re: Why Don't You-?

Did you read my reply to Charlotte? That should keep her
busy reading dull textbooks all weekend. She would hate it if
anybody else appeared to be more zealous than her! Serves
her right.

By the way, I know you well enough. You'll do fine. You can
move in this weekend if you want. God Knows I have
nothing else to do.

Gary relaxed, reassuring himself that she hadn't changed her
mind, and then tensed again as he considered her mail. He'd
do fine? For what?

Rob had finished working with Sam and crossed over to
Amie, who was looking terrified of both the computer and the
trainer. Today she was wearing a high-necked, ruffled blouse
that could only have escaped from a Laura Ashley shop. Her
long hair was pinned back tightly into a large bun that was half
the size of her head; Gary could foresee a severe neck ache
coming to her by the end of the day.

'How are you doing, Amie? Are you experiencing any
problems? You haven't formulated your reply to Charlotte's
message yet, have you?' Rob asked her, hitching up his desert
coloured trousers to crouch beside her, meeting her at her
own eye level. Amie turned her head away from him, fiddling
with first her pencil, then the corner of her new shiny blue
mouse mat.

'All you need to do is click here to get started,' Rob
pointed out as he spoke slowly to her. As he leaned in past
her to touch the screen, Amie flinched away from him. Her
head trembled on the strong stalk of her neck.

Rose returned from her unscheduled break, her careless
strides taking her across the room and close to Rob's back so

that she almost brushed his blond hair with her swinging hand. Gary watched as she slumped back down in her chair. Amie's eyes were fixed upon Rose, and in them he could see a kind of melting anguish, rather like a silent plea was being thrown at the youngest member of the group. Rose met it with an immoveable hardness. Something he did not understand was being exchanged between the two women who sat at his desk, and he felt he lacked the imagination to guess what it was.

At that point Amie got up and walked out of the room. Rob was left mid-sentence, which petered out into a long vowel without any meaning as he watched her walk away from him. She didn't hurry, or cry, or do anything unusual, and Gary didn't immediately recognise that something strange had happened. At least, not until Rob's shocked face registered with him before the trainer shot up from his crouch and strode out after her.

Gary looked around him. Everyone else had stopped in their own movements to follow the action.

'What was all that about?' he asked Rose, who shrugged. Sensing Hilary's eyes on him from across the room, Gary looked up and shrugged at her. Hilary shrugged back. Charlotte and Sam were staring at the path Amie and Rob had taken out of the room as if they might suddenly reappear to play out the brewing drama for the rest of the group's benefit. Charlotte was half out of her chair, but even she lacked the courage to follow them and insinuate herself into Amie's problems without an invitation.

A long minute passed without incident. Gary noticed the flashing of his Inbox once more.

To: Alma Chippendale, Amie Doe, Rose French, Gareth
    Lester, Hilary Black, Charlotte Jackson
From: Sam Spurling

Re: (Fwd) Weekend Activities

Hello again
I think I might be getting the hang of this!
Does anyone here want to come along on a trip? I can
squeeze a few more people in the car. Perhaps we could go to
one of the local attractions that stay open during the winter?

-----Original Message-----

To: Sam Spurling
From: Charlotte Jackson
Re: Weekend Activities

Hi Sam!
I was wondering ... since you say you're not too busy most
weekends, perhaps we could go somewhere together one
Saturday? Keep each other company? It would be great to
get away with a friend for a few hours. What do you think?

Charlotte

He shot an inquisitive glance at Hilary, who gave him a 'not
in a million years would you catch me attending a weekend
excursion with Sam and Charlotte' look in return, complete
with both hands around her neck and her tongue sticking
out rigidly over her teeth. He had to repress a smirk, which
Rose saw and dismissed with a bored scowl. That girl really
wasn't interested in anyone but herself.

The digital clock read 10.02, making it definitely time for a
ciggie. Gary checked he had a packet and a lighter in his
trouser pockets before getting up the courage to saunter out of
the room. He was passing Sam and Alma's desk when Rob and
Amie reappeared and crossed directly in front of him, Rob
leading Amie back to her chair, holding her hand and speaking
to her in soft, soothing words Gary couldn't quite hear. Amie's
eyelashes were wet and she had put her free hand up inside
her ruffled blouse, pulling it out of shape over her stomach.

Amie wasn't quite with it, Gary decided, but his real attention at that moment lay in the chilled grey wind blowing outside and the ciggie smoke he was allowed to breathe in by the main entrance. Perhaps he would discuss it with Hilary tomorrow, after all his belongings were moved in.

Just thinking about that made him fish out his second cigarette from his pocket before he had even finished the first.

Amie

Friday, 3rd November, 1.44 pm

She played with the remaining chip on her plate. It had a series of grey spots, shaped rather like a weeping eye, at one end of its soggy carcass, soaked through with the remainder of the tomato juice from the baked beans. The lessons of her church were too pervasive to be ignored. Amie stabbed the chip with her fork and put it in her mouth, giving it five strong chews before she swallowed it down. There. The plate was cleared.

The restaurant was, as usual, quiet during the lunch hour. Nobody who had eaten there once was eager to repeat the experience, but Amie enjoyed the stodgy food, the peace of the empty chrome tables and the lazy kitchen staff who dumped pie and mash on plates with languid strokes of their utensils. The lunch break was the one hour of the day in which she could relax. The training programme made her feel stupid, and she watched the other group members nervously, trying to understand them, yet keep them at bay. She didn't see how she would ever become a modern working girl when even the most basic flashings of the computer frightened her. It had taken her three hours to type one paragraph on Tuesday. That made her officially the most useless member of the group.

Her anxiety did not abate at home. Her father continued to play his games and keep his own counsel, preaching to her about avoiding the sins of the modern world while knocking back a pint glass of sherry and watching *Big Brother* from the eternal safety of the sofa. Amie felt as if she was a gymnast performing flips on a slender beam for the benefit of the Allcombe audience; one mis-step would throw her to the floor for their amusement. She knew her feet were getting heavier and her ears were ringing under the pressure. She could not stay upright for much longer.

Time for dessert. Amie unwrapped the corner of her King Size chocolate bar and took two quick and dainty bites. She was savouring the sweetness of the caramel and biscuit mixture – just as good as the television had promised her it would be – when she saw Rose pushing through the restaurant doors with her chin-jutting attitude firmly in place.

Rose surveyed the room quickly, working her sharp eyes across the shiny surfaces and dishevelled chair legs, until they rested on Amie. Amie returned her stare nervously, wishing she could dip under the table and pretend that if she couldn't see someone, they couldn't see her. Rose began a slow walk towards her.

Amie ran a freeze-frame of emotions that were overwhelming in intensity. Did Rose want to be friends? Did she want to make an enemy, or find a scapegoat? What would Rose say? What would she find to say in response? Please God, don't let her mention her crying fit this morning. Her utter humiliation was still branded upon her flesh, so that her face was red and scorched in remembrance by the time Rose had pulled out the seat opposite her and flopped down into it.

'You will not fucking believe what just happened to me,' she said to Amie, who could not help but blench at the careless obscenity.

'Really?' she replied, feeling an intense relief that the

conversation was not going to be directed at her. It looked like she was expected to listen, not participate.

'My boyfriend dumped me.' There was a mournful bitterness clinging to her words, but when she spoke again it had transformed into a shimmering anger. Rose fished into her tiny pink bag and produced her mobile phone, brandishing it over the surface of the table. 'He couldn't even be arsed to do it to my face. Can you believe he fucking texted me? Are you leaving that?'

She dropped the phone and swept up Amie's chocolate bar, taking a large mouthful without bothering to unwrap it further. She pulled the wrapper out from between her teeth and dropped it on the table, where it lay, glittering with saliva.

'I'm sorry,' Amie said softly. She had never had a boyfriend, but she could imagine the pain of such an event.

'Too fucking right you're sorry,' Rose spat back through her mouthful of chocolate. 'I'm sorry, you're sorry. Fancy a ciggie?'

'I don't smoke.' Amie wished she could control her automatic wave of fear every time she heard a swear word. It helped to keep her as the outsider of the group, and it made it practically impossible to hold a conversation with Rose.

'Aren't you just the Queen of fucking Sheba.' There was no malice in her tone. She looked hard at Amie, judging her in the way Amie might have once assessed if an apple from the tree harboured a wasp inside it. She had loved to work on the communal farm, watching nature take hold of the land around her and battling it into order. Rose was staring at her long hair, held off her face by a wooden clip, her demure white blouse with the just visible strong white straps of her bra underneath, and her scrubbed pink face.

'Why do you dress like that?'

Amie had been brought up to tell the truth but she couldn't begin to formulate it into a decent answer that would take less than ten minutes to explain. Rose took her pause as a refusal to reply, and her tone altered. The atmosphere of the conversation was darkening, leaving Amie floundering in new territory.

'It's like you're in a pantomime or something. Is that what you are? A pantomime dame? Or the pantomime cow?' The barb wasn't incredibly effective as Amie had never been sure what a pantomime was, but the venom was unmistakable. She willed herself to get up and walk away, but she was magnetised to her chair, pressed into it by the force of Rose's repulsion.

'You should know everybody looks at you and laughs. They really fucking piss themselves when they see you coming. I've seen them. You go past, sailing down the corridor like the fucking Queen, waiting for the computer to work itself.'

'I haven't used a computer before,' Amie explained. Her lunch was sitting uncomfortably just above the waistband of her skirt. When she swallowed she could taste it again in her mouth.

'Where are you from? Everybody has a computer now. Anybody who doesn't must be really fucking thick. Is that what it is? Is everyone in the place you come from really thick?'

'No ... it's just different there.'

'It's just different there,' Rose repeated in a high-pitched voice that filled the restaurant. A few of the serving staff glanced round. Amie smiled weakly in their direction. 'And what was that thing about this morning? That storming out thing? Was that because I didn't reply to that stupid fucking e-mail you sent me?'

Rose took another bite of the chocolate bar and made large chewing movements with her jaw, never taking her stare from Amie, who had been dreading that the interrogation might take this turn. She felt so foolish when she remembered that stupid message she had sent to Rose, and even more ridiculous about the tears it had provoked; tears she could not explain to Rob, who had been quite amazed that anything in his training course could have caused such distress.

She told a lie with a terrible twist of her conscience. 'That wasn't to do with the e-mail.' She knew she'd lie awake at nights over that whopper.

'Good, because that would have been so fucking lame. I mean …' Rose snorted, '… just because I couldn't be arsed to reply to that pleading little mail.' She assumed her high-pitched whine once more, which Amie realised was Rose's attempt at impersonating her Welsh accent. '"I'd really like us to be friends, would you like that? If you would, reply to this mail because I'm too shy to ask you in person." Did you actually think I'd say yes to that? Get a fucking grip.'

Amie stared at her cleared plate, the knife and fork lined up upon it, pointing away from her. She had always been taught to place her cutlery together at the end of a meal to signify she had finished. She reached out and moved the knife, nudging it to a right angle, crossing the fork over the greasy residue on the white plate.

Rose lowered her voice to a soft understanding. 'I get it. I get it now. I see what was going with that whole crying thing.' She leaned over the table. 'You did it to get to Rob, didn't you? You're trying to get into Rob's pants?'

'No!' Her denial was emphatic, and had escaped her before she could control it. All the time Rob had been holding her she had been cringing in his grasp, wishing he would leave her alone but afraid to say it. She felt nothing but distaste for his warm, hard skin and designed platitudes and epithets.

'So what is it, then? What's wrong with you? You're going to have to tell me, or I'll just have to assume it's about Rob, and I'll have to tell him that you're hot for him.' She sat back in the chair, and her sky blue halter neck top rode up to expose a silver ring with a round red crystal, resembling a drop of blood, pierced through her navel. Rose's clothes had been getting less professional and more revealing over the first week of the course, the amount of exposed flesh increasing every day. 'Is it just that you're pathetic? Just say so, then. Say you're pathetic.'

'I'm pathetic.'

Rose blinked. Amie realised she had taken the teenager by surprise with her willingness to capitulate. She felt perfectly calm; the words meant nothing to her. It was only the truth, and she knew no harm could come from speaking the truth.

'All right, then. I tell you what. I feel pretty fucking sorry for you. I feel like I should do the right thing and help you. I reckon I can make you a bit less pathetic. Would you like that?'

'Okay,' Amie said. She needed to leave her old rules behind. It was a question of survival.

'Right. We'll meet here every lunch time, then. You supply the chocolate, and I'll supply the know-how.' Rose was a born leader, Amie realised. Given an opportunity, she endeavoured to squeeze success from it. 'And we can work on it tomorrow as well. You're going on the trip, aren't you?'

Tomorrow was Saturday, and Charlotte's picnic to a surprise destination was taking place. It was meant to be a team-building exercise, although the only other team member attending was Sam, who was the driver. Amie hadn't expected Rose to even consider attending. 'Yes, I'm going. I told Charlotte I would be there.'

Rose nodded. 'She's a cow. We should be in the training room. It's after two,' she said imperiously, and Amie did not think of disobeying her, even though she needed to go to the ladies cloakroom and would be uncomfortable for the rest of the afternoon. She followed the slim teenager out of the restaurant, watching the worldly swing of her hips in her flared striped trousers and the swaying flesh that ran between her top and the visible thread of her cerise G-string. How exactly would Rose go about making her less pathetic?

She tried to shut the door on her creeping fears and prepared to battle her computer for the afternoon.

Alma

Thursday, 7th November, 7.14 pm

'*I've Got a Thing About You*,' Dora said as she held the dog-eared photograph at arm's length and squinted down her nose at it.

'Spot on.' Alma selected another photograph from the piles scattered about her on the faded green carpet and passed it up to her house guest, who was ensconced in the one comfortable chair with a mug of weak coffee balanced on the frayed brown material of the arm beside her.

'Oooh … *The Hottest October*. I loved that one. With Brick Button. He was a handsome devil.'

'Gay,' Alma told her, picking another photograph with care.

Dora sighed with remembrance as she held it gently. '*Taking Off The Tap Shoes*. Winner of the Best Film Oscar 1972. It was my absolute favourite at the time. I made my Ned take me to see it four times. That was back when Allcombe Odeon was still open. It was a palace of dreams to me.'

Alma smiled. 'Very poetic, but it's pretty hard to believe anything in this town was ever a palace.'

'I wanted to be able to sing and dance like you so badly,' Dora continued, shaking her head. 'Back then you were as light as air with the voice of an angel. Did anyone ever tell you that?'

'Only all the agents and blurb merchants in Hollywood,'

Alma replied dryly. The glow of nostalgia was infusing her dingy little flat with a warmth that defied the winter. It was too late for Alma to change her cynical attitude, but she did enjoy Dora's company. The only way she could show it was to keep her in coffee and biscuits, give up her bed for her at night, and spend the evenings reminiscing with the ephemera of the movie world as their beacon.

'Do you do any singing or dancing now?' Dora asked her, putting the photograph down and arranging it into a neat stack with the others on her lap before taking another from Alma's fingertips.

'Nope. I gave all that up. The exercising, the eating right, the kissing butt, the casting couch, the operations. All over with.'

'Operations?' Dora frowned at the new photograph.

'My chin, my nose. I had two ribs removed. And that was before those sorts of operations were safe. It wasn't like it is nowadays.'

'*Tidal Girl*,' Dora enthused, holding up the photo. 'I bought a bikini just like yours and I slimmed for a year in the hope I'd look good in it. I'd already had my daughter by then and I never did get my figure back.' She sighed. 'So why did you give it all up?'

'Would you like another cup of coffee, Dora?' Alma asked her smoothly.

'That would be lovely,' Dora said in an encouraging voice, holding out her mug. Alma rolled on to her knees and then climbed to her feet awkwardly, taking the offered mug. She walked from the living room, down the unembellished hallway and into the kitchen, the whole journey taking less than ten steps. 'I wonder if I could have a drop more milk in it this time?' Dora's voice floated after her.

'Sure.' She turned on the filthy electric hob to boil the third-full pan of water upon it. She never drank coffee herself and so had not bothered to invest in a kettle. The coffee granules, sugar and milk that she placed in equal measures in the bottom of the mug had all been bought specially for Dora. They were products Alma had not expected to find a use for again.

Over the past week Alma had learned how to avoid the questions she did not want to answer. She would offer a drink or a snack, and by the time she had returned to the living room Dora had forgotten what she had been asking. At least, Alma assumed Dora had forgotten, but lately she had seen a slight raising of the cheeks and a knowing look whenever a difficult question was asked, and it coincided precisely with the emptying of her mug. Dora had her wits about her still.

Alma retrieved the whiskey bottle, the only thing she did care about in the kitchen, from the back of the low cupboard which contained instant noodles, packet soups and caramel cookies. She took a mouthful while still crouching next to the open cupboard before replacing the cap and putting the bottle back in its place. Then she decided that one mouthful hadn't quite worked, and repeated the movement swiftly and surreptitiously while the noise from the hob above her increased to become a crescendo of bubbling.

She switched off the heat and poured the contents of the pan into the waiting mug, retrieving one of her two tea-spoons from the sink to give the concoction a lazy stir. Dirty plates and cutlery were threatening to overbalance and de-stroy the careful tower she had built, rising from the lost plug, but that only made her want to rethink her architec-tural skills rather than attempt to wash up. Alma used the sleeve of her purple blouse to wipe up a spill of water from the melamine counter and picked up the mug, taking it back along the corridor to Dora.

Why had she taken Dora to the bar last Thursday? She wasn't sure. She assumed that someone was looking for the old lady, and that the police were probably involved, but that hadn't stopped her for a moment. Perhaps it had been because she could drink more, and openly, in such a place, and also smoke as many cigarettes as she liked. Whenever she lit up in the flat Dora coughed outrageously. Whether it was a real complaint or exaggerated, Alma didn't know, but she had decided to let the old woman have her way for the time being. God knew she had suffered enough in that sinister dump people around here called a nursing home. In the future, though, she would have to get used to cigarette smoke. Alma didn't intend to puff while balancing out of the rickety sash window throughout winter.

'*Anywhere But Arizona,*' Dora enthused upon Alma's entrance. 'Did you really have a … you know ... an affair, with Jim Ace? He was a wonderful actor.'

'All publicity. Jim was a nice guy, but we were both married at the time.' Dora's question triggered, as many of them had, a reminiscence that flew back into her mind from the long unexplored depths. She saw herself and Jim rehearsing the love scene from that movie, standing close together, sipping gin fizzes on the baseline of his outdoor tennis court underneath the stars which always shone so brightly in these flashbacks.

'Shall we practise the kiss?' she had asked him, a trifle breathlessly, for he had been a megastar and she had just been making her name in the movie business.

'Practice makes perfect,' he had murmured before locking his lips on hers. His tongue had tasted of spiced salami, a predilection of his at the time, she recalled. She decided not to tell Dora that.

The door intercom buzzed.

That had never happened before. Six flights of stairs below her someone was pressing the doorbell to her flat.

She looked at Dora, who was setting the photograph down in her lap, straightening it with her thumbs and forefingers so it was aligned with the others. Then she held out her hands for her coffee, which Alma passed over. Life continued without incident for the old lady.

Alma crossed to the intercom, situated on the left of the main door that joined the living room to the stairs. She lifted the handset, placing it gingerly against her ear. Instantly she was listening to the world outside the window with the fascination of a voyeur, and she could hear the shuffle of passing cars and the hissing, fast breath of the person to whom she was about to speak.

'Hello,' she said belligerently, falling back on her usual defence mechanism. Perhaps Allcombe and Dora were erasing some of her harder edges because she heard herself adding, 'Can I help you?' in an almost polite tone.

There was a pause. 'Could I come up?' a woman with a local accent said.

'Who are you? Are you sure you've got the correct address?' Alma replied, taking immediate offence to the woman's tone. There was no way she was going to admit a total stranger to her flat without some sort of explanation. This might be a small seaside town, but she came from a country where four bolts and an alarm system would have been considered a minimal level of safety. Alma had once employed a team of bodyguards and now, in her flimsy flat, just the usual noises of the night kept her awake. She was scared of the dark for the first time in her life; the only time when she did not have the money to assuage her fear.

The woman spoke again. 'It's ... well, it's Angela Fearn. Dora Fearn's daughter?'

Alma pressed the button to unlock the street door and replaced the handset. She turned back to Dora, who looked at her quizzically.

'Your daughter is here,' she said, numb with surprise.

'Oh good!' Dora replied, straightening the oversized green

cardigan she had borrowed from Alma's limited wardrobe. 'She said she'd try to drop round.' Her expression remained benign as she added, 'I spoke to her on the telephone this afternoon.'

'You phoned her? You told her you were here?'

'I thought she might be worried,' Dora explained. There was a knock on the door of the flat. Her daughter had made good speed up the six flights of stairs. Alma walked back to it slowly, in a dream-like state of high drama, and opened it by a hairline crack, then wider.

Angela Fearn was nothing like Dora in her initial appearance. She was tall and had shoulder-length blonde hair with visible chestnut roots. Alma estimated she was in her late forties, and had had at least two children. Her stomach was pressing out against the front of her grey synthetic trousers and her breasts were low inside her white round-necked jumper. She had removed her sensible blue anorak and was carrying it over one arm, holding it like a matador's cape before her. Her large brown satchel was held by a leather strap which ran unflatteringly between her breasts and over one shoulder. Her neck, unadorned, was fat and wrinkled but her face and her cheeks were much thinner than Alma's own.

Still breathing heavily, her eyes were appraising Alma in much the same way, and she was no doubt inventing her own unflattering descriptions in her head, in that way Alma knew women did when they sized each other up at a first meeting.

'Is she here?' Angela asked in a peremptory tone. In reply, Alma stepped aside and gestured to Dora, unbothered and ensconced in the armchair next to the grey storage heater like a queen on her polyester-mix throne. Angela, unbidden, squeezed past Alma's bulk to stand directly in front of her mother, her hands holding her satchel still. Alma banged the door shut, followed her into the room and knelt down, collecting her photographs in armfuls and throwing them into the small cupboard on the opposite side of the heater. Dora helpfully handed Alma the ones she had been holding.

'Are you okay, Mum?' Angela asked briskly, ignoring the activity going on at her feet.

'Hello, dear. I'm fine. How are you?'

'Get your things together. I'll take you back to your room.'

Alma glanced up from her chore and saw Dora's placid expression change to rare exasperation. 'Honestly! I don't want to go back there. I told you that.'

Angela was immoveable. 'I'm not going to discuss this here, Mum. Let's get you back to the nursing home, and then we can have a proper conversation about it.'

Dora put her coffee mug on the floor and gripped the arms of her chair tightly. 'No.'

'Mum!'

'I'm not going.'

Alma straightened up at Dora's side and looked at mother and daughter. They were much more similar than she had originally thought, with those haughty expressions and strict tones; so similar that they had reversed their mother/daughter roles seamlessly. Angela tried to make the rules and Dora defied her while she still had enough strength to do so.

Alma wondered if she would have developed such a relationship with her mother given time, but her mother had been dead for twenty years now, buried in a fancy graveyard on a Hollywood plot. She hadn't thought about her properly for years, remembering the feeling of having a mother rather than the woman herself. Now she wondered for the first time whether she would have been anything like Dora, and whether Alma herself might eventually be that way. Although her own children had made it plain they would never be there to see it.

'We can discuss it, Mum. Nobody wants you to be unhappy. But I think we should stop imposing on this lady first, don't you? We've taken up enough of her time and hospitality.' Angela threw a look at Alma. She was still probably trying to work out exactly what part she was playing in this drama. Alma gave her a calm stare in response. She felt the time had come for her to play her hand.

'Dora can stay as long as she likes,' she said expansively. This was her territory and she felt confident, energised. Dora was her concern too.

'Well ...' Angela ventured, and then her voice grew in volume and confidence. 'I don't think that would really be right, would it?'

'I don't see how taking her back to that shit hole you call a nursing home could be right either, if you want to get moralistic about it. Do you know what was going on there?'

Angela was momentarily silenced. 'If you mean my mother's claims of some kind of conspiracy, I think you should know that she's not totally in touch with reality any more. I'm sorry, I don't know your name?'

The English garb of politeness to cover the most embarrassing situations, Alma thought. She longed to rip it away, to make this English cover-up artist explode in anger. 'You think a lot, don't you? But you don't ever think that maybe she could be right about that place, because that would mean you would have to do something about it. I've been there, I've looked around, and I'm telling you there's something screwy going on in there. Maybe you'll believe me before you believe her, huh?'

Dora piped up in the shocked pause that followed. 'Her name is Jacqueline, dear. She used to be a movie star.'

Angela looked pointedly at Alma, and then at the wood-chip walls of the tiny flat, with the grubby marks and cheap furniture.

'Okay, so maybe she's a little out of it, but that doesn't mean she's not right about the nursing home,' Alma said hotly, although she really wanted to throw off her disguise and reveal her true self in a blaze of glory to wipe the smirk from Angela's face. Quite how she would accomplish that she hadn't worked out, and she knew better than to give way to such impulses anyway. 'Your mother told me that they are killing people and I saw for myself that they were trying to hide something from me. I asked about one old lady and they told me she was on vacation for the day, but they'd already told Dora she had died in the night. Does that add up?'

'They could have made a mistake,' Angela answered.

'Just one thing, yeah, you can call that a mistake. But the whole place was wrong. It was creepy. I was scared and your mother was terrified. I thought they weren't going to let me leave. We had to sneak out of that place. And, even if we are wrong and there's nothing going on, you can't just leave your mother in some place where she's scared out of her mind.'

'Well, I wasn't about to …' Angela retorted, but she had shrunk into herself in the face of Alma's attack and her words carried no conviction. Alma pushed her advantage home.

'Yes, you were, but I think you realise now that it would be cruel and heartless to just dump her back there for the sake of your easy life. You know …'. She was on a roll, and the words were pouring easily out of her as if she was reading an autocue prepared by a Pulitzer winner. '… you should really cherish your mother. She's a wonderful woman. I have talked to her for hours over this past week and we've reached a great understanding. She's made me realise a lot about myself, and she's started to come back to life now she's out of that place. Look at her! She's happy, she's healthy. She needs people around her. She needs you to spend some quality time with her, to take her seriously. Is that so much to ask?'

Dora spoke up again, as cheery and complacent as ever. 'Angela, dear, why don't you sit down? You look a bit shaken. Jacqueline will fetch you a cup of coffee, won't you?'

Angela, silent and white-faced, looked around her for a seat. Alma half-gestured to the wicker garden chair she had nonchalantly stolen from Allcombe Garden Centre two months ago; highly uncomfortable, but she had never expected to have guests in the first place. Angela balanced on it and it gave out a loud creak. 'Coffee would be nice,' she managed to say.

Alma left mother and daughter, silent and rigid, under the paper lampshade she had made herself. In the kitchen she began the automated actions of coffee making once more, including the sip of whiskey from the bottle that was again buried behind the packet noodles. It wasn't so much that she didn't care if Angela smelt alcohol on her breath, but that she was certain that no comment would be made even if she did. Angela's manners were a stronger force within her than her moral outrage. There was no way to break the English reserve.

The bubbling of the pan on the hob began in earnest and Alma poured the water over the cheap coffee granules carelessly before beginning a search of the sink for one of the teaspoons. A voice filtered through from the living room.

It took her a moment to discern whose voice it was; the local accent and the inflexions did nothing to give it away. It was the authority in it that finally convinced Alma it was the daughter to whom she was listening, speaking and pausing in a one-sided conversation with herself. Coffee mugs in either hand, Alma took a few quiet steps out of the kitchen and into the corridor so she could listen at her leisure.

'Well, I thought you should know. It's really up to you how we proceed from here,' Angela said.

So she was giving Dora a choice about her future? That seemed unlikely. There was a pause.

'Yes, that'll be for the best. Are you going to come round?' The tone was too placatory, too anxious to please. Angela was speaking as if to a superior, and she hadn't addressed her mother in any tone but firm so far. 'It's Flat 6, Victoria Terrace, Allcombe.'

In a moment of piercing clarity Alma grasped what was happening and strode into the room, spilling coffee over her sleeves in her hurry. Angela was talking into her mobile phone with calm and authoritative eyes and Dora was watching nervously.

'Who are you talking to?' Alma demanded, legs apart, wrists burning with hot coffee. Angela didn't reply, but spoke into the phone.

'Yes. See you shortly.'

'Who is she talking to?' Alma asked Dora in the same panic. Dora stared back at her in mute astonishment. Alma gave up trying to get a straight answer and waited until Angela had removed the telephone from her ear and placed it back within the depths of the satchel on her hip. The daughter had control of the room now and she made Alma wait for an explanation, which she started with a blunt question.

'You said you were certain something was fishy at the nursing home? Is that my coffee? Thank you.'

She took the mugs from Alma's fingers and passed one to her mother, who clutched it between both hands.

'I wouldn't have said it if I didn't mean it,' Alma defended warily. She couldn't see where this was going.

'In that case the only course of action is to have the place properly investigated,' Angela said.

'So what have you done?' Had she hired a private detective? Perhaps she was suggesting they should solve the mystery of The Paradise themselves; sneak in, take a look around, pump the nurses for information. That might just work, she thought hopefully. She had played a gumshoe before and the reviews had been pretty good – she knew just what to do. This could be interesting.

'I called the police.'

Alma hadn't actually considered that as a possibility. 'You called the police? Just now?'

'They said they'd send someone round right away.' Angela balanced herself upon the wicker chair once more and took a slow, delicate sip of her coffee. Her gestures made it obvious she intended to wait for their arrival.

'They're coming here now?' Alma asked. Her brain was working at a crawl and her fingers had developed a nervous itch. She would have killed for a smoke and a drink.

'Shortly, they said. Thank you for the coffee, Jacqueline. It's lovely.'

'I think it could do with a drop more milk myself,' Dora added from her armchair.

'It's not Jacqueline, its Alma,' she corrected automatically. 'What have you told them?'

'Just what you told me. Let's allow them to deal with the situation as they see fit. After all, they've been involved since the nursing home reported Dora as missing.' Angela smiled warmly at her.

'Oh,' Alma said.

'Do I get to stay here?' Dora asked nobody in particular. Since Angela's arrival she had become a stereotype of the confused old lady quite deliberately, as far as Alma could see. Even when Dora had been terrified she had shown more spirit than she did now. For the first time Alma despised her: she had chickened out of dealing with the present, preferring to live in the past.

Alma strode off into the kitchen. She pulled up the bottle from the low cupboard and took five long mouthfuls of whiskey at once. Then she held the bottle between her breasts, both arms crossed over it as she slid to the floor in a puddle of purple blouse and trousers.

The police would want to know everything. They would want to know her real name, her real details, and Angela would hear it all. Angela would hear it all and tell anyone and everyone about the collapsed movie star in the sixth-floor flat.

There was nothing she could do to stop it.

Hilary

Wednesday, 8th November, 8.34 am

Although she had not been living the nine-to-five life for long, Hilary was becoming aware that mornings were her least favourite time of the working day and Wednesday mornings were her least favourite time of the working week. By Wednesday morning she had given her all and yet there was still at least as much to do again before the weekend became more than a tantalising glimpse of parole.

She poured the milk over the low fat, low taste cereal and ate it efficiently, alternating each mouthful with a sip of freshly-squeezed grapefruit juice. It was about time for Gary to rise and shine. They had fallen into an easy routine as housemates; he cleaned up the kitchen in the evening after he cooked, which he loved to do, and Hilary kept the lounge and bathroom tidy, and the laundry up-to-date.

She had risen earlier than usual this Wednesday. She had washed herself, then tidied and dusted, then dressed in a black shirt and dark blue trousers, blow-dried her hair, prepared her sandwiches – always prawn and mayonnaise – and made her breakfast. Such small, rhythmic actions usually annoyed Hilary. She considered them to be the insignificant minutiae of life and boring in the extreme, but this morning they had soothed her; with the cereal bowl emptying and nothing more to be done her thoughts were straying inevitably to the events of last night, and the very incident she wanted to erase from her mind.

The whole thing was a colossal embarrassment and a terrible defeat to the way she tried to live her life. It had been a pathetic, feminine thing to do, and for that alone it deserved Gary's disdain and her own. She had hardly been able to look at herself while plucking her eyebrows into order that morning.

Above her head the floorboards creaked. They painted a vivid picture; Gary was getting up, swinging his feet out of bed and on to the floor. A series of squeaks and groans told her he was walking to his clothes rail and choosing his outfit, and a loud squeal that he had bent over to tie his shoelaces. The squeals from the ceiling became a rhythm, which meant he was walking out of his bedroom and coming down the stairs. Hilary caught a glimpse of his legs from her standing place next to sink through the open door of the kitchen, and then he was walking into the room, his face still wrinkled from his pillow and his hair spiking up on the side of his head. He looked tired and vulnerable.

'You haven't got long,' Hilary warned crisply, focusing on his shirt buttons so she wouldn't have to look at his face.

'Mmm,' Gary said. He was wearing a dark green shirt with a pink tie and black trousers. Sometimes Hilary could only laugh wryly at his fashion sense, and at other times she wanted to force him to look at himself properly in a mirror before heading out of the house. 'I'm ready.'

'You should really eat breakfast,' she told him, walking

into the hall and picking up her coat and bag from the iron hooks she had nailed to the wall herself. Her plastic holdall contained her lunch and her sports equipment; she went for a run along the promenade every lunchtime in an attempt to energise her body and to remind herself that exercise had once been her life and could be again. So far it wasn't working. 'Come on, then.'

She walked out of the front door and waited for Gary to collect his wallet and step out into the street before locking up behind him. The small fishing boats in the harbour were bobbing romantically, high on the tide, and the stone wall which separated the harbour from the pier was displaying battered metal signs which offered day trips up the coast, even though the holiday season was well and truly over. The sky was overcast and threatening to drizzle, and, as usual, a brisk and unfriendly wind was proving to her that her leather three-quarter length coat offered no protection.

This area of Allcombe was like a ghost town in the American west during a freak ice age. The gift shops were boarded up and the sign for the abandoned amusement arcade on the pier creaked eerily. There was a thick layer of dust over the plates of fudge and the cellophane-wrapped sticks of pink rock behind the unwashed windows. The doors of these small shops were open but she didn't dare to venture inside, half-expecting a gypsy shopkeeper with warts and bad hair would curse her if she touched any of the tacky displays. It was an abandoned wreckage of a town, dormant throughout the winter and waiting for its chance to explode into colour once more with the sun. Hilary wondered if she would still be living here when that happened. She couldn't picture it in her mind.

She wriggled her hands into her wool gloves and began the ten minute walk to the high street, Gary silent and hunched over beside her. They had passed The Slaughter, dark and hung over, and had turned towards the fish and chip shop on the corner, before he spoke.

'Are we going to talk about last night?' Gary asked her. His voice quivered.

'No,' she replied immediately, and was aghast to hear the same quiver in her own voice.

Gary took it in. 'I think we should.'

Hilary stumbled on a loose stone and righted herself with annoyance. 'Look, I'm really sorry, okay? I'm sorry about the whole thing.'

'Why?' he asked her. He looked genuinely surprised.

'What do you mean?'

'You've got nothing to be sorry about. I just wondered if – if it was the first time?'

Hilary absorbed this in silence as they began the slow ascent to the High Street. Her full bag bounced against her lower back with each step. 'No.' She had been dreading this conversation, but now it was upon her she felt almost happy. They would discuss, and then the discussion would be over. 'No, it wasn't the first time it's happened.'

'So you've always had a problem with heights?'

'No … I don't really want to go into how that came about, okay? It's not important.'

'Okay,' Gary demurred. 'I'm sorry I suggested that walk, but you should have said something.'

'Like what?' Hilary said wryly. 'By the way, Gary, I go insane and become a quivering wreck when you put me near a cliff edge?'

Gary swapped his wallet from one hand to the other. They were passing businesses now, encased in the stately Victorian terrace buildings with their crumbling facades lining the High Street and protecting them from the worst edges of the sea wind. 'It wasn't a cliff. It was a hill. And we didn't even go near the edge.'

In a moment of flashback Hilary saw the scene again – the sea crashing far below and the rocky path only a few feet from the tufted grasses that demarcated the plunge into the abyss. She felt again the sweat prickle under her arms and the heat build in her stomach. She could not pretend to herself that if she was back there now she would react differently. The force of her panic had taken her completely by surprise; she had never imagined that a slow stroll up a small hill to look at the view over the harbour would lead to such histrionics.

'You really lost it, Hils. You were shaking and crying. You couldn't get off your knees. I practically had to carry you home.'

Her mouth went dry at the concern in his voice but something in her refused to lay down her pride just yet. 'The vertigo affects me that way sometimes.'

'Vertigo?' Gary repeated incredulously. She could tell he was looking at her as he strode along, so she stared at the uneven pavement directly in front of her. 'Vertigo doesn't make a person completely wig out, does it? It's got to be more than that. Are you getting some help for it?'

'Don't be so melodramatic,' Hilary snapped at him. 'I don't need any help. I just have to remember not to ...'

'Not to go up any hills?' he asked her. She looked up before she could stop herself and met his kind eyes with her own. He was so easy to live with and easier to talk to. She could have told him anything and he wouldn't have laughed at her for her weaknesses.

The clear plastic revolving doors to their destination were busy processing the reluctant bodies of the workers. For every five people who went in one stopped outside to have a cigarette before the working day began, leaning against the red brick wall or squatting on the pavement. Hilary pulled her pass card out of the side pocket of her bag as they reached the building.

'Wait with me while I have a ciggie?' Gary asked her as he squeezed into a small space against the wall to the left of the main door. She stood in front of him and thought about putting her bag down on the ground before deciding against it. Instead she turned up the fake fur collar of her coat with her gloved hands.

'I know you don't want to talk about it, but if you ever do, I'm here, okay?' he said quietly, fiddling with his matches. The other smokers were all busy with their own accoutrements, shielding their lighters from the wind or shifting a cigarette from mouth to hand while picking at their tongues.

'Okay,' Hilary said. 'Thanks. I'm not bonkers or anything.'

'Sure, you're not bonkers,' Gary said, smiling at her. Hilary smiled back. The next thing that came out of her mouth surprised her.

'And I've been meaning to say sorry about the late night phone calls. I hope they haven't woken you up.'

'No probs,' Gary said, and took a long drag of his cigarette. 'Is it someone from New Zealand?'

She suspected he had been listening to those conversations. Could she trust him to keep a secret if she told him the details? Not all the details, and certainly not the worst of the details, but more than she had told anyone else? They had an intimacy now, and she was afraid of it. She was also pleased with it, and she wanted it to continue; she wanted a friend. 'It's Steve, my ex-boyfriend.'

Gary nodded gravely. She couldn't tell what he was thinking. 'Wow.'

'Yes.'

He didn't ask anything so she didn't say any more. He dropped his cigarette stub on the ground and scratched his Adam's apple. 'I know what that's like. Same deal with my ex.'

Hilary failed to see how it could be the same, unless Gary had survived some awful accident that had made him see the pointlessness of life and caused a terrible rift between himself and his girlfriend, but it was an interesting piece of information all the same. So that was who he phoned when she was in the bath; she had heard the low murmur of his voice, speaking as softly as he could manage, and had strained to listen in but had not been able to catch more than a few words.

Hilary felt an intense curiosity, rather like an itch between her shoulder blades, descend upon her. She scratched her back with her pass card and adjusted the strap of her bag. 'Ready to go in?'

Gary was looking at someone over her shoulder with a wary greeting in his eyes. Hilary followed his gaze.

Rose was smoking a cigarette nonchalantly, leaning on one shoulder against the far wall. The revolving doors were between them. She raised her eyebrows at Hilary.

'Hello,' Hilary said. How much of the conversation had she heard?

Rose deliberately turned away from them, wearing a bored expression and very little else. She was wearing lycra again, in day-glo colours, and hadn't bothered with a coat. Her skin was orange except for slices of bright white underneath her arms and around her bra straps; she was obviously a cheap fake tan devotee. Hilary refused to be wary of anyone who dressed so inappropriately.

'Let's go,' Gary said quietly, and they headed into the building to start the day's work, leaving Rose and her sly smile behind them for the moment.

Sam

Thursday, 9th November, 11.41 pm

So he hadn't given up his vigilante ways entirely.

Okay, so he wasn't in costume, but the costume didn't fit him any more. And he wasn't exactly fighting crime, but crime had never been a huge problem in Allcombe and the rôle of bodyguard was more suitable for a man who was no longer at the peak of physical fitness. He was a secret bodyguard. A secret bodyguard for the girl who doesn't realise that she needs one.

The music was deafening. It sounded like six hundred drummers had been told to play at different rhythms. Occasionally a woman would yowl at the top of her voice in a language Sam had never come across in all his travels, and the overall effect made him want to flee the nightclub. It didn't help that the only spot in which he could effectively stay hidden was directly behind one of the unfeasibly large speakers on the far edge of the dance floor. It was the only area that was not covered in whirling spotlights of pink, yellow and green that made his vision blur.

The nightclub was practically empty. Sam supposed Thursday nights were usually slow, and only inhabited by regulars. He had been surprised to learn that Rose was one of those regulars, and even more surprised to see Amie standing next to her. If there had been one person on the course Sam would have guessed would not enjoy pounding modern music and alcohol in large measures, it was Amie. Two weeks of working with her had shown her to be a quiet, conservative and nervous girl, who would blush before raising her voice. Yet there she was, on Rose's elbow, next to the bar holding a bottle of luminous liquid she had hardly touched and wearing an outfit which hardly existed.

Sam did not have a lot of experience with ladies of the night, but he assumed they would dress in the style Amie was dressed in tonight, although he thought they would look a lot more comfortable in that fashion. In an electric blue, glittery boob tube that needed constant persuasion to contain her ample chest, and a white miniskirt teamed with white stilettos, she was making Rose look positively demure, and infinitely more attractive.

He had always thought Rose beautiful, but tonight she was a vision. Her blonde hair was loose and flowing. Her baby pink dress skirted her thighs with a flirty charm. She was holding court with the crowd that surrounded her. Sam couldn't blame them for wanting to be near her; her smile called to him too, but he understood he could only be useful to her at a distance, for if she ever found out about his vigil he suspected she would rip his testicles from his body and throw them over the edge of Allcombe pier.

The dance floor remained empty as the night wore on. The twenty or so youngsters in the club were gathered together between the entrance and the bar, in groups of four or five. In fact, Sam had a feeling they were the same people he had seen queuing up for admission to this very disco – sorry, club – last Thursday night. His eyes grappled with the crowd until they singled out the head and shoulders of the tall lad who had challenged him that time. The lad was standing a few feet away from Rose, his back turned to her, and Sam began to notice how often her head turned in that direction. He wondered if some sort of disagreement festered between them.

From his hiding place he could see Amie shifting on her feet, raising and rotating one ankle at a time. Sam could tell she wasn't used to wearing high heels. Her presence here was extremely puzzling, although Sam had noticed an unlikely friendship striking up between Amie and Rose recently. It had been most obvious at the picnic last Saturday, which

Charlotte had arranged and attended with an attitude that had reminded him of his old school gym master.

The botanical gardens were a nice spot in warmer weather. Thirty miles inland from Allcombe, Sam had often visited them himself, and he had privately thought that arranging a picnic there at the beginning of November was not the best choice for an outing. Armed with a tarpaulin, a raincoat and two umbrellas, he had put a brave face on the proceedings, which was a feat he was quite proud of. Particularly as he had been left to eat drumsticks and garlic bread under one of the umbrellas with Charlotte while Amie and Rose had disappeared into the trees with the other umbrella. They had emerged an hour later in a bedraggled state with a pale Amie clutching a bloody handkerchief to her stomach, and he had spent the rest of the evening in the casualty department of Allcombe's tiny hospital.

Amie had been picked up, and at least he had got to spend some time with Rose, who had explained to him and Charlotte that she had tried to stop Amie from piercing her own belly button with a darning needle but the girl just wouldn't listen. It was then he had decided that Rose needed round-the-clock protection. Violence gravitated to her; she attracted dangerous attention from which she needed to be defended.

Sam glanced at his watch, realised he couldn't see its face in the dark anyway, and put his hand back down. He guessed it would be around eleven thirty, and he was hoping the place would close at twelve so that he could follow Rose to her house and head back home for some much-needed sleep. His eardrums had developed a constant buzzing and his feet were aching. He was also aware that he looked horribly out of place in his brown corduroy trousers and jacket. A comforting thought was that there was one man older than him in the disco – sorry, club – even though that man wasn't wearing any shoes and appeared to be diligently collecting used glasses and returning them to the bar.

Sam shifted his attention to his flies for a moment to check they had not come undone, a common problem with these trousers, and when he looked back Amie was standing in a ring of people, Rose amongst them, who were clapping in a slow and deliberate fashion. Amie was holding a pint glass which contained a drink that had a murky green tint when the whirling lights illuminated it, and she was making a face that did not suggest she found the idea of drinking it appetizing.

Sam watched with disgust as she put the glass to her lips and began to tilt it. The liquid lapped against her lower lip; she took a hesitant swallow, then another. The crowd began to clap faster. For the first time the noise they were making reached him over the music. She swallowed again, her eyes screwed tight against the taste. Again.

Just as Sam was beginning to think she was going to drink the entire pint, Amie pulled the glass away from her face. It was still three-quarters full, but she was wearing a sick expression; she obviously couldn't handle her alcohol. Rose moved in close next to her and her mouth moved. Amie shook her head slowly in response, but she raised the glass back to her lips.

The clapping recommenced. Amie started to take small sips, making tiny movements in her throat. Perhaps thirty seconds passed before Rose reached out and put her hand over Amie's, wrapping it tightly around the glass and jerking upwards so that the trickle of liquid into Amie's mouth became a flood.

Amie swallowed hard, and then the green liquid began to spill out of the sides of the glass and over her face. It ran down her cheeks and her neck, into her cleavage, leaving a glistening stain to mark its path. Rose didn't remove her hand until the glass was empty.

The clapping of the crowd ceased. Amie stood in the centre of them, a sticky mess with a ruined face. She looked at them and they looked at her. Then she convulsed over the pint glass and regurgitated the liquid into it with three heaves of her soaking chest and stomach.

Rose took the half-full glass away from her and Sam saw her mouth twist and move. He had no idea what she said, but it had a profound effect on Amie. She pushed out of the circle and ran out of the club at full speed, an impressive feat in those ridiculous shoes.

Sam watched with interest from his hiding place to see what would happen next. Rose put down the pint glass on the bar, the crowd parting to allow her access. Then she, too, left the disco – sorry, club – with a swaggering stroll that drew his attention to her pert bottom. The tall lad who had threatened him last Thursday followed a few seconds later.

A warning bell sounded in Sam's head. He eased himself out from behind the speaker and sloped round the edge of the dance floor, past the bar, and down the dim corridor that led back out into the street.

Sam looked out cautiously from the entrance, expecting to see the tall lad nearby, but the street was empty. Almost empty. After his eyes had adjusted to the orange glow of the street lights he picked out the now familiar swing of Rose's hips as she walked down the High Street, away from him.

He set out after her, matching the pace of his steps to her own and keeping to the shadows. She was walking away from their office and he assumed she was heading for her home which he knew was uphill, not far from his own house. It was his job to make sure that she got there safely. He could take pride in doing this job well, which was something that was denied to him with clerical work. It was painfully obvious that he possessed no ability in that area.

The terraced buildings on either side of the High Street

were peppered with alcoves and alleyways that led down to the promenade and up to the newer residential areas. Sam had passed about four of these when he saw the tall lad who had left the disco – sorry, club – before him step out of another, about fifty yards ahead of Rose. He must have run down to the promenade, along it, and up again at a fair speed in order to beat Rose's quick pace.

Sam's sixth sense sent a tingle across his shoulder blades. He had often experienced a premonition of danger in the past which had never been proven wrong; he treated his awareness with a respect that had grown from experience. His life had been saved many times over by his instincts, perhaps the most famous example being the Affair of the Fruit Bat, which had been his first encounter, but not his last, with a true supervillain.

He had been pursuing the Bat and had run straight into a carefully prepared trap, following his nemesis into a blacked-out house with fruit placed randomly on the floor in order to trip him up and slow him down. The Bat had been waiting for him with night vision goggles and a fruit knife. It had only been Sam's sixth sense that had saved him. He had experienced the shiver of forewarning, and instantly had ducked down on to the floor, an action that had unarguably saved his life. The fruit knife had swished past the top of his head, missing by a whisker, causing the Bat to lose his balance, slip on a banana, and fall on his own blade. Case closed.

Rose stopped in front of the lad, so Sam continued his slow progress through the shadows, tight against the shop windows. She put her hands on her hips, and then waved one arm in an encompassing gesture. Next she pointed at the ground with one finger. The lad replied with his own arm waving and pointing. Their voices rose to a volume which told Sam a disagreement was taking place, but his ears were not what they used to be, particularly after an evening of loud music, and he found it impossible to distinguish individual words.

His warning bells were clamouring now. As he watched and crept, Rose made a fist with her right hand and swung it with speed and power at the lad's face. A second later Sam heard the crack from the blow and saw the lad's face swing back to her in disbelief. He put one hand to his cheek and explored it.

Sam knew what the lad was going to do. He was moving forward when the swing of the retaliatory punch began its path towards Rose's chin, and he already knew he would be too late to stop it.

Rose stepped backwards and the breeze of the punch passing across her face stirred her hair. By the time the wisps of her loose blonde tresses had settled, Sam had run past her, rugby tackled the lad, and was straining to pin him to the floor with a classical wrestling move.

After a surprised pause his opponent punched him in the kidney twice. Sam was working on pure adrenalin but that could do nothing against such intense and searing pain. It removed every thought from his mind, and he could only lie in the road as the lad climbed out from under him and got to his feet.

'It's that old nutter,' the lad said.

Sam dimly registered the words. At least some element of his brain was still working, even if his body was unable to perform basic muscle actions due to the intensity of his agony. His legs and backbone were on fire. He felt as if a kidney transplant had been performed on him without the anaesthetic.

'God, Matt, you're a fucking prick,' Rose said, and then, miracles of miracles, she was bending down to him and touching him on the shoulder. 'His face is bleeding.' It took several seconds for Sam to realise that she was talking about him. Then he felt a new pain just above one eyebrow and realised he could only see a red mist out of that eye.

'Well, what the fuck did he think he was doing?' Matt shouted.

'He was trying to stop you from pounding me. Can you get up?' Rose moved her small, cold hand to his armpit and Sam made an effort to get into a sitting position for her. It took a while and during that time the pain changed from a constant flood to diminishing waves.

'Give him a hanky for that cut,' Matt suggested, standing behind Sam.

'Who the fuck carries a hanky around?' Rose said. Sam felt obliged to speak.

'I've got one,' he managed to say, even though his teeth and tongue didn't feel like they belonged to him. He pulled the handkerchief from his jacket pocket to show them. Rose took it from him and, squatting on the pavement by his side, dabbed at his cut, wincing as if she was the injured party.

'It's not too bad,' she said, and for the first time Sam heard a softness in her voice. Her knees were brushing his hip; her face was inches from his own. He could have turned to her and taken her in his arms, promised her the moon, told her not to be afraid, that he would watch over her forever.

'Piss off, Matt,' Rose said casually over her shoulder. There was a silence. 'I said, piss off,' she repeated as she played nurse.

'You're not … you're not seriously ….' Matt's thick voice floated from behind Sam.

'Fuck off, all right?' she replied venomously. 'This isn't your business any more.'

'You are sick,' he said brokenly, and then Sam heard his quick footsteps as he turned and left. Sam was alone with Rose.

He was petrified.

'Were you following me?' Rose asked him. Her voice maintained that gentle note. She did not sound angry with him.

He swallowed, fought down his panic, and took a huge gamble. 'I was making sure you're safe.' He swallowed again to clear the emotion from his throat. 'You don't know how dangerous the world can be.'

'So you were?'

Sam moved his head towards her but he couldn't bring himself to meet her eyes for fear of what he might see there. Did she despise him? Would she tell him to stop, to leave her alone? What purpose would his life have then?

'Yes,' he whispered.

'Knowing that you've been out there watching me all night,' Rose finally said, 'makes me feel really horny.'

Sam met her eyes. Behind the glitter and the shadow, under the mascara and the kohl, they were green, and they were looking straight into his own.

'Let's go in the alley,' she suggested, tilting her head towards the dark passage Matt had emerged from earlier. Sam was mesmerised. He could not think why she wanted him to go in there, but he was not going to deny her. He got to his feet and felt her hand slip around him to press into his lower back with the weight of a pebble. They walked into the passage and the dark swallowed them; her hand slipped down to his buttock and he felt her squeeze him roughly. He wanted to speak but could not. She was a stone goddess before him, about to envelope him.

He tried to kiss her and she pushed his face away with a playful hand which began a direct descent down over his body as her other hand increased the pressure on his bottom. He could hardly make her out in the dark and he didn't dare touch her in return. He was overwhelmed by her. He was certain she had at least four hands that were kneading and groping with a precision that did something entirely new to his insides. He had a long moment of dizziness that metamorphosed him. He stepped out of it to become rampant, and he felt so clearly that she wanted him, that she was open to him.

The romantic novels he was so fond of reading made perfect sense now. So this was love, the flow that leads to the crescendo, the not-so-gentle pinching of her fingers, the fly of his trousers that she undid and the tracing of the Y on his Y fronts, and fireworks in his head and trains in tunnels and roses that bloom in the most unexpected of places.

He was part of the dark and part of her, her legs braced on either side of him, her feet pressing against the wall behind him to maintain balance, and Sam was, for the first time, an ordinary man and a superhero all at once, all at the same time. He never wanted to be anywhere else.

He never wanted to be anywhere else.

Part Two

Rob

'Thank you for coming to this meeting. It's great to finally have an opportunity to one-to-one with you,' Rob says.

Sam smiles at him meekly and smoothes his brown tie over his protruding stomach. He is sweating profusely and his smell permeates the tiny magnolia office on the second floor. It's obvious by now that he doesn't wash his clothes often. He wore that corduroy suit every day last week.

Rob categorises all his trainees according to his management technique handbook, and he decides Sam is a type J – 'Behind the Times'.

'Yes,' Sam says softly.

'As you know, this meeting is really about assessing how you're doing at the two week point. I've also got the results of the test you took on basic operating procedures yesterday. Would you like to know how you did?'

'Yes, please,' Sam answers. He crosses his arms and legs into tense jumbles and gives a small shake of his head.

'Right.' Rob rustles his papers even though he has already arranged Sam's test scores on the top of his pile of paperwork. 'You answered ten questions of the twenty questions on the test sheet correctly. That puts your standing within the group currently as the fifth most effective member. That's fifth out of seven workers.'

Sam develops an interest in his shoelaces.

'Now, obviously, that's not exactly where we want you to

be. We want you to be first, and we know you're capable of it. I know you don't feel confident, but that will come in time. And I really have been impressed,' Rob says, leaning forward conspiratorially, 'with the way you've taken to computer work, considering your lack of experience in that area.'

'Thank you,' Sam replies, pulling his earlobe.

Rob coughs and taps a fingernail on the desk. 'So, keep up the good work and see if you can't try a little harder, okay?'

'Okay.'

'Right, that's all. I wonder if you could ask Gary to come in next?'

Sam nods and departs quietly, leaving the door to Rob's office ajar. Rob rearranges his papers and then sits perfectly still, preparing himself, until there is a timid knock, and thin, pale Gary is sliding on to the chair in front of him.

'Hi, Gary. Thank you for attending this meeting. It's great to finally have the opportunity to one-to-one with you,' Rob says.

Gary nods with a tense jerk of his head. He wears a very serious expression that is at odds with his canary yellow tie, bedecked with the large eyes of fuzzy cartoon characters. Rob has decided to categorise him as a type F –'Not Without Potential'.

'I have the results of the test you took yesterday. Would you like to interface with me about them?'

'Not really,' Gary says sheepishly with an uneasy movement of his elbows against the chair arms.

'But you're doing really well!' Rob replies. 'You really are doing very well compared with the rest of the group. In fact, with a score of fifteen correct answers out of twenty questions, you came third. That's quite an achievement.'

'Thanks,' Gary says with a downturn of his ribbon-thin lips.

Rob speaks compassionately to him. 'If there's anything

else you want to discuss I'm happy to do that now. I have put down an extra minute in my schedule just in case. Anything you want to get off your chest? Anything we can do to improve your job satisfaction?'

Gary takes a short powerful breath and lunges into his speech. 'I really don't know if this is the right job for me.'

Rob nods slowly. 'Why is that, Gary?'

'I don't feel very ... involved in the training process,' Gary says, frowning.

Rob smiles easily. 'Well, there's no reason to worry about that yet!' he says joyfully. 'It's early days in the training schedule. And the course does become more involving as you become more skilled. This part of the process is all about mastering the basics – you just need to bear with it.'

'Really?' Gary asks. He fiddles with the knot of his tie.

'So, that's sorted. Keep up the good work!' Rob says heartily. 'And just give me a shout when you've knocked something together for the talent show, won't you? I'm really looking forward to seeing what you'll come up with.'

'Sure,' Gary whispers to his knees.

'Could you send in Alma next, please? Thanks ever so,' Rob says confidently. He watches as a shambling Gary departs, closing the door softly behind him. Then he rearranges his papers and waits.

There is no knock. The door bangs open and Alma arrives as a huge black tragedy in a billowing dress and headscarf that gives her the stature of a Greek widow. She squeezes into the chair and leans her elbows on Rob's desk. Rob has decided to categorise Alma as a type C – 'Not Trying'.

'Okay, so I did crap, give me the slap on the wrists and make yourself feel manly,' she says.

Rob can't catch his breath. 'Well, I, I, er, really wanted to start by saying how happy I was to have the opportunity to one-to-one with you.'

'Yeah, right, whatever. Moving along ...' Alma shoots back with a hand gesture rather like a royal wave. 'I know I failed the test, okay? You know I failed the test. So do me a favour and gimme the short version of the pep talk.'

Rob swallows and presses ahead. 'The test that you took on Basic Operating Procedures yesterday did reveal a shortcoming in your learning curve. Would you like to know how you scored?'

'No.'

'Alma ...' Rob clasps his hands on the desk, nearly touching Alma's fingers. 'Please try to be a part of this. I want to cascade information to you that could really help your performance. I know you want to improve, and I know you can improve. I know you can be one of the strongest members of our group if you are prepared to try.' He leaves an earnest pause after the crescendo of the final word. 'You scored nine out of a possible twenty. That puts you sixth in a group of seven.'

Alma raises her wild eyebrows at Rob. 'You mean someone did worse than me? Thanks for that, Rob. I can feel my motivation increasing just by knowing that fact.'

'Well, that's great,' Rob says, not sure if it's great or not. 'So. That's all for now. Just give it your best and the sky's the limit. Could you ask Amie to join me next? Thanks very much.'

Alma shrugs out of the chair as if it is an effort to move after such an uninteresting meeting, and departs, leaving the door to Rob's office wide open. Rob can't help but scowl as he sniffs the room. He reaches into his drawer and produces a pump action air freshener which he operates vigorously over his head. He replaces the freshener and rearranges the papers on his desk.

Amie knocks and stands, toes level with the change in carpet that signifies the threshold of Rob's office, even though the door is open. They look at each other for a heartbeat.

'Come on in, Amie.'

She moves forward and stands in front of him with her A-line skirt and round-necked, pearl-button cardigan arranged neatly on her pudding basin body. She looks terrified and weepy, red-faced and white-eyed. Rob has decided to categorise her as a type Q – 'No-hoper', although he does feel guilty about it.

'Could you shut the door behind you and then take a seat?' Rob asks her. She obeys, sitting with her hands in her lap and her face angled to the edge of the desk. 'Okay! I'll start off by saying that it's great to finally have this opportunity to one-to-one with you. It means that if there's anything that either of us wants to get off our chests, we can go right ahead.'

Amie looks panic-stricken at the use of the word 'chest', so Rob quickly moves on. 'If there's nothing in particular you want to say, then I'll start off by drawing your attention to your test results from yesterday. Is that okay with you?'

She smiles wanly back at him. His voice drops to a sympathetic, level monotone. 'I'm afraid that the test results showed a problem with your learning process in regards to its efficiency when we compare it to other members of the training group. Your actual score was … seven out of twenty. I'm sorry to have to tell you that was, in fact, the lowest score obtained.'

Rob is looking at Amie and Amie is looking at the desk, both of them sitting in a stillness that is broken only occasionally by minimalist blinking. 'Was there … any reason you'd like to share with me, in confidence, as to why you're not doing as well as we would like? Any family reasons? Personal troubles?'

Amie doesn't reply.

'Because if there were extenuating circumstances we might be able to grant you some leeway for the time being,'

Rob perseveres. 'You don't have to go into detail. We all want to respect your privacy.'

She gives a barely noticeable nod. Perhaps it wasn't even a nod, but Rob takes it as such.

'Okay, so there are extenuating circumstances,' he says with unabashed relief. 'Thanks for sharing that with me. We'll give you as much time as you need to sort yourself out. Why don't we just forget these results? Let's not dwell on the past; you need to concentrate on the future. I'm positive that, in two weeks' time, your results will have improved massively. I'll bet you'll be ahead of the group by then, because, you know, you have that potential hidden away inside you. I can see it. It just needs to be unlocked.'

The pep talk ends and Amie makes no sign of acknowledgement. The silence that follows it seems to have more of an effect on her. She shifts in her seat and finally lets out a soft whine. 'Thank you,' she says.

Rob gives her a smile which he hopes will look optimistic but suspects will look flat. 'You're welcome. Why don't you send in Hilary next? I think we're about done here.'

She gets up and leaves with the bent shoulders of an ageing housemaid. Rob frowns after her and then settles into rearranging his papers. There is a noise and he looks up swiftly to find Hilary sitting in front of him, eyes expectant behind her strict, rimless glasses. He is disorientated for a moment only. Then he collects himself.

'Hello Hilary. Thank you for coming. It's great to be given this opportunity to one-to-one with you.'

'Indeed,' Hilary replies, chin twitching. Rob wonders if she is appreciating a private joke. He has categorised her as a type H – 'Disdainful of Authority'.

'I really wanted to use this time to discuss the results of yesterday's test. Is that okay with you?'

'Absolutely. Press on,' Hilary instructs, so Rob does.

'You scored nineteen out of a possible twenty. That's really wonderful. We feel very happy about your progress and we look forward to a fruitful working partnership upon the completion of the training stage of your new career. Is that how you feel?'

'Of course,' she says. 'Could I ask a question?' Her face is direct and open. 'Did I come first? In the test?'

Rob checks the papers on his desk although he already knows the answer. His fingers twitch over the curling edges of the well-thumbed collection. 'Actually, you came second, but that in no way affects how we view your progress.'

Hilary's eyes narrow and her charming smile winks out. 'I don't need to ask who came first, do I?'

Rob speaks carefully and precisely in reply. 'We think extremely highly of you, and we don't want you to get bogged down in petty rivalries, Hilary.'

'Who's "we"?' she interrupts.

Rob looks at her, unsure of where the conversation is going.

'Who exactly do you refer to when you speak of "we"? Are you using the royal we? Or do you refer to elements within the training group?' Hilary speaks in a clipped, accusatory manner that is harsh and shocking in the tiny magnolia office. She is giving Rob no respect and he no longer feels like the man in charge.

'I mean we at the bank. The company, as a whole,' he explains, trying not to beg for understanding.

'Oh.' Hilary shifts backwards on the chair. 'Of course. Naturally.' She looks pleased with herself. She crosses her legs and smoothes the material of her trousers with a repetitive stroking. She picks imaginary lint from them with her thumb and forefinger. 'Was there anything else you wanted to discuss?'

Rob opens his mouth and closes it again. When he does

speak, he manages to assume the tone of benign command once more and smiles his practised, pleasant smile. 'No, I don't think so. Keep up the good work, and remember I'm always here if you need me. Could you ask Rose to join me next?'

'Rose. Yes.' She eyes him with what looks like suspicion. 'Thank you for your time. I appreciate it.' Hilary then departs as soundlessly as she arrived.

Rob checks his hair with the palms of his hands, and then rolls up the sleeves of his immaculate white shirt with three twists and a fold to keep them in place above his elbows. He rearranges his papers until he is interrupted by a loud and persistent thumping at his door. It opens, and Rose enters in a riot of colour and noise.

She is dressed in a blood-red halterneck dress that reaches, unusually for her, to below her knees. Her pink wedge shoes look precarious but she walks easily in them and her strides to the chair are no less confident than Rob would expect. She is chewing gum with small, biting movements of her lower jaw, occasionally poking her tongue out with a pink membrane of gum stretched tightly around it.

Rob has not managed to categorise her yet. Since meeting her he has established an uncomfortable personal connection with her that has confused his feelings.

'Hi,' she says as she slumps into the chair.

'Hello, Rose. Thank you for joining me. It's great to have the opportunity ...'

'Am I in trouble?' she interrupts. She does not look concerned.

'Of course not,' Rob reassures. 'This is just a one to one session. There's no need to be worried.'

Rose smirks at her shoes. 'A one-to-one? I can handle that.' She sits with her legs apart and her hands in her lap, pushing the material of her dress up over the soft lines of her thighs.

'Can I start by sharing your test results with you? From yesterday?'

'Were they okay?' Rose asks. She is looking around the tiny office, at the papers on the desk, concentrating on them as she tries to read them from her seat.

'They were fine,' Rob says. 'You got fourteen questions out of twenty correct. That means you were the fourth most successful member of the training group at this test. We're quite satisfied with that result at this stage.'

'Pukka.'

'Continue to try hard and you'll find working here a very rewarding experience. Have you got anything you want to add, Rose?'

'Like what?' She leans forward and presses her upper arms towards each other, pushing out her chest. The material of the halter neck is pulled tight to reveal a glimpse of a blue-green tattoo between her artificially lifted breasts and the thin purple band of her bra. Rob looks at it, and immediately switches attention to the strip light on the ceiling, squinting.

'Are you enjoying the training experience?'

'Yeah.'

There is a pause. 'That's good,' Rob says encouragingly, still fascinated by the ceiling. 'Well then. Could you ask Charlotte to join me?'

'Is that it?' she asks him in a surprised voice.

'Yes, that's it.'

Rose pushes out of the chair and stomps away, slamming the door behind her. Rob lets his eyes drop back to the desk and sighs. He gets up, moves around the desk to the other chair and swings it by its back support, letting it drop into a new position on the shorter, left side of the desk. He sits back in his own seat and angles the two chairs so that they are close together, separated only by the corner of the desk. He then rearranges his papers.

There is a sharp and measured knock on his door. 'Enter,' he says, working to achieve a measured voice.

Charlotte enters, closing the door behind her. She arranges herself into the chair, almost brushing knees with Rob, as she unbuttons her slate-grey jacket and smoothes her pencil skirt to provide a picture of elegance and professionalism. Rob has had no trouble in categorising Charlotte. She is a perfect type A – 'Management Material'.

'Welcome to this meeting,' Rob leans in to tell her, with an unprofessional chuckle which he regrets immediately.

'Thank you, and can I just say how great it is to have the opportunity to one-to-one with you, Rob, on a working platform. I've been wanting to tell you how much respect I have for you as a Trainer. You're doing a marvellous job.'

'Thanks, Charlotte. I really mean that,' Rob says, really meaning it. 'Can I say in response that we feel similarly delighted to have you on board. You've become a strong and steady influence on the training group dynamic, and you really are pushing the other trainees forward with your excellent example.'

'It's lovely to be appreciated,' Charlotte tells him gravely, with an inclination of her head. 'I want to do well here, and I feel I could really succeed in this environment.'

'We feel that too.' His eyes are locked on hers in admiration. 'Shall we discuss your test results?'

'Yes please,' Charlotte says, with no anxiety Rob can see.

'You scored twenty. That was out of twenty. One hundred per cent correct. It was just wonderful to see a paper where it was obvious that the trainee is really benefiting from the information cascaded during the process.'

'All credit to you!' Charlotte enthuses in return.

'Now, Charlotte, you did the hard work. I just helped you to find your feet.' His fingers twitch involuntarily towards her arm.

She gives him a glimmer of a smile and then her face falls into a serious, woeful expression. 'My only concern is ... have you got time to discuss this now?' she asks.

Rob is delighted to be needed. 'Charlotte, I have as much time for you as you need. You know that,' he reprimands, linking his fingers together on the desktop and forming a triangle with his thumbs. 'What's troubling you?'

'I'm doing well on this course, I do know that. But I'm worried about what happens when the course is over.'

'You have no reason to be,' Rob reassures.

'You see?' Charlotte says, her lower lip wobbling. 'You're always there to help me along. I don't know how I'll do when you're no longer my manager.' She bursts out as an afterthought, 'I need you, Rob.'

She puts one hand on the corner of the desk with her palm facing upwards, open. Rob responds automatically by sliding his own hand over hers.

'You really have no reason to worry. Don't you know I'll always be there for you when you need me? As far as I'm concerned you're my responsibility for as long as you remain in the company. And maybe even beyond then.' She nods gratefully at his words and he gives her a beaming smile.

'Can I ask you something?' Their hands are still together, motionless on the desktop.

'Anything.'

Charlotte screws her eyes together and purses her lips. 'We have a great working relationship, don't we? We really connect in ways that enrich the business experience above and beyond what could be expected. Do you agree?' She takes a breath. 'What I really wanted to ask was – can we be friends? Good friends? Not just colleagues? I need a good friend. Someone I can rely on, someone who'll support me. Someone I can ... I can ...' She pauses and then the word erupts from her. 'Love?' She modifies hastily. 'Love and trust?'

Rob feels an uncontrollable and pleasurable spasm in his stomach at her words. He wants to confide; he wants to be her rock. 'Don't you know we have that already? That I consider you to be one of my closest friends? I feel I know you so well, Charlotte. All the terrible things you've been through. You've been so brave and I feel honoured to have your confidence on those times. We are friends, good friends.'

He clenches his hand around hers and lifts it to his lips. He kisses the knuckle of her ring finger. Charlotte freezes. Rob looks up at her as he feels the contraction of her muscles and sees the fear on her face. Still holding her hand, he slides out of his chair and drops to his haunches in front of her. His shoulders are level with the edge of his desk.

Charlotte explodes into tears. These are not pretty, hand-kerchief-dabbing tears, but a tidal wave of water from her eyes, nose and mouth, with gasps and hiccups as she is forced to fight for breath through this emotional onslaught. Her face has collapsed and she makes honking noises.

Rob is taken aback initially, but then he reassures himself that such passion is a wonderful thing in a person. He drops her hand and then, hesitantly, puts his own hand on her right knee. 'Come on, now,' he says awkwardly, feeling her bony kneecap through her skirt.

The sobbing eventually slows. She manages to speak, interrupting herself with hiccupping and slurping. She puts her index finger underneath her nose. 'I'm sorry.'

'There's no need to be,' Rob murmurs. It's all he can do for her.

'They're sending a representative over from Salzburg to talk to me,' Charlotte says in a rush. 'In two weeks' time. I think they've reached a decision. I'm terrified.'

Rob straightens up and sits back in his chair. 'Oh, Charlotte.'

'Could you be there?' she asks him. Her face contorts as she waits for his answer, which is not long in coming.

'No problem. Anything to help. After all ...' He puts out his hands to her and after a moment's hesitation she slips her own inside them, wet with clinging mucus. Rob does not flinch, even though the reality is overwhelming. 'What are friends for?'

'Thanks so much.'

Rob gets up slowly, brings her to her feet, and leads her to his office door. 'Go take a break. Take as long as you need. And then back to work with you. We need you.'

Charlotte nods with a small, one-sided smile. She buttons up her jacket, straightens her skirt, lifts her chin, and leaves the office.

Rob feels complete. With a tilt of his head and an out-stretched palm, he blows a sweet kiss after her.

Charlotte

Monday, 13th November, 10.54 am

She didn't want to think about what had just happened. She didn't understand it, and she wanted it to go away.

She was a mess. The wall of mirrors in the ladies' toilets reflected a collapsed, crimson face with crinkles and a mop of light blonde hair that would not be reasoned with. She tried to pretend to herself that a splash of cold water and a light combing would restore order, but somehow she knew her façade would not so easily be rebuilt.

Charlotte turned on the tap and looked at the water spilling out of it, falling around the chrome plug hole before being sucked down it. The last time she had cried that way had been at age eighteen. Her A-Level exams had not gone to plan and the morning on which the results fell on to the doormat had brought the kind of disappointment she had spent a lot of time trying to avoid since then. The memory of that failure, even now, brought with it a knife wound of shame. She hadn't worked hard enough and her results had reflected that.

What she hadn't expected was that her grades would not be high enough to ensure a place at university, and it was that knowledge, and the realisation that she might not be about to escape Allcombe and her parents, that had triggered hysteria.

Charlotte winced as she remembered clearly how she had wailed, the carefully opened envelope still clutched in her hand, and the embarrassed desperation of her parents to reassure her. They were people who did not admit to having emotions. After they had sat her down, presented her with a strong cup of tea and patted her twice on the back, they had left the house and not come back until after sunset. And they were not the sort of people who left the house at all unless they had somewhere specific to go.

Luckily, by their return, she had summoned the courage to phone the university and had been told they were still prepared to offer her the place if she wanted it. A tremendous relief then; a huge waste of emotion in retrospect, and she cringed away from it whenever it reasserted itself into her mind.

Crying solved nothing. It simply made her look unattractive, and so she had resolved not to do it again after that awful day. At least, not to do the realistic kind. Why she had broken that rule at such a crucial moment, and in front of such a crucial person, was not so much of a mystery to Charlotte as she would have liked it to be.

Something was worrying her, and it wasn't, for once, a job or a man. It was another woman. It was Rose.

Charlotte stuck her hands into the icy flow of water from the tap and let the cold turn her fingers numb. Bloody Rose French. The stupid, ignorant girl who had no idea of what real life was like, and no desire to learn. She had never been out into the world. She had never even left Allcombe. She had no intelligence, so it had to be a natural talent for nastiness that enabled that bleach bottle casualty to get under Charlotte's skin so effectively.

So perhaps a picnic hadn't been the best idea for November, she could see that now, but Rose's smirk had been constant throughout the entire day. Charlotte had wanted to ask her why she had bothered to come at all, but the girl had disappeared into the bushes with her intellectual equal, Amie, and after that they had been forced to rush to the casualty department because of her stupidity. The smirk had been unwavering as they had waited for Amie. Stuck in a small white reception room with Sam and Rose, her ability to make pleasant conversation had petered out within minutes.

The smirk was not the part of the day that really bothered Charlotte. Rose had waited for Sam to excuse himself and wander off to hunt for coffee before playing her trump card. Charlotte could remember the conversation word for word.

'You with Rob?'

What an opener. A lightning attack from nowhere; a feigned interest that was difficult to attribute immediately to malicious intent. She had parried deftly. 'Why do you want to know?'

'Just thought you could do better than a slapper like him.'

Charlotte had made herself smile after the initial shock of the word had died away. She had tried hard to disguise the wary quality of her voice. 'Do you mean he sleeps around? That's not true. Who told you that?'

'Nobody had to tell me,' Rose had replied with a shrug of her shoulders, and then Sam had returned from his fruitless search and the conversation had ended as abruptly as it had begun.

Charlotte turned off the tap and punched the metal button that started the hot air dryer with controlled fury. All that week, and throughout most of this week, she had dismissed Rose's insinuations. She had watched Rob and found she had no obvious reason to doubt him. He looked at Rose with no special interest; he hardly looked at her at all.

Why, then, at that wonderful moment she had planned and worked for, when Rob had taken her hand and called her his friend, why had she seen Rose's smirking face once more and felt the bitterness of distrust rear up inside her? It was that emotion that had destroyed her. It was the fact that Rose had controlled her behaviour, and had ruined the one good moment in her life, with her evil insinuations and laughing eyes.

Rob could never bring himself to touch a girl like Rose. She knew that. But why would Rose want to make her think that he had? Charlotte decided, as the hot air dryer wound down from a soft whine into silence, to give the matter more thought. She left the ladies' toilets no happier and no wiser.

Gary

Wednesday, 15th November, 10.17 pm

The basement was a good place in which to rehearse, or it would be as soon as he got around to having a heater installed. They had not removed their winter coats, and Gary had found that he needed fingerless gloves in order to play his guitar effectively. Still, even with the wind circulating freely above their heads and the damp trickling down the brick walls around them, the basement had its advantages. One was the fact that it was free. The other was that the kitchen was directly above them, and the lure of hot coffee and biscuits close by had led to far longer rehearsal sessions than they had ever managed before. Even Donna had lasted for two hours last Tuesday, which was a record for her attention span.

Not that this had led to any noticeable improvement. He had discussed the issue with Hilary, and she had come up with an excellent, and unexpected, suggestion; a suggestion he was going to implement tonight. He played the opening bars of the number he had been working on and nodded Donna in.

'Millicent,' she sang into the microphone, curving her thin body around it and twining her hair over her face, 'The world was what you meant ...'

The band stumbled through the chord change, all playing at a different tempo, looking to Gary for musical leadership. He winced at their individual noises.

'But now the dream's all bent, oh Millicent,' Donna sang meaningfully. Then she stopped and dropped the microphone away from her skinny purple lips with a pained grimace. 'It stinks,' she said.

The other band members stopped playing in a clatter of misplaced beats. She pushed her hair back into a nest of black strands around her long, pale neck and stared Gary down with a truculent energy. 'It stinks. I'm not singing it.'

Gary lifted the guitar strap over his head and set his most prized possession, his Gibson Les Paul in worn cherry-mahogany, back on its stand before sliding his lime green plectrum underneath the strings with an accompanying harmonic twang. 'You're not even going to try?' he asked her wearily. This was an old battle of wills that had always been more tiring than productive. Donna liked to be in charge and she liked to be right, but Gary knew she liked both of those things more than she liked to think. This had always worked to his advantage in these regular skirmishes.

'I don't see why we need to rehearse any fresh material,'

she said airily. Lozza put down his sticks and sighed. Paul sat down on the white plastic garden chair behind him, his bass guitar across his lap. Only Sock, the keyboard player, remained poised at his instrument, even though they all knew from experience this wasn't going to be resolved quickly. Sock always had been the most optimistic of the group.

'Power Cord is not going to be just another cover band,' Gary said, keeping his voice light and his eyes on his amplifier.

'That's what people around here want, though,' she told him with a pointing finger. 'It's just not what you want.'

She really was irritating. 'Should we do what you want, then? Should we do Alanis Morrisette rip-offs for the next fifty years?' There was a sarcastic edge to his words, so much so that for a moment it was almost as if Hilary had thrown her voice from the kitchen. Gary would never have dared to say such a thing before. He was beginning to like the new, confrontational, him.

Donna changed tack. 'I can't practise down here. The acoustics are all out.' She waved a skeletally thin arm at the bricks of the basement, slimy against the bright, swinging light of the naked bulb hanging high above them all.

This time, unusually, Lozza spoke up. The round, strong drummer with an immaculately trimmed, sand coloured goatee made a lot of noise when playing and was prone to sighs and coughs to get his point across, but hardly ever decided to say something directly during a band argument. 'It's free though, Don,' he placated.

'And there's a loo, and you can have a drink when you want,' Paul joined in. Tall, sensible, and older than the rest of the group members, he was a classic bass player. He wore blue jeans, white trainers and a Queen T-shirt. Nobody had ever seen him in anything else.

Sock, the thin, nervous keyboard player completed the line

of defence. 'My Dad did say he was pleased to have his garage back.' They had been using the garage as an emergency practice site for the last three weeks after the lock-up had fallen through.

'It's too cold,' Donna protested. 'It's doing damage to my vocal chords.'

Gary assessed her. He felt distant from the room, as if he floated above it, as if he was looking down on them from a hole in the kitchen floor next to Hilary. He was no longer the boy who, fresh from a break-up and a failed attempt to escape Allcombe, had hesitated to approach Donna in case she had thought he was making a move on her. At the time she had been the only person willing to sing during one of The Slaughter's rare karaoke nights, and that had been enough for Gary. Now he was beginning to realise he could do better than an untalented teenager who liked to pretend she was a star in the making.

'Donna,' he said to her firmly, 'your vocal chords are not worth keeping warm.'

Lozza, Sock and Paul collectively held their breaths.

Donna's cool, gothic exterior dropped away to reveal the pinched fishwife underneath. She was indeed an Allcombe girl. 'Your guitar is not worth plugging in,' she retorted nastily, 'and this song is definitely not worth fucking singing.' She raised her hands towards Gary and slowly, maliciously, tore the lyric sheet down the middle. The two pieces drifted on to the cement floor, landing with the copied words side up.

Gary bent down and retrieved the pieces. He looked at Lozza, who was sitting behind his drum kit wearing the avid expression of a man who has just realised the world's most exciting television programme is on. Lozza was a haulage man for a local brewery and his parents were happily married; he didn't usually get to see confrontation on this level. Gary smiled at him and Lozza blinked in confusion.

He turned on Donna. 'Are you saying you are definitely not going to sing this song?'

She lifted her chin and clenched her fists. 'Yeah.'

'And – just to be clear – you're saying you won't rehearse down here any more?'

Donna looked sideways at the other band members, twisting herself like a bent paperclip around the microphone stand. She seemed to sense that she was in a dangerous situation but could not work out why. Gary knew he had never given her any reason to think of him as a threat; that fact had to work to his advantage. 'That's right,' she said.

'Well then,' he said, and an elegant line that probably came from some old film sprang to mind. 'Then we are at an impasse.' It was as if this wasn't his life at all and no consequence could come of any action of his today. He no longer needed to be understood by Donna, or the band, or Allcombe. He was beyond them all.

Lozza cleared his throat and spoke again. This was turning out to be a most unusual rehearsal. 'Perhaps we should call it a night? Go away and, you know, all calm down?'

Paul and Sock looked both relieved and disappointed. Lozza shifted behind his drum kit. Gary sought to keep them together. He hadn't yet achieved his objective. 'I really think we should resolve this now,' he said with inner confidence. They froze, unused to the tone of leadership from him.

Donna glared at him. 'You really get off on bossing us around, don't you?'

'And, let me guess,' Gary replied sweetly, 'You're sick of it.'

He had never seen her look uglier. 'You read my mind.' She looked quite capable in that moment of lashing out at him, and Gary blenched before remembering that she liked to think of herself as too much of a lady to resort to violence. It was obvious that she cherished a mental image of herself as a punk version of Audrey Hepburn, but she was actually an anorexia-ridden teenager with a penchant for cheap makeup. Gary made a mental note to share that witty thought with Hilary later and played his trump card.

'Okay, then. You've made your feelings clear. Thanks for your honesty.' He turned to the three lads and shrugged. 'We might as well pack up.' Everyone looked blankly at him, so he made it clear. 'If we can't agree now, there's no point going on with the band, is there?'

Lozza, Paul and Sock looked at each other. Donna glared at everyone in turn. Gary affected a casual quality he didn't feel. 'You might as well push off now, Donna. We'll pack away. I'm sorry things didn't work out.' She shook her head and opened her mouth. Gary immediately interrupted her. 'I think it's all been said now. Go and find another group. Don't worry about us. You're better than all of us, anyway.'

Donna frowned, her heavily plucked eyebrows drawing together to form a strong circumflex across her long forehead. Her glossy purple lipstick drew attention to the question that was teetering on her tongue, but she didn't ask it. Instead she climbed the stairs and left the basement, her leatherette coat sweeping the concrete and her hair once more hiding her expression from the remains of the band.

In the silence that followed, Gary strained to catch the exchange between Hilary and Donna in the kitchen. He couldn't make out the words, but he could translate Hilary's murmur as a concerned question and Donna's tone of flat denial that followed. Just as he had expected.

Sock moved first. He switched the keyboard off and stretched out his shoulders. 'S'pose I better head off, then.' Lozza pulled at his jumper and Paul began to sort through the tangle of electric cords around his feet. Gary stood, head cocked, waiting for his cue.

A voice crept down the stairs. Gary's body was tuned to it; his demeanour told the others to stop and listen. The voice intensified. It had a power and a range that Donna had always lacked. It became rougher as it grew louder; it did not have Donna's sweetness, but it was compelling in a different way. The singer was expressing *Little Wing* with a clarity that made the sound hurt inside his chest.

'Who's that?' Paul whispered under his breath, not daring to swamp out the voice.

Gary left some moments before replying. 'It must be Hilary.' He met the eyes of each group member in turn. They were all captivated, all statues with frozen faces.

Lozza whispered, 'She's really good.'

Gary gave a half-smile. This was something he had already known. 'Do you think ...?' he began to ask, and then ground to a halt. 'No. She wouldn't.' He cast a querying glance over the band, asking them to fill in the gaps. 'Would she?'

Paul said quickly, 'Why not?'

Lozza said at the same time, 'You could ask her?'

Sock followed them both up with a firm, 'Yeah.'

Gary widened his eyes. 'You sure, guys?'

'Yeah,' Sock said again, and the others nodded.

'Hold on,' Gary told them, and began a low creep up the stairs so as to not detract from the voice. It was developing a Joni Mitchell edge through the continued singing that he was eager to explore.

He opened the basement door and emerged from under the stairs into the more muted light of the hall. Hilary was waiting for him in the doorway to the kitchen, and she stopped singing as soon as he appeared, shutting her mouth tight. There was an excitement in her face that he could feel he was mirroring with his own. In jeans and a V-necked T-shirt she looked younger, even with the glasses firmly in place and her hair scraped back against her skull. She looked more like his own age, and her anticipation increased that illusion.

Gary closed the basement door and leaned back against it.

'Well?' she asked him, quietly and breathlessly, her hands on either side of her stomach.

'It worked,' he said. 'You're in.'

She yelped once, her hands reaching out to clasp his fore-arms. He had not imagined this moment of success, but his body reacted to it as though he had been mentally rehearsing the action. His arms slid up around her hips to clasp behind her waist, and he pressed her into him so that her breasts were against his chest and they were breathing against each other, his face turned to her neck and her lips close to his ear.

She let him hold her that way until the intensity of his delight had passed and embarrassment began to set in. He had walked halfway into the ocean; now he didn't know whether to turn back with wet shoes or take the plunge and try to swim. In the agony of indecision he missed his chance. She took the lead and pulled away.

'The Millicent Song I wrote did the trick, then?' she asked softly, half-smiling.

'Spot on. Donna won't be coming back.' Gary couldn't meet her eyes as he said, 'I suppose we should get started?'

He opened the door for her and stood aside to let her descend in to the basement ahead of him, watching the sway of her hips and the way she handled his band.

Amie

Friday, 17th November, 4.31 pm

Amie had recently discovered that she possessed the gift of calm.

When she had been living within the confines of The Nation, she had been shielded from the outside world totally and the idea that it might somehow break through had terrified her. She had believed herself to be the kind of person who would freeze in a bad situation; that, when threatened, she would curl up into a ball and whimper. She had often imagined that she would not make a noise if she was dragged by her hair into a dark alley and violated. Any assailant could do as they pleased with her because her fear would make her as good as an accomplice, and who would believe afterwards that it was against her will? She had been horrified by such thoughts, and yet her mind had returned to them as if fear was a box she could unlock if she scratched against its surface.

Now she knew she would never have to worry about fear again.

In difficult circumstances, it turned out that she did not control what she did. Instead the sure hands of an emotional auto-pilot reached out and grabbed the joystick, and Amie had discovered she had only to do as the voice she heard coolly instructed. Only when the situation had passed did the saviour disappear, and she would once more become the Amie who took half an hour to decide on whether to drink tea or coffee.

Even her moments of apparent panic had been planned by the auto-pilot. When Rose's needle had pierced her navel, a dry voice in her head had suggested that the only way to get Rose to take the injury seriously would be to fake a fainting fit. And the incident in the club with the pint glass – the running away had been an inner suggestion from her helper. He understood dangerous situations better than she did. She trusted him to keep her alive.

Her auto-pilot was with her now. Somewhere inside there was fear, but he was keeping it under control so she could do what she needed to do. But this time it was not for her own benefit, but for her father's.

Her father was in the hospital, the telephone at work had

told her, and she needed to get there as quickly as possible. Not Allcombe Hospital, but the cardiac unit that was half an hour's drive away. He must have collapsed on the building site; he must have had a heart attack, Amie had filled in for herself.

Then, blessedly, her auto-pilot had appeared. He had persuaded her to collect her things and go home. He had asked her to call a taxi, which would be with her shortly. He had then suggested she should get together some items for her father: a pair of pyjamas, some clean clothes, a book. Not that her father had read a book since they had left Wales, but the television was too heavy to carry.

Amie had deliberated over which book to take. She had wanted to bring him *The Bible*. She hoped he would want its comfort, but the inner voice reasoned that if he wanted it, he would ask for it. It couldn't be thrust upon him now. Her fingers had twitched over it twice, fighting her auto-pilot, but in the end Amie had conceded and picked up *The Wind In The Willows* instead. It was the only other book in the house.

Under the sink she had found a plastic bag bearing a supermarket logo, and had put *The Wind In The Willows* inside it before creeping upstairs to her father's bedroom to look for some clothes. He did not allow her to come up here on her own. There was a wash of guilt as she pushed open the door, but she had been brought up with guilt and Amie did not allow it to stop her now.

The room was a mess. She had expected that. She had seen him get less and less concerned about his personal appearance, and she had not imagined that his attitude to his personal space would be any different. There were dirty clothes scattered randomly over the unmade bed and the once beige carpet. The sash window, badly painted and peeling, was closed, and the smells of sleep and sweat had intermingled. The small sink opposite the door was decorated in swirls of stubble, and the mirror that was attached to the wall behind it no longer reflected due to the snowstorm of toothpaste and shaving foam that had dried hard to its surface.

There was only one place to look for clean clothes, and that was in the small, white chest of drawers under the window. It had been there when they had moved in, along with the bed and sofa, the fridge and cooker, the crockery and cutlery. They possessed no household items; even the television was rented. Amie skirted the rumpled bed and wrestled with the stiff top drawer. It decided to leap from closed to open so suddenly that it came out of its hole, and Amie was left holding it in mid air by its mock bronze handles. She lowered it on to her lap and surveyed its contents.

There was a set of pyjamas, clean and folded, along with five pairs of pants. They were pristine and unused; she recognised them as past birthday presents from The Nation. They were an order who believed in useful gifts. She took them all and put them in the plastic bag.

Her father's behaviour had changed so much and so quickly; his untouched clothes were a testament to that. He had always believed in being properly dressed, even in bed, yet he had put these things away and decided he would never use them again. Not just clothes, but also faith and community had been banished, the tools with which he had raised her. Because he had finished with them he expected her to do the same, but it was not so easy for her to put aside these things. Perhaps it was because she had always had them in her life. Perhaps it was because she had never been given a good reason for discarding them.

She was finally beginning to identify the feeling that had been dogging her since moving to Allcombe. It was anger. She had seen it expressed in other people; Rose exhibited anger loudly on a daily basis. She said it was healthier to get it out into the open. Amie wondered if that was true. She wanted to find out.

'Shit,' she said experimentally. 'Shit shit shit shit shit.'

She felt guilty, but no less angry. She decided to try a stronger word. 'Cocksucker.'

Her little voice, her Welsh accent, turned the words from expletives into apologies. So she couldn't swear effectively. She only wished she could do something else to express her anger, like have a healthy conversation about the cause of it, with the butt of it. He was lying in a hospital bed; it was possible that she would not ever get the chance to ask him why they had left.

Immediately her auto-pilot kicked in and told her she had only to pack belongings and wait for the taxi cab. Worrying was not going to help.

It was in that moment of reinstated and artificial serenity that Amie saw the piece of paper that had been lodged behind the back of the top drawer and was now poking out from the space left when she had removed it. It was white and small, and it had been folded once, asymmetrically. She realised it was an envelope.

Amie's anger level shot upwards meteorically. She couldn't believe her father would be so unimaginative about secret correspondence as to stuff it down the back of the only drawer in the house. It was like a plot twist in the hackneyed religious novels The Nation were allowed to read. She suddenly felt convinced that he had wanted her to find it; that he had left it in such an obvious location in the hope that he would be caught. He had hoped she would air his dirty laundry for him, and judge him accordingly.

She detested this machination and she refused to give in to it. Amie decided not to look at the letter.

She picked the drawer off her lap by its handles and tried to slam it righteously back into position. It lodged itself at a strange angle at the lip of the hole and refused to go in any further. Amie struggled with it as an idea occurred to her:

God was stopping her from returning the drawer to its original position because she was fated to read that letter. It was a reasonable enough explanation, and one by which she felt reassured.

Amie yanked the drawer out again and placed it on the carpet beside her. Then she reached into the hole and took the envelope between two fingers, extracting it from its hiding place with the delicacy of a surgeon.

The Allcombe address had been handwritten in a large and clear style, using a light blue pen. It looked honest on the off-white, good quality paper. She removed the letter within, straightening its creases with the flat of her hand before allowing her eyes to slide over each word. For some reason she did not want to rush this.

Dear Adam,

So her father's first name was Adam. How fitting. To her he had always been Papa, to others in The Nation, even her mother, he had been Reverend, or Sir. Never Adam.

> I had to steal your address from Peter's records, so that's yet another sin I have committed because of you. I'm writing to tell you that I don't care. I would do the same again. I don't regret it and I still love you.

So that was it.

Amie felt a sincere and complete relief that unburdened her of all her worst doubts. Her father had fallen in love with another woman after the death of his first wife, Amie's mother, and had not been able to cope with the guilt of those feelings. That meant there was a clear reason for this near-death experience. He was meant to get better, see the error of hiding from his emotions and return to The Nation.

> There's only one thing that makes my soul beg for forgiveness, and that is my son. I think you have always

known that he is our son, our Abel. I hope every day
that he will inherit your strength, your charisma, and
pray that nobody else will see it in him. They may
know about our transgressions but they do not know
how far we went or for how long. That alone keeps
him safe within the walls of The Nation.

Amie had known Abel well. They had played together as
children. But he was twenty six years old, the same age as
her. Amie's mother had died ten years ago.

I dread to think what life is like out there for you. You
weren't given a choice, and I understand your decision
to take Amie with you. She is the one child you can
publicly claim as your own.

All those children who will, God willing, never know
who their father really is. And so we have all made a
mockery of The One True Separatist Nation, The
Nation you led and have been forced to leave. All of
us that you once loved in your special way agree that
you have only to ask us to come to you and we will,
bringing your children with us, leaving our husbands
behind. Only part of the secret was uncovered by
them. We will tell them the rest and start again only
with you, as one family, if you desire it.

The letter was signed in the same hand. Underneath, in the
same pen but in differing scripts, were eleven other signa-
tures, all women Amie had known, and with children of
ages spread from seventeen down to mere babies at the time
she and her father had left.

Amie replaced the letter in the envelope and put it back
into position. She picked up the drawer and this time it slid
smoothly into place with no effort. Now it seemed less like
the work of God and more like the fact that her muscles had
relaxed due to shock.

Auto-pilots were amazing things. Her auto-pilot was busy telling her that she did not need to start thinking right away about what she had just read; that she should present a calm and loving face to her father in his time of sickness. He was telling her that there would be time later to have the unavoidable confrontation.

She tried to follow his sensible instructions. She got to her feet and picked up the carrier bag, half-filled with the meagre detritus of an abandoned life; a few clothes, a book. There wasn't even a photograph to add to the pile. The only personal belonging she could find was the letter, and although Amie found herself wishing she was the kind of woman who could take such an item to a hospital bedside, she could not do that to him. He was still her father, and worthy of respect for that reason alone. He was, apparently, worthy of that respect from quite a few people.

Names started to pop randomly into her head. The names of children she had played with, prayed with, studied with. Children she had looked after as they had grown. Abel. Rachel. Leah. Zachariah. Once she started to list them, she could not stop. Phillip. Jason. Paul. Sophie. Thomas.

The distant hum of a car grew into her thoughts and crowded out the list. She wished she had a pen and a piece of paper close by; Amie wanted to get it all down so that she could look at it and begin to make sense of it. She wanted to list her possible relatives. She wanted to draw a new family tree.

Amie snorted with a sudden attack of humour and a car horn beeped outside the window. Of course; the taxi had arrived. It was time to go to the hospital and hold her father's hand.

Alma

Monday, 20th November, 9.55 pm

Somebody had fed the jukebox, and a noise was blaring out from the speakers on the walls above the bar. It cut through her appreciation of the remains of her pint of real ale and the last drag of her cigarette. It turned her mind to other thoughts, which was the last thing she wanted.

Dora was back in the nursing home, where she belonged, where she should have been left at the beginning. Back at The Paradise, where the sheets were changed every other Tuesday and the piano had been left untuned for decades. Alma had promised to visit but she had lost faith in Dora's ability to take her away from both their worlds any more. Dora had seen her drink, and seen her beaten verbally by her daughter; was it any surprise that the old woman could no longer see her only in the golden haze of nostalgia?

Alma raised her eyebrows. She was a regular: that was all it took. The barman turned to the stereo positioned behind the dripping optics and the orange fairy lights, and tweaked at the volume dial. The noise receded enough to allow her to finish her pint and her cigarette in relative serenity.

The raising of her right index finger set the barman in motion once more. He took her glass and started to fill it from the pump with the slow, steady pulls that demonstrated his skilled boredom with the task. He let the liquid fill up and over the glass until he was satisfied with the foamy head, and then placed it back in front of Alma. She looked up from the cigarette she was lighting to accompany it. 'Cheers, Max.'

He did not reply. She had made it clear early on in their relationship that she was not the talkative type. They had quickly come to the understanding that classified him, for Alma, as the perfect man; he gave her alcohol and asked no questions.

It was a quiet night in The Slaughter, but then Mondays always were. She preferred it that way. There were only the types of faces with which she felt comfortable. The soft, fallen lines of the forgotten old men and the expanding bellies of the middle-aged disappointeds were a lot easier to deal with than the hopeful anger of drunken youth, pretending to know it all and thinking that pretence would get them somewhere. It was not that she hated to see their judgement of her as she sat at the bar and blocked their way, but that she hated to feel herself judging them. She wanted to believe that youth had its own purpose – when she saw it up close she remembered it was God's trick to make procreation possible.

The jukebox clicked off, the song at an end. Max was having a conversation about soccer with the man in the raincoat on the corner stool. He was always in place, with his patient spaniel slumped beside him, no matter when Alma arrived. He had a thinning face and an uncontrolled spattering of white across his hair, eyebrows and moustache, and he liked to talk about his spaniel. It was easy to tune him out.

A chill on the back of Alma's neck told her that the main door to the bar had just been opened. She pulled her knitted, floor-length, emerald green cardigan around herself as she heard the door close behind her. Even as she registered it, she felt a new presence beside her at the bar and a vibration through the brass rail on which her feet rested that told her someone was climbing on to the stool next to her.

She held her pint glass and turned her head fractionally to get a look at the newcomer. It was the last person she had ever expected to find in a pub.

'Angela Fearn,' she said in sarcastic welcome, lifting her voice on the final long syllabic drawl. She lifted her glass and toasted her before taking a long swallow, trying not to show how much this surprise had made her need it.

'Alma Chippendale,' Angela replied in the same tone,

making it clear how she felt about both the surroundings and the false name. 'Mother told me you had brought her here.' Max, who had approached her to take her order, faltered in his professional smile. They were creating a strange vibration between them that he could not have failed to miss. Angela turned to him and ordered a glass of white wine, giving Alma the opportunity to weigh up her opponent.

She was sitting bolt upright on the stool as if her back was unused to being without support, and her head was tilted back, as if trying to stop the smell of cigarette smoke and debauchery from sneaking up her nose and penetrating her brain. She looked like the kind of woman who wasted good money on plug-in air fresheners and decorative toilet roll holders. Alma thought she was probably an office worker who gave to charity and thought she had a stressful life.

'Mother also said you haven't been to visit her.' Angela spoke suddenly once the glass of white wine had been paid for with the careful sorting of exact change from her satchel, suspended on her hip by a thick leather strap that ran over her sky blue blouse, between her breasts. The wine sat on the bar forlornly, looking unloved.

Alma dragged her attention away from it and concentrated on her reply. 'Not yet. I thought I'd let her settle in first.' She lit another cigarette without thinking, and registered Angela's distaste at the habit.

'She's quite settled. She would love to see you.'

Alma shrugged and did a tap dance on the balls of her feet against the brass rail. A mischievous, rebellious urge seized her and she blew a mouthful of smoke over Angela, who refused to acknowledge it. 'Maybe I don't want to see her,' she said casually, spite-ridden.

The meaning of the words were misunderstood. 'The police did a thorough investigation. There was no evidence to suggest anything untoward was happening there. And I did warn you that Mother had a problem distinguishing reality from fantasy. Can we go somewhere else to discuss this?' she asked.

'Haven't finished my drink,' Alma replied, reasonably, she thought, raising her glass.

Angela swallowed in a reflex action, but left her own drink untouched. She looked around the pub, peering into the darker corners and taking in the long, empty benches. 'Do you know I've never been in here before? It's not at all how I pictured it. It has a bad reputation.' She said it conversationally, with a hint of surprise.

'Well, gee whizz, we're sorry to disappoint you! I guess you were expecting a hotbed of hookers and dealers,' Alma retorted, feeling her mood lift. So Angela was nothing but a prude who pretended to be above the messier side of life, but was in fact only afraid of it. Now Alma felt superior she was ready to hear whatever it was Angela wanted to say. 'So why did you come here now, if it's all so shocking to you and your English virtues?' She smiled at Max, raincoat man and dog, who all smiled uncertainly back at her, watching the action.

There was a squeak as Angela rearranged herself on her stool, ending up with her legs crossed to make her look even more uncomfortable than before. 'All right, I'll get straight to the point,' she said in her high, clipped tones. 'We both know, through the information you provided to the police and to my mother, that Chippendale is not your real name.' Angela hesitated, and the state of panic Alma had reached when she had thought the disclosure of her real name was imminent faded slightly. The worst, however, was yet to come. 'If you could be bothered to visit my mother you'd find that she is terrified and that no-one, particularly not me, can reassure her. That is because you allowed her to believe that her story of abduction and murder might have some credence, although the only abduction that happened was her own.

'Obviously, I would like to take her out of The Paradise, but I cannot afford any of the other nursing homes in Allcombe. Since this mess is, at least in part, your fault, I came here to find out if you intend to help her in her current predicament.' Angela ended her speech and closed her mouth so tightly that pressure lines formed underneath both cheeks.

Alma waited for a specific request, but none was forthcoming. Since Angela could not name a specific form of aid, Alma decided, after stubbing out her cigarette, to offer the kind of help she felt happiest providing. 'Okay, I'll go and talk to her, I'll tell her everything's all right, not to worry, yadda yadda yadda …'

Angela's expression told her that was not what was required. 'Well, that would be lovely for mother, obviously,' she said, 'but really she needs something more material. More financial,' she finally brought out of her mouth, and looked infinitely relieved that she had managed it. She even took a quick sip of her white wine, pressing her lips together as she replaced the glass.

Max shifted towards Alma, and she did not have to ask him to refill her own glass once again. She had developed a taste for real ale and appreciated the time it took to drink compared with a whisky sour, her previous tipple. She would have expected to have drunk at least eight sours in the time three pints took her. The evenings passed a lot more quickly now; she did not feel she had to count time before she could reasonably order another. Angela clutched her satchel in alarm against the speed of her drinking, but she was the only one in the bar who cared, and she was an outcast here. It was easy to defy her. 'Boy, are you way off the mark,' she told her, using her 'I'm right and you're wrong' smile. 'I don't have any money. Why do you think I'm stuck here working for peanuts?'

Angela did not look in the least bit surprised. 'I gathered that. I've been to your flat.' She said it with a smug disgust, as if it had been a unique pleasure to discover an ex-movie star living with stolen garden furniture and photograph albums as her only possessions. 'I did think there might be some way to help that you hadn't yet considered. How about going to the press?'

So Angela wanted her to sell her story, make a spectacle of herself to the newspapers in order to provide that most basic commodity, money. The answer didn't even need to be considered.

'No,' Alma rapped out. Then, in case that wasn't enough, 'Not ever. Not in a million years.' Her voice came out louder than she would have liked, and she realised she had the attention of the bar again. Now she was the one to wish the conversation had taken place elsewhere; Max, raincoat-man and dog felt less like her adoring sideline fans and more like a jury, waiting avidly for a slip-up in her defence. 'No press.'

Angela looked prepared for that answer too. She unzipped her satchel and removed a shiny cream pamphlet from its depths. She didn't look at it. She simply placed it on the bar next to the newly refilled pint glass. 'Prices are on the back,' she said, returning to her mode of polite tyranny that Alma now understood was not reserved exclusively for Dora.

Alma looked at the pamphlet without deigning to touch it in case it looked like a commitment. It was a long rectangle, the stiff card folded twice with its front page an expanse of cream with embossed italic gold lettering upon it, shaped into a curve to slide around the top of an oval two-thirds of the way down. In the oval was a pen-and-ink sketch of a large building that resembled a castle in its crenulations and flag-poles. Flightily sketched pine trees had been added to bestow a fairy tale quality that Alma took for granted the building did not actually possess.

The lettering stated, 'The Allcombe Grand – Nursing Home,' in a caring and efficient style. Alma had never seen the building in Allcombe, but she could tell that the fees would have to be large in order to give out freely this quality of brochure.

'No,' she repeated. It did not seem to be reaching Angela's ears.

'I've written my number on the back. I'll expect to hear from you by next Friday. If you haven't come up with any alternative financial arrangements by then I'll assume you're compliant in my contacting of a newspaper.' Angela sounded so reasonable. She looked so reasonable, with her easy-to-style haircut and her gold stud earrings, her flat shoes and her round-necked sweater. It was hard to believe what was happening. She got off the bar stool, hopping down awkwardly, and rearranged her satchel to her satisfaction.

Alma had been in this movie before. She knew the next line. The next line was, 'This is blackmail!', delivered in outraged and impatient tones. It wouldn't come out. While she struggled with her vocal chords Angela left, abandoning her once-touched drink, walking with the jilted movements of an actress who had not been given her expected cue and could not think of anything to say in its stead.

Max stepped in. 'Did she just try to blackmail you?' he asked Alma. So it seemed fate could not be baulked. Somebody had to deliver the line. 'Who did you used to be? What's your real name?' This was what happened when the apparent inconsequentiality of a person vanished; a natural curtain that existed between them and others vanished with it. She was somebody important to the other drinkers now, and she was attracting a crowd. She never understood why people were always looking for somebody to do tricks for them, to take their boredom away instead of dealing with it themselves.

So much for real ale and understanding barmen. Now she had to return to whisky sours drunk on her garden furniture and the pull of her photo collection. That would give her far too much time to mull over her current problem, although she already knew she wasn't going to do anything about it. She didn't have the money, and if she did she would have spent it on drink and cigs.

She half-suspected Angela didn't have the guts anyway. And why should anybody believe her? Angela had nothing but the word of a frightened and lonely old mother to back her up. Let her see if she could get rich on that.

Alma shrugged off her stool and put the last of her money on the bar, guessing it would be enough. Then she downed her pint with fluid grace. 'Mind your own beeswax,' she told Max, the raincoat and the dog, who was now sniffing round her ankles in an interested way. With a final thought she took Angela's wine and downed that too before picking up the pamphlet and abandoning the locals to the tidal swell of gossip.

Hilary

Thursday, 23rd November, 11.49 pm

The meal had been eaten and the wine had been drunk. She knew she was putting on weight and she knew this was a sign of happiness, but still, even during these timeless hours before they went to their separate beds, when they prevaricated over the kitchen table and talked with a frenzy, she clung to the belief that she was a troubled woman. Hilary had discovered it was easier to live that way. Then happiness was not an expected thing; it was a sudden wallop over the head with a large pink mallet that made it impossible not to smile, just like the children's television show she had grown up with and despised as fluff.

Now Hilary was beginning to suspect happiness was important to her, no matter where it erupted from.

This thought occurred to her only after the third glass of wine, at about eleven o'clock every night, and the revelation died again by the summons of the alarm clock the next morning. Then she woke with her old ideas firmly back in place – that it was important to have a handsome and successful boyfriend, to have a real career and to hold strong opinions on every subject and look down on those who didn't. In the mornings she remembered the reasons why she couldn't be attracted to Gary.

Right now, this evening, past eleven o'clock, everything he said and did looked pretty good. And she wanted him to be thinking the same thing about her.

He was summing up. ' …and she would never really be interested in what I had to say, you know? I could never really discuss opinions with her. We always just had to agree,' he said with intent eyes, his brush of ginger hair sticking up in right angles from his head.

Hilary nodded knowingly. 'It was the same with Steve. Exactly the same,' she said. 'He thought every disagreement was the end. He couldn't accept that people can be together without operating from a joint brain. I think now, in retrospect, he wanted a clone more than a girlfriend. He didn't want discussion. He just wanted a mutual patting of egos.'

Hilary watched Gary toy with the fork on his empty plate. His terrible leadership tactics with the band had begun to seem cute, and his huge socks, coupled with the fact he had decided to start cultivating a trimmed goatee, now appeared interesting to her. He pushed the fork on the plate with rhythmic movements. He was coming to the end of his speech again.

'… It's like the signs of being in a bad relationship, isn't it? It's funny how you can never see it at the time. You always want to struggle on when really it would make so much more sense to say enough. Why do you think that is? Why do you think we both persevered?'

Hilary loved it when he asked her a question this way, as if she was an oracle and he had travelled for miles to glean wisdom from her. And it was also heartening to see how his vocabulary was improving; she put that entirely down to her own influence. She rested her eyes upon his with sagacity as she formulated her answer. 'We're all looking for something to complete us, don't you think? Something to prove to us that we're not alone. Perhaps a relationship gives you a glimpse of that, no matter how unsuccessful it might be. So we're not willing to let it go.'

At least, that was the theory she had shared with Steve as they had watched couple after couple who refused to see their unsuitability during nights out in New Zealand. She remembered how her friends had tagged along behind them as they had walked together, hand in hand, and she had laughed at the jealousy emanating from them, the loneliness and anger that oozed from them because one of the pack had dared to find a soul mate. But it was natural to move on: she had always moved on.

'You're so right,' Gary said with admiring intonation. 'We carry on because we see a shadow of the real thing. But we really need someone who sparks off us, someone who we can discuss matters with and learn something new from, in order to be completely happy. With Millicent, she always made it so clear that she considered music to be ...'

Hilary toyed with the remains of her own tagliatelle. This talking so candidly of partners was a new thing, but it had taken a strong hold of both of them. For the past two nights, last night after band practice, they had each revealed the peccadilloes of their old relationships with the glee of children unwrapping Christmas presents. They treated each small failure as a pearl of wisdom that they carefully passed back and forth.

She didn't really believe that listing faults could help

them discover a formula for a successful relationship, but she did enjoy the intimacy of a shared goal and, a new thing for her, the pleasure of open conversation that held nothing back. Nothing except the abseiling accident and the death of her friends, she mentally corrected herself. And perhaps it was approaching time to share even that.

'… But you have such a gift for singing, for music, it's really amazing, you know? And it's just another thing that we have in common? We have such a lot of things in common.' Gary was leaning forward and his eyelashes were quivering. The way he held his breath told her he had been working himself up to this moment. He fell silent.

The microwave, positioned on the pine cabinet next to him, was flashing 11.57. Hilary thought suddenly of Cinderella, of acts that must be completed before twelve or the opportunity would slip away forever. She was catching his urgency. The kitchen was warm and dry, lit only by the four mismatched candles on the table that it had become their habit to eat by. Outside the street was quiet, so quiet that there was only the hum and swish of the automatic movement of the sea.

11.58, and he was stretching out his left hand towards her, sliding out of his chair. She couldn't look him in the eyes. She felt a white-hot embarrassment surround her, but it couldn't penetrate her determination to let this happen. It was definitely the wine, but she still wanted it, no matter how she would feel tomorrow morning, and she suspected she would feel awful.

He was leaning back against the table beside her and his hand was a breath away from her face. She thought, *If he tries to kiss me without first removing my glasses then I'll know this is all wrong*. It was so important to her that he should take away her analytical face and leave her vulnerable to him. That was the only way she could picture them together tonight.

11.59. His hand was trembling against her cheek and

then he was moving behind her ears, at the arms of her glasses, with the clumsiness of a man who has never worn them. He knocked them forward with a quick, nervous movement and they slid to the end of her nose. He grabbed them and put his thumb over one of the lenses; a distracted part of Hilary's mind made a note that they would need cleaning later while the rest of her smiled. He had done it right. She let him see her smile and take it for encouragement. It was all right that he should lean toward her, smell her, start to move in for the kiss.

There was a baby softness to his lips that were hardly touching hers and he left them there without movement, without attempting to probe, as if wanting her to get used to him. Hilary wondered if it was really even a kiss. It was a new and delicate experience; she let herself unfold into it and only then realised how tense she had been. Now she could relax. Now they both could.

The telephone rang.

It was attached to the wall just a few inches from the back of Hilary's head and it was a screaming alarm bell that made her jump back. Gary overbalanced in panic and put one hand on her plate and the remains of her tagliatelle.

Hilary turned to the phone so she wouldn't have to look at his struggle to retain dignity. Her lips felt hot and tender. She had to resist the urge to touch them. She reached for the receiver.

'Hello?'

There was a pause. 'Hi, Hils. How are you doing?'

Steve, phoning to check on her. His watchdog sense had certainly struck gold this time. She heard Gary struggling with the plates behind her, sending cutlery skittering to the floor. 'Hi Steve,' she said, and all movement behind her stopped. She faced the wall resolutely.

'Just phoning to see if you're still up?' he asked her. There was an edge to his voice. Something was wrong. For a moment she had the ridiculous thought that he somehow knew about the kiss. She pushed that thought aside. He was in New Zealand. Not even light could have reached New Zealand in that time.

'I told you before, the phone is in the kitchen. So if you phone me, I have to be up, okay?' Gary resumed his clattering behind her. She felt inordinately sensitised to him. Her neck, back and bottom were tingling with his proximity. 'Look, I was just about to go to sleep. Can I talk to you some other time?'

'I – um – need to talk now,' he contradicted. Most unlike him. 'It's kind of important.' He cleared his throat, something he only did when he was very nervous. He knew that whatever he was about to say would displease her. 'Open the door.'

'What?' Hilary asked sharply, her mind working overtime and arriving at one, very undesirable, conclusion. 'Why?'

'Open your front door.'

She dropped the receiver on to the table and turned. Gary was hunched over the dirty plates with the expression of a skivvy who was expecting a whipping. She pushed past him, left the kitchen and took five steps to the front door. Before she could allow herself to chicken out, she turned the dead lock and threw open the door.

A tall figure stepped forward into the light thrown outwards by the hallway. The blurred outline coalesced into Steve.

'Surprise!' he said. He sounded nervous. He knew her well enough to know how she hated surprises. Then he stepped forward again so he was on the threshold of the house, his tanned, conventionally handsome features rearranging themselves into a frown. 'Where are your glasses?' he said.

Sam

Sunday, 26th November, 3.05 pm

Allcombe Park on a Sunday afternoon was an experience that changed throughout the seasons. In spring the children wore adorable red and yellow mackintoshes, picked daffodils, and left muddy footprints on the rungs of the slide. In summer there were green and pink dresses and dungarees, and they danced around the swings with the joyous swagger of bees who have found nectar. The mothers would sit complacently by the fuchsias. In autumn there was a dwindling in numbers. Occasionally a small figure encased in brown or black would appear, dragging an unwilling mother to the roundabout and making her push it into action for a few minutes.

In winter it was deserted. In winter it belonged only to Sam, and he could sit on his cast iron bench with the arm rests that curled into lions' paws and imagine that the children played on in their rainbow patterns, their high voices calling out his name, asking him to join in.

Whatever the season, and whenever possible, on Sunday afternoons he would fill the pockets of his hooded anorak with mint imperials and head to his bench for a few hours. This had been his habit for years and he had never seen fit to share it with another person before, not even his father. This was his sacred time; a time when he could watch the very children for whom he wanted to make it a better world. He could see them, safe and happy, and know that they would not be kidnapped by The Baby Snatcher or blown up by The Recreational Area Rogue, because both of those villains had been stopped by him. He, Sam Spurling, had improved the world. He had not done it for praise or glory. He had done it because he could, and because of his private Sunday afternoons.

He didn't know why he had decided to break that rule of privacy today.

He tightened the drawstring of his hood against the possibility of drizzle and redid the knot of his tartan scarf. It was a cold afternoon. The sun had already decided to desert him and a uniquely British dampness was setting into his bones. The iron bench was hard and cold, and his corduroy trousers offered no protection.

The Park stretched out before him, a skeleton of the living, breathing thing Sam had seen it become in warmer times. The small slide joined on to an activity area in front of him – a playful castle in primary colours was the newest apparatus. Coloured beads swung from the open drawbridge and ladders balanced against the ramparts. Behind it lay the swings and the roundabout, old and metallic, with peeling paint and rusted chains. From his bench Sam could see them all, and beyond them the main gate to the park, encased in privet that ran stubbornly over the strung wire.

Beyond the gate lay a hill that stumbled down to the promenade and the sea, or up to one of the shabbier new estates. Sam knew that Rose lived in one of those houses. He was hopeful that, by giving her only a short downhill walk, she would be more likely to make their meeting this afternoon, and to be in a good mood if she did attend. When she was in a good mood she was all the more likely to let him touch her.

Sam shifted on the bench and kept his attention on the gate. He knew it wasn't morally right, but he couldn't give up such pleasure. He was powerless against her. Just like the time that Burp Boy had tricked him into a dry cream cracker eating competition, robbing him momentarily of his own special power, Sam had no way to protect himself. When she told him to follow her in to a dark alley or somebody's garden shed, his feet moved and his body responded joyously. Within the space of a week he had learned to hate himself and live for those moments.

His trouser area responded even as he thought about it. He could picture exactly how, at their last meeting in the early hours of Saturday morning, she had slapped him on the back of his head, connecting with his bald spot, as she had demanded, 'Harder! Faster!' He always did his best for her. He contended with his father's outraged voice reverberating within his skull, but never considered not doing as she asked.

She was at the gate. It swung open with a creaky harmonic.

She had made an allowance to November by wearing a faded denim jacket that fit snugly around her shoulders and waist. Sam caught a glimpse of something violet and skimpy underneath it. Jeans in the exact shade of the jacket belled out over her pink high heels with open toes, and her hair was held back from her face by a plastic pink Alice band. He handbag was beige and squashy, no bigger than her fist.

Rose caught sight of him, and he raised a hand in welcome, which she ignored. She looked over her shoulder and made a gesture before walking through the open gateway and across the play area with unswerving pace. In her wake appeared another girl – sorry, woman – who scuttled along obediently in her exact footsteps.

Sam watched them both approach with a pang of disappointment. His trouser department took a dive. Rose was as confident and beautiful as ever. Her companion, trotting like an old dog in pursuit of a young mistress, struggled to keep the requisite four paces behind her. She was taller than Rose, and had copied Rose's style, which only revealed more clearly to Sam her deficiencies. She had bad skin and her hair had been the victim of an attack by a home bleaching kit. She had no grace on her illogically-high heels, and her bottom half was at least two sizes bigger than her top half in her tight jeans and denim jacket. She was a mutant clone of Rose that had managed to bypass all of the charm of the original. She was still walking towards him by the time Rose had arrived and slumped down on to the bench, a hand's width from him.

'That's Kelly,' Rose said by way of a greeting. She hardly ever did the traditional hello, Sam had learned. She examined her flaking nail polish as Kelly crossed to stand in front of them both with a belligerent scowl on her short mouth. Her front teeth protruded on to her lower lip and she stood with her weight slung on to one hip, in modern, lazing, fashion.

'Hello,' Sam said to her. Kelly stared at him with disgust written in her crinkled nose and forehead.

'Budge up,' she said to Rose with a local twang, and Rose shifted closer to Sam to make a space for her friend, shooing him with her hands so that he was squelched up on one buttock against the curling arm of the bench. This wasn't at all what he had been hoping for.

Rose exchanged looks with Kelly. 'Told you,' she said, and Kelly nodded with the sympathetic eyes of a confidante. They had been discussing him. Sam felt a shiver of fear. A pouncing anger emanated from both of the girls, as if they were about to commence combat to the death with him. And Sam knew he couldn't count on his own wits and guile when it came to dealings with Rose. He only had to look at her tiny ears and jutting chin and he melted.

'I've got something to tell you,' Rose said. Her hands were in her lap, her gaze focused on the swings jumping in the sharp November breeze, backwards and forwards, backwards and forwards. She was nervous, he realised with a flash of understanding. He was deeply surprised; he had thought her immune to such emotions.

'I'm pregnant.'

Sam's feet quivered in their lace-up shoes. His mouth refused to sit in a straight line and he couldn't find a place to put his hands. He shoved them into his anorak pockets and then pulled them out again, scattering mint imperials randomly over all three of them. Kelly started popping them into her mouth as she retrieved them; Rose brushed them off her lap to the grass beneath where they nestled like wrens' eggs.

He had never imagined this possibility. He had assumed that he was infertile, that he had lost his potency due to the long years in which his testicles had been severely underused. Yet within a week he had managed to impregnate her. He recognised the new, shameful emotion uncurling within him as pride. It stood up, straight and tall, and blossomed in a flower of happiness.

'Say something,' Rose commanded. The park gate, which Kelly had not bothered to shut, creaked wilfully in the wind.

'Would you marry me?'

He didn't know where that had sprung from. Then he remembered the one speech his father had given him, on his eighteenth birthday, about this subject. He had muttered the stock phrases, such as doing a lot of that in the bathroom could make you go blind, and it would be despicable to go getting a nice girl into trouble but, if you did, you should do the honourable thing. Sam supposed those embarrassed aphorisms had created more of an impact on him than he had previously thought.

'Okay,' Rose said immediately, with an exhalation of breath.

The future had just taken a strange and wonderful turn. A new path lay before him that he had never dared to dream about even imagining. Organisation, and white dresses, and rose petals, and then a mother and a baby. And a father and a husband. He got to have it all. He felt like dancing, like singing, like hanging off a lamp-post Gene Kelly style and shouting to everyone that life could start anew.

He picked a mint imperial off the slope of his chest. Kelly was whispering in Rose's ear, who listened and then spoke on cue. 'My Dad's kicked me out.'

Sam felt expansive and lightheaded. Nothing was beyond him. 'Move in with me,' he said. It was almost a statement instead of a question. He could be a confident father figure in this new life.

'Okay,' Rose said. Kelly leaned over and whispered once more into that tiny ear. A strong spike of wind thrust the swings into squealing pendulum motions. What a beautiful place the park was, Sam thought. He would treasure it, always. 'If anyone says anything,' Rose began haltingly, stopped, and then restarted, 'If anyone like Matt, or anyone, comes up to you and says anything, just ignore them, right? They don't know what they're talking about.'

She wasn't making any sense. Newly pregnant women have a lot of adjusting to do, Sam told himself. Things were happening inside her that he could not begin to comprehend. He wanted to touch her, but she had the attitude of an ice sculpture and the watchfulness of a radar installation; he feared any move towards her would ruin the perfection of the moment. He was more than content to simply count his blessings today. He had a fiancé and a baby on the way. He felt he could not reasonably expect a hug as well.

Rose stood up, her back straight and her expression brittle. A heartbeat later, Kelly followed suit. 'Right, we're off. I'll bring my stuff round later.'

'Okay,' Sam said, anxious to please her and desperate to get her to stay for a moment more. 'Um ... so I'll see you tonight?'

Rose and Kelly lit simultaneous cigarettes from Kelly's lighter and began the walk back across the play area in single file, Rose, naturally, leading the way. Sam watched them disappear out of the gate.

She was moving in tonight. He had to get home and rearrange things. His superhero memorabilia would need to be hidden away, for the time being, at least. Until Rose was happy and settled. Then he would tell her everything, just as his father had told his mother about his life as The Amazing Screw. Rose would have to be prepared if the baby was a boy; the talent was always handed down to the Spurling men and manifested itself around puberty. Then, with love and understanding the boy could learn to use his rare gift, whatever it might be, for good. And Sam would retrieve the Symbol of Superdom from back of his sock drawer and pass it on to his flesh and blood, as it had been passed on for generations before him.

Maybe he could even don the cape and helmet once more himself. After all, there would be no better way to teach his son than through personal experience.

But enough of the future. For now it was enough to know they would be together forever.

Charlotte

Monday, 27th November, 4.41 pm

Mr Forth's office was surprisingly spacious considering it was situated above a television repair shop. On her first visit, when she had returned to England from Austria, Charlotte had been expecting a grand, pillared building that would speak of morality and justice; instead she had found an untidy series of rooms with no legal tomes lining the walls and no barrister's wig on a stand, waiting to be swept up on the way to court.

At least there was an impressively large desk strewn with

papers, and green leather armchairs, and also an efficient secretary sitting in the hallway, so perhaps that explained why Mr Forth assumed such eminence with his clients. He was just as invulnerable and crotchety as she had remembered, although she had assumed that her memories had made a caricature of him as time had passed since their first official meeting.

With Rob sitting beside her in an immaculate three-piece suit, Charlotte felt endowed with a confidence that refused to be daunted by her imagination. His precise appearance complemented her own dark grey pinstripe. They looked like the perfect professional couple, which everyone knew was not a force to be trifled with lightly.

She gazed out of the window as Mr Forth prepared them for the meeting. The view was a bland one. In this insalubrious part of London there was a second-hand car salesroom and a very unwelcoming fast food outlet directly opposite, both of which she would never have chosen to frequent. They had a dirty quality, as if the once bright paintwork had been soaked in the grime from the car exhausts that ran alongside them constantly. The passing people all wore stiff-necked depression that suggested they had been dipped in the same filth and then left to dry.

For the first time Charlotte wished for the clean air of Allcombe. Then she recalled that the air had been just as pure in Salzburg, and she decided to wish for that instead.

'...they have already arrived and are, at present, waiting in the boardroom,' Mr Forth continued in an instructional tone of voice. He was leaning back in his chair with his fingertips pressed together to make a pyramid of his hands. His slow tone reminded Charlotte that she was paying him by the hour. 'I though I'd prepare you beforehand as to the identity of the key participants in the discussion today?'

He raised his eyebrows at Charlotte, who inclined her head in agreement. At least he wasn't one of those men who instantly deferred all decisions to other men. Rob was being treated by Mr Forth as nothing more than an observer, which was how she wanted it. 'The head of human resources for your previous employer has flown over from Austria specifically for this meeting. As I'm sure you're aware, her name is Susannah Medley, and she has already intimated to me that she is hoping we can settle the personal injury claim today with a mutually acceptable figure. As I have already advised, Ms Jackson, I feel an out-of-court settlement would be the best option rather than a drawn-out affair that may, or may not, go in your favour on the day.'

He took a deep breath. 'Also present, with your agreement, will be Mr Michael Miller.'

Charlotte felt a strange tingle of recognition in her stomach as the name passed Mr Forth's lips. Rob must have seen some reflection of it in her face; he put one hand on the arm of her chair in concern. She wondered what her expression was showing.

'There's no cause for concern,' Mr Forth continued. 'It's quite common in these cases for the company to insist that the accused admits culpability and apologises to the ... er ... victim. If you feel unable to accept such an apology then I'll simply instruct that he be removed from the meeting before it commences. There is no obligation. Would you like to take a moment to consider?'

'Yes,' Charlotte said immediately, 'If you would give us a moment.' Mr Forth removed himself from his comfortable chair and his office. Charlotte watched Rob out of the corner of her eyes until he turned to face her with concern in the softness of his mouth.

'You don't have to do this,' he told her, wearing his beautiful, earnest expression. 'You've been braver than anyone could ever expect. There's no need to do more.'

'I'm going to see him,' she said. She had made up her mind

immediately; she needed this interval only to dissuade Rob from attending. She couldn't risk him hearing what Mike might say. 'I want to do it alone. Can you wait here for me?'

'Wait here? But ...' Charlotte realised his dimples showed in his frowns as well as his smiles. His blond hair had been contained with some sort of gel which had taken away the fluffiness and marred his perfection. She wanted to tell him not to wear hair products again. 'Why? I thought you wanted me to be there? For moral support?'

'I know, but I feel really strong. Really,' she persuaded. 'I would hate myself if I didn't take this last step on my own. And I'll need you afterwards. Will you wait for me here? Please?' Charlotte smiled her most winsome smile and saw him melt into it.

'I'll be right here for you.' He took her hand and squeezed it. He had taken to the role of protector and Charlotte could tell he did not want to relinquish it; she felt momentarily guilty that she was denying it to him now. But she had not foreseen Mike's presence – she needed to be sure Rob and Mike did not meet.

Charlotte pulled her hand out from under Rob's and gave him a sweet smile goodbye. Then she straightened her suit and strode out of the office to meet Mr Forth in the impersonal corridor beyond. She surprised the solicitor with her sudden appearance. He replaced a large blue handkerchief, on to which he had been clearing his nose, in to his suit pocket. 'Ms Jackson. Are you ready?'

'Lead on, Mr Forth.' The time for nerves was past. Now was the time to show what she was made of. She pictured herself as a gigantic statue depicting a woman of indomitable courage; a Boadicea of the business world. Let Mike Miller say what he wanted. Her demeanour alone would make them disbelieve him and fall at her feet instead.

They passed the efficient secretary at her desk and stopped

outside a set of double doors in dark, impressively solid wood, Charlotte halting in the tracks of Mr Forth's shuffle. When he opened the doors and ushered her through, she was as prepared as she could have ever been.

A long, polished table stretched down the length of the boardroom. The size of it took Charlotte by surprise; she had imagined a small round seating arrangement with stackable chairs which led to bumping knees with the opposition. Again the façade of the building had misled her. It occurred to her that this room was the heart of Mr Forth's business. The impressive quality of the negotiation room had to give him a significant home court advantage.

Certificates and gold leaf documents had been framed and placed with precision and regularity along the yellowing walls, starting from behind the double doors and continuing to the four tall, narrow windows that looked out over the same street she had observed from the office. There were no other adornments. The impression was of age and exactitude, and it could not have failed to have an effect on the two people sitting opposite the double doors with their backs to the windows. Charlotte knew they came from a world of primary colour desks and sky-blue walls, where modern meant efficient. They were being confronted with age and seniority, and she knew them both well enough to know that they were uncomfortable with it.

Susannah Medley was smiling her welcoming smile at Charlotte as Mr Forth pulled out a chair for her on the nearest side of the table. Charlotte mentally reviewed what she knew of the woman as she took her seat and unbuttoned her jacket to reveal her brilliant-white blouse with mother-of-pearl buttons.

1. *Efficient – high work turnover.*
2. *Intelligent – quickly promoted within company.*

3. *Prefers to work with men – all HR underlings have been male since her appointment.*
4. *Attractive in a severe kind of way – see point 2.*
5. *Likes to be boss. Will try to control the meeting.*

Charlotte decided to let the other woman take the reins of the discussion. Let her lay her cards on the table and make an offer. Charlotte would keep her poker face and her silence, and allow Mr Forth to take on the messiness of negotiation. He had already been given his orders; he knew what Charlotte considered to be an acceptable outcome.

Mike Miller had shot to his feet as she and Mr Forth had entered the room, and had waited for her to take her seat before perching nervously back upon his. He was now seated directly opposite Charlotte, moving his gaze only from his own reflection in the immaculate tabletop to Ms Medley with, Charlotte thought, sycophantic attention. He looked more like a trainee than a fast-track manager. That satisfied Charlotte and reassured her that he was not present to play any major part in the negotiations. She observed him in the way that one could observe hissing cockroaches behind glass at a zoo.

Ms Medley and Mr Forth fussed over the organisation of coffee and paperwork, while Charlotte listed mentally what her observation of Mike told her:

1. *Late thirties. Looks good for age. Raven hair, blue eyes, sharply dressed. No change there.*
2. *But has bags under eyes. Not sleeping well? Stress at work? Department suffering without me, perhaps?*
3. *Carries no notes/documents. Table is clear in front of him. Is not here to be a player.*
4. *He won't make eye contact. He's afraid of me.*

With that realisation, Charlotte succumbed to an explosion of triumph. He had nothing over her now. He was destroyed.

She elegantly sipped the coffee that had been placed in front of her. Mr Forth was engaged in opening swipes with Ms Medley, the crocodile smile still rigid upon her lips. Charlotte felt no need to get involved. She let time pass over her, concerning herself with taking perfect mouthfuls of the passable coffee and revelling in her victory. Opposite her sat the man who had destroyed her life, taken her job, her pride. He appeared so weighed down with guilt that he could hardly stop the bowing of his shoulders. He was sinking lower and lower into his chair.

She was looking forward enormously to his public apology. Charlotte wanted him to grovel openly so that she could, perhaps with the lightest absolving touch of her hand that would haunt him forever more, forgive him.

Lost in thoughts of revenge and retribution, Charlotte did not catch exactly what Mr Forth had said to her. She only became aware that the room was waiting for some kind of response. To forestall her own embarrassment, she took a gamble and blurted out, 'Yes.' It was a reflex more than a decision.

Mr Forth leaned over in his own chair beside her in order to speak softly into her ear. 'You're in no way obliged to listen to what Mr Miller has to say.'

So they were at the apology stage already. 'That's fine,' Charlotte whispered back. Something in her tone must have convinced Mr Forth. He nodded his assent to Ms Medley as Charlotte checked her posture so that righteousness emanated from her impressively straight back.

She wasn't expecting Mr Forth and Ms Medley to get up and leave the room.

There was a moment of blind panic. Only dignity kept her in her chair, and even that, her last stronghold, nearly crumbled when the double doors closed and Mike's eyes shot up to lock on to her. She had forgotten how blue they were, how penetrating. Her heart accelerated to light speed. She felt her heavy duty deodorant sting her underarms. She could not see how the man sitting opposite her would be able to stop himself from doing some injury to her.

He remained seated, but it was a dangerous stasis. He did not even blink; only his mouth moved, and his voice was an approximation of control that could not quite avoid trembling on the final syllables of his words. 'I've been forced to resign. Were you aware of that?'

He waited for her reply. She had to find the voice to reply.

'No,' she said, and could not banish her own nervous tremor. She wished she had the bravery to voice her pleasure at his loss, but it wouldn't come. If his eyes had been cold she might have been able, but they were the eyes of an intimate and tender lover; there was a caress contained within them that horrified and reprimanded her.

'I'm back in England for good. I don't know who will employ me now. Was that what you wanted? For me to be unemployable?' He asked it genuinely, without sarcasm, and that forced her to try to formulate some sort of response. She picked up her coffee cup to stall, but it was empty. In desperation, she told the truth.

'I think so.'

She saw layers of emotions within his eyes, none of which were the obvious ones. When he spoke again he had to lick his lips before they could function. 'So what now?' He said it tentatively, with great import.

'I don't understand,' Charlotte stammered.

'What now? You're in a different job. I'm unemployed. We're both back in England. Did you do it so … so we … would be even? So we could be equals? Because I think I could understand that, if that was the reason.' He was stretching towards something, trying to make her say something. Charlotte retreated to a comfortable place.

'I can't formulate any sort of reply to your question when you're not giving me accurate information on which to work. You'll have to be more specific, Mr Miller.'

'Cut the crap, Lottie,' he replied immediately, in a louder voice than he had used before. For the first time he moved. He leaned in toward her, his hands with their ragged fingertips splayed out towards her on the table-top. She seriously considered calling for help, even as she recollected how precise Mike had always been about the state of his fingernails. Seeing them bitten and unkempt appalled her. 'No businessspeak. You've won, okay? Can we please treat each other like human beings now? Can we talk about the future?'

Charlotte had a flash of understanding mingled with terror as he stressed the word 'future' so peculiarly. She had to act immediately in order to regain control. 'If you come near me ever again I'll go to the police. I'll get a restraining order,' she threatened, although to her own ears it sounded weak.

He raised his eyebrows, as if they were playing a board game and she had made a move that was surprising. She had seen that expression before. The circumflex of his brow flooded her with memories of Salzburg that she had no time to sort. 'Knowing you, Lottie, I'd say that was your way of telling me it's over.'

She knew the first rule of business so well that even in panic she could not break it. Play cool. Dominate the situation. Hadn't he taught her that? 'What's over?' she asked him haughtily, and was rewarded by the collapse of his self-control. She had pushed him over the edge.

'What's over?' he repeated slowly. 'What's over?' He sounded like a victim of shock. He closed his eyes and rocked back in his chair. Charlotte felt the relief of the removal of his stare like a cool wind against her skin. He stayed in that position as he began to talk again. 'I can't believe this didn't occur to me before. You're ill, Lottie. You're ill. You need help.'

Mike genuinely believed that? She had to resist the urge to throw the coffee cup at him. She was sure nobody would have blamed her for it. 'You're right, Mr Miller, you have left me needing help. I needed to regain my confidence, my ability, and my trust, after what you did to me. And now you see fit to torture me again with this mockery of an apology – well, you just can't see it, can you? I'm going to survive your harassment. You're never going to get the chance to do this to another woman again.' So much for graciousness. So much for shaking his hand. All that was shaking was her head, in tiny movements, as if in denial of what she had just said. She loathed her own weakness.

'And that's what you really think, is it? That I harassed you?' he replied slowly after her words had transmuted to a ringing silence. She was beyond answering him for fear she would cry. Charlotte could feel tears waiting to explode on to the scene and ruin all of her hard work, so she stared him down instead, refusing to break away from his grave gaze. 'Then, I am sorry. I'm genuinely sorry.'

Mike lifted his right hand from its place, flat on the table in front of him, and extended it towards her, his thumb and fingers rigid. So he wanted to shake hands, now that she was incapable of it. He had robbed her of her victory and he wanted to rub it in. Charlotte bore his mockery for as long as she could. When he made no move to drop his hand, she forced herself to get up from her chair and walk to the double doors. She rattled the handle before managing to turn it and admit Mr Forth and Ms Medley back into the boardroom.

They re-entered with characteristic professionalism and the meeting resumed with no mention of the conversation which had taken place without them. Mike lowered his eyes back to the table top and resumed his demure act that Charlotte now knew to be a sham. She was incapable of speaking of it, even though she wanted badly to tell her solicitor that something had gone so very wrong with the whole process and she had been damaged yet again. She was beyond help. She had been made into a victim once more.

Negotiations took place around her; she could not see why she needed to be present at all. The more time passed in that room, the more Charlotte succumbed to despair. Her bubbly and irascible personality deserted her and she was left with nothing to hold on to – no indomitable spirit, no management technique: no sage words from any mentor could be recalled. There was only herself; a small woman with big feet at a long table with nothing to say. This was as low as she could have ever imagined she could get.

Beyond tears and beyond hope, with the voices of Mr Forth and Ms Medley droning on indistinguishably, Charlotte discovered something new within herself, something disturbing. Her memory began to fire images at her that could not possibly have happened. As she tried to reject them from her consciousness, they coalesced into specific events that were potent and rich in emotion and detail. So many came to her that she lost the room and her place in it entirely; she was involved only in the battle for control of her own mind, and she was vaguely aware that she was losing it.

The memories were of Salzburg. All of them occurred in places she knew to exist and in which she had spent time. The Augustine Beer House, with its large pewter tankards of wheat beer and vaulted wooden halls filled with carousing students. The coffee house opposite Mozart's birthplace and overshadowed by the brooding and dark-walled castle. The circle of gnomes in the Mirabell gardens with their individual expressions that had always made her laugh. How could Mike have found his way into those precious places and why did he smile out of them at her now? In her memory he touched her in a proprietorial fashion and she enjoyed it. She enjoyed his kisses, his touches, and they were carefree and open together with their hands clasped and their hips bumping as they strolled.

The memories were so clear that she could recall whole conversations intact; each cadence of his voice, each change in expression, and those details were undeniably infused by the incredible attention paid by a woman in love to the object of her desire.

'That about wraps it up,' Mr Forth said, touching Charlotte's shoulder and bringing her back to the boardroom. Ms Medley was collecting her papers together. Mike was standing with his back to her, looking out of one of the windows with stiff shoulders. Her newfound memories told her his upright carriage was a sure sign of anger and resentment, something he had always been terrible at expressing openly due to strict and uncommunicative parents.

Stop it, she told herself strictly with a sharp jerk of the head that attracted a frown from Mr Forth. 'We'll have something for you to sign in about half an hour. Are you amenable to waiting in my office until then? I'm sure we would all rather get this matter settled today?' He continued to scowl at her. There must be a vacant look in her eyes, Charlotte realised. It took everything she had to nod her approval, get up out of her chair and walk out of the room whilst Mike's back dominated her thoughts with its anger and helplessness.

He had a birthmark under his left shoulder-blade, she remembered as she forced her feet to walk. He had a kink in his backbone just above his buttocks where he had fallen down the stairs as a child. He had told her that story as they had eaten würst at a stall outside the cathedral on a spring day. She had offered to kiss it better. It was impossible, but it was all ingrained within her. It was as if she had watched three thousand home movies simultaneously or read fifteen books in a second. It was knowledge that was suddenly, irrevocably, there.

She needed to burn these vivid lies out of her with a searing heat; she needed to cauterise herself to stop this leak of guilt and love that was oozing out of her. She reached Mr Forth's office and opened the door.

Rob was standing there, looking out of the window. She didn't know what the strong, straight lines of his shoulders meant.

He turned around as she shut the door and took in the pain on her face. He opened his arms to her.

She straightened her back and strode over to him. Before he could respond she grabbed the knot of his tie and stripped it apart, throwing the silk snake of material to the floor. She put her fingernails on the side of his neck and pulled his face into hers, sucking at his lips and tongue. She used her weight and his surprise to move him backwards to the desk. She worked at his waistcoat and forced her fingers through the gel in his hair as he trembled. It was at the moment she reached for the zip of his trousers that he responded, by touching her hands with his own, as if asking a question of her.

As a reply she kissed him hard, strong, and this time he kissed her back, his hands moving from hers up to her blouse and the mother-of-pearl buttons. She helped him to undo them; they didn't have long.

Gary

Monday, 27th November, 4.41 pm

'So the talent show is scheduled for December 23rd, the day after we break for Christmas, and Rob thought it would be good if everyone could get involved … um … unless they really don't want to,' Gary told the group. He knew he sounded lame; he had no talent for public speaking even when he felt confident. Now, with his self-belief at a new low, this gathering had been yet another piece of bad news, communicated via e-mail for him to find this morning. Rob had asked him to chair the meeting because, apparently, an emergency in London had summoned him.

How unsurprising, Gary thought bitterly, that Charlotte should pick the same day to phone in sick. They were probably licking each other's egos in an expensive hotel room somewhere.

'We know what the basic act will be. My band has agreed to come along and play, and Hils is going to do the singing. We need everyone else to think of something they could do, like, maybe, be a backing singer or maybe just play a comb and paper or a tambourine ...' He petered out and looked at the people slumped around him on the bright green sofas at the back of the cafeteria, chucking down coffee or staring at a point two inches above his head. Only Hilary was giving him any real attention.

Sam spoke up in his usual soft, hesitant manner. It had not escaped anyone's attention within the group that he had begun to arrive and leave every day with Rose, even though she blanked him if he ever tried to talk to her and moved away if he ever tried to sit next to her. Nobody was quite sure if he was a stalker. Gary felt sorry for him; he was beginning to resemble a choke-chain trained dog in his wary attention to Rose's every move. 'Have ... have you picked a song?'

'Not yet. If anyone has any suggestions they'd be gratefully received,' Hilary spoke up. Her voice was clear and confident. She should have been chairing this meeting, not him. 'We thought perhaps a sixties tune with an easy chorus, maybe? So everyone could join in? A Beatles track, maybe?'

Gary looked at the group from his uncomfortable stance in front of the coffee machine. They were divided between the two sofas, which were arranged in a chevron in front of him. Rose and Alma were sitting on his left, both wearing faces that intimated how distasteful they found their proximity to one another. Rose's bare thigh was pressed against Alma's bulk. She was balancing a coffee cup on one of her crossed legs. Alma had folded her arms over her stomach like a complacent Buddha. The sofa really wasn't big enough for both of them.

Hilary and Sam shared the other sofa. Hilary was perched on the very end. She seemed to be trying to leave some space between herself and Sam, and from the moue of her mouth Gary could guess why. Sam was wearing the same clothes to work again. He must regard brown corduroy as the company uniform. The smell was reaching a point where people would veer away from him when he walked past them in the corridor. It was the e-mail joke of the team this week.

It was a relatively small meeting, thank God. Amie had been signed off work indefinitely with family issues, Rob was in London, and Charlotte had phoned in sick. Gary wished he had the courage to phone in sick too. He dreaded every work day. He knew without doubt that he was no administrator and he was incapable of reaching the heights of bullshit required to become a manager. The nine-to-five existence gave him nothing but an irritable bowel and a thirty cigs a day habit. He had been staying for Hilary, but now his last reason to stay had been taken away from him.

Steve would meet her after work today, as he always did, and if Gary liked he could follow them home, just as he was free to follow them to work each morning. Then Steve would cook for Hilary and they would eat in the living room so Gary could cook his own meal. He would eat slowly in the kitchen, straining to overhear what they talked about in low voices.

At eleven they would go up to Hilary's bedroom, and then he would stay in the kitchen for a while longer. On the worst nights he would hear the ceiling creaking rhythmically above his head and know they really were a couple in every way, and he was an outsider who they wished would find somewhere else to live.

It had taken Steve just four days to establish his place in the household. He had arranged ways to take up all of Hilary's time so that Gary never got to spend a moment alone with her, and he had done it in such a way that any complaint would have seemed childish beyond belief to Hilary, the one person he wanted to impress.

Gary had only one weapon in his arsenal, and that was the band. It was his bargaining point; the only reason he was allowed to ask for any of Hilary's attention. On rehearsal nights he could call her down to the cellar and be near her, even though the other band members were always present. Still, he could look into her eyes with the pretext of discussing the lyrics, and brush her hands with the pretext of adjusting the microphone for her.

It was those moments that gave him a shred of hope. She never pulled away. She never let her eyes drop from his and never shyed from his touch. In fact, in those precious seconds her entire demeanour seemed to be geared towards passing on a secret message to him that he lacked the ability to understand. So he guessed; he guessed she was asking him not to give up on her yet, to let her have time to sort out her life. He looked through her rimless glasses and into her pleading eyes and hoped he was transmitting his own message in return – the message that he would wait for her for as long as she needed. The message that he would always be waiting for her.

'I've always had a soft spot for *When I'm Sixty-Four*,' Alma drawled. With her accent, it was impossible to tell whether she was being sarcastic or not. Gary was beginning to think she was always being sarcastic.

'Not really the kind of tune my band can play,' he explained. 'Think a bit rockier, a bit more guitar-based?'

'Don't ask me,' Rose said, even though nobody had. 'I hate all that kind of music. I'm not going to play the comb and paper in some lame talent contest.' At least she hadn't used her usual array of swear words. She crossed her arms over her chest, bumping elbows with Alma.

Sam looked at her nervously. 'Perhaps I ought to … um …. I'm really quite busy with other concerns at the moment, so maybe I ought to pull out, too.' Rose refused to look at him. Gary felt a surge of annoyance at Sam's desperation to please.

Alma jumped on the band wagon. 'Yeah, count me out,' she said lazily, unbuttoning her black cardigan to reveal an off-white T-shirt that bore the slogan 'Beached Whale' complete with a drawing of a whale in a bikini.

'So nobody's interested, then?' Gary asked, trying not to sound too pleased. This could mean extra time alone with Hilary, if he could persuade Rob that they needed to practise during work hours as well.

'Don't worry, Gary-boy,' Alma said, heaving herself forward to the edge of the sofa and assuming a sumo-like position in order to lift her bulk to a standing position. 'Charlotte will definitely want in. And Amie, I reckon. She's a joiner.'

Alma was right. Even if Amie didn't return from compassionate leave, there was no way Charlotte would miss out on getting involved. That woman would do anything to put herself in charge and in the spotlight. She was addicted to power; either getting it for herself or shagging it. Gary wondered if Rob had worked out what the others in the group had deduced from the beginning of the course – that Charlotte wanted him for his key to the executive bathroom.

'Right, that's it,' Alma continued, heading off to the glass doors of the cafeteria. Rose took that as her cue to leave and Sam popped up from his sofa as if he was attached to Rose by a string. Only Hilary remained sitting, trying to give strength to Gary's position as leader of the meeting.

'Alma!' he called after her. She ignored him. 'But it's only half-past four!' She didn't even bother to turn around. Rose replied for the both of them.

'Yeah, but by the time we've closed down the computers and gone to the bogs, it'll be five, won't it?' she said, slinging her miniature orange handbag over her shoulder. Her intonation made it quite clear that she was not expecting Gary to respond.

Sam stopped and offered one more comment. 'You could do *Wild Thing*. By the Troggs,' he suggested optimistically. 'I always loved *Wild Thing*.'

'Since you're not going to be involved I don't know why you should have a say,' Hilary replied tartly, giving him an evil stare from her position on the sofa. Sam looked punctured.

'Yeah, thanks,' Gary said. 'We'll think about it.'

Sam went out, his neck craned as he tried his hardest to follow in Rose's exact footsteps. That left Gary alone with Hilary. This was the moment he had been waiting for since Steve had appeared on the doorstep.

She stretched in a casual fashion, and then surprised the hell out of him by making extraordinarily intense eye contact. It rooted him to the ground even as she began a mundane conversation. It was as if there were things she couldn't bring herself to say, and she was trying to place them directly in his mind. 'So ... that didn't go quite as Rob would have liked, I'd guess.'

'No.' To cover his embarrassment, Gary stooped and started to collect the used coffee cups together on to the brown plastic tray on which they had arrived. 'Still, it could be worse,' he offered in a jolly, comedic tone.

'How?' So she was prepared to be the straight man in order to preserve this comfortable conversation.

'They could have actually wanted to get involved. Can

you picture it? Like – Alma wailing away in the background. Sam standing behind Rose with a hard on, Rose wearing red leather hotpants and demanding to do a Britney Spears number ...'

Hilary laughed appreciatively for a little too long. She shifted position on the sofa.

'Do you want me to move out?' Gary found himself asking in a belligerent rush. He continued to stack the coffee cups as if his life depended on it; he prayed he wouldn't run out of them.

'No,' Hilary said in a measured, disappointed voice. 'At least ...'

'You do want me to move out?' He shot up from the tray and stared at her. She stood up so that she was meeting his gaze at eye level.

'I said no. It's just that ...' It seemed to take an effort of will for her to confide in him. 'I'm worried that you're finding it uncomfortable with Steve always around.'

That had to be the understatement of the year. 'No, no. He's a nice bloke.' Gary felt his eyelashes flutter at the blatant lie, and he had to force himself to maintain eye contact.

Hilary was as strict in her appearance as ever; hair tied back, glasses in place. How could those eyes so completely contradict that guise of self-sufficiency? They were wounded and pleading. The strip lighting overhead revealed the tired patches that were spreading underneath them.

'You still okay for rehearsal tonight?' he asked her, to stop her walking away.

'Yes. That's fine.' She sighed and gave another one of her mock-stretches. 'I'd better be going. Steve will be waiting.'

A million questions sprang into Gary's mind. He only had time to pick one; strange, then, that his mind opted for, 'He's meeting you from work again, then?' He even managed to make it sound petulant.

She nodded. 'We'll probably go for a walk or something. I'll be back in time for rehearsal.' She didn't move. Was there something else she wanted to say? Gary waited on a knife edge of anticipation. 'See you later.'

She left, dragging those bleeding eyes away from him. He watched her walk away, through the doors and along the glass-partitioned walls of the restaurant with the slow, balanced steps of a martyr. His frustration at her and himself was enormous. Why couldn't she say what she wanted to say? Why couldn't he make her tell the truth? He despaired of ever getting an honest reaction from her.

The only thing that kept him hoping was the kiss. She had kissed him: he hadn't imagined it. She did like him. He tried to feel certain of it.

The hours stretched ahead until rehearsal, and the chance to try to reach her once again.

Amie

Wednesday, 29th November, 7.45 pm

Amie cowered behind the sofa. She could see a ten-pence piece, an escapee slice of carrot, and a cobweb lurking underneath it. She was dreading the appearance of a five-inch-long hairy spider at any moment.

The banging on the front door stopped. There was a four second pause before the banging on the living room window commenced.

'Open the fucking door, Amie.' Rose's bored, loud voice was as clear as if she was standing over her. Amie contorted with the effort of remaining silent. 'Stop fucking around.'

It had been an instinctive reaction to hide when she had seen Rose approaching the front door by the glare of the porch light. She cursed herself for not closing the curtains at the moment night had fallen; then she could have ignored Rose's demands easily. She thought about it, and decided that it would never be easy to ignore Rose. And she really didn't want to ignore her. She just wanted a little peace tonight; peace to think about her critically ill and morally reprehensible father. Peace she wasn't going to get.

'Amie,' Rose whined in a sing-song voice, mimicking her Welsh accent. 'Amie.' It was as close to charm as she had ever heard from Rose's lips. It didn't last long. 'Amie, I can fucking well see your feet,' she said with the barest sliver of patience.

Amie uncurled slightly on her side and looked past her ankle-length skirt to the polished black leather of her lace up shoes. They were poking out beyond the end of the sofa. She shuffled up on her knees to get them hidden and then re-alised how ridiculous that must look. Although she would have loved to just accept that ridiculousness and stay where she was, she found herself climbing up from her hiding place and moving to the front door, assiduously avoiding looking at Rose through the window.

The door lock was stiff. It took a long moment to open; a moment in which Amie heard Rose mutter as she approached. Even so, Amie didn't have an inkling that she had more than one guest until she was face-to-face with the evidence.

Rose was standing with attitude on the doormat, and she was flanked by two people Amie had seen before during her one disastrous trip to the local nightclub. One was Rose's muscled ex-boyfriend, Matt, and the other was her syco-phantic, gangling friend. Kelly, that was her name. They were both taller than Rose by a head at least, and both were stooping in deference to her.

Rose was wearing a black dress adorned with gold buckles on the shoulder straps and around her hips. Her black strappy sandals revealed lime green toe polish which matched the shade of her tiny bag, clutched in one taloned hand. Her blonde hair was scraped back from her face into a high pony tail, and the narrowness of her eyes was emphasised by her liberal application of eyeliner. She was impervious to the teeth-grinding cold of the December night.

She smiled warmly. She had to be in a good mood, Amie assessed. Matt and Kelly had straight lines instead of mouths. They weren't sharing her mood. 'How's it hanging?' Rose asked her. 'Aren't you going to ask us in?'

Amie moved backwards to let them pass through the hall and into the living room, aware of the dusty and unkempt condition of the place. She had been spending all day at the hospital and had not been given either the opportunity or the inclination to clean up. She suddenly became aware that she was wearing yesterday's clothes and had not taken a bath for two days. She hoped Rose had not come round to attempt another update on her appearance. As Kelly, the last of the small group, disappeared into the living room, Amie closed the door quietly and pulled at her blouse, hoping to smooth out a few of the creases.

'Got any booze?' Rose's voice carried out to her. Amie hurried in to find all three of them standing between the sofa and the television, facing her. They looked like a police line-up.

'No. Sorry.'

'None at all?' Rose asked incredulously.

'No.'

'Fucking hell,' she said. 'We'd better have a whip round, then. Come on.' She dived into her miniature bag and produced a five pound note, gesturing for the others to do the same. They followed her instructions, Matt checking the pockets of his trousers and Kelly rummaging in her copycat bag, until both had produced similar amounts. Rose was looking expectantly at Amie. 'Cough up,' she instructed.

On her auto-pilot, Amie went back into the hall and searched the pockets of her duffel coat for money. Armed with all she had, three pound coins, she returned and passed the money solemnly to Rose, who handed the entire amount to Kelly. 'Right, Kel, nip down the offie and get us some Mad Dog or something.'

Kelly held the money at a distance in the palm of her hand, as if she was afraid to take responsibility for it, but she did as she was told. She obviously knew better than to contradict Rose, good mood or not.

Rose waited for her to go, and then bestowed a brilliant smile that showed her barely yellowing teeth on Matt and Amie in turn. 'This is going to be a great party,' she said with a teasing edge before slumping down on to the floor and leaning back against the television support. 'Aren't you going to congratulate me?'

'What for?' Amie managed to say. This was the first party she had ever attended; she had assumed planning and invitations were the basic requirements, but apparently a small house and enough cash to buy Mad Dog, whatever that was, would do just as well. Rose did appear to be genuinely in the mood to celebrate about something. Her eyes kept flicking to Matt, who had taken a seat upon the shabby sofa. He seemed to be the only person who had any control over her. Or perhaps, Amie thought, it was that he was the only person whose opinion Rose actually cared about. Amie hated the idea. She saw Rose as the ultimate free spirit, not to be curtailed by anyone.

'I'm engaged,' Rose said, pouting. Amie felt a pang of sorrow.

'Congratulations,' she stated conventionally to Rose and Matt, and was rewarded with a hostile stare from Matt and a titter from Rose.

'Not us,' she told Amie. 'We're not engaged. I just asked Matt along to help me celebrate. You want to help me celebrate, don't you, Mattie?'

Matt's back was towards her; Amie could not see his face, and for that she was glad. Amie didn't know a lot about modern relationships, but she knew a lot about sin, and she knew there was an act of cruelty taking place in her living room. Her stomach was writhing as if she was a spectator in a torture chamber, seeing each turn of the wheel or every flick of the switch. A dizziness passed over her. She was not used to such things, although she had begun to realise that they were part of the outside world.

'I've got some crisps,' she said, to break the painful silence. 'Shall I put them in a bowl?'

'Fucking A,' Rose said. Amie didn't know what that meant but from the tone she could gather it was positive. She was glad of the excuse to escape into the kitchen, even though it was only a few steps away and did not hide her from either of her guests. It was just enough distance to give her breathing space. Rose obviously thought so too; she immediately began a private conversation with Matt as if Amie had disappeared down a long corridor into the distance. She wondered if Rose was already a little drunk.

'So aren't you pleased to see me?' she asked Matt in a little-girl voice. Amie resolutely rattled the kitchen cupboards and kept her attention on finding the crisps and a clean bowl. The demon in her strained to listen in.

'God. I just don't *believe* you,' Matt replied. Amie could hear his affront. 'I told you, you don't have to do this. I told you I'd take care of you.'

'With what?' Rose said smartly, all innocence gone. 'With your dole cheque? Do you want me to move in with you and your parents? Or are you offering to make an appointment to get rid of it? Because I told you, I'm not doing that.'

There was a silence. Amie didn't even dare to open the crisp packet she was holding. She heard movement; maybe somebody sliding across the carpet? 'This doesn't need to change anything,' Rose caressed in a lower, softer voice. 'He's harmless. He doesn't have a clue. He's even going to give me a lift home from here later. Just because I have to be practical, doesn't mean ...' Her voice lowered another notch and Amie couldn't hear the words. She didn't dare turn around; she was afraid she would see something so immoral that she would lose all of her personal goodness instantly. She wanted so badly to turn around, but she didn't dare.

The sound of a more scuffled, peremptory movement finally convinced her to face her fears. She swung around with her eyes shut and the bowl of crisps held in front of her like a shield. 'Crisps are ready!' she trilled, before releasing one eyelid by a fraction.

Rose and Matt were hand in hand, and she was leading him out of the living room. She met Amie's one open eye with an expectant and alive gaze. Matt was looking at the floor. 'I was just going to show Matt where the loo is,' Rose told her.

'But you've never been here before,' Amie said.

'Yeah, don't worry, we'll just find our own way,' Rose dismissed her, tugging on Matt's hand, who complied with her demand to move out into the hall and then up the stairs.

Amie moved dazedly to the sofa, holding the bowl of crisps on her lap. She heard her father's bedroom door open and shut. She wished she could turn the television on and turn up the volume but the devil within her demanded to hear what was happening upstairs.

The bed squeaked once. There was a high-pitched, muffled laugh. The bed squeaked again.

Amie was aware that her upbringing had been puritanical to say the least, but recent events had put the sexual act firmly at the forefront of her attention. In the outside world it was everywhere; used to sell shampoo and raise television ratings, to tell people what to eat and what to wear. Her infallible father had fallen victim to his own. And now Rose was expressing hers upstairs. It was so wrong, and yet it was so thrilling to be so close to it. Rose lived for the moment and had no time to worry about eternal damnation or forgiveness. That was the powerful thing about her.

By the time Kelly returned the squeaking was regular and increasing in pace. She appeared in the living room with a plastic bag slung on one wrist and a handful of coins on her still outstretched palm with no warning; she must have left the front door open. She had the manners of a barn animal, Amie thought, and then was shocked at herself for being so unkind.

Kelly sloped into the living room and dropped on to the carpet in front of the television, in almost exactly the same spot as Rose had occupied earlier, scattering the change and the carrier bag beside her. Then she sighed, opened the bag and retrieved a large, flat bottle of pink liquid from which she took a long swig. Her face screwed up as she drank, and the hiss she produced after she had swallowed made Amie suspect that the process was painful.

Kelly was a photocopy of Rose blown up to A3 size. She wore the same clothes and affected the same moods, but Amie could tell she was actually a cheery, uncomplicated girl who yearned to be a dark and violent goddess. She was like the people in The Nation, but she wanted to escape from that fundamental uncomplicated view. Amie understood her.

'Want a sip?'

'No thanks.'

'Can I have a crisp?' she asked. Amie passed the bowl to her and she took one, nibbling on it until it had disappeared. The creaking upstairs was speeding up to a rhythm a little faster than her heartbeat. 'Have they been up there long?' Kelly asked her, with no hint of embarrassment.

'Five minutes?'

Kelly nodded. She took another swig of the liquid and considered the giggles and creaks coming from above her head. They were getting to the point where Amie felt she either had to make loud conversation to mask the sound or admit defeat and listen to the entire performance.

'Rose told me about your Dad,' Kelly said suddenly. 'How is he?'

Amie hadn't known that anybody other than Rob had really been aware of her situation. 'He's not any better, thanks.' She wasn't sure what she was thanking Kelly for. It just slipped out.

Kelly shrugged as if that was to be expected. 'So what was it? Stroke?'

'A heart attack.' Just saying it made it more real. A week had passed and he wasn't improving. If anything, he seemed worse, lying there with determination written on his chalk face as if he was concentrating on being ill to block out everything else. He hadn't opened his eyes or said one word to her since it happened. It was as if he could tell that she knew his reason for leaving The Nation (or getting kicked out, she reminded herself).

The squeaking had reached the point of no return, turning the bedspring noise into an intense whine. Or perhaps that high-pitched squeal was Rose. It was difficult to tell, and it was impossible to hold a conversation until it ended, which it did, mercifully quickly. Not that Amie really wanted to hear what Kelly had to say, but at least now she could relax slightly. She uncrossed her legs and took another crisp out of the bowl before passing it back to Kelly.

'My Uncle had a heart attack last year,' her guest said.

'Was he okay?'

'Nah, he karked it. He left me one of his old medals.' She finished her crisp with delicate bites and washed it down with Mad Dog. She had worked her way through a third of the bottle. 'They won't be long now.' She sounded as if she spoke with the voice of experience.

There was a scuffling in the hall, and then a voice that Amie knew but could not place floated through into the living room. It was deep, male, and burdened with both the local accent and the dead weight of embarrassment.

'Hello? Anyone in?'

Sam Spurling popped his head around the door to the living room and smiled nervously at Amie and Kelly. 'Hello,' he said. 'I didn't know this was your house.'

'Rose is just using the loo,' Kelly said, catching Amie's eye as she stood up from the carpet. 'I'll go and tell her you're here.' She escaped from the room as quickly as possible, leaving Amie alone with Sam. He was wearing a pair of very blue jeans with a central crease down each leg and a tartan shirt underneath a plastic mackintosh. They were obviously new clothes. He had combed his hair and her nose informed her that he had even bothered to wash.

'Girls in the loo together!' he said heartily. 'Rose asked me to pick her up so she didn't have to walk up the hill. I suppose she's told you our news?'

He was almost grinning at her. Suddenly all the pieces clicked together. 'You're engaged? You and Rose?'

His grin widened in confirmation. There was a pause before Amie remembered what it was she was supposed to say. 'Congratulations.'

'Thanks. I can't quite believe it …' She watched his face as he made an inner decision to blurt out whatever else it was he wanted to say. 'I'm going to be a father.'

The pieces Amie had just clicked together were rearranging themselves in her head to form a completely different picture. She hoped she had enough control over her face to be expressing anything other than what she was feeling.

There was an urgent clattering overhead, which moved down the stairs and then Rose burst in with Kelly trailing behind. She looked energised and radiant. There wasn't a line of guilt on her face; she appeared so unrepentant that Amie wondered for a moment if she could have really been doing something immoral upstairs.

'Ready to go?' she said to Sam by way of a greeting.

All of his attention had moved on to her as she had arrived and now his bloodhound eyes and slightly open mouth were the epitome of a mesmerised man. 'Ready if you are.'

'Well, then, get a fucking move on,' Rose told him in an exaggeratedly patient tone. He started forward with an apologetic smile at Amie. She watched him go, squeezing past Kelly who lounged in the doorway as if awaiting her own personal instructions. Then she spoke to Amie. 'I'll come round next week, yeah? If your Dad's still not better by then.'

'Okay. Thank you,' Amie said automatically as Rose departed with confident strides, motioning to Kelly to follow along.

Amie waited until she heard the front door shut before getting up from the sofa and carrying the empty bowl to the draining board in the kitchen. She returned to the living room and knelt down on the carpet in front of the small pile of coins that had been left there; somebody had taken the Mad Dog.

Four pounds and a penny had been left behind. She hovered over it uncertainly. It felt to Amie like some sort of illicit payment; a subtle, menacing back-hander that was meant to guarantee her complicity in her father's house being used as a den of iniquity. She couldn't bring herself to touch it.

There were footsteps on the stairs, thumping down in to the hall. It was only then she remembered Matt, and understood his reason for waiting upstairs until the others had departed. Amie looked up at the doorway from her crouching position on the carpet, her chest bent over the money, as he appeared with a downturn of his mouth.

For the first time Amie really looked at him. He was tall and brown-haired, with a trace of a carefully trimmed beard that looked more blond in colour. His face was a strong, square shape, with an almost Roman nose. He had two earrings in his left ear, tiny golden hoops, and he wore a collarless sapphire blue shirt over black drainpipe trousers. There was a separate quality to his blue eyes under his generous eyebrows that seemed familiar to her, and directly contradicted everything she had assumed about him.

He filled the doorway as he stood within it. 'I should get going.'

Amie got up from the carpet and smoothed her blouse. She felt hot and scratchy, and very aware that she was alone with him. She didn't know what to say; she wished he would go away and take his guilty, abstracted look with him.

'She wants to be secure,' he said suddenly, as if stung into a response in the face of criticism, his lips twisting. 'Every woman has the right to be secure. Financially, I mean. And she's right about me. I can't look after a baby. It'll be better this way.'

Amie felt her face fall into disapproval at his show of weakness. This was not how men were meant to behave. He wanted her to reassure him. She didn't know how to do that, and she wasn't sure she would have wanted to if she did. She couldn't think of anything to do but look at the wobble of his Adam's Apple.

'I'm going now,' he said into the silence. He shifted his weight and then took a step backwards.

Amie tried hard to make the socially required move. 'I'll see you next week.'

Matt threw her a strange look before walking out. The front door opened and closed quietly as she translated the look as despair and resentment. Perhaps she was wrong, but he might have been asking her for help in some way; it could have been a plea for complicity, or even a plea for moral correction. It was just possible she had failed him.

It occurred to her as she began to unfold the sofa into a bed that she did not have to be silent about this matter. A threadwork of options branched out in front of her, and only one of them involved obeying Rose.

Rose was amazing. Rose was free of so many of the conventions by which Amie felt so fettered. Amie wanted to be Rose, she could see that now. She wanted the fulfilment of desire without the bitterness of guilt. She wanted to think only of herself, but she was beginning to realise that she would never gain that ability.

She had seen the blind optimism on Sam's face and the betrayed acceptance on Matt's. Rose was like Amie's own father. And they were not the only people who had a right to be happy.

She pulled the sofa-bed so that it slid into position over the money on the floor. She hadn't decided whether to take that payment yet.

Alma

Saturday, 2nd December, 8 .57 am

She had a hangover. Not that the sensation was a new one, but it had been a while since she had experienced one in these proportions. It was beyond head-spinning and stomach-churning; it was a dog-shit-on-the-tongue and shish-kebab-into-the-brain kind of hangover. It was the inability to move coupled with the burning need to move so she didn't choke to death on her own vomit. It really hurt.

Alma moved, ignoring the urgent pain messages she was receiving, into an upright position. She cracked open an eye. She didn't recognise a single thing she saw.

She opened the other eye, wrestled with her stomach, and took a good look around. It was definitely unfamiliar territory; an impersonal, medium-sized room with a battered wardrobe positioned next to a bay window portraying a swatch of sea and sky. The walls were decorated with a floral blue wallpaper – tiny forget-me-nots in rings and swirls, a dated design – and the carpet was a faded dark blue. Alma had a particularly good view of the carpet as she was still lying on it. It had been a long time since she had slept on the floor. No wonder she couldn't feel her legs.

She twisted around to peruse the rest of the room. A dressing table, as beaten-up as the wardrobe. An ajar door through which she could glimpse a toilet and a bathtub with no frills. Dated brass light fittings and a framed print of a chocolate box watercolour that depicted a windmill in a cornflower field. And a double bed over which was thrown a rumpled bedspread in the same pattern as the wallpaper. Wrapped up inside the bedspread was a mixture of lumps and curves that could only belong to a human body.

Alma had seen this movie. Jane Fonda was in it. A woman wakes up after a bender and discovers a dead man lying in bed next to her. Alma tried to remember what Jane had done about it; she had a feeling that Jeff Bridges had come along and saved the day. She doubted Jeff would do the same for her.

The bump in the bedspread rolled over. Alma found that just as disturbing as her initial belief that she had been alone with an unexplained corpse. Now she had to face another person.

She defied her hangover and got to her feet. The view

from the window became the familiar sight of Allcombe promenade in the bare light of the early winter morning, deserted by all life but the pounding of the iron sea. That meant she was in one of the Victorian terraced houses on the sea front. It didn't prod any memories, except unwelcome ones of Dora. It occurred to Alma that maybe this was The Paradise and she had spent the night with Dora – perhaps this was Dora's room. But it didn't look familiar, even if her memory wasn't what it used to be.

The bump rolled and sat up, revealing a youngish man with dark, curly hair and an impressive growth of stubble. He was still dressed – at least, he was on the top half, which was all Alma could see. He was wearing a crumpled white shirt with the top three buttons undone, revealing the beginnings of an extremely hairy chest. The care with which he manoeuvred himself suggested to Alma that he was not feeling particularly well after last night either.

Even so, he was much better looking than she had ever expected to pull again. She was beginning to wish she had stayed the night in the bed rather than on the floor.

With an effort, he managed to focus on her and give her a cheeky smile before clapping one hand on his forehead and sinking back down into the horizontal position. She realised that the hangover was for her benefit alone; he was suggesting he felt as bad as her, but he wasn't much of an actor. Alma could tell a fake hangover from a real one in a second. With a fake one you rolled around dramatically. With a real one you stayed as still as possible and hoped aspirin would magically appear.

'I don't suppose you'd mind,' he said from his prone position, 'fetching me a glass of water since you're up and about?' It was a London accent, a mixture of Queen's English with cockney barrow boy. She thought he was putting that on, too. She had a vague recollection of disliking this man.

'Get it yourself,' she told him. 'You're only faking.'

He sat upright and grinned at her once more. Her first impression, of a handsome and pleasant young man, was turning out to be mistaken. In fact, he was a grating little wanker. 'Very astute of you.' He unwrapped himself from the bedspread, revealing beige trousers and black socks, and leapt energetically from the bed into the bathroom, closing the door behind him. Alma heard running water.

'Do you know where you are?' he called.

She didn't dignify it with a response. Instead she moved to the bay window and tried to gauge her position on the sea front. It looked as though she was in one of the better-kept hotels near to the beginning of the pier, only a stone's throw from The Bosworth Slaughter. Alma sniffed her clothes and discovered the smell of the pub upon them. Yet she was sure she wouldn't have gone back to The Slaughter after what had happened there last time. It didn't make sense.

She searched the pockets of her candy-striped trousers for a cigarette but found nothing but two pound coins; the remnants of her last pay-packet. As usual, upon realising that a smoke was not immediately available, the desire for one became all-consuming. She pressed her lips together and considered her escape options.

The bathroom door opened and the man reappeared after what had to be the quickest wash and change of clothes in history. He was now wearing a beige T-shirt with black trousers and had shrugged off any tiredness with a mere splash of cold water. That meant he had to be only in his mid-twenties, Alma estimated. He leaned in the doorframe on one elbow, lounging as if to let her admire his youth and health. He really was a tosser.

'Cigarette?' he said, holding one out to her with an amused smile. Alma shuffled over and snatched it from his fingers; it had already been lit. She hated to be so predictable. Still, she took a long drag in relief. Her headache immediately seceded; now she could begin to think. She felt she could begin to play him at his own game now she had control of her brain once more.

'Busy in The Slaughter last night,' she said in a deliberately conversational tone. Let him think she knew exactly what had happened last night.

'How would you know?' he asked her. She clashed eyes with him. He moved to the bed and lounged back upon it in a languid pose, smiling to himself. She wanted to punch him.

That thought brought an instant of revelation. She was fairly sure that she had punched him. She had punched him, late last night, on the promenade. She had socked him in the stomach and he had doubled over, retching and cursing. The memory gave her real satisfaction. 'How's your stomach?'

He flinched and his façade cracked a little before he could find the self-control to reply breezily, 'A little bruised, I think.' He was back in charge as he added, 'And how's your head?'

Alma guessed he wasn't referring to the hangover. Then it came to her. When she had turned away from his curled-up agony last night, he must have leapt up and hit her on the back of her head with something heavy. She could remember an intense flash of pain and then nothing more. Strangely enough, the memory didn't alarm her. She felt a weird pleasure that he had not taken her punch like a gentleman. 'Sore,' she said.

'You went out like a light. I was worried about you,' he told her with no attempt at sincerity. 'So I carried you up to my hotel room. I say carried ...' he added, '... in actual fact I had to enlist the help of four strong men who luckily were on their way home from the pub. They moved you after I reimbursed them appropriately for their labour. People don't ask many questions around here, do they?'

Alma took a long drag of her cigarette and sized him up. He had a sharp way with words and a penchant for poking people where it hurt, but underneath it she suspected he was a little boy who enjoyed pretending he was older. She could take him. She had played politics with the big boys – she had been a Hollywood player. There was nothing she didn't know about pretensions and put-downs.

A name popped into her head and she decided to risk it. 'That's why I like it here, Sebastian.'

He raised a perfectly groomed eyebrow. She had been on target; his name was Sebastian. Sebastian Storey, if her memory was correct. 'Perfect for a superstar who wants to be forgotten, I suppose, Jacqueline.'

Damn. He had just trumped her again. And he knew her secret. How was that possible?

That was the missing link Alma needed. Something in her head clicked and her memory of last night flooded back in a shocking Technicolor puddle.

Angela. Dora's daughter. She had threatened contacting the press, and somehow she had actually found the balls to follow through on her threat. Alma hoped she had been paid well for that titbit of gossip.

The man lounging on the bed across from her was indeed Sebastian Storey, but now Alma knew what that name meant. Sebastian was the entertainment correspondent for Britain's biggest tabloid newspaper, *The Mercury*. His printed word made or broke reputations. He had to be rubbing his hands together with glee at this story, and she knew enough of him to know that he would not miss out on such a scoop simply because it might destroy one washed-up woman's life.

She had already been on the tail-end of six pints when he had strode into The Gloucester Arms, the only other pub in Allcombe and generally visited only by tourists who were prepared to pay through the nose for warm scrumpy. He had introduced himself to her. She had shouted at him and he had shouted back. They were thrown out of the pub, and had continued to shout at each other outside. They had come to blows on the promenade, and now she was in his hotel room. She had handed him the story of a lifetime.

'Enough games, methinks, Jackie. Let's order some coffee and talk about this reasonably,' he offered, looking around him for a phone. 'Buggeration. No room service. I don't know how you stand this village.' Defeated, he let his head drop back on to the bed and spread his arms and legs as if making a snow angel. 'So tell me – do you enjoy being a clerical worker?' He pronounced her job title with the kind of distaste usually reserved for talking about internal parasites and rapists.

'There's nothing to tell. There's no story here,' Alma persuaded. 'I'm just doing a boring job to make enough money to drink myself out cold at nights. Not inspirational. Not chicken soup for the soul. Nobody wants to read about a story like that.'

'Because if you really do enjoy clerical work, then I won't tell you about the possibility of a new job offer that's come your way. A job offer in *show business*.' He stressed it with reverential relish.

Alma knew that tone. This job, whatever it was, was an earner. He was talking about more money than she could ever make as an administrator. She strived to play it cool. 'I'm listening.'

Sebastian leapt from the bed to land next to her, closer than she found comfortable. She backed towards the window, and he followed her until they were side-by-side, looking out over the view. He even put one hand on her elbow to steer her into position. 'First we would need to come to an agreement regarding *The Mercury*'s interests in all of this,' he suggested as he perused the promenade. 'Something along the lines of ...' He thought for a moment. 'We get the exclusive; you, in your tiny hovel, office work, the whole shebang. Then we announce your comeback. We'd need an interview for both, of course.'

He raised an eyebrow at her. He knew she'd be a fool to turn it down.

She hesitated. There had to be a catch. 'You don't get to talk about the drink problem,' she said unequivocally.

'Of course not,' he soothed. 'As if we'd be so tasteless. We're looking for a more inspirational take on the washed up has-been.' He squeezed her elbow, adding with a casual air, 'If you don't want to play ball, I quite understand. We'll just go for the traditional angle– you know, long lens shot of the faded legend doing something repulsive like eating corn-flakes out of the box or rummaging in their crack, and forget the interview and the job offer. I was sure you'd rather avoid all of that if you could.'

So she didn't really have a choice at all. In that case she'd make sure she was getting the best out of the deal. 'What are we talking about? How much?'

Sebastian looked triumphantly bored. He let go of her elbow and crossed to the bed, crouching to search underneath it. 'You get yourself an agent and let them worry about that.' He retrieved his shoes and slipped them on his feet. 'Shall we go and find some breakfast? Does anyone around here do a good wheatgerm shake?'

'Just tell me what the comeback offer is,' Alma said as he reached for his expensive sunglasses by the bedside and adjusted them on his nose to his satisfaction.

'It's fab. British television at its best. A reality show. Imagine – a counselling group for minor celebs who were on other reality shows and now can't cope with being nobodies again. They're looking for someone to host. I said your name and the producer went wild.' He opened the door to the corridor outside. 'You know, Jacqueline, this place really does have a kind of backwater charm. It's a shame its too far away from London to commute.'

'You wanna live here?' she asked incredulously. She couldn't think of anyone less likely to settle in a town where a meal out meant fish and chips on the sea wall.

'I wasn't thinking about me. I was thinking about you. Once we've run the first article you'll have to chuck in your little job and move up to the Big Smoke.' Sebastian gestured impatiently for her to join him. 'Come along, Jackie, let's get to work over breakfast. I'll ask you some preliminary questions.'

'Don't call me Jackie,' she grumbled as she stomped after him. 'It's Alma.'

'Fabulous!' he crowed, ushering her out of the room ahead of him. 'What a story this is going to be!' He shut the door behind them with a gentle control.

Part Three

Rob

'Look at it,' he says. 'Touch it.'

They all look suspiciously at the telephones that have been installed on their desks overnight.

'Don't be afraid of it,' Rob says reverently. 'It's not an enemy. The telephone is your friend. It is the instrument by which we communicate our needs.'

Hilary snorts and then alters it to an unconvincing cough. The rest of the group are wearing expressions that range from uncomfortable to terrified. This part of the course always inspires the most fear. They are about to become the front line.

'Here's what we're going to do,' Rob continues. 'We're going to have the calls usually taken upstairs by team eighteen patched through to these phones this morning. We're going to listen in as each person here takes a call, because when we listen, we learn. Any questions, concerns?'

Sam raises his hand over his head, revealing a dark discoloration of his shirt under his arm. 'I don't know if I'm ready … I mean … what if they ask something I can't answer?' Gary nods in nervous agreement.

Rob shrugs and shifts his position on his desktop, where he sits when he wishes to address his trainees. He is wearing a dark green suit with a gold, embroidered waistcoat and immaculate brogues. He has lost some of his accommodating nature recently; he is no longer interested in holding hands at this stage of the course. 'You know everything that I can teach you. The things you have left to learn can only come through practice and experience. It's time to jump in the deep end and start swimming.' Gary and Sam still look unconvinced, so Rob sighs and takes a different approach. 'If you get stuck, put the caller on hold and ask for assistance. That's all you need to do, and I'll be right here. And have a little faith, okay, guys? Faith in my training methods if not in yourself.'

Gary and Sam have the kind of wide, pleading eyes associated with children waiting in line for an injection. Alma and Rose are bored and blank; strangely enough, their attitude has also crept over Amie's usually round cheeks and clear complexion. Hilary and Charlotte look poised for action.

'Are we ready? Then let's do it,' Rob says. He swivels on his desk to reach for his own telephone, punching in a three digit number and talking matter-of-factly into the receiver. 'Hi, it's Rob. Yes. Patch them through one at a time. Yes. The hunt group number. Thanks.' He replaces the receiver and raises his eyebrows at the team. 'Any moment now. Be prepared to listen and learn.'

An awful silence settles over the room.

With a shrill demand a telephone rings. There is a moment of barely restrained panic as everyone tries to identify the first victim. It turns out fate has decided upon Hilary.

She is cool today, as she is every day. She is wearing a black shirt with black trousers and her hair is pinned back into a plait. She does not look at the other trainees; throughout the course she has hardly given notice to any of them, except occasionally to bestow a mocking half-smile. She does not hide her disdain for what she obviously thinks is a pitiful attempt at a training course. Rob likes her against his better judgement.

She takes a deep breath as the phone reaches the third ring, the company standard on which it must be answered. Then she picks up the receiver and clips out a professional greeting. 'Good morning, Customer Services Department, you're through to Hilary Black. How may I help?'

She picks up her dark blue fountain pen and slides the standard issue telephone message pad they were all presented with this morning across the desk to the ideal writing position. She flicks off the lid of her pen and starts to make notes on the paper. The rest of the group watch in morbid fascination, as if observing an autopsy. 'Yes. I see. Yes. Do you have an account number? Right.'

She types into the computer with one hand and peruses the information that flashes up on the screen. 'Could you confirm your full name and address for me please? Yes. Thank you. Okay, I'll get that sent out to you as soon as possible. Thank you very much. Goodbye.'

Hilary puts the receiver back into place and makes some notes on the pad. She only looks up when she is finished, and then she pretends casual surprise at finding herself the centre of attention. 'They wanted a statement,' she explains. She moves in her chair to face Rob. 'Do I just put the telephone message in your tray?'

'That's right.' Rob leans over and takes the message from her, deliberately brushing past Charlotte as he does so. He drops it into a new red plastic tray which appeared that morning on his desk. 'Well done, Hilary. That was spot-on.' He gives her a thumbs-up in a dated and affectionate gesture. He is disappointed when Charlotte coughs and looks away. The rest of the group watch silently.

The phone rings. This time it is Amie's.

Amie has been on compassionate leave for two weeks, and she was not the strongest candidate to begin with. Rob is convinced she is going to fail the course, unless she tries again on the next training program. Rob was ready to take her into his office, and for her to emerge crying, but she has bemused him with her change in attitude when she un-expectedly appeared for work this morning. Her clothes are the same, clean and dated, and her shoes still squeak, but she does not lower her eyes and shrug her shoulders. She stands up straight, and does not look afraid.

She picks up the receiver immediately, on the first ring, and speaks in monotone. 'Good morning, Customer Services Department, you're through to Amie Doe. How can I help?'

There is a long pause during which she says nothing, just listens. She does not look at the computer or attempt to take notes. Just at the moment when the tension has reached a point of idiocy, she speaks without interest. 'I'll just put you on hold.' She presses a button and turns to Rob.

'Is there an extension for the complaints department?'

Rob nods. 'Press recall, then dial three zero zero.'

Amie does so, and does not wait for a reply. She simply puts down the receiver to connect the caller to the department. Rob cannot quite believe her actions. 'Does anyone have any feed-back for Amie?' he asks the group. Nobody replies, not even Charlotte. Rob has to answer his own question. He can't help his mask of amiability from slipping to reveal irritation.

'She started well, but then it began to go downhill when she forgot to make her positive noises. Remember the strong words we talked about? Words like "yes", "right", "I under-stand"? It's very important to gain the friendship of the cus-tomer. Then she transferred the customer without explaining what she was doing. That's going to cause misunderstandings and delays for the next person to touch that call. Can you appreciate that, Amie?'

Amie raises her head and stares straight ahead, giving no sign that she has heard. She has stony eyes and a clenched jaw. A rogue vein throbs in her throat. Rob loses his pity for her.

The phone rings. Sam looks panic-stricken. For a moment he jumps out of his chair, as if to escape, but he manages to control himself enough to pick up the receiver and speak. He smells slightly better than usual and his fluff of golden hair has been combed to lie flat. He looks as if he has lost a little weight. His transformation at the hands of Rose is the talk of the group, Rob knows, although nobody has dared to ask him directly about his relationship with her in case Rose takes offence.

'Good morning, Customer Services Department, you're through to um … Sam Spurling … um …. How may I help?'

He listens intently, and grabs at his pen and message pad in an effort to bring them under his control. 'Yes … yes … of course … well, if you'll hang on for a moment I'll just check for you.' He turns to Rob with a desperate haste. 'How do I change someone's address?' he asks, a drowning man clutching at the neck of the good swimmer.

Rob measures him up. 'You know we've already learned this, haven't we?' he says. Sam wears a forlorn expression. 'Get the account number, check the details, F2 on the keyboard, input the new postcode, and search.' Sometimes Rob wonders how he maintains his calm.

Sam repeats what he has been told. The rest of the call goes smoothly. As he thanks the customer and replaces the receiver a smile of ecstatic relief passes over his face. He has survived; he looks as though he doubted he would. Rob does not say anything, although he would dearly like to vent his annoyance.

The trainees who have completed their tasks are floppy and spent; the others, who have not yet taken their calls, are tense and upright on their chairs.

The phone rings on Alma's desk. She does not look stressed. She looks bored and hungry. Rob has never seen her as anything else. She is wearing a buttercup-yellow shirt and her dirty white bra can be seen through the gaps between the buttons. Her fingernails are filthy and she smells of stale beer.

Her voice is filled with an energy that surprises everyone. 'Hi there, you're through to Customer Services and I'm Alma Chippendale. How can I help you out today?' It sounds subtly wrong; layered in mockery. Rose smiles appreciatively and Charlotte grimaces.

Alma replaces the receiver without saying another word. She looks as uninterested as ever.

'What happened?' Rob asks incredulously, ready to toss his temper away this time.

Alma shrugs. 'Wrong number.'

Rob opens his mouth, and then shuts it. Then he opens it again. 'Okay.' He cannot object to that, however suspicious it might sound.

Alma slumps backwards in her chair and yawns as another phone rings. The colour drains from Gary's face. He always seems to be on the point of nervous exhaustion, and recently it has been getting worse.

He waits for the three rings. 'Good morning, Customer Services Department, you're through to Gareth Lester. How may I help?'

The person at the other end of the phone is a loud speaker; the voice, but not the words, can be heard clearly by Rob across the room. Gary is instantly and irrevocably lost in confusion. 'I'm sorry, I can't … sorry? I beg your pardon? Would you repeat that, sir? Do you... so you... do you have an account number?'

Rob, sensing danger, moves up to stand behind Gary. The caller continues to talk at top volume without apparently drawing breath. Amie moves her chair backwards, away from the noise. Gary is scarlet in the face. 'I can't... I can't... ' he says to Rob in anxious despair, who leans over and plucks the receiver from his hand. He will have to save this one himself.

'Hello, sir? I can't help you unless you slow down, please.

Take a deep breath. That's right.' Rob's voice is the epitome of empathy. His gentle touch never fails to work. The voice lessens in volume and vehemence. 'Yes. I understand. I totally understand.'

Rob gives a master class in controlling the angry customer. Some members of the team listen and some, the usual culprits, don't. The call takes over five minutes and by the end of that time, when the customer has been passed to the appropriate department, he is a lamb who laughs heartily at Rob's jokes. Rob knows he has done a wonderful job.

Gary has turned from scarlet to green. He is puffing queasily. 'I'm really sorry. I just couldn't get my head round it.'

Rob pats his shoulder. 'No harm done, Gary. These things happen to us all occasionally. You'll get another go.'

Gary's face changes from green to yellow, probably at the thought he will have to go through this again, but Rob cannot negotiate on this point. Rob looks away from Gary's mouth as it works with emotion. For a moment it looks as though he might even cry.

The phone rings. Charlotte answers the call and deals with it immaculately, as he had expected from her. It's not even really worth the effort of listening in. Gary remains the focus of attention as he struggles to control himself. Rob keeps a hand on Gary's shoulder, but keeps his body at as much of a distance as he can manage. His eyes are upon Charlotte's back as she finishes up, writes her message and walks it over to the red plastic tray before returning to her chair.

She is dressed in a sky-blue trouser suit and has lightened her hair a shade. She has always been constant in her business manner but lately there has been a brittle quality to her smile and she hasn't answered as many of Rob's questions as he would have liked. She won't take his calls either. She was his high-profile success story, keeping the heat off the other trainees' backs. Now she is slipping in her devotion to her career and it is becoming obvious to Rob that the others have no interest whatsoever in their own careers.

Gary hiccups and shakes off Rob's hand. 'I'm fine,' he says to no-one in particular. 'I'm okay.'

The phone rings. Gary jumps, but it is the phone next to his. It's Rose's turn to practise her manner with the customers. She waits until the third ring, and picks it up. 'Good morning, Customer Services Department, you're through to Rosemary French, how can I help?' She adopts Queen's English perfectly, and sounds, with that authoritarian tone, a little like Penelope Keith. Confidence was never going to be a problem for her.

She is wearing her red halter-neck dress, and her affectation for tight, revealing clothes has led to a revelation in the group that has made her the centre of their attention. She is putting on weight. Everyone has been looking at the growth of her breasts and the curve of her stomach, and it has become impossible to think of any explanation other than that she is pregnant. At least three months pregnant, maybe more, the other trainees speculate in their e-mails, to which Rob has managerial access.

Rose is as defiant as ever – she smokes incessantly and has been seen drinking in The Slaughter on the weekends – but there is a definite bump that grows a little larger every day, no matter how she abuses her body.

'Yes. Yes, that's right. Yes. Okay, that'll be fine.' She grabs her chewed biro and writes messily on the pad, ignoring the lines and the boxes upon it. 'Yes. Yes. I've got it. Yes. Right. Okay. Thanks for calling.' She checks her message as she ends the call and then swivels on her chair to face Amie.

'That was the hospital,' she says, reading from the pad. 'They said they were extremely sorry to report that your father died ten minutes ago and would you mind coming up to collect his possessions.' Then she tears the used sheet of paper off the pad, wads it into a ball, and throws it into the bin.

Amie doesn't immediately register the words. She is un-moving and uncomprehending. There is a long silence.

'I'd better go,' she says suddenly, looking at Rob. 'Is that okay?' Rob has been shocked into inaction; it takes him a moment to remember his rôle.

'Of course. Of course. I'm so sorry. Would you like me to come with you?' he asks her in his best caring and sym-pathetic voice.

She shakes her head and gets out of her chair, stumbling over the leg and righting herself slowly. It has broken her self-control; she expels a harsh breath and reddens around the eyes. She looks around wildly, as if she has forgotten where the exit is.

'Poor thing,' Rob overhears Sam whispering to Alma, as if discussing a puppy that has been run over.

'Jesus,' Alma says in a loud voice.

Amie is looking at Rose for some reason. Rob knows she'll get no sympathy from Rose. He moves to Amie in con-cern. He puts one hand on the small of her back and the other on her arm. He leads her out of the room, slowly, one footstep at a time.

Nobody says anything, not even Charlotte, as he walks out of the training room with his arm around the girl.

Hilary

Thursday, 7th December, 10.32 pm

She lay in bed.

She could have slept if she had put her mind to it – there was nothing Hilary couldn't do if she put her mind to it – but she wanted to think over the events of the evening. Maybe if she dissected them into fine detail she would be able to file them away without anxiety.

Fat chance. She was destined to replace one set of neuroses with another. Or, more precisely, she was destined to know people who would make sure that she would forever replace one set of neuroses with another. Gary was one of those people, and the events of tonight had proven to her that Steve's arrival on her doorstep had been the lucky escape of her life.

She always slept on her back with her arms crossed over her stomach, on the left side of the bed so that she could be near the lamp and her glasses, which she always placed on the bedside table last thing at night. Steve was a much more regressed sleeper: he curled into a ball and thrashed from side to side most nights, muttering and getting caught up in the duvet. He dreamed vividly and then deliberately forgot what he had been dreaming about upon the instant of awakening. Hilary dreamed in black and white and struggled to recall everything so that she could remain aware of what her sub-conscious was trying to tell her.

This was just one of the ways in which they differed, and a great example of why she should be with Steve. They did not complement each other: they challenged each other. They made each other try to excel.

He had been the catalyst and the instigator of her decision to face her fear of heights today, and the past along with it. His physical presence was a goad that made her want to reach for him and outshine him; during their time apart, she had forgotten just how good he was for her.

There were other things she had chosen to forget: his attractiveness, for one. Even during her initial spurt of annoy-ance at his appearance on her doorstep, his body had im-pacted upon her awareness with the freshness and force she had felt at their first meeting at the outward activity centre back in New Zealand.

He wasn't much taller than her and he had a slimness that perhaps wouldn't appeal to every woman, but his muscles were well-defined and his hair was a mass of natural golden curls that fell down to the blade of his chin. The hairs on his arms and legs were golden too, and in summer he always wore shorts that would reveal a graze or a scrape on one or both of his knees, proof of a constant devotion to his own physicality. There was an energy that sprang from him and demanded her attention.

She wondered now why she had ever thought their relationship would survive on the phone. At a distance he was only a hesitant voice with a reticence that sounded like laziness when he spoke to her; in person he had no need for words. He would hold her hand and tickle her palm with one finger, or jump at her from behind a door to give her a fireman's lift to the bedroom. Such actions were more than enough.

He was nothing like Gary. She had been nurturing the feeling that she would remember Gary fondly from a distance upon her return to New Zealand and maybe even wonder, when Steve was out of the house, how life might have been with him. It could have been an occasional fantasy during which she could pretend she was a different person with different priorities, but Gary had effectively killed that fantasy tonight.

She had been sure, at least, that his friendship would be a constant. She had been looking forward to telling him her news; she had expected him to be ecstatic that she had conquered her problems.

Hilary lay perfectly still and refused to fidget. Her eyes were open in the absolute dark of the bedroom. She didn't need to see the heavy velvet curtains, or the circular Turkish rug that lay under the sturdy dark wooden posts of the bed in order to protect the varnished floorboards. She knew her CD collection was next to her favoured self-help tomes on the wall of shelves between the door and the window, which looked out over the quiet lights of the pier. This was her room and everything was in place except for her emotions. Some internal tidying-up was required.

The image that kept returning to her from that evening was Gary's face, as he sat in the kitchen with the mismatched candles lit around him, a plate of barely-touched pasta in front of him, with defiance and belligerence clinging on his back and moving him to the kind of anxious state that never did anybody any good. He had looked as if he had done nothing for hours but brood on things that were beyond his control. Hilary wished he had settled for a hot bath and an early night instead.

'You'll never guess where we've been,' she said upon entering the kitchen, trying to create a little jollity to brighten the gloom he was emitting.

'Where?'

She hadn't wanted to tell him when he was in that mood, so she went on the attack instead. 'What's up with you?'

He looked her straight in the eye and said, 'You missed rehearsal.'

What had she said then? She couldn't quite remember; something genuinely apologetic. She had never meant that to happen. Steve, who had been removing his boots in the hall, burst into the kitchen and caught the strained atmosphere in a moment.

'What's going on?' He had never been one for letting tension build over time.

Gary refused to meet his eyes, so Hilary answered, 'I missed the rehearsal this evening.'

Steve pinched his lips together in concern. 'I'm so sorry, mate. I didn't have an eye on the time. But there's a good reason why – have you told him why?' he said to Hilary, who remembered mutely shaking her head to discourage him from blurting it all out. Luckily, he had taken the hint.

Gary waited with the barest hint of patience on his face. Hilary had to swallow before she could speak to him; the situation was making her nervous. 'I'm moving back to New Zealand,' she said. She saw no point in leading up to it gently.

He had taken it with a frozen expression that only just verged on polite. Steve must have pretended not to notice it; he was certainly not blinkered enough to miss it, even if he was overjoyed with the way things had turned out today.

'Back to training as an Outward Bound instructor ... that's what she's good at. She wasn't made to sit behind a desk and take phone calls,' Steve said, smiling at her, filling the silence with his easy, confiding manner. Gary had swivelled in his chair so that his body faced them, quivering and taut.

'Outward Bound? But what about the ...' He didn't finish his thought, perhaps because he suspected Hilary hadn't told Steve about her phobia. She was unpleasantly surprised to learn he thought she could be so dishonest.

'We went up the hill tonight,' she said shortly, not wanting anything more to have to be said about it.

Gary shrugged in a liquid, expressive rebuffal. 'And now you're cured?'

Steve tensed beside her. He hated to be questioned or made to feel foolish as much as she did; Gary was denigrating them both. She suddenly decided not to care about his righteous anger, or his accusatory manner, or his wrathful stare; she wanted to walk away from it all.

Perhaps it was at that moment that Hilary had decided irrevocably that she would return to New Zealand with Steve. It was certainly at that moment she had walked out of the room and left the two men alone in the kitchen; she had gone up the stairs and into the bathroom, and had run cold water from the tap until it was an icy flow over her fingernails, just to distract herself from the disdain she had heard in Gary's voice.

She hadn't heard a thing from downstairs, as far as she could remember. Nothing out of the ordinary had made her rush back to the kitchen, she was sure. She had turned off the tap in the bathroom, dried her hands and walked down the stairs at a slow pace. The front door had been open. She shut it, and returned to the kitchen.

Gary was alone. He was sitting on the floor with his straight legs splayed apart and his back hunched over, the top of his buttocks pressed against the metallic green door of the oven. He reminded Hilary of a bean bag doll that had been dropped on to the wooden floor by a careless, distracted owner; the illusion was only dispelled when he made a spluttering sound from his nose and moved his shivering hands over his stomach with concentrated care. He was in pain, she realised as she stood in the doorway, and then she moved towards him and crouched by his side, unsure of what to do.

'What happened?'

Gary flapped a hand and tried to push himself to his feet. Hilary found herself grasping his elbow and hoisting him back on to the kitchen chair that he had occupied all evening. Once in a more comfortable sitting position he seemed to find it easier to breathe; even so, it still took him a time to manage to speak to her.

'He hit me.'

'Steve hit you?' She immediately felt ridiculous for not suspecting such a thing would happen if she left them alone. Gary had been aiming for a fight since they had stepped through the door; she should have known he would get more than a verbal slap-down for baiting Steve.

He nodded confessionally and tried to put his head on the table even though the remains of his pasta dinner were still directly in front of him. He only jerked back at the last moment, wincing at the sudden movement, and gulped down air.

'Did he punch you?' Another nod. 'In the stomach?' Gary gave a strong, downward affirmation of his head, and then he tucked his chin into his chest as if coiling himself up to gain strength.

'What did you do to him?' she asked, and his head snapped back up to register outrage at the question.

'What did I do to him?' he repeated in a strong voice. He had recovered quickly. So Steve hadn't hit him that hard after all; he had been lucky.

'You know what I mean,' she told him. 'What did you say?' She was acting the schoolmistress but she felt the fear of the naughty child. It was possible Gary would have told Steve about the kiss; she was just beginning to realise that he was capable of such pettiness.

'I didn't say anything!' Gary defended. 'I said that nobody is cured of a phobia that quickly, that's all.'

'So you think I'm lying?' Hilary pulled back the nearest kitchen chair so it was a few feet from Gary, and sat upright upon it, her arms and legs crossed.

'I don't know what I think!'

Gary always backed down. He was the rodent he resembled; hiding in his hole and skittering away from any trap, real or imagined, with a sixth sense of self-preservation.

Hilary couldn't recall exactly what she had said to him then, but she was sure it was some kind of witty put-down, like, 'That's painfully obvious' or, 'What a surprise!'. And then she had told him that she was sorry she had missed rehearsal, and maybe he should start looking for a replacement singer as soon as possible.

'When are you leaving?'

'I'll hand in my notice tomorrow. I'll have to wait and see what Rob says about a leaving date.'

'But soon?' he prompted. She nodded once, looking at the electronic display of the time on the microwave, as she had once before in this room. It was 11.56: the time of the kiss. Fate was pernicious; it was demanding that she realised the similarities between the two moments. She felt an unusual pouring of warmth from herself towards Gary – he had been close to her once, and perhaps she should be more accepting of the fact that he was not adjusting immediately to her change in circumstances.

Gary ruined her flush of temporary sympathy with ease. 'So you want me to move out, then?' He had such a miserable little mouth and self-pitying gaze.

She was unmoved by his display, and his personality no longer charmed her. She wished Steve would return from wherever he had gone to regain his cool. Or, more accurately, she wished she could join him there instead. 'Well, I don't know. Can you afford to buy this place? I'll give you a special discount.'

He took her comment as an insult rather than a jest, and she wasn't surprised. She hadn't felt very funny when she had said it. 'So where I go now is just a joke to you, is it?' he replied with an injection of poison that stung her. 'So it was all just a laugh at my expense?'

'That's not true,' she bit back.

'You just ... go off with Steve and draw a curtain over this period of your life? Maybe think of me fondly once a month? Maybe write a letter every six?' He grabbed the plate from the table and took it to the sink, dumping it down with a clatter that attained the volume he could not allow himself to reach with his voice. 'You know what you want now, and Steve can give it to you?'

'Steve supports me and there's nothing wrong with that,' she replied, searching for calm.

'I didn't know you needed to be supported. I thought you were independent and proud of it.'

'Fat lot of good it did me,' Hilary retorted. 'Moving to

Allcombe, taking this job, trying to forget the past, the accident. It's all been one long series of mistakes.'

Gary stood still, leaning back against the sink, two footsteps away from her. 'Sorry to hear the whole thing has been so terrible,' he whispered. He left the room. She heard him head directly to his bedroom and close the door behind him.

He stayed there all night, not making a sound, not even when Steve returned and knocked on his door to apologise. He hadn't even played his guitar. There had been only silence emanating from the bedroom across the hall; an ominous affirmation that neither of them was forgiven, or was likely to be. It looked as though she would not be allowed to remember Gary fondly after all.

He was still silent now, although she wasn't lying awake to listen out for noises. Yet she almost wished she would hear just one reassuring sound from his room; the soft strings of his guitar or the sound of his voice making a late night call to his ex-girlfriend – anything but this complete withdrawal from her.

But in retrospect, when she examined all that had taken place that night, all that had been said and done, she did not feel that she had behaved badly. Gary had been the unreasonable one. He had refused to be pleasant to Steve, and had refused to discuss the situation openly with her.

If he wanted her to stay why didn't he just say it? Why didn't he ask her to be his girlfriend straight out, rather than insinuating that she couldn't possibly be cured of her phobia, and couldn't possibly return to New Zealand and pick up where she had left off? She had thought he understood her, but he had been thinking only of himself. He wanted her to be a big fish in the small pond of Allcombe, swimming around with him and not trying for anything better. He wanted her to make him feel like a man.

Hilary wanted to get back out there, to start to experience

life again. She could do that with Steve's help. Gary wasn't offering help. He was only offering himself and all his problems to add to hers.

So there really wasn't a choice to be made. She could count herself fortunate that Steve had returned and had found her worth fighting for. She pulled the duvet up over him and pressed herself against the roll of his back, determined not to move again.

She wouldn't wait for Gary in the morning. He could walk to work alone.

Sam

Saturday, 9th December, 3.23 pm

'It'll do,' Rose said, 'for now.'

'I'm sorry I didn't ask,' Sam said nervously. 'I thought it would be better as a surprise.'

'I only like big surprises,' Rose replied, looking at the tasteful red gold, diamond cluster ring that was sitting pertly on the third finger of her left hand. 'I told you before – check with me first. We'll have to take it back and exchange it.'

Sam cursed himself. 'And I'm really sorry about the bedroom thing.' He shifted forward from his faded rose-print armchair to be closer to her. She was sitting sideways with her legs thrown over the arm of its equally battered twin. The circular seventies-style coffee table, with asymmetric wooden legs and a glass top, was between them, and lying discarded upon it was the empty ring box.

It was early afternoon but the room was dark and damp, as it was at any time of day or night. Sam had never thought to do anything about it before, but now he was aware of how the unwashed lace curtains at the one small window, and the engrained dust on the bulb in the wicker lampshade above them, made it difficult to see Rose's delicious unlined heart-shaped face and adorable pointed chin. She didn't look right ensconced in one of these old armchairs; she needed clean, bright lines surrounding her to show off the growing curve of her stomach, which had practically doubled to his eyes in the last two weeks.

'Yeah, well,' she said, scratching her neck with her long fingernails, which were painted orange today to match her three-quarter length trousers, 'I didn't know you were such a dirty old man on the sly.'

'I thought ...' He battled with intense embarrassment and the desire to explain himself so that, just once, they could reach an understanding.

'Well you thought wrong, Sammy. You can fucking well wait until we're married before we share a room. What kind of a girl do you take me for? I want to do this properly or not at all.'

That was the veiled threat that she could deliver so effortlessly and that could turn him into her unquestioning drone. She had all the power. She could leave him in a moment. The confusion he felt over her sudden denial to let him so much as touch her was matched only by his impotence to change her mind.

Things would improve once they were married, he knew, but the ceremony was three months and hours of organisation away; organisation that was filled with the possibility of causing offence to her that might make her change her mind about the whole thing.

'Have you got your room ready yet?' she asked him.

'Are you sure you want to swap?' he stalled. 'My bedroom might be a little bigger, but there's no sink in it.'

'Big fucking deal,' Rose said. 'That sink's blocked anyway. Every time I turn on the tap this thick brown water sits over the plughole and refuses to go down. Let's swap now.'

She swung her feet down and pushed off from the armchair even as Sam attempted to delay her. 'Well, I haven't quite got everything together yet. Perhaps I'll have another look round before we swap over.' He was hopeful that if he could put off the change-round for a few days she might forget the idea. He was reluctant to move into the room, and the bed, that his father had died in. It would feel like an admission of his mortality.

Rose stood over the coffee table and looked down at him. 'Nah, let's do it now. I'm going over to Amie's in an hour.'

'Amie's? Wasn't it her father's funeral this morning?'

'What do you want her to do? Wear black for the rest of her life?' Rose shot back. 'And I've told you before – don't question me. Come on and get your stuff.' She wasn't irritated, not really. The tone was mild even though the words were harsh. Sam obeyed, jumping out of the armchair and making the remains of the springs squeak miserably. He knew when he had lost a battle.

It was a large house but most of it was in a state of dilapidation. Only two of the four bedrooms were in a usable condition. Sam had the money to fix the rest, he didn't doubt, but it had never seemed important before. Now, as he walked up the curving staircase and passed all the doors of rooms that he had not entered for years, he decided to look into renovating and repairing for the little life that would soon be curiously trying these handles.

Rose was ahead of him and didn't hesitate to walk into his room on the second landing. He followed her and stopped just inside his bedroom door as she stood in the centre with her hands on her thighs, looking about herself with a grimace.

He saw it as she must; a room with nothing to recommend it to a young girl – sorry, woman – who was accustomed to colour and light. The wallpaper had lost its pattern and had become little better than peeling brown paper, just as the once red carpet was worn through to reveal the skeleton lattice of its threads. The double bed had sunk in the middle from his weight, and was covered by an ancient patchwork that had been passed down through the family. The bay window was filthy and one pane was cracked through its centre; the paint on the sill was shrinking away from the light. The large oak wardrobe threw its shadow over the room, a hulking but exhausted beast with two large round brass handles that stared malevolently straight ahead.

'Christ,' Rose said. 'Still, at least it's better than the other room.' She looked at Sam with a casual glance that brought him an involuntary step closer to her. 'Have you packed up all your stuff?'

He gestured at the large cardboard box at the foot of the bed into which he had placed his few personal possessions – his clothes and the photograph of his parents that had been taken fifty years ago on the unrecognisably clean doorstep of this very house. At the bottom of the box, hidden under his clothes, lay his costume and helmet. 'I think so.'

'Go on then.'

'Sorry?'

Rose jerked her head at the door, making her pigtails dance. 'Take your box and piss off,' she commanded without a shred of self-doubt in her voice or body.

Sam picked up the box, balanced its weight on the ledge of his stomach, and turned away. He began a slow walk across the landing to his father's old room, dreading to open the door and claim that space as his own.

'Sammy! Get back here!'

He obeyed that impatient bark immediately. She was crouching in front of the huge open wardrobe, its doors forming a backdrop around her.

'What the fuck is this?' she asked him without bothering

to turn around. He had to move close up behind her, holding his breath, in order to see into the wardrobe and identify what had claimed her attention and caused the offence.

It was the bottom drawer in the wardrobe; his abandoned sock drawer. Open and bared to the dim light of the room, it looked like a sad and deliberate collection of strange fashion. A woollen tartan sock nestled with a stretchy luminous green exhibit that had a hole in its toe, inside a nest of mainly brown and grey sock leftovers.

He had forgotten to clear it out, but it hardly merited such attention as it was now receiving. He had always experienced problems in keeping pairs of socks together, and had decided upon the drawer as a place to keep singular socks when they turned up, reasoning that eventually he would match up long-separated pairs with this tactic. Seven years later he was still waiting to reunite a pair.

'Sorry,' Sam said, wanting to explain about the whole sock process but knowing he wouldn't get further than a few words before Rose's impatience would be triggered.

'God, you weirdo,' Rose muttered, not without fondness, he thought. 'Take your ... collection ... away.' She took a double handful of the socks with the brusque, necessary distaste of a housekeeper who must touch a pile of vomit in order to clean it up, and straightened so she could place the socks upon the contents of the cardboard box he was still holding. Then she bent down again to scoop up a second handful.

'What's this?' Instead of giving him more to carry she leaned closer in to the drawer so Sam could no longer see over her shoulder. She reached in with a thumb and forefinger extended to make a pincer and removed something. It was only as she turned towards the window and the small amount of light it provided that he recognized the object, and an overload of adrenalin transfixed him to the floor.

She was holding a small blue velvet bag that fit snugly into one of her hands. It was tied at the neck by a drawstring of gold rope that her fingers were already manipulating.

'It's nothing,' he said, aiming for a relaxed tone and achieving only a high-pitched squeak of tension. 'It's nothing important.' He wanted to put down the cardboard box but his fingers wouldn't release it and his body wouldn't move. All he could do was watch her tear open the knot and empty the contents of the bag in to one of her small, eager hands.

'Fuck me,' she breathed.

It was the family treasure; the Symbol of Superdom. The object which was passed to the firstborn son of each generation of Spurlings when he identified his power and came into his inheritance.

It was a large, heavy, ancient gold ring into which was set a ruby the size of Rose's thumbnail.

And it was too late to do anything other than explain to her the reason why such an item was in his possession, and hope that she would understand. 'Rose, listen to me,' he said in a wonderfully calming voice that he did not recognise as his own.

'Fuck me,' she said again, with no less wonder than the first time. He put down the cardboard box and grasped her under the armpits, lifting her to her feet and half-carrying her over to the bed. She was docile and unresisting; all her attention was on the ring. It was as if the world around the ruby had ceased to exist.

He put her down and she sat quietly on the end of the bed. It seemed possible that she might just listen to his story. 'Rose, I have to tell you about my family; about the ring and my family, okay? It's something that goes from father to son. It's a symbol of power. Do you understand what I'm trying to tell you?'

Her eyes slid from the ruby up to his face. He had to tell

her. 'There's a lot more to me that you know. Listen. When danger strikes, when I'm needed, I have a tremendous gift. I can save people. Don't you understand?'

He stood up straight, and told her the secret he had thought to keep hidden always. 'To you, I'm mild-mannered office clerk Samuel Spurling. But, in the hour of need, I'm the Death Defying Sputum.'

He stepped back and waited for Rose to speak.

Charlotte

Saturday, 13th December, 9.04 pm

Charlotte's mind was firmly on the new mental list she was perfecting. It was entitled, 'Reasons Why Rob Is Not An Acceptable Boyfriend', and it grew longer every time she observed him.

1. He phones me at odd and inconvenient times.

Only this evening he had phoned twice to check she was on time for their date, speaking to her mother on both occasions because she had decided to no longer accept his constant intrusions. And on the occasions when she did speak to him, he invariably had nothing to say. All he wanted to do was talk about meaningless, unimportant things like how he was missing her and how many times he had thought about her that day.

2. He is always looking at me, making both of our jobs suffer as a result.

Two days ago Sam had asked him a question regarding telegraphic transfers and Rob had asked him to repeat it because he had not been concentrating. Charlotte was certain he had been staring at her breasts instead of paying attention to his trainees. It was difficult to maintain professionalism in such circumstances, she knew, but he wasn't even trying. She was the only one striving for dignity in the hell-hole of Allcombe.

3. He keeps referring to the Salzburg Incident.

Which was extremely irritating, as she had settled the matter and, as far as she was concerned, it was now closed. She never wanted to think of it again, but in any private moment Rob would lower his voice a tone or so and mention gravely how she had overcome such adversity to be doing so well now. It made her want to staple his head to her desk.

4. Rose.

What was happening between him and the teenage slut? Too many inconsistencies had come to light for her merely to dismiss Rose's claims of inside knowledge. Rose seemed to know things that only Rob could have known; she was either sneaking into his office or sleeping with him. It had to be the office. Weird as he was becoming, Rob would never go near a girl like Rose. Surely he realised the risk of catching a disease was too high.

Four points on the list so far, and more were destined to crop up. The scale was overbalancing; the relationship was becoming more troublesome than rewarding, more unfulfilling than pleasurable. And now there was another factor to consider. The letter.

She had it in her handbag now, resting against her left ankle under the table. It was too important a letter to be left in her bedroom for her mother to find during one of her incessant 'tidying' sessions. This was not something she wanted to discuss with anyone until she had made her decision.

'Garlic bread?' Rob asked her. She shook her head. 'Wine?'

'Mmm …' she demurred, '… perhaps a bottle of house white?' She addressed the waiter directly, who was a good two sizes larger than the uniform into which he was squeezed. He had to be a local.

'Do you want to order your mains now?' the waiter asked, after laboriously writing down her decision with his tongue poking out between his teeth.

'The double pepperoni is good,' Rob said.

'I'll just have the salad bowl buffet option,' Charlotte said.

'I'll go for the double pepperoni,' Rob confirmed, and it took the waiter another thirty seconds to write that down before shuffling through the blue plastic tables and chairs to the undoubtedly filthy kitchen.

Allcombe's only restaurant: the Pizza Parade. It was deserted, and hygienically unconvincing. Their window table had a tomato stain across the length of the paper tablecloth and the floor felt sticky underfoot.

Overall, it added up to reason number five.

5. He has no taste.

She was aghast to discover that, for all his well-turned-out clothes and groomed speaking voice, Rob still considered this place to be an acceptable venue for a romantic meal out.

Although perhaps she was being a little harsh on him. Perhaps she should fish a little to ascertain if he really did think this was a restaurant of choice, or if he was making do with the only place available.

'Not much of a choice,' she said, indicating the menu, which lived in a clear plastic holder on the table top. It had been laminated so that greasy finger marks could be wiped away; it didn't bode well for the quality of the food. 'Still, I suppose it impresses the locals.' She kept her eyes on his face so she could gauge his reaction.

He smiled back and looked out of the window at the street lights and the occasional passing car.

She tried again. 'I mean – small town problems. Were

there any decent restaurants in the place you lived before you came here?'

'I've always lived in Allcombe,' he said.

6. He's a local.

He had hidden his roots well, even though he did not seem embarrassed by admitting to them now. She hadn't suspected this for a moment. 'But ... how did you get this job? As a trainer?'

'I went to university in Plymouth. I lived there during the week and came back here every weekend.'

'But you were so confident in London.'

He smiled at her warmly. 'I don't mean I've never been out of the West Country,' he explained. 'I've travelled. I've just always preferred Allcombe. It's my home.'

The wine arrived and the bottle was plonked down on to the table between them. Rob, who was obviously used to such service, picked it up and poured a large measure into her glass, then his own. Charlotte didn't even want to taste it; it was as clear as water, with a slight fizz, and she had the suspicion it was a bottle of cheap Spumante masquerading as a house white. Spumante gave her a blinding headache.

'Speaking of London ...' she said. It occurred to her how little she actually knew about Rob. If she could have been wrong about one thing, she could have been misguided about others. '... Rose knows.'

There was an unmistakeable glint of guilt which he covered quickly. 'Knows what? About the trip? About your harassment case?'

She did wish he would stop referring to that. 'Maybe. She made a crack yesterday about day trips to London and so on. It seemed to me she knew more than she was saying.'

Rob was still, his hand around his wine glass, his eyes as blue as an unpolluted ocean. Something was whirring away inside him. 'Okay, look, we started this relationship on a totally honest footing and I want that to continue, so let me tell you something in strictest confidence about Rose.'

'You slept with her,' Charlotte said.

'No! God, no! How could you think that of me?' Rob looked so traumatized at the suggestion that Charlotte decided he had to be telling the truth.

'What, then?'

'She was my brother's girlfriend.' He took a mouthful of wine. 'For a while; not any more, I don't think. I'm not sure what's going on between them now. Matt says she's moved in with Sam Spurling, but, knowing Sam, I can't imagine …'

'No,' Charlotte said. 'Or, at least, I don't want to imagine it.'

'No.'

'But why would that mean she knows about London?' she asked, wanting to gauge the extent of Rob's mistake.

He looked down into his glass. 'I think maybe … Matt's been asking me about work, about the trainees, about you … and then telling Rose whatever I told him.' He raised his hands with his palms facing her when he saw her outraged expression. 'I've stopped telling him anything now. I didn't realise he couldn't be trusted, but I know now.'

'Any information you have about your staff is meant to be strictly confidential,' Charlotte told him, surprised and dismayed that she had to. That was another fault on the list, and perhaps the clincher.

7. He is bad at his job.

He couldn't keep a secret; he couldn't maintain professional confidentiality. He was no better than the trainees. He had gossiped and given away personal information just to make conversation. No wonder Rose always had a smirk on her face – she had obtained the measure of Rob a long time before Charlotte had.

'I know,' he said miserably. 'Nothing like this has ever happened before. I've betrayed my trainees. I've started a relationship with one of them. It's just not good business. I suppose I could lose my job if it got out.' He looked small. He was no longer her brilliant, dependable, rock-like Rob. He was a sad man in a job he did not deserve to keep after he had abused his position so despicably.

A thought came to Charlotte that she did not immediately reject as unfair – Rob Church was just another incarnation of Mike Miller, and she had fallen for the same tricks all over again.

'I've got a headache. I might just go,' Charlotte said, retrieving her handbag from under the table.

The sympathetic dimples appeared, but this time they failed to charm. 'Let me walk you back – I'll just get the bill.'

'Don't bother,' she said, and then made herself soften a fraction for the sake of appearances. 'I'll see you at work tomorrow.'

She wanted to get home and re-read her letter from Susannah Medley, particularly the part about how much the Salzburg company had suffered without her presence and the mention of the fact that Mike's old job was up for grabs and she would be the perfect candidate.

She left before Rob had a chance to say another word.

Gary

Wednesday, 13th December, 8.00 pm

'So she's not part of the band any more,' Lozza repeated. He had already taken his place behind his drums and had his sticks in his hands. He looked most unhappy that music-making had been thwarted, but he didn't seem to be really absorbing what Gary was trying to tell him. Neither did the other band members; Sock was pressing a switch on his keyboard repeatedly and Paul was fiddling with his amp.

All the lads had liked Hilary and had enjoyed her constructive presence far more than Donna's. They weren't saying much, but their careful, quiet movements told him that they were listening closely and trying to comprehend what this meant for the future of the band.

'So she's going back to New Zealand,' Lozza repeated.

Gary sat on the third step of the staircase that led up to the kitchen, ignoring the aching cold that spread through his jeans from the icy stone. He had said what needed to be said. He didn't want to talk about it any more.

'So you have to move out and we have to find a new place to rehearse,' Lozza repeated. He was still grasping his drumsticks.

Sock looked up from his button-pressing and addressed the basement in a too-loud voice. 'My Dad won't let us back in the garage. He loves having that garage back. He's started putting pictures on the walls and he's getting a Black & Decker Workmate for Christmas.'

'All right. We'll find somewhere else,' Gary said.

'Where?' Sock demanded.

'Just take one thing at a time, okay?' Gary hated the fact that he had to do everyone's thinking for them. Just once he wanted one of them to come up with an idea.

'So Hilary's not the singer any more,' Lozza repeated. Then he actually said something new. 'So who is the singer?'

'Not Donna,' Paul said, looking up at the basement door as if Donna was about to burst through it and scream at him for disrespecting her.

'No, not Donna.' Gary held together the tiny scraps of courage he had managed to protect from Hilary's savage jaws and dared himself to talk about his plan; the plan that had germinated on the night Steve had attacked him. 'I'm going to be the singer.'

Amp fiddling, button pressing and drumstick twiddling began again in earnest. So they didn't think he had what it took to be a lead singer. That was fair enough: he didn't know himself. But he had learned not to rely on any woman to deliver his dreams for him. He would make them come true himself.

'Let's do a number,' he suggested. Paul straightened up, Lozza grinned, and Sock braced himself as Gary picked up his guitar and set up the microphone with shivering, clumsy fingers. He needed to start with an easy one, one he knew so well that he could concentrate on delivering the kind of performance of which he hoped he was capable.

'*Wild Thing*,' he said over his shoulder at the others. It was only three chords; if he couldn't sing that, he couldn't sing anything.

He'd never even done karaoke before, and he was relieved when, with the band behind him, he reached the first words and they flowed out of his mouth, into the microphone, and emerged clearly and strongly out of the black mesh of the amplifier.

He was going to make it through the song and, he realized, through the next week and year and through his life on his own terms. He had grasped that he needed to be responsible for what he wanted out of life and, as he poured his soul out through his voice box and sent it reverberating around the freezing basement, he discovered that he was not incapable. He was afraid, but that did not make him incapable.

The final chord faded away and, ears ringing, Gary turned to look at the faces of his friends.

Lozza's eyebrows were drawn together and his lips were pursed. He looked as if he was trying to drag the answer to a difficult crossword clue from the back of his brain.

Sock and Paul were both looking at Lozza.

Gary felt the tread marks of foreboding sprint across his shoulder blades.

'So you're the new singer ...' Lozza repeated.

The others looked at him expectantly.

'... but you're pants,' he finished, with the plaintive confusion of a child who had seen a parent do something morally wrong.

'That did suck,' Sock inserted into the pause that followed.

'Yeah,' Paul added.

It was time, Gary decided, to reconsider his options.

Amie

Wednesday, 13th December, 8.17 pm

The door was locked and the curtains were shut. There was no way Rose was being admitted to her father's house tonight.

Amie wouldn't have decided upon this course of action herself, even though Rose had broken the news of her father's death in such a callous fashion and made her realise that they never had really been friends at all. It was only because someone else had asked it of her that she had found the strength to keep Rose out.

Matt was sitting next to her on the sofa, his eyes fixed on the chat show on the television screen, playing at a reduced volume, but his ramrod spine and cocked head told her that his attention was pinpointed on the street outside. Rose was late for their weekly appointment. That was not unusual, but Amie wished, for Matt's sake, that Rose could have been on time just this once so that his ordeal could have ended sooner – Matt's fingers were biting through his trousers and into his knees, and his teeth were clenched as if wired shut.

She reached out impulsively and put her own fingers on his arm. He flinched, but smiled back at her. Then his smile was immediately destroyed by the peremptory knock at the front door.

Amie put her hand back in her lap and listened. Matt needed her to be the one in control; he needed her help. She had to be capable of resisting Rose, of stopping her from hurting anyone else. She had to teach Rose that the world could not be had on her terms alone.

'Amie!' Rose called. 'Open the frigging door!'

She banged for entry. Matt jumped with each thud as if it was a gunshot.

'Oh, for Christ's sake,' she heard Rose say. Her impatience was legendary. A moment later Amie heard the traipse of her high heels approaching the window, and her fingernails clinked against the glass. 'Get a fucking move on! Amie!'

When nobody replied, Rose lapsed into silence. Amie knew better than to relax; she had never thought Rose would give up so easily. She would merely be reconsidering her tactics.

'Matt?' she said, 'Matt? Are you in there?' Amie was amazed at her sixth sense for these things; it was no wonder everyone was so afraid of her. 'Matt, you fucking prick, let me in!'

Matt had adopted the utter stillness of a meercat on sentry duty.

'Matt? You can't be serious.' She sounded almost vulnerable. 'I've explained the whole fucking thing to you – you can't be fucking serious about this.'

Matt's shoulders caved and his neck drooped, but he remained on the sofa. Amie wondered if he was thinking the same thing as her; that Rose could turn emotion on and off at will, and she could not be trusted simply because she had brought a catch to her voice.

There was a tremendous thump. Amie thought that Rose must have flung herself bodily against the door, so loud and solid was the reverberation through the house.

It was her parting shot.

Amie thanked God. If Rose had tried anything like that with the window she would have ended up standing in the middle of the living room in a shower of glass. Instead her high heels took her away, and the ordeal was over.

Amie put her hand back on Matt's elbow and he looked at her with bleak eyes. Then he slumped back into the cushions on the sofa and rubbed his forehead with his thumb and middle finger.

'She's gone,' Amie whispered to him.

'Don't open the curtains,' he pleaded.

'I won't. I won't.'

But she was uncomfortable, touching him on the small sofa in the low, flickering light from the television. She wished she could be left alone now, but she didn't have the heart to kick Matt out immediately. He evoked strange feelings in her: pity, compassion, camaraderie, and something deeper that she did not want to identify and that was squirming to the top of her emotions.

'I just couldn't deal with her today,' he confessed, still talking in a whisper.

'Why not?'

'I dunno. Sometimes she gets me so ...' He petered out.

Amie knew she couldn't help him by avoiding talking about the issue. 'It's your baby, isn't it?'

He nodded, curving his back and shielding his face from her with his hand.

'Did you tell her that you wanted to help her raise it? That you want to be a family?'

He dropped his hand and stared at his knees. 'I don't know that I want to be a family.'

So what did he want? He wanted her to kill it? Or stay on her own and bring the baby up without any help at all? Amie was surrounded by death and deceit. She felt choked by it. She saw Matt with fresh vision. He was only concerned about himself too. He didn't care about his baby, or about anyone else. The selfishness of this world appalled her.

She got up and turned on the living room light switch, making the room blare into blinding electric incandescence. Then she switched off the television.

'What are you doing?' Matt demanded.

'I'm sick of hiding in my own house and I'm sick of being used by everyone. You come here and then decide you don't want to see Rose. Well, fine. You should have told her yourself. This isn't a sanctuary for anyone. MY FATHER HAS JUST DIED!' It was the first time she had ever raised her voice.

She looked at the dirty curtains and the dated turquoise carpet that had come to represent her life, as Matt squirmed behind her.

'Sorry about your Dad,' he finally said.

'Thank you.' It didn't help to know that her father had refused to make peace with her and was certainly burning in hell now and forever more.

Matt swallowed noisily. She couldn't turn to face him; she felt disgusted by every person on the planet, and she could not control her expression. 'I just ... I really need a friend right now,' he said quietly.

'You want me to help you?'

'Yes. I suppose.'

'Then read this.'

Amie moved from the window, past the sofa, without looking at him, and retrieved the letter she had been writing and re-writing all day from the kitchen counter. She had not thought she would show it to anyone, or explain her actions to anyone, but Matt had provoked her into it. She wanted him to look seriously at himself; to try to make a decision about how he could help himself.

She passed him the letter and then sat back down on the sofa beside him so that she could watch his expression as he read it.

At first she could tell only that he was concentrating – he obviously wasn't a great reader – and then, on about line four she guessed, a deep, creased frown ran across his eyebrows. It remained there until he reached the last third of the page, and, surprisingly, a smile began to break through. When he smiled she was drawn to him like a tourist to sunshine; the most charming dimples appeared in his cheeks and the blue irises of his eyes widened in pleasure.

'You're actually going to send this to him?'

'Do you want me to?'

Matt handed the letter back to her with delicate care. 'Yeah.'

She hadn't expected that response. 'You're sure?'

'Yeah.' He pulled at the material of his collarless shirt and redid a button that had slipped its noose. 'You're not going to ... to stay in Allcombe after this, are you? She won't like it.'

His fear of Rose would have been funny if Amie didn't feel it too. 'I know. I'm not staying.' Saying it made it a fact, but she really hadn't felt there had ever been a choice since the death of her father. There wasn't enough money to stay, anyway. She simply couldn't afford to live on her earnings alone, and she faced the fact that the only reason she had been delaying was that she didn't know what kind of welcome she would receive at her chosen destination.

'Where are you going to go?'

'Back to Wales.' Amie folded the letter once and placed it on the arm of the sofa.

'You've got family there?' Matt asked.

Amie thought about the question. There was no way to describe to a heathen like Matt what The Nation meant to her. She supposed family was a close enough approximation to the support she had felt from living with others according to the will of God, until her father had dragged her away. 'Yes.'

He moved his hand, very slowly, to take one of hers. His palm was hot but his fingers were cold; she couldn't pull away from such tenderness, from a man's touch. 'Can I come with you?'

He leaned in closer to her. She felt him willing her to give in to him. It was intoxicating to be so close to a man who did not live by the same rules as her, who wanted to make her agree with him and would do anything to achieve that.

Then she realised it was a game to him.

He wanted to escape Allcombe and he thought seducing her would give him the way out he needed.

He deserved Rose.

'No,' she said.

He let her hand go and threw her a petulant look. 'Why not?'

'Believe me when I say you wouldn't like it.'

'I can make my own decisions,' he told her, getting to his feet.

'You haven't so far. Look …' she said, standing up so that he wouldn't tower over her and gain an advantage in the conversation. 'I am sick of living in this place and I am sick of being used. Can I suggest that you think over what you want out of life? Because I've thought it over and I don't want to be an administrator and I don't want to be Rose's friend and I don't want to be your friend.'

Matt looked at the blank television screen, as if the confrontation wasn't happening, but she could tell from his pinched nostrils and his stiff shoulders that he was listening to her.

'Now, would you mind going away?'

He absorbed her request in silence. Then he asked, 'When are you leaving?'

'Tomorrow, okay? I'll post the letter and then I'll go.'

He nodded twice, and then shrugged and gave her a care-free smile, as if their previous conversation was now forgotten. ''Bye then.'

''Bye,' she said, feeling an awful lot less sure of herself than she had ten seconds ago. Nonchalantly he walked away and out of the house. She just didn't understand him; she supposed he had tried, and failed, to get his own way and this was his attempt at saying 'no hard feelings'. She didn't get it, but she decided she wasn't going to waste any more time trying. And she wasn't going to think about his smile any more.

Amie intended to disappear without saying goodbye and without giving notice at work. She wanted to be back in a place where people still recognised the difference between good and evil. She just had to hope that, because of her time outside and the legacy of her father's mistakes, she had not been categorised as evil.

Alma

Thursday, 14th December, 4.55 pm

The complete silence of intense concentration had stretched on for fifty-nine minutes, and Alma was more than ready for it to come to an end. She had given up thirty-two minutes ago, according to the clock on the wall over Rob's head, and had waited as patiently as she knew in order to give the others the chance to succeed at the test. Personally, she thought that was extremely good of her.

'Okay, that's it. Everybody drop your pens and place your

papers face down on your desk in front of you,' Rob announced after checking the clock. 'And once you've done that, you can call it a day. Alma, could I have a brief word with you before you go?'

Alma sat in her chair and leaned her elbows on the desk while waiting for the rest of the trainees to leave. Rose and, surprisingly, Charlotte were the first out of the room. Hilary was next – everyone knew she had given in her notice but she had asked to take the test anyway, strange girl – and Gary followed after her. Sam, with depression tattooed on his forehead, finally placed his paper on the edge of his desk and slumped out. Amie had not turned up at all.

This final test had held no fear for Alma. Her future was assured; it wasn't in administration, and it wasn't in Allcombe. She would have been surprised to have got one question right. She knew she hadn't answered more than five. Most of the neatly printed examples of customer behaviour she had simply drawn a line through, and striking them out had made her feel great, as if she was denying them the right to have a hold over anyone. Or, at least, over herself.

It was a totally different world from the one in which she had first sat in this room, on the very first day of the training course. In this square meeting place, on the fourth floor, with the window looking out to sea, she had met a selection of strangers who had represented the bottom of the trash can to her; people without hope and without prospects. She was quite proud that she had avoided any real socialising with them, and she had climbed up over them to start her career again.

'How do you think you did?' Rob asked her. He was moving around the room, picking up the papers from the evenly and exactly spaced desks. He was as beautiful as ever; yet although there was no sag to that gorgeous bottom or firm chin, his personality had recently acquired a definite droop. Alma blamed Charlotte. That girl had a blood-sucking look about her.

'It's anybody's guess,' she replied easily. She knew what Rob really wanted to talk about.

The newspaper article had been printed yesterday.

He contrived his collection so that hers was the last paper he needed to retrieve. He stopped directly in front of her and left her paper between them as he placed the others on the desk beside her. Then he grabbed a nearby chair and turned it so that he could sit before her, his hands on his knees, and his face, complete with charming dimples, close to her own.

'Was that article in the paper the other day really about you?'

This was the first time she had been asked about it, although she had seen many people look sideways at her, and a few had stopped and stared. Just like old times, really.

'Yeah, it's me,' she said.

He seemed unconvinced, and then grudgingly surprised. 'Wow.'

'Yeah.'

'Should I call you Alma or Jacqueline?' he asked her. 'Is Alma your real name?'

'Jacqueline's my real name, but you can call me Alma.'

Rob pulled his eyebrows together and then smoothed them back out with a deep breath and his business smile. 'Well then, Alma, I've had a word with my manager and we've agreed that we'll offer you all the support necessary in order to make you feel comfortable in your rôle here.'

Alma smirked. 'Gee, thanks, Rob.'

He leaned even closer and spoke softly to her. 'And, on a personal note, I'd like to say how very generous an offer I find that to be, considering that you didn't disclose any such information about your past on your initial application form.'

For a moment she had thought he was going to compliment her, or ask for her autograph, so nicely it was phrased. So that was how Rob reprimanded people: Mary Poppins-style. He opted for a spoonful of sugar to help the medicine go down.

'Oh, sure. I would have got the job if I'd told you all this. You would have thought I was a nut.'

'Well, that's probably been taken into account by management. It wouldn't surprise me if that's the reason you still have a job.' He stood up and took her exam paper from the desk, sliding it on top of the others. 'Just so long as you're clear that this doesn't warrant any special treatment.'

He still thought he was better than her. Alma knew she should have waited until the second article, announcing her comeback to television, was published but she wanted to wipe that sanctimonious smile off Rob's face. 'Actually, Rob, I'm not planning on staying around much longer.'

He insisted on behaving like her boss. 'Are you finding the course difficult?' he asked her in his caring voice.

'You know, someone should help you pull that stick out of your ass. No, I'm not finding it difficult. I just don't give a shit,' she said, feeling a tickle of glee in her throat.

He absorbed this. 'Do you have another job lined up?'

'You could say that,' she told him. Experience had taught her not to crow about a job before the contract was signed, no matter how much she wanted to.

'Can I take this as your resignation, then?' he asked her. It seemed she had forfeited the right to his concern. For a moment she almost felt sorry.

'Could we just let things slide for a while? Just keep it quiet until after Christmas?'

He shook his head, she couldn't tell whether in disapproval or denial. 'The results of this test will be announced at the end of next week, before we leave for the Christmas break. If you haven't passed it then I can't help you. You'll be sacked whether you want to let it slide or not. It's in your contract.'

His eyes contained a warning; he turned away, picked up the papers and returned to his position under the clock without another word.

Alma refused to give him seniority over her. She didn't care that she had no chance of passing the stupid exam, and she told herself sternly that she didn't care if she was sacked.

Still, it would have been nice to have succeeded in normal life as well as stardom. But she had made a mess of the whole thing. She just had to hope that her return to the public eye would last long enough and pay well enough to keep her in booze and ciggies, because she knew now that she would never be able to return to the little, nine-to-five life. It was too tough to live that way.

She got up from her desk and exited with as much dignity as she could muster, refusing to worry about the future. She had never worried about it before, and things had turned out okay so far, albeit with a few hiccups.

'See you tomorrow,' Rob called out after her.

'Whatever,' she said, not bothering to turn around.

After a ride in the incredibly slow elevator and a short walk through the plastic pot plant hell that was the lobby, Alma was outside and squinting against the orange street lights, trying not to lose her footing on the frost that covered the sidewalk. She stopped by the revolving door and looked around for any reporters that might be lurking nearby. She liked to keep her eyes open for any opportunity of publicity.

She was still hoping that Sebastian Storey would talk the paper into running another article in which she could dish the dirt on her ex-husband and her kids. She was aching to get some revenge on the family who had deserted her. In moments when a drink wasn't readily available, mentally rehearsing what she might say on the subject actually made life bearable.

She had considered also talking about the Dora Fearn incident, but that episode left her with a creeping embarrassment when she thought about it now. And chances were that somebody might approach Angela as a follow-up, and that would lead to disclosures about drinking habits. Alma had considered herself a heroine to that old lady at the time. Now she saw it on the same level as her drinking – both had made her lose control of herself.

The Dora incident was definitely best left in the past.

There weren't any journalists waiting for her, but Alma's scanning eyes did pick up the familiar figure of Rose, who, with no protection against the freezing wind and totally unsuitable shoes to combat the slippery layer of fine frost, was talking to a man Alma did not immediately recognise. Then she realised he was the guy who was always waiting for Hilary at this time; her foreign boyfriend, if Alma remembered correctly.

He was a dish. Definitely not local: he was more tanned and blond than any Englishman Alma had met, and he didn't seem to be burdened with the usual inability to talk to the opposite sex. He was doing a good job of chatting comfortably with Rose, which was a rare feat.

Alma listened in to their conversation. She always felt a mild curiosity when she saw a good-looking guy. Back when she was a goddess of the screen, she would have walked straight over and introduced herself. Now she kept her distance so as not to scare him away.

'Hils shouldn't be much longer. She just had to pop to the loo,' Rose was saying, sweet as a strawberry. Alma had never heard Rose refer to Hilary as 'Hils' before. She recognised a move when she saw it. Rose had better hope Hilary didn't catch her playing this game; the tall, serious brunette was pretty well muscled and not blessed with a great sense of humour.

'Thanks for letting me know,' the foreign guy said.

'Doesn't Gary usually walk home with you as well?' Rose asked with a pretence of innocence that Alma saw through in a second.

'Um ...' He looked uneasy. 'He used to.'

'Doesn't he live with Hils? With you and Hils, I mean?'

'Right now he does, yes.'

'And he did before you arrived? Live with Hils?' she pressed.

'Well, yes.'

'I thought so. They're really close, aren't they? They spend all their time together in work. You're really cool to be laid-back about something like that. Most blokes wouldn't.'

'No, I guess not,' the boyfriend said. He was looking a little vulnerable.

'And you seem really chilled about their whole relationship thing – you know, before you and Hils patched things up ...' Rose left a theatrical pause. 'You did know about that?'

'Um ...' the guy said.

'Oh, God, I've just put my fucking foot right in it, haven't I?' Rose looked at her wrist, as if a watch should be there. 'Look, it was nice talking to you. Say hi to Hils for me.' She raised one hand and wiggled her fingers in a coquettish fashion before turning in Alma's direction and spotting her in a moment.

Rose walked towards her while rummaging in her tiny bag to produce a cigarette. In fact, she produced two. A lighter followed, and both cigarettes were lit. Alma didn't know what shocked her more: the random act of cruelty towards Hilary and her boyfriend, or the random act of kindness towards herself. Both were inexplicable.

Alma noticed the extreme gooseflesh on Rose's bare arms from the cold, but the girl didn't even shiver. Up close, Rose's stomach was a dome that pushed itself out under her tight skirt and demanded attention. She tried not to stare at it.

'Why did you say that to him?' she asked as she took the proffered cigarette and put it to her willing lips.

Rose took a deep drag, held it, and exhaled with her head tilted back to the sky. Then she shrugged and smiled. 'For fun.' She held Alma's eyes with her own, and Alma saw no concern there; no shadow of remorse or doubt. The girl was free of all personal responsibility for her actions. Not even Alma had learned that trick.

The revolving door swished and a short, silver-haired man in an immaculate suit and raincoat, who Alma thought she recognised but couldn't place, emerged. He glanced at Alma and then shot a look of meaning at Rose before climbing into the back seat of a long, black car that was waiting at the kerb.

'See you tomorrow,' Rose said immediately, and walked away after him with a severe grace that was peculiar and beguiling. She got into the car and it pulled away without a sound.

Hilary's boyfriend was still waiting in the frost with a stunned expression and one hell of a conversation ahead of him. Alma put out the cigarette under her heel. She didn't want anything from Rose; she didn't even want to admit to playing the same kind of games when she had been younger. She particularly didn't want to admit that she would still be playing them if she had the looks for it.

Instead she concentrated on imagining her second shot at stardom as she began the walk home.

Hilary

Sunday, 17th December, 10.01 am

'Is that the last of it?' she asked.

'Yeah, that's it.'

Hilary stood on the pavement outside her house with her rucksack leaning against her knee. Gary was holding his guitar case as he emerged from the front door. She should have known that would be the last thing he would move back to his parents' house. It was certainly the thing that was most important to him.

It was an exceptionally bright morning, with an icing sugar layer of frost over the boats in the still sea. Allcombe harbour resembled the Christmas cards she had already sent out this year. Only as Hilary was about to leave did the town reveal its picturesque side to her; she could finally understand why people travelled to see it. She entertained for a moment the idea that she would return one day as a tourist. Then she dismissed it. Life was too short to return to the same place, particularly a place like this.

'I've got a present for you,' she said. She bent over her rucksack and undid the plastic toggles which held down the top flap to extract the small, precisely wrapped gift she had chosen, complete with a snowman shaped foil tag. Hilary gave it to him, and he put down his guitar case on the doorstep in order to take the present in both hands.

'Wow. I really wasn't expecting anything,' Gary said, reading the tag.

'That's all right. I didn't think you'd get me anything anyway,' Hilary pre-empted.

He met her eyes and smiled for the first time in days. She didn't know if it meant he was asking for forgiveness or giving it and, unusually for her, she wasn't bothered either way as long as she could have this moment to take away with her. She wanted a happy ending.

'I'm really sorry about how things worked out,' she said, and for a moment she meant it.

'Me too.' Gary opened his mouth and paused; perhaps he changed his mind about what he wanted to say. 'Can I open this now?'

'It's a Christmas present,' she told him, 'so you can wait until Christmas.'

'Oh, okay.' He transferred the present to one hand and picked up his guitar case with the other, but she was reluctant to let him leave just yet.

'It's not a very good present, anyway.' It was a new set of strings, three multicoloured plectrums and a book about Jimi Hendrix. On the title page of the book she had carefully written an inscription: 'To Gary, The only other person I know who really appreciates Jimi'. It sounded a bit pathetic now, and that was the reason she didn't want him to look at it.

'Where's Steve?' he asked.

'He's at the estate agents, just dropping off a set of keys. He shouldn't be much longer.'

'Is everything okay?' he asked her with a strange emphasis.

She knew immediately what he was getting at, but didn't understand how he knew, unless he had been listening to conversations that really didn't concern him.

'What do you mean?' she asked carefully.

'I was speaking to Alma,' Gary said with determination, 'and she told me she had overheard Rose speaking to Steve …' He left the sentence hanging, but there was no need to say any more.

'So everyone knows?'

'I don't think so,' Gary attempted to reassure. 'Alma told me in confidence. She thought I should know.'

'Well, I don't see why. It's pretty much a private thing, I would say.'

She had offended him. He looked at the pavement, and then off in the direction of The Bosworth Slaughter. 'I should get going.'

Hilary felt panic that he should leave her in this mood. It forced her into honesty. 'Look, I told Steve that I ... had been tempted while he was away, and he was fine with it. He said that he knew I'd been really confused and it was understandable.'

Gary absorbed this confession. 'He's a good bloke,' he admitted, as if it hurt him to do so.

'Yes, he is.'

'And were you?'

'Was I what?'

He looked directly into her, daring her to tell him a lie. 'Were you tempted?'

She wanted to give Gary a glib answer, but she reassured herself by holding in her head the knowledge that this was probably the last time they would ever meet, and it couldn't be such a bad thing to tell him something that anybody with a little more self-belief would already have known. 'Yes, I was. I really was.'

Gary stood a little straighter and glanced up into the clear winter sky. She watched him take some deep breaths, and when he looked back to her he had a smile behind his eyes that could not have been faked.

Hilary felt a wave of relief. She had given him something real from their time together: the ability to respect himself. Perhaps because of her he would be on MTV in five years' time instead of serving fries in a fast food outlet or, worse still, stuck answering the phone in Allcombe.

'I could still kill Rose, though,' she admitted. 'And I would, if I had time.'

Gary laughed, and she laughed with him. It was like before Steve had arrived. It was good, and open, and honest, and she remembered why she had liked Gary so much. It was pleasurable to stand there and joke about something that really wasn't very funny at all.

'Anyway, here's my e-mail address.' She broke the mood deliberately, reaching into the back pocket of her jeans to produce the slip of paper on which she had written out her details earlier. He took it between the fingers of the hand which held her gift to him. 'Make sure you tell me everything – all the gossip, how the band's doing …'

'Yeah, I will.'

A car sounded in the distance. It grew closer. This was her last chance to say goodbye properly. Before she could allow herself to think it through, she moved in close to Gary and placed a soft and timid kiss on the bottom of his cheek. Then she stepped back, feeling the mark of his stubble against her cold lips, and watching the surprise on his face.

'Good luck with everything,' she said.

The rental car appeared around The Slaughter and drove up to the house to park outside. Steve didn't turn off the engine; instead he raised his eyebrows at her. They were already running late to get to Heathrow.

'I've got to go,' she said, a little breathlessly.

Gary had the same tone in his voice. 'Listen … I hope it all works out for you.'

'And for you.' She picked up her rucksack and carried it to the boot of the car. She was only taking the bare essentials now. The furniture would be sold with the house and the remainder of her possessions shipped over later.

'And good luck with everything at the bank. The course, the test results …' She had asked Rob to e-mail her own results to her. She wanted the satisfaction of passing the course. Besides, it gave her another skill-set, and she was not

foolish enough to think her problems with adventure training had simply vanished. She had a long way to go before
her confidence would be fully mended.

Gary gave her a self-deprecating smile from the pavement as she slammed the boot and moved to the passenger
door. She knew he felt he had done badly at the test, but
then she didn't think he had ever really wanted to succeed
at it.

'And I hope the performance at the talent show goes
really well. Sorry to be leaving you in the lurch with that.'

'Yeah, well,' he said. 'Take care.'

He sounded blank, she thought, as she slid into the car
beside Steve. When she rolled down the car window and
looked back out at his drained face and panicked eyes, she
realised why. He must have forgotten about the show.

'Oh shit,' he said. Hilary wondered for an embarrassing
moment if he was about to beg her to stay merely to sing for
him and get him out of trouble.

'We've got to go,' Steve said.

She gave Gary a wide smile. ''Bye, then. Don't worry about
the show. I'm sure Rob will understand that you haven't had
a chance to sort anything out.'

'Do you think so?' Gary pleaded.

So he wanted her to spend her last moments in Allcombe
reassuring him. She was remembering why she was glad to
leave him behind. In a moment of perversity she decided not
to play his game this last time. 'Mail me soon, okay? 'Bye!'

She wound up the window and turned to Steve. 'Let's get
out of here,' she murmured, and refused to look back at the
house or the figure standing in front of it as Steve reversed
out of the road and turned the car around by The Slaughter.

This part of her life was over, Hilary told herself as they
drove away. It really was over, and she was glad.

Sam

The exam had not gone well, and Sam had been brooding about it since. He could never remember which key to press; the computer had never become his friend. It had remained as mysterious and distant as a super villain, and F2 had always called to him when he was meant to be pressing the Control key instead.

At least the stress of the past week had motivated him to restart his exercise regime. The intense sweating and run-away breathing of his daily jog made it impossible to worry about anything other than his own survival. He had forgotten how the incredible pain of one hundred press-ups and one hundred sit-ups could focus one's mind, to the exclusion of everything else, on one's own mortality.

As usual, Rose was leaving it until the last moment to come downstairs and begin the walk to work. Her mood was always worse in the morning, although it wasn't much improved in the evening. At least after work he could speak to her and she would speak back rather than shout.

It was getting worse now she was unable to get into most of her clothes. It seemed lycra could only stretch so far, and she was reluctant to buy new, practical garments. He would have paid out for as many as she wanted; he would have loved to see her in a rosebud-covered dress and flat brown clogs, or maybe in elasticised waistband jeans with a prim-rose yellow blouse, but he was afraid to suggest it.

Sam didn't want to be called a mental case again. He didn't want to give her any excuse to look at him as if he was the stain on the bottom of the toilet again. He had decided to keep the peace and keep silent, and give her everything she wanted until she accepted the truth about the ring and his family.

She had laughed at his heritage. He knew she was pregnant and uncomfortable and going through changes he couldn't imagine, but he still couldn't quite forgive her for that. And he couldn't forgive himself for not forgiving her. Forgiveness and rehabilitation were meant to be the trademarks of The Death-Defying Sputum.

Sam finished the last of his toast and tea, and checked his wristwatch. The time to leave had already passed; he wanted to call to Rose to hurry. An important meeting for the training team had been scheduled for that morning – it had to be the results from the final exam and the allocation of the trainees who passed into existing teams. He knew he couldn't shout out to Rose, so instead he put his cup and plate in the sink and went to hover in the hallway instead.

The post was already on the doormat, which meant it was early or Sam was late because usually he didn't get to see the post until he returned from work. He really would have to find some courage and say something.

'Rose?' he called up the stairs, and then, a little louder, 'Rose? Are you coming? It's getting late.'

There was a muffled reply. He didn't know what she had said, but at least she knew that time was moving on. Sam couldn't consider leaving without her. He had to hope she would not be much longer. He did feel absurdly pleased that he had managed to say anything to her at all. He saw it as a positive step forward.

He picked up the post from the hessian-weave doormat that was older than him and flicked through the usual selection of bills and circulars. He never got anything interesting. At least, he never had before. Today seemed to be the exception. There was an envelope, handwritten in a sloping, feminine style quite unlike anything he had ever seen before. It was a surprising and unwarranted work of art. He almost didn't want to open it. A rip in the envelope would spoil its majesty.

But if the envelope was this good, imagine what the letter might be. Sam opened the sticky flap as carefully as he could and slid the matching paper from its sheath so that he could read the message in the same immaculate hand.

Dear Sam,

I'm sorry to have to break this news to you, and to break it in such an impersonal way, but I feel you should be informed about the character of your fiancé.

To put it bluntly, you are not the father of her baby. The father is her old boyfriend. She is using you because you are in a position to look after her materially. I don't know if she loves you. Can I suggest you consider if you want to continue to make plans for marriage, as she might be aiming to divorce you to get your money?

I should also tell you that Rose has been meeting with her ex-boyfriend every week in order to conduct a secret liaison with him. I do not think these meetings have been innocent.

Please feel free to show this letter to Rose. I am leaving today and won't be returning to Allcombe, so she can't do anything to me. I wish I could say the same for you.

Best wishes,

There was an elegant squiggle for a signature at the bottom of the page that Sam could not immediately decipher. He stared at it. He wanted to know who was capable of spreading such malicious lies that were designed purely to wound.

Rose had told him, that day in the park when he had proposed, that something like this might happen and he had kept himself prepared. Now the hot surge of fury that erupted from his belly told him that nothing could have prepared him for this attack. He wanted to find the writer and spit in their face.

That feeling was erased a heartbeat later. The signature gave up its secret to him, and he could no longer believe that the content was a lie.

Amie Doe had written the letter.

He didn't know Amie very well, but he knew enough to know that she was honest. Sam had spent a lifetime looking into the faces of people and determining the criminals; Amie had the eyes of an angel and the walk of a girl who knew she had nothing standing between her and heaven.

So where did that leave him?

There was a thumping above him, and Rose appeared on the first floor landing. She was a vision of health and success; forgoing her usual skimpy outfit for the pink suit which Sam remembered from the first day of the Induction Course. With the jacket buttoned, her pregnancy was hidden and she looked demure, with her clean, scrubbed skin and pinned-back hair.

She descended the stairs with self-confident grace. 'Ready to go?'

Sam couldn't think of anything to do other than what Amie had suggested in the letter. He handed the piece of paper to Rose without a word, and watched her as she read it for herself.

She flashed a puzzled look at him before scanning the letter. Her self-control never wavered and Sam could pick up no emotion from her; her lips moved as she read, but her eyes remained trained on the paper and her body was relaxed, right down to the last line. When she looked back up at him, she was no more tense than she had been before he had given the letter to her.

'Yeah, it's kind of good timing that this arrived today,' Rose said without pause, 'because I was going to talk to you about it anyway.'

'Oh,' Sam said. She gave the letter back to him.

'Do you want to do this now or do you want to wait until after work? Because we are running a bit fucking late, but it's up to you, you know?'

Sam could not understand what was happening. He opened his mouth and stammered words came out, beyond his control. 'L ... let's do it now.'

'Okay, right,' Rose said, putting her splayed hands on her thighs and looking him directly in the eyes. How could she look at him that way if she had something to hide? It must all be some huge mistake that she could explain away in a moment.

'The engagement's off and I'm moving out after Christmas,' she said.

It was as though he had fallen over a high, straight cliff. His stomach contracted and his limbs felt tight and cold, as if a strong wind was blowing against them. The ground was rushing up to meet him, but not yet, he prayed, not yet.

'Is it true?' he wondered.

'Yeah,' Rose said. He realised she wasn't only talking about her statement but about the contents of the letter from Amie. He had only been trying to comprehend the unreality of the moment, but now the ground was coming up fast and it was impossible to breathe without gasping. 'I was just trying to do the best thing for the baby, but a better offer has come up ... I would be a fucking muppet if I didn't take it, wouldn't I?' But she wasn't really asking; it was a figure of speech he had heard her use before.

'What offer?' Sam asked. His future was over. This freefall

into oblivion left him with nothing; no wife, no baby, no continuance of the family name. She was taking it all away.

'I'm not allowed to say yet. You'll know by the end of the day, anyway. We should go. We're really fucking late now.' Rose sounded exasperated, as if it was all his fault.

In that moment he saw something in her long, curving fingernails and accusatory glare that he should have recognised a long time ago. She had never cared for him. She had never lost her cool with him; she had never looked at him with anything other than calculating eyes.

It was understandable. She had a life inside her that had to take precedence over everything else, including her own feelings. He so wanted that life to be his responsibility too.

'I don't mind that it's not mine,' he said, in a burst of desperate inspiration. 'Let me raise it. Or stay, and we'll raise it together. I'll do it either way. I have money.'

Rose opened the front door and turned back to him. She was an outline of darkness against the bright glare of the morning. Tears rose into his eyes as he fought to see her face against the perfect, cold lightbulb of the sun.

'Could you be any more embarrassing?' Rose asked him.

So that was definitely it.

No more Spurlings. No more superheroes.

It had all been a ridiculous dream; as ridiculous as expecting a girl – sorry, woman – like Rose to love him.

Sam was consumed by the desire to purge himself of his stupidity; to make a gesture that would prove to Rose that he accepted the situation and would not embarrass her any further.

'You should keep the ring.' They had upgraded the engagement ring to a very expensive and flashy, diamond-laden piece of jewellery that was, even now, sitting proudly on her finger. He wanted it to be a gift to her and the baby. Maybe his money would do them both some good.

'Yeah, I know,' she said. 'I've got it already. I took it out of your weird sock drawer this morning.'

Not that ring. He hadn't meant that ring.

'Come on. Let's go.'

She walked out into the winter sunshine. Sam watched her from the familiar, long untouched dust and cobwebs of the hallway. He had just realised she was not a good girl.

Part Four

Rob

'I'll start by making the announcement about the final exam results,' Rob says flatly, 'and then I've got another announcement to make to those people who passed.'

He can't make it sound like good news; to make such news sound like good news is beyond even his control. He scans the group, sitting in their allocated seats in the training area. They are exhibiting all their usual characteristics, not knowing everything is on the verge of change.

Alma is slumped back in her chair, her hands on the front of her woollen green cardigan, stretching it over her chest. She is wearing heavy eyeliner and mascara, and a strong and artificial smell of violets wafts from her hair. She shows nothing but a hint of smugness in her perusal of him and her team mates. She smiles constantly, as if certain that everyone is worshipping her from afar.

Sam does not appear to be nervous, which is a surprise. He keeps his head down, his nose pointed at the desk, his shoulders hunched. His position makes his bald spot obvious. It shines with his sweat, and resembles a wet egg in a nest of blond feathers.

Amie's chair is empty again. Rob has heard nothing from her. She did not sit the exam, and he's sure she wouldn't have passed anyway. He sent a letter to her house, asking her how she was after the death of her father, but received no reply.

Gary is the most obviously nervous of the group. He shifts and fidgets constantly, his long fingers twisting through his hair and playing with his chewed biro. He can't control his mouth; it grimaces and then slips from side to side. He worries his lower lip with his long yellow incisors. His eyes move along the lines that divide the brown floor tiles around Rob's feet.

Rose is calm. He knows she has every reason to be. She is dressed in perfectly acceptable business attire, even if the skirt is a little short and her legs bare, and she is keen to flash those slightly orange thighs. Her hair is scraped back into a long silver pin that glitters under the strip lights.

Hilary's chair is empty. Already Rob is missing her calm, sardonic presence. He would have found it soothing today. He would have liked to have allied himself with her amused distance, even if it was unprofessional. But her amused distance is on the far side of the world by now.

Charlotte will not look at anyone, particularly not him. She is sitting alone, separate from the others. She is beautiful in a pencil skirt and a severe black jacket with an ivory blouse that has a perfectly behaved collar arranged over her lapels. She is very pale. She won't speak to him any more, and when he looks at her his professionalism slips. He doesn't want to think about fragile china dolls high on dusty shelves when he looks at her, but that's what he sees; she has killed his ability to remain detached in the training room.

Rob leans over his desk and selects the paper that contains the group's results from his basket.

'I'm going to read out each name in turn, and tell you whether you need to stay in this room or go to the restaurant. Then I'll speak to you in two separate groups, okay? Any questions?'

Nobody speaks.

'Then here we go. Alma, please stay here.'

She yawns, nods in acknowledgement and scratches at her stomach.

'Sam, please stay here.'

He looks past Rob with a dazed countenance.

'Gary, please go to the restaurant.'

Gary leaps up and walks out of the room, pumping his arms and quivering with adrenalin.

'Rose, please go to the restaurant.'

Rose bestows a glittering smile upon him that lets him see the small pink jewel she has glued to one of her front teeth, and then she sashays out.

'Charlotte, please go to the restaurant.'

Charlotte straightens up and adjusts her jacket. She walks out without looking anywhere but at the space just before her toes.

That leaves only Sam and Alma to deal with in this room. They are already sitting at the same desk. Rob moves over to it and sits opposite them so he can speak more informally. They both have to know what was coming, but neither of them looks concerned. Sam doesn't even look awake.

'I'm afraid I've got some bad news for you. You didn't pass the test. Would you like to know your final scores?'

Alma shakes her head but Sam says, 'Yes please.' He says it in an empty monotone, but at least he's trying to make the best of the situation.

'Okay. Alma, you scored thirteen per cent. Sam, you scored forty-four per cent. The pass mark was seventy per cent.'

They look at him. They don't seem to be aware of what is about to happen next.

'So, according to the terms of your contract, the company is now able to terminate your employment with no required notice period. Basically, guys ...' Rob says slowly and clearly to avoid misunderstandings, '... that's it. Get your stuff together, clear out your desks, give in your passes at the reception desk and thanks for all the effort you've put into this company. We're sorry it didn't work out better.'

'You mean we leave right now?' Alma asked.

'That's right. It wouldn't be productive to have a drawn out notice period.'

'What about the show?' Sam asks. Rob is not immediately sure as to what he is referring. Then he remembers something that had long since fallen to the back of his brain: the talent show. It is scheduled for tomorrow night. 'Can we still go? As a goodbye to the rest of the group? The rest of the group are still going, aren't they?'

'I suppose so. I don't know.' He takes in Sam's defiant face and Alma's bored one. 'I'm sorry, Sam, I just don't think it would be a good idea.'

'What do you mean?' Alma snaps. 'Why can't we go?'

'To be honest, I don't think either of you have earned the right to attend. Please try and remember that you are no longer part of this company,' Rob says, with an edge to his voice. 'I'm sorry, I have to get back to my trainees. Remember to hand in your passes on the way out.'

He gets up and strides out of the room, along the temporary corridor and through the hammering workmen, to the restaurant, concentrating on what he is about to say and in what order.

His team is gathered on the green sofas. No-one has fetched coffee from the machine. No-one is talking.

Rob forces a brilliant smile on them as he arrives. 'Congratulations! You passed the course!'

Gary shows relief, which is surprising considering the company he's in. With Charlotte in the group Rob thinks Gary could have worked out for himself that he's a successful candidate.

'As a reward you get to have a long lunch today. You can go now and come back at two this afternoon. Then we'll go over what happens next if you decide to stay with the company after the announcement I'm about to make.'

Charlotte is looking at the buttons of her jacket and Gary is devoting all his attention to Rob. Rose is completely unbothered, but then he knows she knows what's coming next. She probably knew about it before Rob did.

'What time is it?' Rob asks Charlotte.

She checks her wrist watch. 'Twenty past eleven,' she says coolly.

'Well, we're a bit early, but I don't suppose it matters. This announcement is being made to the entire work force simultaneously, okay? It's very important that you listen carefully, and I'll take any questions you have at the end.'

Rob produces a piece of official company paper from his jacket breast pocket and unfolds it. He reads directly from it.

'The service we can give to our customers is the most important part of our organisation. We are a company that aims to provide the best service for all. This includes our employees and our shareholders.

'This has been a difficult year. Changes in the global financial climate have affected many companies, and we are not the only banking and investment organisation that must now make structural alterations in order to maintain our position as a market leader.

'Therefore, the decision has been taken by the Board of Directors that the call centre and associated customer services arm of the business will be relocated to Bombay. This will enable us to cut costs for the benefit of the shareholder and the customer.

'We are keen to retain as many of our valuable work force as possible through this necessary transition. Therefore any employee who wishes to relocate to

Bombay is encouraged to approach their line manager for an application form; every chance will be given to them to reapply successfully for their current position. Please note that remuneration and pension rights may be affected; please speak to your line manager for details.

'On a personal note, the Board of Directors would like to thank all employees for being so supportive and dedicated to providing customer service. We couldn't have made it work without you.

'Redundancy packages will be unveiled in the New Year. Until then, have a very merry Christmas and best wishes to you and your family.

'Seasons Greetings,

'Rolf Chester'

Rob folds up the piece of official company paper and slips it back into his pocket. His voice is as clear and strong as it has ever been as he asks, 'Are there any questions?'

Gary half-raises one hand with a jerk. His face is off-white compared with the red shock of his hair. He looks as though he has been electrocuted. 'So we've passed the exam but we're out of a job?' he asks. He keeps looking at the others as if they will illuminate the situation, but Rose and Charlotte are both silent and unmoving. Rob would even go so far as to say they look uninvolved; he expected it from Rose, but Charlotte is a different matter. Doesn't she care about anybody any more? He wants to shake her to get a response.

'You have the right to reapply for your job if you want to relocate,' Rob says.

Gary laughs without humour. He appears to be taking the news badly. 'Relocate to Bombay? Bombay, India? Is anyone going to relocate to there? Are you going to?'

Rob says quietly, 'No. I'm not going.' Charlotte looks up

at him, and he holds her gaze with a question of his own. She knows what he's asking.

She shakes her head. 'I'm not staying with the company.' Rob didn't really expect she would – her mother told him about the letter from Austria offering her a job – but it's still a shock to hear it.

Rose moves forward on to the edge of the sofa with a wiggle of her hips. 'I am,' she says.

'You're moving to India?' Gary says incredulously. Charlotte transfers her stare to Rose, who nods once, with pleasure.

'I've got the job of Personal Assistant to Rolf Chester when he transfers over. It'll mean a lot of travel between London and Bombay. I probably won't be out in India for more than three months a year, Rolf says.'

'But what about the baby?' Charlotte says, envy and disbelief shot through every word. Rose looks affronted that somebody should finally have the nerve to mention her pregnancy.

'So what about the baby? You of all fucking people should know about discrimination,' she says sharply to Charlotte, who freezes into icy outrage. Rob opens his mouth to defend her and then shuts it again; it is his fault that Rose knows these things. 'I have every right to get a promotion.'

'When did you interview? Who told you about the position?' Charlotte demands, leaning over Gary to gesture at Rose with thrusts of her splayed fingers.

'Rolf did. I met him when we were both having a fag break outside. We got talking and he said he was looking for a new assistant who he could get along with. Then he offered it to me.'

'You mean you offered it to him,' Charlotte shoots back, her chin pushed out.

All pretence of refinement slides off Rose in a second. 'Oh yeah?' she sneers. 'Well, you're no fucking different, you sanctimonious bitch.'

They both look ready to lash out physically. Gary cowers between them, trying to melt into the sofa and escape any damage that might be about to happen. Something needs to be done quickly.

'Let's all just calm down,' Rob intervenes.

Rose turns on him with bared teeth. She is electric and unrestrained, revelling in the chaos she is causing. 'Don't you fucking tell me what to do any more either, you prick,' she slices through him with precise savagery. 'You've got nothing over me. You're not my boss and neither is your fucking brother. And you couldn't go to Bombay if you wanted, because they're not offering you a new contract. Rolf told me you would have been sacked by now if it wasn't for the move.'

Rob has a desire to punch her in the face, just to get her to shut up. It would be an unprofessional release and he manages to control it. Charlotte and Gary are watching him. Charlotte has guilt and terror in her wringing hands and peeled-back lips. Gary has become an uncomprehending statue.

Rose is stroking her skirt with one hand and watching him, a half-smile on her face. She thinks he is just like his brother – a plaything, a person who will respond to her whims and take her judgement – and she has managed to control him, just as she controls Matt. He underestimated her. He did not understand her capacity and her lust for violence; he was misled by her youth, and by the blonde hair and pink suit.

He wants to punch Rose and he wants to plead with Charlotte to talk to him, but Rob can do nothing but cling to his professionalism, even if it is a punctured and fast-deflating life raft. It only has the energy left to keep him afloat as he buttons his jacket and walks out of the restaurant with no intention of returning.

Charlotte

Saturday, 23rd December, 3.12 pm

The organist was halfway through murdering the theme from *Gone With The Wind* when the coffin was sucked into the furnace. The vicar closed the two white panels to veil the proceedings, but that only concentrated Charlotte's mind on exactly what was happening behind them. The body of her great aunt, her grandmother's sister, was being burnt into ashes so that it could be scooped into a little pot and scattered over a weedy rose bush in the garden of remembrance by the crematorium car park.

At least it had happened before Charlotte had returned to Salzburg. The timing had saved her from having to return when just commencing her new managerial position. It was not that she was pleased about this unexpected death of her family member; it was only that she wanted to try to find the good angle of such an event.

The organ droned on. Charlotte recapped her own, very definite ideas about her own funeral:

1. *Burial, not cremation.*
2. *No organist ruining a piece of music she loved. A tape recording of something classy instead, maybe a Whitney Houston number.*
3. *A decent eulogy by somebody with a great speaking voice. In her daydreams Patrick Stewart turned up to talk about how wonderful she was, so perhaps she ought to marry somebody with that kind of voice to be sure of a great send-off. She was sure she wouldn't marry somebody without an amazing speaking voice anyway.*
4. *A dress code. She hated it when people turned up in any colour other than black.*

Simple rules for a simple ceremony. She could imagine it

perfectly, just as she could always mentally take out and polish her blueprints for her wedding day and retirement dinner.

Such thoughts got her through the rest of the service and out into the nearly empty gravel car park. Her mother was talking to her aunt, both of them holding large white handkerchiefs although their eyes were dry. Her father was chatting to an older woman Charlotte didn't know; probably someone from the retirement home. Charlotte wanted to get home and start packing, but she had to wait for her parents. They had driven her here and it was ten miles back to town.

She caught a flash of movement at the back of the car park and looked over to the one car that had been left there, next to the well-trimmed privet hedge and the gate that led into the memorial garden. It was a metallic-blue Ford Focus and the driver was leaning on the open door and holding up one hand to summon her attention to him. His blond hair and expensive suit were as initially appealing as the dimples in his cheeks. Charlotte had to fight hard against her initial response to smile back.

She checked on her parents. They looked as though they would be a while yet, fielding the sympathies and commiserations. She had no excuse to avoid him. She pulled her winter coat around her, tied the belt in place and strolled over to meet Rob.

He closed his car door and locked it as she approached, never letting his own smile waver. He was the king of the smile. It was a technique that could hide a multitude of emotions; he had to be masking rage right now. Charlotte hadn't wanted this confrontation, but now it was upon her she focused on his face and watched carefully to see how he intended to handle it.

'Hi,' he said as she got closer.

'Hello,' she replied coolly. 'How did you know I'd be here?'

'I phoned yesterday to speak to you and your mum said you'd be here today. She said it was okay to turn up.'

Her mother's interference was not surprising, merely irritating. She knew her mother didn't want her to return to Austria, and was probably hoping that Rob could talk her into staying. Charlotte hated that kind of attitude; the idea that a man could control her actions. It was never going to happen to her.

'Shall we take a walk?' he asked her, quite formally, holding out one arm to guide her past the gate and into the remembrance garden. She stepped through and he fell into place beside her. They assumed the traditional slow walk of the bereaved around the struggling rose bushes that twined around the wooden plaques staked through them.

'Your mother said your great aunt passed away,' Rob said in a low, respectful voice. 'I'm sorry.'

'Thanks. It was my Great Aunt Dora. She was in a nursing home but nobody was really expecting it. It's all been a shock to my Aunt Angela. She'd just got the money together to move her to a better home, with a larger room, more nurses.'

'It must have been a shock for you, too,' Rob said.

'We weren't close,' she replied. She wasn't really feeling much of anything. 'What did you want to see me about?'

Rob kept walking at the same sedate pace. 'I wanted to say goodbye. You're leaving for Salzburg soon, aren't you?'

So he knew. It had to be her mother's interference once more. 'Yes. Pretty soon,' she admitted. There was no point trying to hide it.

'Well … there was no future in Allcombe for you.' He said it as if it was a piece of home-grown wisdom that he had learned painfully and was passing on down to her. 'And not for me either.'

Charlotte let him collect himself as they walked underneath a series of trellises on which the rose bushes were faring a little better. 'Have you thought about what you'll do next?'

'Not really.'

She made a non-committal sound. She didn't know how he could discuss it so calmly, without any animosity towards her. Mike Miller had been the opposite: angry and penetrating. This was harder to deal with. She couldn't tell when the explosion would come, if at all, with Rob.

'So, anyway, I came to tell you that I hope we can still be friends,' he said. 'You've made the last three months bearable, even though things didn't … work out.'

'If you feel you can be friends, I'd like to,' she agreed.

'That's good.' He adjusted his tie. His knuckles were white. 'As a friend, can I ask you a question?'

Now that they were doing the friend thing, Charlotte couldn't really say no. 'Of course,' she agreed, not without reservation.

'Did you decide things weren't going well between us before or after you got the job offer from your old employers in Salzburg?'

'I really don't want to rehash the past, Rob, it was just … wrong to get into a relationship and that's the end of it,' Charlotte said. 'I should get back to my parents now.'

'Of course.' He had impeccable manners, as always. They started back out to the car park. He had such a convincing façade of confidence, ability and charm, but she knew better. Sometimes it was difficult to remind herself of that fact, particularly when he was being so courteous, even after everything that had happened.

They reached his car and he retrieved his keys from his jacket pocket. 'Are you going to the talent show tonight?' he asked her.

'No, I don't think so.'

'No.' He looked at the sky. 'Me neither.' There was something else he wanted to say; she could see it in the way he opened the car door and leaned upon it as if he needed the support. He bit his cheek and then launched into it.

'I know you don't want to talk about what's happened, Charlotte, but I just have to get this off my chest to someone. I hope you understand.' He shook his head from side to side. 'I can't believe that Rose has got away with it. I should have said something when I first found out she was seeing my brother. I should have known not to confide in him ... I don't know. Now she's got a great future and I'm lucky not to have been fired.'

'I don't understand,' Charlotte said. 'What has Rose got to do with it?'

Rob tilted his head in surprise. 'I thought you knew. She told the boss about us, and about me telling my brother private things about the trainees. God knows why she did it. I mean, I know I did the wrong thing, but it didn't deserve this.'

Charlotte didn't know what to say to him. Rob seemed to be asking her for some kind of reassurance that she wasn't able to give. He was looking at her and she could not respond. Eventually he looked away.

'Well, anyway. I'll get your address from your mother once you've settled,' he said, his voice back to gentle normality. He flashed his dimples at her. 'Maybe when things calm down here I could come and visit?'

She couldn't stand him smiling at her so hopefully, not realising the truth. 'No,' she said.

The smile disappeared. He half-reached out to her, and then his arm dropped back to lean on the car door once more. 'Why not?' he asked.

'Because Rose didn't report you to Rolf Chester. I did.'

'I ...' he said, and then stopped. He got behind the steering wheel of his car and closed the door. He was looking at the windscreen wipers.

She had done the right thing, Charlotte reassured herself in the face of his stunned disbelief. He could not be trusted. He gave away secrets, and he had seduced her, which he had no right to do. She had been making sure that he would not do it to anyone else, ever again.

She felt an ache creep up over her left temple. The stress was bringing on a headache. Perhaps a minute passed before she realised Rob wasn't going to speak to her or drive away. There was not going to be a confrontation, and she did not get a chance to explain her actions.

Charlotte walked back to the funeral party and stood beside her mother, refusing to turn around when she heard Rob's engine start and the car drive away.

Gary

Saturday, 23rd December, 8.33 pm

'So this is it,' Alma said. 'Are you okay?'

Gary bobbed his head. He was too nervous to speak, and too wired to make any other gesture. He couldn't believe he was about to do this.

His guitar strap was tight against his shoulder and he was carrying his wire to plug into the amplifier that was already on the makeshift stage. He could hear the large and noisy audience cheering and clapping the current act; it sounded like a series of poor impersonations of the well-known managers. It was disconcerting to be given such proof of the other employees who worked on the floors above him, divided into teams of which he would never be a part. They had all been given the same news yesterday about the company's relocation to India; no wonder they were blowing off steam.

The glass walls of the restaurant had been covered over

with black cloth and, waiting in the kitchen that was serving as a backstage area for the talent show entrants, Gary felt a nervous energy that he hoped would infuse his performance.

'Thanks for agreeing to do this,' he said to Alma and Sam.

He had returned to the training room yesterday after the relocation announcement and had found them both sitting there after having been effectively sacked. Alma had moaned at him and he had confided in her his problem with the talent show. She and Sam had kindly offered to help.

'You don't know how it's going to go yet,' Alma said darkly. Then she laughed at his doubt. 'Just wait to the end to thank us, okay?'

She was so calm. The talk around the training group was that she had actually been some kind of celebrity back in America; he could believe that now. He had no idea what her singing voice would be like, but her confidence was infectious. Gary was scared and he was charged up, but he wasn't terrified.

Sam wasn't in such a good way. Gary had provided him with a tambourine and instructed him to try to keep to the beat, and twenty minutes ago Sam had accepted those instructions with a curious blankness that had surprised Gary. Now Sam kept looking at the tambourine and experimentally shaking it as if it was a mutant growth on his hand that demanded extensive examination.

'Are you okay, Sam?' he asked. Sam looked up in confusion. 'Do you know what you have to do?'

He took on a look of determination that Gary had never seen in him before. 'Yes. I know what to do.'

Gary hardly felt reassured, but there was no time left for worrying. The crowd had upped its cheering and clapping, and the managerial impersonators were walking back into the kitchen, bursting with energy and laughter, congratulating each other and commenting on the audience.

It was time to get out there.

He looked at Alma and Sam. 'Ready?'

'Lead the way,' Alma said. Sam nodded.

Gary held his breath as he walked out of the kitchen with his semi-acoustic guitar clutched to his side, and pushed through the dividing black curtain to step on to the area that was usually home to the stainless steel food counters, but tonight was a makeshift stage.

He squinted against the bright white lights that had been erected above the stage, but his lack of vision did not make him any less aware of the hush of the crowd in front of him, a much larger crowd than he had been expecting. He could feel the weight of so many eyes upon him as he crossed the stage to plug in to his amplifier. A sweat had broken out on his face and was stinging his underarms. This was by far the greatest number of people he had ever performed for.

Alma strolled up to the centre of the stage and rolled up the sleeves of her voluminous royal blue shirt as if preparing herself to get down to business. She took the microphone and moved its stand to the side of the stage before casually returning to her prime position.

Sam edged on to the stage with the tambourine held before him like a shield. His eyes were searching the crowd until they fixed themselves on the middle of the front row. As Gary's own eyes adjusted to the lights he discovered the object of Sam's attention. Rose was sitting there, next to her new manager and the Head of Customer Services, Rolf Chester. They were both very well dressed in complementing outfits, and Rose was baring a large amount of pregnancy-enhanced cleavage.

The look Sam was giving her was so intense that Gary wondered how she could bear it so calmly, but she merely returned it without blinking.

'Hit it,' Alma murmured over her shoulder. Gary counted himself in under his breath and began the introduction; a light strumming that he knew well. This was one of his favourite songs to play, and he had no worries about his own ability. He just had to hope that Alma and Sam would be capable of matching him.

This was it: the moment in which Alma had to open her mouth and sing. He prayed that they were not about to look ridiculous.

'Busted flat in Baton Rouge, waiting for a train, And I's feeling nearly as faded as my jeans ...' Alma sang on cue, and then she was past the first lines and riding along the lyrics and the rhythm with a total conviction in what she was doing.

It was as though somebody had turned up a lamp to its very brightest setting, at the point at which it must explode or wink out to nothing. She expanded and filled the stage, and then went beyond it to dominate the entire crowd without ever seeming to try. Gary thought the world had stopped breathing at her command. She controlled them all, and his fingers were jumping on his strings in response to her demands, just as the tambourine was in exact counterpoint.

'Freedom's just another word for nothing left to lose, Nothing don't mean nothing if it ain't free ...' Alma sang so intensely that he could have worshipped her forever. The feeling was so powerful that he felt he was being sucked into her. 'You know feeling good was good enough for me, Good enough for me and my Bobby McGee ...'

The voice was pure Janis Joplin: a bottle of bourbon and fifty-cigs-a-day-sandpapered-throat heaven, so strong she needed no microphone and no accompaniment. But, even beyond that screaming, raw talent there was a stage presence that made her mesmerising. Everyone was looking at her and she was looking right back at them.

Gary began to understand. This was her revenge on the company. She was proving that she was so far beyond any of them in talent and personality that their dismissal of her was like an insect stinging a planet. She would be fine without them.

But that wasn't quite enough for Alma. They reached the free-flow part of the song and as Gary and Sam continued playing she began to speak.

'I've got a few special appreciations I need to say to y'all this evening,' she said, 'so let me thank the following people from the bottom of my big old heart. First of all, thank you to the company for hosting this great event and then telling me that I wasn't good enough to attend it.'

The people who weren't listening clapped, and a few who were frowned. 'I'd also like to thank the company for putting me out of a job, and let's not forget to thank them for moving all of the operation overseas so that everyone here tonight could soon be out of a job too.'

That got a ragged cheer from some areas at the back of the crowd. People sitting closer to Rolf Chester and Rose looked uncomfortable. Gary watched as Rose sneered. The atmosphere had soured, and Rolf Chester shifted but did not turn around to identify the booing culprits.

Alma wasn't finished. 'And, on behalf of the band, I'd like to thank Rose French.' She pointed her out to the audience. Rose stared back at her, her chin lifted. 'Thank you Rose, for all the extra special help you've given to my band members over the last months.'

Gary had reached the end of the song and there were no more notes to play. He petered out and his fingers halted. Sam came to a confused stop and stood self-consciously with the tambourine on his thigh. Alma had yet more to say. 'Thanks, Rose, on behalf of Gary Lester, whose love life you interfered in just because you felt like some fun. And a big thank-you on behalf of Sam Spurling, who you got engaged to for his money and then dumped on when a bigger fish came swimming your way.'

A few people in the audience laughed. Many of them were craning to get a look at Rose.

'And on that note, people, have a good Christmas and goodnight!' Alma finished in a spurt of triumph. She turned to Gary with satisfaction as the crowd erupted into noise. It had been an incredible performance. She had the kind of stage presence he had always wished for.

She jerked her head towards the kitchen. Gary nodded, and looked round for Sam.

Sam had moved to the very front of the stage. He leaned over, and his head and shoulders slid out of the lights. From his position Gary could just see his mouth moving, but he could not hear what was said – he doubted if anybody could have over the noise of the audience. And then Sam did something so unbelievable that Gary would have called anybody else who told him about it a liar.

He spat on Rose.

That would have been bad enough, but this was no ordinary spittle. It was like a gigantic flying jellyfish that landed squarely over her nose and mouth and stuck instantly to her skin.

She shot up from her chair and clawed at it with her fingernails. Rolf Chester and the rest of the front row got up and clustered around her, hiding her from Gary's view. Everybody else seemed to start running around and shouting; there was a crush of bodies in the aisle as people crowded forward to get a good look at the largest and stickiest gob of spit that anyone had ever seen.

Sam ran off at a speed that amazed Gary. Alma dropped the microphone and ran off after him.

Gary's instinct for self-preservation kicked in. He unplugged his guitar and ran at top speed after them, following Alma's rolling back and scuffling legs through the kitchen and out of the fire exit. He kept going around the side of the building until Sam, and then Alma, slowed and stopped in front of him, and he came to a halt beside them.

They were all gasping for breath, Sam leaning on his knees and Alma with her head and hands against the brick wall of the building. Gary bent double and worked hard on trying to regulate the sharp, uncontrolled movements of his lungs, his guitar trapped between his chest and thighs.

Then they were all laughing, all working off their adrenalin rush and not quite believing what had happened.

'You are cool,' Alma said to Sam admiringly.

'How did you do that?' Gary asked in awe. 'Did you put something in your mouth before we went out on stage?'

Sam, grinning and wild, shook his head happily. 'It's just a natural talent I have.'

'You gotta tell me how to do that some day,' Alma said. Then she looked at Gary. He could see the whites of her eyes shining in the darkness. 'And you were great. You can really play.'

Delighted, Gary repaid the compliment. 'But you can really sing. You blew them away.'

Alma smiled and managed to straighten up. Her breathing had slowed to normal. 'Do you think we won the talent show?'

Gary smiled back at her. 'I think we're lucky not have been lynched.'

'I think we'd better get out of here,' Sam added.

They were all alive in a way he had never experienced before; glowing and beyond worry. He felt a pain in his stomach when he thought of how he had nearly never had this experience; how easily he could have shared so much space and time without ever once finding out that Alma and Sam were the only people on the training course who could make him feel happy.

It was a feeling he didn't want to let go yet. Alma winked

at him. 'I think we need to celebrate,' she said. 'I'll buy you both a beer.'

She held out her arms. Sam took one and Gary took the other. They set off to The Slaughter, talking about all the things that might happen next.

Epilogue

Amie, clothed in the hessian robe of the Leader, looked down at her congregation. She loved them all. They were her family.

◆

Hilary checked the safety harness, took a huge breath, and launched herself over the edge of the cliff.

Abseiling was the only way she could escape Steve for five minutes.

She hummed *Little Wing* as she descended. At times like this, in moments alone, she always ended up thinking about the happiness she had felt while she was in Allcombe, singing with the band, Gary strumming his guitar behind her.

◆

Gary stepped into his tiny London flat and put his guitar case on the floor. Alma had loaned him the money to get set up; now he needed to find a band, record a demo, and start making the rounds at the record companies. It was his responsibility to make this work. He felt good about that.

◆

Alma fended off the questions of the reporters with practised ease as she left the television awards with her gold statuette tucked under her arm. The show was a huge hit, and she had decided to take a three-year contract with a leading soap opera as a follow-up. After all, life in Allcombe had taught her a lot about real trauma and despair, and she wanted to bring all that to the small screen. At heart, it turned out she was a glass half-full kind of a person.

◆

The Death-Defying Sputum looked down over the cliff edge at the burglars' hideout. Then he put his spit-producing helmet on his head and leapt over the precipice to face his destiny.

◆

The baby had been crying for three hours, the telephone was ringing incessantly with business queries she had no idea how to answer, and Rolf Chester had introduced some bitch called Katrina to her yesterday, saying he needed another assistant to 'lighten the burden'.

Rose was feeling something new. She wasn't sure what to call it. Perhaps it was regret.

◆

Charlotte scanned the faces of her new team and launched into her precisely-planned introduction.

'Hello everyone. My name is Charlotte Jackson and I'm your new manager. We're going to begin today by getting to know each other a little better. Let's start by playing a game called Three Things About Me.'